Dance with the Enemy

Rob Sinclair

Vesey Manor Publishing

Find out more about Rob and his books at:
http://www.robsinclairauthor.com

Books by Rob Sinclair

The Enemy Series:
Dance with the Enemy
Rise of the Enemy
Hunt for the Enemy

The James Ryker Series:
The Red Cobra
The Black Hornet
The Silver Wolf
The Green Viper
The White Scorpion

The Sleeper 13 series:
Sleeper 13
Fugitive 13
Imposter 13

DI Dani Stephens series:
The Essence of Evil
The Rules of Murder

Other:
Dark Fragments

Chapter 1

Maybe the psychologist had been right. Maybe he *was* an addict. Who else would put themselves in these positions willingly? Knowingly?

He had the man in a hammerlock. It was a classic submission hold. Its ease of application, and the fact it could be used from an upright position, meant it was a favoured hold of bouncers and law enforcement the world over. Logan was in neither of those professions, but it was a move that he had found to suit many purposes nonetheless.

He pulled the man's wrist further up toward the shoulder, feeling the resistance as the shoulder joint was pushed to bursting point. The man let out a yelp at what was becoming an inevitable outcome. His friends, just five yards in front of Logan at the other end of the bar, continued to look on, forming a physical barrier between Logan and where he wanted to be – the exit.

'Move out of my way. Now,' Logan said. 'Don't think for a second I won't do it.'

Despite the threat, the man's three friends stood their ground. They weren't about to back down. But they weren't looking like they were about to make a move either. For now, it was a stand-off. Neither side wanted to take it to the next level.

Yet.

Logan looked them over, one by one. Rednecks would be a harsh way to describe them. They were probably just average working guys letting off steam on a weekend; albeit guys who were bulked up through steroids and overuse of weights, and fuelled by alcohol and God knows what else. Each one of them

2

was big and menacing. And judging by the non-situation that had started this, they were looking for a fight tonight.

And for no sane reason, other than he was who he was, Logan was prepared to grant them their wish. He wasn't the tallest or the strongest guy in the world, but he could handle himself just fine. Despite the odds, he still fancied his chances against this lot.

'I warned you,' Logan said.

He pulled the man's wrist further, as hard and as fast as he could, pushing against the resistance until he heard the tell-tale pop as the man's arm dislocated from the shoulder. The way it suddenly flopped in his hand told Logan it had probably dislocated at the elbow too. The man shrieked in pain and slumped to the floor as Logan let go, readying himself for the next stage of his latest battle.

The three friends, wide-eyed and staring, looked shocked at what had just happened. Maybe their macho stand-offs didn't normally go this far. And yet they continued to stand their ground. Logan was a little surprised by that.

But then he saw it. The man on the left. It was nothing more than a flinch. Maybe just a twitch, even. But it was enough for Logan. Enough to tell him that this wasn't over yet. And that man was now his next focus.

But just as Logan was about to leap forward, something unexpected happened.

He heard the noise before he felt anything. A dull thud. He was on his knees before the searing pain in the back of his leg took hold. Then came the thud again. This time pain shot across his back.

In an instant, unable to stop himself, he was face down on the floor.

He tried to stand up, but the combination of whisky and whatever had just hit him was too much. Instead, he just lay there, hearing the thuds that kept on coming. Feeling the pain with each strike, but unable to muster a response. He saw boots crowding around him. Saw them pulling back and kicking him. Pulling back and kicking. The thuds kept on coming across his back.

He took a boot to the face and felt his lip open up, blood pouring into his mouth. The blows kept on coming but Logan didn't move. He wasn't sure he could anymore. He closed his eyes, wondering how things had gone so wrong this time. Maybe he was losing it. Maybe he had never really got it back. He had been out of action for too long. Five months had gone by now since his last fateful assignment. Five months of hell.

His mind began to wander, his awareness of the blows raining down on him fading. Before consciousness left him, he felt a slither of an unlikely smile form on his face.

The psychologist *was* right. He *was* an addict.

But it wasn't the fighting that he was addicted to. It wasn't the pain either – he was no masochist. Too many years had gone by living a life that wasn't a life at all. He didn't want to be *their* machine anymore. He couldn't. That was his addiction – the clamour for some sort of normality. He just wanted to live and to feel like everyone else did. Nights like this, in a twisted logic that made sense only to him, allowed him that.

He just wanted to be normal.

And yet he knew that would never be the case.

Chapter 2

The motorcade edged along the Voie Georges Pompidou on the banks of the Seine, heading back toward the American Embassy. Three identical black Escalades, one after the other, the vehicles almost twice as heavy as regular models due to the extensive armouring. Six agents from the United States Foreign Service were in the three cars, each of them armed, carrying SIG Sauer P229 pistols with twelve-round magazines.

It was heavy protection. But it needed to be.

The Foreign Service was responsible for running all of the US foreign embassies, consulates and missions. Its special agents were responsible for the safety and security of visiting US diplomats, amongst other duties. Today, the special agents attached to Paris were assigned to protect Frank Modena, the eighty-third Attorney General of the United States of America.

The official threat level for Modena's trip was minimal, but the embassy had insisted on taking necessary precautions given the high-profile nature of his visit. Everyone in the world knew of the subject matter that he had come here to talk about. And almost everyone had a strong view on it.

Modena, a well-built, silver-haired man, was sitting in the back of the second Escalade, along with his much younger assistant, Laura. The midday traffic was heavy and they meandered along, passing some of the most famous sites of Paris – of Europe. Undoubtedly, the road they were on passed along what was one of the most spectacular riverfronts in the world, with its rich history and eclectic mix of buildings. In the world's capital of romance, the River Seine, and all it had to offer, was the epicentre.

All of this was lost on Modena, however, who was deep in his own thoughts, reflecting on the speech he had just given to a room full of delegates from across the world. All things considered, it hadn't been at all bad.

Modena's eye caught a young couple, strolling along the riverbank, arm in arm. They stopped and embraced each other. Together with the scene that surrounded them, the iconic buildings and leafy parks, it was like something straight out of an art-house film. It sparked thoughts in Modena's head about what the evening's antics with his assistant, Laura, might entail. But he had no intention of heading out for a romantic walk. Everything he wanted tonight would be found within his luxurious hotel suite. He glanced over at Laura and caught her eye. She gave him a meek smile then looked away coyly. Gazing out the window, she lifted up the skirt on her leg just a little, as if she knew exactly what he had been thinking. Modena felt the rumblings of arousal begin.

But his daydreaming was rudely cut short when, without warning, the driver slammed on the brakes and the vehicle came to a sudden stop. Modena shot forward, his belt catching and jolting him back into his seat.

'Jesus, Bridges!' Modena shouted to his driver. 'What the hell was that?'

'Sorry, sir. The car in front stopped suddenly. Looks like an accident up ahead.'

Modena tutted and rubbed the back of his neck. He'd not taken to Bridges at all. The guy looked barely old enough to drive, never mind be a special agent. He was tall and fair-haired, all skin and bone. Not exactly a threatening presence. Where did they even get these kids from?

Modena carried on nursing his neck. He had an old whiplash injury from a previous car accident. Even after six years, any unexpected movement sent waves of pain through his upper spine.

'Sorry, sir,' Bridges said again.

'That's okay,' Modena said without conviction. He leaned his head into the middle of the two front seats so that he could see out through the windscreen. But he couldn't see what was up ahead. They had come to a stop only inches from the first of the three cars in the motorcade, which was now blocking the view. 'What do you think the problem is?'

'Can't really see,' said Carlson, the agent in charge of the convoy, who was sitting next to Bridges. 'But there are some flashing lights up ahead and Roberts just called over to say there's a crash up front on the Place de la Concorde.'

Carlson was everything Bridges was not. Ex-military, he was stocky with a furrowed brow and chiselled face. He looked like he meant business and he looked like he'd seen it all. Modena had liked him immediately. Probably because he was the kind of man Modena wanted to be seen as, rather than the pen-pusher that he really was.

Modena heard sirens coming from behind. He turned to look out of the back window and saw an ambulance trying to come through. But the traffic was too tight and the cars were struggling to move out of the way to let it pass.

Slowly, the cars directly in front began to pull to the side. After the lead Escalade had squeezed forward, Bridges did the same and mounted the kerb to allow the ambulance to pass.

The ambulance came to a stop again just past the front Escalade. Modena assumed the cars further in front were still blocking the way.

'Idiots,' Bridges muttered. 'I never understand why people can't just do the simple thing and pull over so they can get past.'

Carlson huffed in agreement.

Two police motorcycles came up behind the ambulance and they too were now stuck. Modena moved forward in his seat to get a better look. The ambulance was still just past the first Escalade, its lights and sirens still blaring. The motorbikes were parked one behind the other, right outside Modena's window.

After a few moments, the back doors to the ambulance opened.

'Looks like they've had enough,' Modena said.

But he did a double-take as the doors opened fully to reveal two figures dressed from head to toe in black. They had balaclavas over their heads, leaving just their eyes and mouths exposed.

Modena's mind began to race as he tried to figure out what was wrong with the scene. 'What the hell is going on here?' he said, a fraction of a second before it clicked.

'Oh shit!' was all Carlson could say as the two figures lifted assault rifles to their chests.

'Get down!' Bridges screamed at Modena.

The two figures from the ambulance opened fire on the front Escalade, but Modena, stunned, was unable to react. The thudding sound from the volley of fire seemed to reverberate through his entire body. His world in slow motion, he turned to see the man who had been on one of the motorcycles walking toward the third Escalade. The other was pointing a gun directly at Modena. They both opened fire on their targets and Modena jumped as the bullets ricocheted off the armoured vehicle.

'Oh my God!' Modena shrieked. 'We're under attack! Jesus! We're under attack!'

All around, pedestrians began to scream and run for cover. Some of the people in the cars in front and behind were jumping from their vehicles and running too.

Modena finally put his head down to his knees. It was only then that he heard Laura crying in terror next to him. 'Frank, what's going on?!'

Modena didn't respond.

'We need immediate assistance!' Carlson shouted into his radio. 'Repeat, we need immediate assistance! We're taking heavy fire! Bridges, you have to try to get us out of here.'

Modena couldn't keep his head down any longer. He had to know what was going on. He lifted his head again just as Bridges put the Escalade into reverse and pressed the accelerator. The car jerked backward two yards, crunching into the front of the third car. He pushed the stick into drive and they lurched forward three yards into the front car. He carried out the same manoeuvre again, trying to create enough of an angle to get them out. The other two cars remained stationary, their drivers making no apparent attempt to move away from the danger.

Modena wasn't sure if that was out of choice or because they were already dead.

After the initial round of fire at Modena's vehicle, both of the motorbike gunmen were now firing on the third Escalade. The two ambulance men were still firing on the front car. In the momentary respite, Modena couldn't help but feel a wave of relief, despite the predicament.

'What are we going to do?' he shouted.

'Just stay calm,' Carlson shouted back, sounding anything but. 'And keep your head down!'

'We're armoured, right? They can't get us. Right?'

'Look, we're armoured, but those rifles will cut through here eventually. These vehicles aren't made for heavy fire. We have to get away from them.'

Modena, ignoring Carlson's instruction, kept his head up to see what was happening. He watched as the front passenger door of the first Escalade opened and an agent fell out onto the ground. Modena's first thought was that the agent was already dead. But then he hauled himself up against the wheel arch, trying to give himself some cover from the attackers at the opposite side of the car, his gun held at his chest. The ambulance men must have seen him escape the car, though. While one continued to fire on the vehicle, the other made his way cautiously to the front of the car.

Modena heard the crash as the glass on the driver's side of the first car gave way. He looked on in horror as the attacker moved forward, still firing on the stricken agent in the driver's seat. Seconds later, with the driver of the first vehicle surely dead, the attacker turned his attention to Modena's vehicle and began firing again – aiming low for the bonnet.

Bridges tried again to manoeuvre enough space to get out. 'Just once more should do it!' he said, desperation in his voice.

The agent who had escaped the front car was still hunkered behind its wheel arch. With a sudden head of steam, he stood up, firing his weapon at the second ambulance man who was just a few yards from him at the front of the vehicle. One of the shots hit the attacker in the shoulder and he stumbled backward. But the agent hadn't been quick enough and the attacker had managed to get off four rounds with the rifle. The agent could do nothing as each of the bullets hit his mid-section. Modena watched in horror as the bullets tore right through him, four neat exit holes appearing in his jacket, arranged in a cluster, only inches apart.

Almost in slow motion, the agent's lifeless body slumped onto the ground in a heap.

Laura let out a whimper at the sight of the agent going down. Both Carlson and Modena turned to her in unison.

'For God's sake, get down and stay down!' Carlson screamed at them both.

Laura did as she was told, but Modena was frozen. Bridges finally managed to manoeuvre enough space to get out. He pressed the accelerator all the way down and the car shot toward the first ambulance man, who only just managed to jump out of the way. The Escalade, with nowhere to go, crashed into the back of the ambulance. Bridges carried on stamping on the accelerator, the engine revving and the tyres screeching, sending up plumes of thick smoke. But the ambulance didn't move an inch.

He looked behind and started to reverse. Modena looked behind as well. In addition to the two abandoned motorbikes, which were now directly behind them, there was also a panel van that had pulled up about ten yards behind them, blocking any planned exit. The Escalade swept backward and knocked the first motorbike clean out of the way. There was a crash as they hit the second motorbike, which was pushed along, caught on their rear bumper. But their escape was cut short once more as they crashed into the stationary van.

Modena was thrown back against his seat and felt the jolt of pain surge through his neck again. This time, he didn't even think about nursing his injury. Bridges pounded as hard as he could on the accelerator, but the van wasn't going to be moved. He then tried desperately to put the car back into drive, jolting the gear lever in and out, in and out, pressing his foot down hard on the accelerator each time he did so. Each attempt let out a low-pitched whine, but produced no movement.

'There's no power!' Bridges shouted, still pushing the gear stick in and out of drive, but to no avail. 'The engine – it's dead!'

'Okay. We need another route out of here,' Carlson said, his voice still calm and steady, unlike those of the other occupants. 'If we get out your side, you can provide covering fire while I move the rest of us away.'

Modena, hearing the agents' conversation but paying no attention to their words, looked to his right. The windows of the third Escalade, with which they were now parallel, had caved in, just like the first. The two agents in the front were motionless, their faces bloodied and bowed.

'Oh God, no,' Modena said, putting his hand to his mouth.

And then, just as it had been at the start, everything went silent. A deathly silence. No screaming, no shots ringing out now. But Modena's mind was racing too much to understand why.

Was he already dead?

In the silence, Laura looked up again. Tears were streaming down her face, leaving a trail of black from her mascara. She let out another whimper and flung her head into Modena's lap. Her boss didn't react, just looked on aghast at the scene of carnage in front of them.

The four assailants were crowded around the front of Modena's car. Their weapons were still drawn but they were no longer firing. Carlson and Bridges looked at each other then back out at the gunmen without saying a word.

'You have ten seconds to get out of the vehicle,' one of the armed men shouted. The leader, Modena assumed. He was speaking in English, with what Modena thought was a southern English accent. Modena hadn't expected that. It seemed out of place. 'Ten seconds or we start firing again. And you can see what happened to your friends.'

'What the hell are we going to do?' Modena said.

Carlson and Bridges looked at each other again. They were both armed. But they weren't in a position to fight these men, who had both superior numbers and superior weapons.

'I don't think we have much choice,' Carlson said. 'We do as they say. There's no sign of any help coming in the next ten seconds and we're not exactly equipped to fight these guys.'

'A minute ago you said we should get out,' Bridges said. 'I'll cover you. We can still do that.'

'It's too late!' Carlson snapped. 'We should do what they say.'

'No,' Bridges said, shaking his head. 'We have to try to fight. It's what we're trained to do. There's only four of them.'

'And how do you suggest we do that? There are four assault rifles aimed at us. As soon as we made a move, it'd be over.'

'Our job is to fight. If we go out there, they'll just kill us anyway,' Bridges said.

'No, our job isn't to fight, it's to protect.'

'Giving up isn't the same thing as protecting.'

'It's the only choice we have.'

The confidence now exuded by Bridges surprised Modena. Maybe he'd been wrong about the young agent. But he had to side with Carlson on this one. The thought of running out there in a volley of fire was making him feel nauseous. The path of least resistance would be his choice every time.

Carlson, taking the lead, put his hand on the door handle, opened his door and stepped out. Bridges hesitated but then put his hand to his door and began to open it. Modena and Laura looked at each other, wide-eyed. Neither made a move for their doors.

'Keep your hands in the air!' the leader of the armed men said.

Carlson did as he was told and stood up straight, facing toward the men.

'I'm Special Agent Carlson of the US Foreign Service. I'm responsible for these passengers. What's going on here? What do you want?'

'What do we want?' the leader said, sniggering. 'Not you.'

He pulled his weapon up and squeezed off one shot. The bullet hit Carlson in the middle of his face, creating an exit wound in the back of his head the size of an orange. Blood, flesh and bone splattered onto the Escalade and all around as Carlson's body fell to the ground.

Laura put her hand to her mouth and gave a muffled scream. Bridges, reacting on instinct, quickly shut his door again. He turned and began to move toward Carlson's door to try to shut that too. But he had no chance. One of the attackers was already there, his rifle pointed through the open door at the agent's head.

Bridges looked up into the barrel of the gun.

'Please ...'

But before he could say another word, the attacker fired. The bullet hit Bridges in his temple as he tried to turn away. The high-calibre round at close range was like a baseball bat smashing a watermelon. Bridges's head all but exploded, thick liquid and mushy flesh covering the inside of the car, Laura and Modena, who both screamed and immediately started clawing at their face and clothes, trying to remove the mess.

Taking just a second to readjust, the attacker moved his rifle toward Laura and fired again. The sound in the confined space was deafening. Modena shuddered, his ears ringing, his head going into a spin. Disorientated, he shot out of his seat as Laura's bloodied, limp body fell into his lap. He crawled up against the inside of the car, trying to get as far away as he could. As he fumbled for the door handle, the ringing still in his ears, he couldn't take his eyes off Laura's lifeless body. The mess of bone, blood and flesh that used to be her face.

Finally, his hand grasped the handle and the door came open. He tumbled out onto the ground, gasping for air. Barely a second later he was dragged to his feet by one of the attackers.

'Please. Please don't kill me,' Modena begged, putting his hands together in prayer. 'Please, I have a family.'

'We're not going to kill you, Frank,' the leader said matter-of-factly.

One of the men came forward. Modena didn't flinch, didn't move an inch, as a small sack was placed over his head.

'Not yet anyway,' the leader added. 'You're coming with us.'

Chapter 3

5th October

Logan sprang upright in his bed. He was panting heavy breaths and his body was damp from sweat. He threw the covers off and shivered as the cold, conditioned air hit his skin, sending a wave of goose-pimples across his body. After a few moments, his breathing began to slow down as his mind recovered from the horrors of his sleep.

It had been the same dream as before. The nightmare that he had nearly every night. Except that it wasn't really a dream at all. It was worse than that. It wasn't a figment of his imagination, but a replay of the most heinous moments of his life.

He closed his eyes and felt the throbbing in his head. He was hungover. Usually alcohol would help him to have a dreamless night. But he only rarely allowed himself that luxury – that was the coward's way out. And last night, even the alcohol hadn't saved him from the nightmare.

Opening his eyes, he looked over at the empty space on the other side of the bed. He was alone. Was that a surprise? He had half expected it not to be empty.

He turned back to face the other way and winced in pain. It felt like he had daggers in his shoulder blades. That wasn't from the drink.

With pained movement, he reached out and turned on the bedside lamp. A rush of memories from the night before flew through his head: beer, whisky, a girl. A bar brawl. Las Vegas, that's where he was. The city of sin.

The flashes were enough to remind him why he was feeling so rough. It hadn't just been the drink. He had taken a beating. There had been at least four of them and they had gone to town on him. An unseen attacker had taken him down from behind. A cheap shot. But he probably deserved it. In any case, Logan's cuts and bruises would be gone in a few days. Their friend would have to get used to using only his left arm for the next few months.

Despite the beating, Logan had still ended up back in his hotel room. He didn't know how. The last thing he could remember was lying on the floor in the bar as blow after blow came his way.

Logan got out of bed and headed toward the bathroom of his hotel suite to get some water. The inside of his mouth was so dry it felt like sandpaper. He poured himself a glass from the tap and downed it in two large gulps. The water barely touched the sides of his mouth, which didn't seem to lose any of its dryness.

He closed his eyes again, but then immediately wished he hadn't as the images from his sleep tore through him once more. The cold stone floor. The shouting all around him. The feeling of the blade against his flesh, cutting into him. The bloodied and lifeless body within touching distance, Logan powerless to help.

He opened his eyes, escaping the nightmare. His hands were shaking. He felt dizzy and had to grab hold of the sink with both hands to stop himself toppling over.

After a few deep breaths, the sickly sensation began to dissipate and he felt able to let go of the porcelain. He turned the cold tap to full force and used his swollen hands to splash water onto his face, feeling his mind awaken as he did so.

Snippets of memories from the night before continued to come back to him. A girl. What was her name? Caroline. That was it. A nice name. A nice girl. Shame about the guys she normally chose for company. After Logan and Caroline had spent a couple of hours talking, drinking, laughing together, some meathead had slapped her backside as she went to the toilet. Turned out he was a local, she was a local. Logan wasn't. It was Logan's British accent that had first drawn her interest. In the end it had probably only contributed to his downfall. He'd tried to be the knight in shining armour, out to save her. But his courageous efforts hadn't turned out in his favour.

Maybe the night would have panned out differently if he'd kept his head and walked away. With her. But he hadn't. The fight had found him, as it so often did. And he'd woken up alone. Again.

The sad thing was, he had enjoyed her company – she had made him feel alive for those few hours. Feel normal, even. Just two people sitting in a bar, having some drinks, talking. That was normal, wasn't it? But in his clamour for that very feeling, he had blown it all to shit.

He knew that he was anything but normal. Normal people hadn't lived half of their lives in a cocoon, isolated and separated from the real world. They had families and friends and they felt emotions like joy, happiness, pain, sorrow and fear. He'd spent his entire adult life bereft of those emotions. Ever since the agency had shown him how to control his feelings. No, not control his feelings – they'd trained him to ignore them altogether. They weren't needed for what he was. For what he had become.

Until five months ago. When everything had changed.

Now he could feel emotions once again. But he was filled with so much angst, anger, regret, shame – so many feelings coming to the fore that he didn't know how to control. And sometimes he wished he was still the zombie he had been for the last eighteen years – almost half of his life.

He drank another glass of water and looked at himself in the mirror. His six-foot-three frame meant he had to crouch slightly to get a good look at himself. Dried blood was caked on the side of his face. The wound that it had come from still glistened up in his hairline, discolouring the close-cut mousy-brown hair around it. His normally sparkling green eyes were bloodshot, his right eyelid swollen almost completely shut. His bottom lip protruded awkwardly, making his face look lopsided. Not to mention the three-day stubble and other obvious signs of wear and tear from too much alcohol and too little sleep that aged a normally handsome face.

He looked a mess. And not just because of last night's wounds. His life's scars marked his entire torso, and were a stark contrast to his normally clear and unblemished face. The ones from five months ago were by far the most severe.

How would a beautiful woman like Caroline react to seeing those?

She had seemed pretty interested in him last night, though. In their brief time together he'd found he could talk to her like he could to very few people. She was a free spirit, no inhibitions. She was young and naive about the world, but she also had an unerring confidence to which Logan had immediately been attracted. It'd been easy to talk to her. Probably for the very reason that she didn't know anything about him.

She had liked him, he had liked her. Although she fit the mould for so many of the women that Logan had seen over the years, he felt there was something different about her. All those others had come to nothing. After the initial excitement had died down, there was really nothing of substance in any of Logan's previous relationships. But he knew that was almost entirely because of him. He'd never got to the point where he'd been able to let anyone into his world. But maybe this time it was different. He wasn't the same person he used to be. He may have messed up last night, but what did he have to lose in giving it another go?

He made up his mind: he would definitely go and see her tonight at the club she said she worked at. See if he could be lucky for a change.

Logan's mobile phone began to ring. Hesitantly he walked out of the bathroom to the bedside table, unable to avoid limping on his bruised legs. He picked up the phone. It was Mackie, his boss. He felt himself lose two inches as his body deflated.

He knew what this meant. There would be no Caroline. Not this time.

'You know I'm on holiday, don't you?' Logan said, answering the phone.

'Logan, I'm afraid men like us don't do holidays. We both know that. And anyway, I'd hardly call what you were doing last night a holiday.'

'What's that supposed to mean?'

'What do you think?'

It didn't take him long to work it out. Logan felt his cheeks blush with embarrassment. Mackie had sent someone to keep an eye on him. Someone had been watching him last night. They had probably been watching him from the moment he landed here three days ago. Logan winced at the thought. Not just because Mackie had felt it necessary to do that, but because Logan hadn't spotted the watcher at all.

He really was losing it.

'And it's just as well I had a man on you,' Mackie said, breaking the silence. 'What do you think would've happened if he hadn't been there? You certainly wouldn't have been waking up this morning to five-star luxury.'

So that explained how he had ended up back in his hotel room. Mackie's man had brought him back here. Kept him out of trouble. Babysat him.

Logan felt his temperature rise as anger took hold.

'Are you intentionally trying to ruin your career, Logan?' Mackie was saying. 'I'm not always going to be around to bail you out.'

Career? It was hardly what you would call a career. He was their machine. He did what they told him. He always had. And this just proved how they saw him.

'I can't believe you did that,' Logan said. 'So this is what it's come to? Now I have to have my hand held wherever I go?'

'Well, based on last night, quite clearly, yes.'

Logan thumped the wall in frustration. The skin on his knuckles split and his hand began to pound, but he was oblivious to the pain.

'Logan, you've got to understand. You are what you are. We still need you. *I* still need you. But things aren't like they used to be.'

'I assume you're not calling just to give me grief,' Logan said, eager to change the subject before the conversation turned to things he didn't want to think about.

'I thought maybe it was time you came back. I have something for you.'

Logan's head began to whir. It was like a ton weight had been lifted off his shoulders. On hearing Mackie say those words, five months of frustration and torment suddenly vanished. And yet he knew feeling like that was contradictory to everything he'd been fighting against for the last five months.

Was this really what he wanted? Was it what he *needed* to get his life back on track?

'So what do you think? Are you ready?'

'Yes. Of course I am,' Logan said, without a moment's hesitation.

He knew that it wasn't true, however much he wanted it to be. But what else was he going to say? Maybe this would get him focused again. He would never be the same man that he used to be, and he didn't want to be, but this was still what he was.

'Good. I need you back here right away.'

'So, what is it?'

'Well, when I said you're needed here, what I really meant was, you're needed in Paris.'

'Paris? What's in Paris?'

'Yesterday Frank Modena was.'

'Frank Modena? Who's that?'

'Frank Modena is the Attorney General of our chums over the pond. Have you not been watching the news?'

'Sorry, but I've not been keeping up to date with current affairs. It was you that sent me away on holiday, remember? Something about it aiding my recovery? And anyway, Frank Modena being in Paris is of concern why?'

'I said he *was* in Paris. Past tense.'

'Okay. So where is he now?'

'That's what I need *you* to find out.'

Chapter 4

6th October

Charles McCabe opened the walnut door to his riverfront office to
see his assistant, Peter Winter, hovering over the large oak desk. It
was almost nine in the morning and McCabe, or Mackie as he was
known by all those close to him, was already in a bad mood from
having to fight his way across central London on the underground.
The weather was unseasonably warm and public transport hadn't
seemed to get the message. The underground had been like an
oven with heaters on full blast and Mackie was a sweaty, wet mess
by the time he arrived at his office.

'What do you want?' he snapped at Winter.

The young man looked up apologetically and started shuffling
some papers on the desk.

'Mackie, I mean, sir, good morning, sir.'

Mackie shut the door behind him, took off his coat and hung it
on the coat stand. He carried on to his desk where he sat down on
the large black leather chair. As ever he was well-groomed and
smartly dressed, though his pinstripe suit jacket only just buttoned
up around his protruding belly. He had thick-rimmed glasses and
dyed brown hair, neatly parted, which made his face look ten years
younger than he really was.

'Sir, did you get my message?' Winter said, sounding
flustered.

The blank look on Mackie's face gave away the answer.

'There's a committee meeting in five minutes. To discuss the
Modena situation.'

'What?!'

'I tried calling you, sir.'

It wasn't the fact he hadn't got the message that was the problem, it was more the unexpected timing of the call. Mackie was one of six commanders at the Joint Intelligence Agency, or JIA, a secretive intelligence organisation funded equally by the UK and US governments. The commanders were responsible for managing a group of intelligence agents and the JIA's operations were overseen by a committee made up of a senior intelligence official and a politician from both the UK and US. A ten o'clock meeting was unusual, given that it would only be five a.m. in Washington. And the timing could only mean one thing: a problem.

'Okay,' Mackie said, fingering his goatee beard, a bad habit that he had been trying hard to rid himself of. 'What do you know?'

Winter went on to give Mackie the little background he had. Although his title was that of personal assistant, Winter's role was much more than that of a traditional secretary. He was essentially being primed to one day be a commander himself. He looked like a typical young executive with his neat suits, designer shoes and pristine appearance, but underneath there was substance to him as well. He was articulate and intelligent and also brilliantly manipulative when he needed to be. Mackie liked him a lot. Winter's confidence and unerring enthusiasm reminded him of himself when he had been that age. Mackie, now in his fifties, had never been a field agent, but he'd worked so closely with them for over thirty years that he felt like he knew and understood their roles just as much as they did. No, in fact he understood their roles even more than they did, because he saw the bigger picture too.

Winter sat down on one of the two chairs at the front of the desk and Mackie dialled into the conference call. They were two minutes late and the last to join the call. Mackie got the impression that the four committee members had already been deep in discussion.

Although he was answerable to the committee, he'd never had any qualms in ruffling feathers or challenging them. As far as he was concerned, he knew more about the JIA than any of them – he'd been one of the original commanders when the agency was set up, long before any of the current committee members came on board. And so, after the usual pleasantries, Mackie dived in head first, as always.

'Do we have a problem?' he said.

There were murmurings on the phone before Jay Lindegaard, the current committee's longest-serving member and a lifelong CIA bureaucrat, took the lead.

'It's not a problem, Charles,' Lindegaard said in his thick Deep South drawl. 'We just need to understand how you're handling the Modena case. I'm sure you can imagine this is being taken very seriously here.'

'Of course I know that,' Mackie snapped. 'It's been taken care of. That's all you need to know.'

'And who is your lead agent on this?'

Mackie was fully aware that everyone on the call knew the answer to that. It was surely the entire purpose of the call after all.

'It's Carl Logan,' Mackie said.

'That's what we heard. I have to say, we're a little uncomfortable about this.'

'He's my agent. Let me handle it.'

'You know we can't afford for this to go wrong,' piped up John Sanderson from SIS, or MI6 as it was still routinely referred to by all and sundry. Sanderson was the only committee member that Mackie really had any time for, even if he was becoming soft and disinterested as he neared retirement.

'Exactly,' said Lindegaard. 'Just look at everything in the press recently and all these ridiculous leaks – the intelligence community is already under attack. The last thing we need is an unhinged and incompetent agent on the loose in such a high-profile case. What happens if our whole operation is blown wide open?'

'He's the most experienced man I've got,' Mackie said.

'He's been out of action for five months,' replied Lindegaard. 'And from everything I've heard, he's a mess. I've seen many agents removed altogether for far less significant problems.'

'I know what I'm doing here,' Mackie declared, not wanting to argue the points. The truth was that even he was doubtful of Logan's state of mind. How could he not be? But he had to trust Logan – trust in the ability that Mackie knew he had. Logan deserved the chance. It wasn't like his problems had been of his own making. And even if it came back to bite him, Mackie owed it to Logan. Mackie had given Logan this life. And it was his actions that had led to Logan's fateful assignment ending the way it had.

'You realise if you're wrong about this, it's not just his neck on the line,' Lindegaard said.

'I know. He's ready. There's nothing more to say.'

There was quiet on the line for a good ten seconds. As ever, the two politicians on the committee, Philip Greenwood and Randall Curtis, had been silent throughout. Although Mackie understood the necessity to have some link to the powers that be both within the US and the UK, their presence on the committee was merely a token gesture to ensure they were informed of activities, rather than their having any meaningful involvement in matters in which they had no expertise.

'Okay,' Sanderson said. 'We're bowing to your judgement. For now. He's got one week. And we expect daily updates on his movements and his progress. If there's anything amiss, he gets pulled. Permanently.'

'He's my agent, not yours,' Mackie said through gritted teeth. 'I decide when he gets pulled.'

Mackie pressed the mute button and swore at the phone. Winter was unable to hide his smile.

'We're already giving you the benefit here, Charles,' said Lindegaard. 'Please don't make out that we're the bad guys.'

'Just let him get on with it,' Mackie said, after unmuting the phone. 'Winter will keep you abreast.'

Mackie ended the call without another word and let out another tirade of abuse at the machine. He stood up, adjusting the waistband of his trousers to cover his stomach as he strode over to the window of his office.

'Please tell me Logan has sobered up enough to have left Vegas by now?' he said to Winter.

'Yes, sir,' Winter said. 'In fact, he boarded a flight from Newark last night. He'll be landing in Paris shortly.'

Mackie was pleasantly surprised to hear that. He'd half expected Logan to still be in a drunken stupor in some rundown casino. But, unusually, Mackie also felt incredibly nervous. It was only natural that the more pressure the committee put on him over Logan, the more he began to doubt his own judgement. Was Logan really ready for this? He didn't know, but he would find out soon enough.

'Okay. I should get moving,' Mackie said. 'I need to get to Paris. Now.'

Chapter 5

Five months of physical recovery, recuperation and rehabilitation. Even without considering the recent spate of bar fights, it had been the most gruelling five months of Logan's life. And the mental rehabilitation, which he knew deep down was nowhere near complete, had been more like torture.

During those months he'd endlessly questioned where his life was heading, unsure whether he really cared about living at all. But now he was back. The call had come and he had obliged. He wouldn't go so far as to say it felt *good* to be back. But it certainly felt familiar. And it felt like it was what he needed. Whatever this case was about, he had a point to prove. He might not be a machine anymore, but he could still do this. He had to still be able to do this. When it came down to it, being an agent was all he had in the world.

So why was he feeling like it was a step too far, too soon?

'Good morning, sir,' Logan said to Mackie as he walked into the makeshift office, trying his best to act as if this was nothing more than a routine work day. 'I would say it's good to see you but I don't like lying to people.'

'Could have fooled me,' Mackie retorted, not looking up from the desk at which he was sitting. 'Half your job is about lying to people.'

The modern desk looked out of place in what was actually the lounge of a rundown Parisian apartment. Logan hadn't been here before, but it was much the same as any other safe house he had ever been in.

It was located in Saint-Denis, a largely industrial suburb. Many parts of the area were surprisingly deprived given the close proximity to some of Paris's central tourist traps. There was the odd exception, such as the Basilica Cathedral of Saint Denis, with its rich history dating back to Roman times when it was a cemetery – the archaeological remains of which still lie beneath the cathedral. By and large, though, it was far from the romance and historic architecture that Paris was so famous for. But that was the same for any city. The *real* city, the bowels where the thousands and millions of people lived, was never what you saw on the picture postcard. And yet it was those areas that made the cities.

The safe house was in an area made up of narrow streets of nondescript, post-war housing. Together with the littered streets, graffiti on the walls and un-weeded yards, it was clear that this was one of the less prosperous parts. From the outside it was an unassuming apartment block, and on the inside it was much the same. There was no high-tech security here – just an agent in an unmarked car across the street and another stationed in the hallway of the apartment. They didn't need anything more than that. Why bother drawing attention to the place?

Logan hadn't recognised the man in the hallway as he came in, but then that wasn't unusual. The fewer people you knew – and, more importantly, the fewer people that knew you – the longer you'd be in this game.

Logan shut the door behind him then headed over toward the desk.

'Logan, you look terrible,' Mackie said, finally looking up from the pile of papers he had been reading. It wasn't just his normal banter either. He looked genuinely concerned by Logan's dishevelled appearance.

'Thanks. That's quite a welcome,' Logan said, well aware that Mackie was right.

Logan had headed straight to McCarran Airport after speaking to his boss the previous day. Unable to get a direct flight into France, he'd stopped off at Newark. From there he'd taken the redeye to Paris. He had only managed to get a couple of hours' sleep on the flight, and although some of the swelling on his face had gone down, it was still heavily bruised. To add to that, he had heavy bags under his eyes and the three-day stubble he'd had in Vegas was now almost beyond being stubble.

He was used to travelling at short notice; it was part and parcel of the job. But when you put into the mix the two days of boozing, the fight and the lack of sleep, it was all the more gruelling. Logan felt as rough as he looked.

'What happened to you?' Mackie asked.

'Don't ask,' Logan said, shaking his head and sitting down on the simple metal chair opposite Mackie.

'Don't fob me off. This isn't good, Logan. I thought you were over there getting yourself straightened out?'

'I was. I am.'

'Not in the way I meant,' Mackie said, the anger in his voice rising. 'You're treading a fine line. We can't have your antics drawing unwanted attention. You know how bad that could be. For you.'

Logan got it. But what could he say? He was a mess and everyone at the JIA knew it. His current appearance, bruises and all, only confirmed what everyone else was already thinking.

'I'm surprised they've let me come back,' Logan said, referring to the committee members, who he was sure would have raised their eyebrows at Mackie's decision to put him on the case.

'It was my decision, nobody else's. So tell me what happened.'

'Didn't my babysitter fill you in?' Logan said.

'Don't play games with me, Logan. I want to hear it from you. Just what is going on with you?'

'There's *nothing* going on,' Logan said, trying to keep his cool. 'I'm fine. It was just a scrape. These things happen.'

Mackie laughed sarcastically. 'You're right there. These things always happen to *you*.'

'Is this all you brought me here to talk about?' Logan said, standing up and taking a step toward the door. 'If it is then I can think of better things to do.'

'Sit down!' Mackie bellowed, getting to his feet. Logan stopped in his tracks. Mackie was a good six inches shorter than Logan but he had a certain presence that made people stop and pay attention. 'I haven't brought you back here to play games. This is serious business, Logan. And if you think I'm giving you a hard time then it's because I have to know that you can handle this.'

Sheepishly, Logan did as he was told and sat down again. He couldn't let this opportunity pass him by. Whether he was ready or not wasn't the question, as far as he was concerned.

'No offence,' Mackie said, sitting back down, his voice calm again, 'but couldn't you have shaved at least?'

Logan sensed that this time Mackie's comment had been more upbeat, trying to lighten the mood between them. That was his style – though Logan knew Mackie would never let anyone win an argument, or even worm their way out of one.

'I'm sorry, sir,' Logan said. 'I didn't realise I worked for an employer that disallowed facial hair. And you might not have heard, but they don't give out inflight razor blades these days.'

'Look, I mean … your clothes … what's up with your clothes?' Mackie said, just the slightest smile now visible.

Logan was wearing a pair of jeans which were threadbare on the knees and backside, an old pair of white trainers which had taken on a brown tinge many months ago, and a black turtleneck sweater.

'I've been on holiday. It might surprise you but I didn't take any suits with me. And anyway, this jumper is brand new. I just bought it in Newark airport 'cause I knew you'd do this. It was either this or my orange Hawaiian t-shirt.'

Mackie smiled and laughed, easing the tension in the room for the first time. 'I guess you did me a favour there.'

Despite his mood, Logan couldn't help but smile as well. Mackie had made his point. Logan had understood it.

'So where's Winter?' Logan asked, though he was glad he wasn't here. Logan couldn't stand him. The guy was ten years younger than Logan but already thought he ran the place.

'He's still in London. Why?'

'Just curious. Are you going to tell me what we're doing here?' Logan asked. 'Why do we care about some politician?'

'He's not technically a politician. He's a lawyer.'

'That's just about as bad.'

'Well, he's a pretty important lawyer. And very influential. Now, this case has come to us from the very top.'

'You don't say.'

'I do say. The Attorney General is the US's most senior law enforcement officer. He's also very close to the president. He's been kidnapped, and that causes a major headache. Not just because of what he knows, but because of who he knows.'

'So who is doing the official investigation then?' Logan said, referring to the fact that the JIA's involvement would be known to no-one in the outside world.

It was quite simple, really: the US and UK governments used the JIA to carry out black-ops and covert operations under the radar. Plausible deniability. But that didn't mean it was some sinister organisation charged with carrying out questionable dirty work that would have conspiracy theorists drooling. Just an organisation that was far enough removed to give its agents the room they needed to carry out operations as they saw fit. Or at least, as their governments saw fit.

Logan was a field agent, one of the most experienced that the JIA had. He guessed his role fell somewhere in between that of your classic spy and a private investigator. His skill was in doing whatever it took to get a job done, whatever the job may be.

'The Police nationale will be performing the official investigation,' Mackie said, 'but it wouldn't surprise me if the FBI and CIA didn't try to wangle their way into this one somehow, given who the victim is. Probably the FBI on the official side. Now, you're reporting directly to me, so keep well away from anyone else on this one unless I tell you otherwise.'

'I know that,' Logan said. He didn't need to be taught to suck eggs. The JIA rarely had any legal jurisdiction for their operations, so they generally steered well clear of any team carrying out a parallel local investigation. 'So what do you know?'

Mackie pointed at the two boxes next to his desk, which Logan could see were crammed with loose papers and files.

'This is what we know,' Mackie said, standing up and walking toward the coat stand near the door. 'Looks like you've got some reading to do. You've got three hours.'

Without looking at Logan, Mackie pulled his coat from the stand and walked out of the door.

Chapter 6

Frank Modena opened his eyes. His vision was blurred from the last beating he'd taken. His left eye was virtually closed up. It made it even harder to see in the windowless room, which was only sparsely lit by a single overhead bulb. Modena couldn't see behind him, but the room in front of him was completely empty. The poured concrete floor had pockmarks and chips taken out of it, suggesting the room had seen heavy use at some point. On the exposed brick walls were large patches of mould and mildew which, in the dim light, seemed to take on a sinister appearance, and there was an odour of damp and decay in the room.

Modena's hands were tied behind him, fixed to the chair that he was sitting on, and each of his ankles was tied to a chair leg. He couldn't move. Though it didn't really matter, because he didn't have the strength to try.

He'd been tied to the chair since he arrived at this place. They hadn't yet fed him, or moved him at all. He had lost his one last dignity a number of hours ago when he had been unable to hold his bladder any longer, much to the amusement of one of his captors.

When they had put the sack over his head and thrown him into the vehicle, Modena had used the movements to try to keep track of where they were going, seeking some comfort in at least knowing in which direction they had headed. But it was harder than it seemed. Within minutes, he no longer had any idea of direction. At a guess, he thought they'd driven for close to two hours before they'd finally come to a stop and dragged him into this hellhole. He had been taken down some steps, so he assumed he was in the basement of a building, but he had no idea what kind of building it might be. It could have been a barn or a city-centre skyscraper for all he knew. But there was so little noise, so little indication of the outside world, that he had no way of determining which it was. After arriving here it had been several more hours before the captors had taken the sack off Modena's head. And then the beatings had started.

None of them had yet shown their faces, always wearing their balaclavas. And they hadn't used any names for each other. He'd seen four attackers when they'd taken him, but he guessed there must have been at least two others involved: one driving the ambulance and another to drive the panel van that he'd been hauled into. But since he'd been in this room, only three different people had been in. Even though he hadn't seen any faces, he'd used their sizes and shapes as a guide. Though given their identical clothing, he supposed there could have been more than three if two or more of them were of a similar build.

One of them definitely seemed to be the leader, or at least was the most senior of those who had been in the room with him. The same one who had spoken to him before they had taken him. It was quite easy to tell him apart from the others. He was big in all directions, like a heavyweight boxer or a wrestler, and he had a deep, bass voice. A real thug.

Modena was straining to see through his swollen eyes. But with the sparse light he could tell he was alone in the room. For now.

Minutes later, though, the door opened and in walked a figure carrying a small object up to his chest. Modena winced, initially mistaking the object for a gun, but as the figure came closer he realised it was a plate. In the other hand was a glass of what looked like water. This man wasn't the leader. He was too short. Too thin. Modena felt the slightest twinge of relief.

'It's time for you to eat,' the man said. He spoke in English, though it was heavily accented. Modena would have guessed he was Arab, Middle Eastern, but he really couldn't be sure. It was the first time he'd heard this voice, but he thought he recognised the shape of the man. So that would still make it only three who had been into this room with him.

'Please. Why are you doing this?' Modena asked, though he wasn't really sure that he expected an answer.

The man put down the plate and held out the glass of water to Modena's lips. He began to tip it up, most of the water splashing down Modena's front as he frantically lapped at the cool liquid. When the glass was empty the man put it down and picked up the plate.

'You need to eat,' the man said.

He thrust a spoon toward Modena, who initially resisted, but then parted his lips and let the spoon be pushed into his mouth.

'There you go. Not so bad, is it? Ha! I could be feeding you your own shit and you probably wouldn't care right now.'

Modena had no idea what the food was. It didn't seem to taste of anything at all and he swallowed it without chewing. He stared into the man's dark eyes as he ate, not sure what he was hoping to see. He saw nothing.

After six mouthfuls he began to feel his stomach heaving. He closed his lips tightly when the spoon came back toward him.

'Last chance,' the man said. 'You don't want any more then I'm out of here. Your next visitor might not be so friendly, though. You ask me, I'm better company than some of those guys.'

He wasn't wrong there. He was the only one of the three so far to have not used Modena as a human punchbag. Modena opened his mouth and took one more spoonful. He dry-heaved as soon as he swallowed the food, struggling to keep it down.

'Whoa there,' the man said, laughing. 'Looks like you've had enough then. Don't want to make a mess of that nice suit you're wearing.'

'Why are you doing this?' Modena asked, trying to keep his mind off the pain in his body from the beatings and the sickness in his stomach from the food.

'Not for me to say. Just do as you're told and you'll get out of this. If you don't then things are going to get a whole lot worse for you. You know that, don't you?'

'I just want to go home.'

'You want to go home?' exclaimed a booming voice, followed by fake laughter.

Modena hadn't heard him come into the room. It was the leader: the foghorn voice and his size were unmistakeable.

'You'll go home when we get what we want from you,' he said.

'Just do what he says. You'll get out of here if you do,' the thin man said to Modena, almost in a whisper, before he got up and made for the door.

Modena was actually sad to see him go. He had been the only one to show any form of kindness. All the others had done so far was cause him pain.

The foghorn man strode up and laid a fist into Modena's stomach. He bowed his head and exhaled deeply. He knew the guy hadn't put his all into it, but the blow was still enough to send Modena's head into a spin. The food sloshed in his stomach, pushing up his gullet toward his mouth. He managed to hold it down – just.

'You do what we ask and you'll be going home,' the man said. 'You don't, and ... well, you know the rest.'

A punch was thrown into Modena's chest. The pressure sent his heart into a panic. It felt like it was about to explode.

All they had done so far was beat him and say the same thing to him: 'Do what we ask and you'll go home.' The only problem was, they hadn't yet asked him anything.

'I'll do whatever you want,' Modena said through jolted breaths. 'I have money. Is that what this is about? I have lots of money. I'll do whatever you want.'

The man leaned down to Modena and whispered into his ear. He was so close that Modena could feel the warmth of his foul coffee breath against his cheek. Modena struggled not to gag at the smell.

His swollen eyes opened as wide as they would go as he listened to what the man had to say. Listened to what it was that they had kidnapped him for.

'That's what you want?' Modena said.

The big man stood up again, a wicked smile visible beneath the black balaclava. 'That's what we want. You give us that and you're on your way home to wifey.'

Modena shook his head and opened and closed his mouth a few times before the words finally came out. *'That's what this is all about!'* he hissed. Anger rose up inside him and a strength returned to him from somewhere within.

But as quickly as the feeling had come, it was taken away from him again when a right hook from the big man landed on his head. It caught Modena on the ear and sent a ringing noise coursing through his brain. It took him a moment to recover, but before he could say anything another fist was thrust into his stomach. This time, despite his efforts, he couldn't stop as he retched and sprayed sticky, acidic vomit over his legs and onto the floor.

'Fuck me!' the man said, laughing. 'That's grim!'

Modena heaved a few more times, until there wasn't anything else in him to come out.

'Look, it's pretty simple, Frank. That one thing will save your life. In fact, that's the only thing that's going to.'

Modena spat out a mouthful of phlegm. It didn't take away any of the foul taste. 'But ... you don't understand. I can't do what you're asking. I can't. Because I don't know it ... I don't know how!'

'Oh, you *will* do it,' the man snarled, an instant before his fist caught Modena on the side of his head again. 'Or you'd better start praying.'

His head filled with pain and confusion, Modena was only partially aware of another strike to his head before everything went black.

Chapter 7

The boxes Mackie left contained copies of everything the local police had compiled so far. The investigation had only been ongoing for three days but they'd already pulled together a vast amount of data. But for all the pieces of paper, there really wasn't much to go on. They had endless details about exactly how the crime had taken place, including numerous witness statements. But there wasn't a single lead as to who had carried out the attack, why they had done it or where Modena now was.

The majority of the witnesses had seen or heard very little, mainly because most had either fled or kept their heads well down through fear of getting caught up in the melee. Together, though, the statements had allowed the police to re-create the events of the attack in some detail: how many perps there were, how each element of the assault had occurred, where the vehicles and people were located throughout, who had said what and when.

On top of that, there were numerous other pieces of information within the file analysing the scene: where the shots were fired from, what type of guns had been used, how many different guns had been fired, which ones fired the killer shots. The police had worked exceptionally fast to pull so much detail together in such a short space of time.

But none of it would help unless there was a lead to go on. All of those details would be crucial to any criminal case against the perpetrators, and would be vital in obtaining convictions. They were the difference between reasonable doubt and a lifetime in prison. But Logan hadn't been brought in to secure convictions. He'd been brought in to find the Attorney General.

Logan turned around when he heard the door open. It was Mackie. He took his coat off and hung it on the stand before walking over to the desk. Logan looked at his watch. Three hours, five minutes since Mackie had left. He'd been so engrossed in the files he hadn't once stopped to look at the time.

'So where do we start?' Mackie said, putting a brown paper bag down in front of Logan which contained a large cheese and ham baguette.

Logan picked up the sandwich and took a bite before answering, both because he hadn't eaten in hours and because he wanted to think his response through. He hadn't had anywhere near enough time to finish reading the files. And in truth he was lost as to where to start.

'Modena was here to discuss Guantanamo Bay,' Logan said.

'You, me and the whole world know that.'

'He was delivering a speech at the Hôtel de Ville,' Logan carried on, fully aware that Mackie probably knew all this, but it was helping him form his thoughts. 'The new guys at the White House are closing the place down. Or so they say. You ask me, it'll probably take them a few more years yet, and then all they'll do is carry on the same activities somewhere more private. Call me a cynic if you will.'

'It's what the world wants to hear.'

'Yeah, but closing the place down doesn't make the bad guys go away.'

Logan had some sympathies for what went on at Guantanamo Bay. He knew that his own job would probably be derided by those same people who protested against the existence of the facility. He had never had a problem with the things he'd done. Not until recently, at least. Did he agree that everything he'd done in his life was for a greater good? Maybe, maybe not. But someone somewhere did, otherwise he wouldn't have been given his orders. And in his line of work you couldn't really say no.

'There's the obvious hypothesis – that the kidnapping is linked to terrorists,' Logan said.

'It's certainly the route the press are taking. And the local police too. I take it you're not buying it.'

'Maybe. Maybe not. Either way, we're not seeing the whole picture.'

'How so?'

'Too many things are wrong. Where do I start? There's been no contact with the kidnappers, no ransom. Why such an elaborate attack? It was carried out in broad daylight. They used assault rifles and killed seven innocent people. Just to get to a politician?'

Logan stopped and took another couple of bites from his sandwich.

'The attack was all so over the top,' he said after swallowing another big mouthful. 'Certainly not how I would have snatched someone. You should know. You've had me do it plenty of times. You do it as quickly and effortlessly as possible. And that means not doing it in broad daylight, in a heavily populated area, against a heavily protected target where there are likely to be lots of witnesses and lots of casualties. Not to mention the planning and the money required to hire and train all your men and commandeer the vehicles needed.'

'Yes, I get all that,' Mackie said, standing up, a frustrated look on his face, and moving toward the sash window behind the desk. 'But do you have anything to go on?'

Logan thought for a minute before answering. There was one loose thread he wanted to pull on. But he was reluctant to raise it for fear of being shot down. And for fear of it being a non-starter. He'd been brought back into the field to prove himself, and there was no doubt he was already feeling the pressure.

'One thing,' Logan said eventually. 'The crash that was staged at the Place de la Concorde. It was a hit and run. They've looked for and can't find the offender, but the police haven't even spoken to the victim yet. We should dig into him a bit, see what there is.'

'The motorcyclist? He's still in hospital. He'll never walk again, apparently.'

'Yeah, I know.'

'You think he wanted his leg smashed fifteen different ways?'

'It's not unthinkable that he was part of it.'

'But it's much more likely that he wasn't.'

'I don't agree,' Logan said, going on the defensive. 'This whole thing would have fallen apart if that crash didn't happen at exactly the right time and place. Yeah, they could have crashed their car into anyone, but it's not exactly a high-speed junction. A simple car prang and everything would have moved on within minutes. They wanted gridlock. It had to be a serious incident.'

'It's possible, but it's hardly a smoking gun. Check it out by all means. But if it doesn't fit then move on. We don't have time on our side.'

Mackie sighed and came away from the window and sat down at the desk. He took out his tablet computer and began tapping away. Logan finished his sandwich and quickly rifled through the remaining files. But nothing else jumped out.

Checking out the motorcyclist had to be worth a shot. He knew that the lead was tenuous, and might prove ultimately to be worthless, but as Mackie had always told him: you take the low-hanging fruit first. And he had to start somewhere. Right now, just doing something was better than doing nothing. He needed to find his feet again. Mackie might not have been explicit but Logan was being tested. If he failed here, it would be the end of the line for him. And that made him uncomfortable because this case was anything but usual for him. He wasn't a detective. Having to eke leads out of nothing was not his strength. But he had to play the hand he'd been dealt. He had to make this case work somehow.

As Logan got up to leave Mackie stopped what he was doing. 'Please keep me abreast, Logan. I want to know what's happening at all times.'

Logan didn't respond. He knew he was under the spotlight and his every move would be watched and scrutinised and there was no point in fighting it. He was just going to have to grin and bear it. He headed toward the door. But Mackie wasn't quite finished yet.

'And, Logan ... just be careful out there.'

Again, Logan said nothing. He rolled his eyes as he walked out of the room, then carried on out of the safe house.

Once outside, he made his way to the apartment of Jean Vincent, the motorcyclist who'd been knocked off his bike at the Place de la Concorde. That crash had started the sequence of events which had led to Modena's capture. Vincent was still in hospital, but Logan didn't want to speak to him yet. He wanted to pay a visit to Vincent's apartment, where he lived alone, to see what dirt he could find. Anything that might link him to the attackers.

His counter-surveillance techniques second nature to him, Logan took a circuitous route on foot and on the Paris metro from

Saint-Denis to Montparnasse where Vincent's apartment was located in a quiet back street. Logan had no reason to believe there was any heat on him, but in his line of work there was no such thing as being too careful.

Although in close proximity to the main Parisian tourist traps, Montparnasse had a more leisurely feel with many residential apartment blocks and quaint cafés and bars. In years gone by it had been one of the main artistic centres in France where many of the world's most respected artists chose to live, and the area still carried a bohemian air.

The apartment block that Logan headed to was a five-storey building built in the pre-war years with wrought-iron balconies and ornate decorations on the outside window arches. It was clear, though, that the building had seen its best years and was now falling into disrepair. The main entrance to the building had neither a doorman nor a secured main entrance and Logan casually walked into the foyer, eyeballing the layout as he went. There was a wide central staircase which Logan began to walk up – Vincent's apartment was on the third floor.

As Logan left the stairs onto the dimly lit corridor, he took just a moment to take in his surroundings. He wasn't sure why but he could feel his nerves begin to take hold. Like a child would with a comforter, he put his hand to his side and felt the bulge where his gun was. A Glock. JIA agents didn't have standard issues as such, but the Glock handgun was about as standard as they got.

The trouble with being in Logan's line of work was that he didn't have any kind of security clearance because most of his identities didn't really exist. He couldn't take a gun through airport security like some law enforcement officers could, and that made carrying weapons across borders difficult. As a result he would typically pick up a weapon soon after arriving in a country from a pre-determined source. This Glock had been ready for him at the safe house when he arrived.

The importance of de-arming before cross-border travel and re-arming after had been drilled into Logan from early on in his career. Having had to do it for years now, it was nothing more than a mild inconvenience. There was a well-told story of one agent who had fallen foul of the system which had always stuck in Logan's mind. The agent, working on a case against a gang involved in people trafficking and weary from months of non- stop travelling around Eastern Europe, had turned up at airport security at Heathrow carrying a concealed handgun. He had simply forgotten he still had it with him. After causing quite a commotion, which made the national news, he was eventually charged with a whole host of firearms-related offences and sentenced to four years in jail. Whether to set an example of him, or whether it was just the way they did things, the JIA never intervened in the process, never came to his aid at all. The agent ended up spending over two years in jail before being let out on parole.

When Logan was younger, the part he liked most about the story was how the agent never once tried to defend himself by claiming to work for a government organisation. He didn't try to persuade the police, the judge or the jury that it was all part of his job. Didn't ask them to check out who he really was. He never asked for help from anyone. He just accepted his punishment, almost as if he acknowledged that he had done wrong by not following the JIA's rules. Two years of his life gone and he had accepted it as though it was a slap on his wrist. That, to Logan, spoke volumes about what working for an organisation like the JIA was all about. When he was younger, he had admired that – had admired both the JIA's and the agent's response to the situation.

He wasn't so sure he felt the same way about it anymore.

Would they just sit and let him rot if he was banged up in some archaic foreign jail? He already knew the answer to that. If it suited them, then yes, they would. The trick of course was not to get caught. But nobody is perfect.

Logan shook his head, realising he'd let his mind wander. He needed to focus. He carried on down the corridor, which was deserted, and approached the door to apartment 3d, one hand still on his Glock. In his other coat pocket he had a small torsion wrench and a set of picks. Simple tools that would allow Logan to pick an array of household locks within seconds. But he came to a stop on the near side of the door when he realised it was already ajar. As he looked more closely, the splintered wood on the door frame made it clear that the lock had been jimmied.

He looked around, up and down the corridor, his senses on high alert. No signs of anyone else. He stood there for a few seconds, listening for any sounds coming from within the apartment. But there was nothing. His heart rate was quickening nonetheless. He inched forward, pulled his Glock from his trousers and held it out, using the barrel to push open the door further. And as it opened to reveal the studio-style apartment inside, Logan felt a pang of satisfaction when he realised this lead might be worthwhile after all.

Because Logan didn't believe in coincidences.

And it was quite clear that someone had ransacked Jean Vincent's apartment.

Chapter 8

'Is it done?' bellowed Reggie, an oaf of a man whom Johnny worked for from time to time as a 'security' consultant. Reggie wasn't shouting, his voice was just naturally raucous. He was six foot seven and weighed almost twenty stone and his voice matched his appearance.

'Yes, of course,' Johnny said, entering the lounge and sitting down on the empty three-seater sofa adjacent to Reggie. 'It's not going to be a problem anymore.'

'Okay. Good. Make sure this is the end of it. No more cock-ups.'

Johnny could tell that Reggie was fuming inside but, somewhat unnaturally for him, he was keeping it below the surface for now. It wasn't Johnny's fault that things looked like they might have turned south. Well, not entirely. And at least he'd taken the initiative in sorting the problem out. He was pretty sure that they now had the collateral to keep the problem under wraps.

'How's our friend?' Johnny asked.

'Asleep, apparently. I've not seen him for the last couple of hours – too many other things to worry about.'

'Yeah, well, one less thing to worry about now.'

'One less thing to worry about?' echoed an unfamiliar voice from over by the door.

Reggie and Johnny both turned their attention to the man standing in the doorway. He was slight, and dressed in beige trousers and a blue turtleneck. He had silky black hair and a manicured black beard. His voice was smooth and his upper-class English accent belied his Middle Eastern origin. Johnny had never met him before, and he wasn't much to look at, but Johnny knew all about this man. He was someone you really didn't want to get on the wrong side of. Although Johnny hadn't until now come face to face with him, he knew Reggie and the others had been in contact with him for some time. And he could tell by the unusually pleasant look on Reggie's face that even the big man was wary of him.

'Johnny, I don't believe you two have met,' Reggie said, getting to his feet and walking toward the newcomer.

'No, we haven't,' the bearded man said.

Reggie shook his hand before ushering him into the room. 'This is Johnny. He works for me,' he said, pointing toward Johnny, who was now on his feet.

'Johnny, this is –'

'I know who he is,' Johnny said, timidly shaking the bearded man's hand but not daring to look him in the eye.

'You said there was one less thing to worry about?' the bearded man said.

Reggie and Johnny looked at each other, aware that he must have been listening to their conversation. Johnny could see the look of unease on Reggie's face. As confident as Reggie was, it was clear he was scared of this man. Johnny felt the same. He'd heard about the grisly fates of his many enemies and he really didn't want to be one of them.

'There's nothing to worry about now,' Reggie said. 'It's been taken care of.'

'What's been taken care of?' the man asked.

'It was nothing. Just a problem with one of our men.'

'What was the problem?'

The bearded man's tone was calm and as smooth as his hair. But his placidness was unnerving. Reggie looked over at Johnny again, who was squirming away. The question had clearly been aimed at Reggie and Johnny wasn't going to bail him out. He really didn't want to delve into the trouble he'd just been sorting out because he knew it made them look amateurish.

'Nothing really,' Reggie said, scratching his head. 'Someone wanting more money than they were promised. But it's sorted now.'

The bearded man smiled at Reggie and then at Johnny. 'Well, that's good to hear. We don't want anybody getting greedy now, do we? So, you've taken care of him?'

'Yeah, we've taken care of it,' Reggie said.

'No, I asked have you taken care of *him*?'

Johnny knew exactly what he meant.

'No. It's too difficult to do that right now,' Reggie said. 'Let's just say we've made provisions so that he can't do us any harm.'

The bearded man shook his head. 'That's not the same thing at all, though, is it?'

'We're trying to be careful here,' Reggie said, the forced softness in his voice waning. 'We don't need any unwanted attention.'

'Just get it done.'

'Don't you think it'll be a bit obvious?' Johnny blurted out, surprised at himself for speaking up. 'We can't just leave bodies lying around here, there and everywhere.'

'Bodies are only a problem if you're not careful and make a mistake,' the bearded man said, shooting a glare at Johnny.

'And just how do you expect us to do it, then?' Reggie said, struggling now to keep his pleasant tone.

The bearded man flicked Reggie a stare that spoke volumes. 'Well, I would suggest you do it something like this.'

The man lunged toward Johnny, sweeping behind him and grabbing him around the neck with his left arm. He whipped his right arm from around his back, a gleaming hunting blade in his hand. He wrenched Johnny's head back and pushed the blade onto his exposed neck.

'You put the blade here,' the man said.

The knife dug into Johnny's neck, just below his left ear. He felt a sharp pain as the blade was pushed against his skin and shivered at the sensation as a line of blood ran down onto his clothes. He began to shout and writhe, but despite his superior size over the bearded man he was helpless.

Reggie stood motionless, his mouth wide open.

'And then you take the blade and you cut from ear to ear, like this.'

The bearded man's tone had now switched to a menacing hiss. He swept the knife across Johnny's neck, nicking the skin, making Johnny wince.

'You want to go nice and deep at the start. You're not looking for a mere flesh wound.'

He placed the knife back up against Johnny's skin, pressing against his larynx.

'You can easily cut a man's head off with a knife like this. The hardest bit is the throat. You can open it up with ease, but to cut right through you need to press down hard – don't just rely on the blade. Or if you want, go in at the side first, and force the blade out to the front. Either way, you should be able to cut through in one go.'

He pressed the knife further into Johnny's neck, cutting deeper into his skin now. Johnny was in a panic. Surely he wasn't going to do it? Not here, like this?

'You can take his head off if you like, but it's messy. And it's not for everyone.'

The man pulled the knife away and released Johnny's left arm. Johnny fell in a heap on the floor, whimpering. He felt his neck then looked at his bloodied hand.

'He cut me!' he shouted. 'He fucking cut me!'

'Just get it done!' the bearded man spat, his whole face contorting with anger. Then, quick as a flash, the look was gone again and his eerie calmness returned. He swept his hair back, away from his face. 'Now. Where is dear old Frank? I really am dying to meet him.'

Chapter 9

Having first checked Vincent's apartment to make sure he was alone, Logan spent a few minutes searching the place for anything of interest. He had no idea how Vincent fitted into the wider picture of Modena's kidnapping, but given the ransacked apartment his instincts were screaming at him that Vincent was in some way involved.

After leaving the building, Logan made the decision to head to the Saint-Joseph Hospital. It was time to speak to Vincent himself. Apply a little pressure. However it was that Vincent fitted into the attack on Modena, he was surely only a small cog. So Logan needed to find a bigger cog. And he was good at persuading people to talk.

The hospital was less than two miles away from Vincent's home, so Logan decided to walk. He needed the fresh air and the exercise would hopefully wake him up – the long flight the night before was quickly taking its toll.

The weather was pleasantly balmy and the sun in the clear sky beat down on him as he made his way, making him feel warm and clammy even though he wore only a jumper on top.

He called Mackie as he walked and explained what he'd found.

'Anything useful to go on?' Mackie asked.

'Not much. No phone, wallet, computer. An angry letter from his landlord about unpaid rent, but other than that, not much correspondence.'

'Damn it. What were they looking for?'

'Who knows?'

'So you've got nothing.'

'I didn't say that. I've got a phone number you should check out. It was on some scrap of paper stuffed in his jeans pocket.'

'Okay. Anything else?'

'Two receipts from a bar. One was with the phone number. The other was in his rubbish bin.'

'Bar receipts. Jesus, you're really scraping the barrel there, Logan.'

'Maybe. But why would Vincent be visiting a bar in Clichy-sous-Bois? It's not exactly his local. And it's not an area known for its thriving nightlife.'

Logan had never been there before but he knew that Clichy-sous-Bois was one of the most deprived areas of Paris. A hotspot for gang-bangers and career criminals.

He stopped at a busy crossroads and, conscious of the people milling around him, he waited for the lights to turn before he carried on the conversation.

'What about at your end?'

'Well, I have to admit,' Mackie said, 'it looks like you might have been right about Vincent. We've done some digging and some things here don't look right.'

Logan felt a wave of relief. He'd half been expecting a berating for having wasted everyone's time with nothing but a phone number and a couple of bar bills.

'We've been through his bank accounts, his mobile phone records. There's nothing significant coming in or out of his bank account. To be honest, this guy wasn't a big earner. But he's not drawn out anything for almost two weeks now either, which looks odd.'

'Actually, it stacks up nicely,' Logan said. 'It means he's come into some money recently. Cash.'

'My thoughts exactly.'

'And his phone records?'

'Well, let's just say this guy keeps some pretty lousy friends. What was that song about drug dealers on speed dial?'

Logan laughed. 'Any of them look like they could be of interest?'

He stopped at another set of lights, still looking around him. Up ahead he spotted the hospital looming large.

'We're still working through the list,' Mackie said. 'As you know, big players are pretty careful, so we're only talking about a handful of low-level pushers and guys with misdemeanours here. But like I said, Vincent keeps some poor company. So we need to find who he works for, and who they work for.'

'You know, there's not really anything yet to actually link him to the attack on Modena. Given his friends, his apartment being broken into could have been to do with anything.'

'You really believe that?' Logan said, feeling a little deflated.

'I'm just saying it's possible.'

'Okay. I guess there's only one way to find out. I'm on my way to see Vincent now.'

'Logan, just be careful,' Mackie said, sounding just a little concerned. 'I mean, please be discreet.'

'I'll do what I can,' Logan said again, dashing over a side road just in front of a slowly approaching car. He tried his best not to rise to Mackie's gibe.

Logan gave Mackie the details of the number he'd found and the bar receipts, and ended the call just as he approached the hospital's main entrance. It was a modern, glass-fronted building that looked more like a corporate office. But behind the impressive façade it was much the same as any other large inner-city hospital: long, winding corridors, sterile colour schemes, confusing and utterly ineffective signage, and the distinctive smell of illness and disinfectant that only exists in such places.

Vincent was in an open ward on the second floor of the main building, having had surgery on his left leg the previous day. Logan headed to the bank of lifts and then up to the second floor. He exited and walked toward the double doors that led into the ward.

As he entered the ward he did a split-second recce of the area. Logan didn't have a photographic memory but he was good at taking in his surroundings. While other people might fill their memory banks with phone numbers, birthdays and sports statistics, he was much more adept at memorising details in the short term; the layout of locations he went to, faces, clothes, things like that. Being aware of everything that was going on around him was an essential part of the job. It was a learned skill rather than something that had always been with him. After years of training and use, it was now second nature, to the point that it was almost subconscious.

The ward was centred around a long corridor with numerous small, open ward areas off it and also a number of doors which Logan guessed led into the private ward rooms for more serious or long-term residents. The reception desk was a few yards down the corridor, though there was a waiting area and a vending area on opposite sides of the corridor before that. Logan knew that the receptionists wouldn't let him through to visit Vincent if he asked, but that wasn't a problem. All it would take was a little patience. So many people come and go in hospitals that an unfamiliar face rarely draws attention. The majority of staff are there to serve the patients' needs and are necessarily distracted by that. On this ward, the only people in Logan's way were the two receptionists. And he knew it wouldn't take long for them, too, to be distracted.

So Logan waited, milling around the vending machines, looking for the right moment. He eyed the people passing through, staff and visitors alike. But then a teenage girl in the waiting area caught his attention. She was nestling her head against the man sitting next to her, who Logan guessed was her father. Logan couldn't help but stare. At first he wasn't sure why. There was just something about her. And then it clicked.

Her long, dark hair. Her perfect skin. *Those eyes.*

She looked just like *her.*

Logan's heart skipped a beat. He felt his hands begin to tremble. He took a step back, his legs unsteady, his hand reaching out for something to hold on to. He was unable to take his eyes off the girl, all of a sudden oblivious to everything else around him. Within seconds, sweat droplets began to form on his body, the same way they did each time he slept. His mind began to take him to a dark place. That place where he had first seen her, five months ago.

The day he almost died.

She hadn't been so lucky.

Lost in his own thoughts, the ward was quickly becoming stifling. A trickle of sweat ran down his cheek. His whole body was stiff. He was locked in place, unable to move. It was as though Logan's mind was taking him into a waking nightmare, the images of that fateful day flashing before his eyes.

A voice echoed in his head. At first he thought it was part of the nightmare. But then he heard the voice again and some clarity began to return. Again came the voice, from right next to him, and as quickly as the nightmare had started, it began to fade. Logan looked down at the boy standing by his side and apologised, moving out of the way of the vending machine that he had been blocking. The boy put some money in the machine and pressed a button, and a chocolate bar dropped down.

Logan peered over at the girl again, the nightmare now vanquished. She turned her head and, just for a moment, their eyes met. She noticed Logan staring. Seeming just a little unnerved, she quickly averted her gaze and started up a conversation with the man she was sitting with.

Logan looked away too, back at the reception desk, trying his best to keep his head clear. He didn't need any more unwanted distractions. And it wasn't long before he saw his chance: one of the receptionists was called into the back office while the other was dealing with a very animated old French man. Logan glanced around and then quite simply walked past the reception desk and headed down the ward's corridor.

Mackie had already given Logan the number of the private room that Vincent was staying in. Looking at the numbering system on the doors, Logan knew that Vincent's room would be toward the far end of the corridor.

As he walked along, Logan kept his senses on alert. Interns scurried about in front of him, and nurses strolled along the corridor confidently. A whole mob of trainees following a consultant stood to one side to let Logan pass. But other than that no-one paid him any attention. Few other visitors were in the ward, Logan noticed.

But then, as he neared Vincent's room, someone caught his eye. The man, wearing blue jeans and a brown leather jacket, was of a similar size and build to Logan, though even with his face partially obscured by a baseball cap Logan could see the man was a good ten years older. He had a confident walk but he was anxious, his eyes darting from left to right, an uneasy expression on his rugged face.

Logan kept his gaze on the man and their eyes met briefly as he walked past. Logan's instincts were already screaming at him.

He quickened his pace and found room 9d. He turned the door handle and stepped into the room. Long white curtains were drawn around what Logan guessed was Vincent's bed. He moved toward them and reached out to move the drapes aside.

'Oh, shit.'

Logan's heart thudded in his chest once again. But this time his mind wasn't playing tricks. The grisly sight before him was all too real. And the blood-soaked sheets, together with the gaping wound in Vincent's neck, which was still oozing thick liquid, told Logan all he needed to know.

The man with the baseball cap. It had to have been him.

A split second later Logan was sprinting back down the corridor.

The consultant's posse were milling about by the reception desk and Logan screamed at them to move. He barged through without waiting for them to do so, oblivious to their shouts and cries. He pushed open the double doors and headed for the stairwell. There wasn't time to wait for the lift. He took the stairs two, three at a time, and crashed through the doors at the bottom, almost taking out a startled old lady.

Running through the central reception area, he was only briefly aware of the bystanders who had stopped to stare at him. Logan looked left and right as he ran, scoping out exits or routes of escape, but there were none that he could see – only the main entrance.

Exiting out onto the street, Logan finally stopped. He was panting, out of breath. He scanned the street, up and down, his brain calculating the options, determining which way to go next.

But in the end he didn't go anywhere. Logan shouted in frustration and hung his head.

Because he knew it was too late.

The man was gone.

Chapter 10

After regaining his composure, Logan left the hospital immediately. He wanted to be well away before the police arrived.

He was supposed to be operating covertly, and running amok through the ward where a man had just had his throat cut wasn't exactly inconspicuous. He knew Mackie was going to give him a hard time about it. But in the moment he'd lost his head. There was no doubt in his mind that the man he'd seen in the ward was the culprit. And Logan had been so close to him that he'd got carried away with the situation.

The training Logan had received for his job, all those years ago, had been all-encompassing. He'd been extensively coached in surveillance and counter-surveillance, a whole host of armed and unarmed combat skills. He was proficient in nine martial arts, had been instructed in the use of knives, handguns, rifles and countless other small arms. There had also been psychological training: learning to control his body and its reaction to external stimuli. They'd taught him survival techniques and how to keep himself alive. He'd learned to handle extremes such as heat, cold, thirst, hunger, pain and physical endurance, and how to control and suppress his feelings.

He used to be proud of each and every one of the traits he'd developed. He'd thought they made him a better man. But they had made him into a living, walking, talking machine. A robot. Something which carried out orders.

Everything was different now. The speed and clarity of mind that had once come without forethought had been tarnished. He was now rational and emotional and acted on instinct.

He was human again.

The only problem was, humans make mistakes.

And by creating a scene in the hospital, the spot where a bloody murder had just been committed, Logan had done the exact opposite of what his boss had told him to do.

There was also the doom-and-gloom feeling of knowing that the man who'd killed Vincent had got away. But, as unlikely as it would have seemed to him beforehand, it was the sight of the dead, bloodied body that had bothered Logan the most. It had physically shaken him. Until recently, the sight of a dead body wouldn't have moved him in the slightest.

Logan headed to the Hotel Brittanique to gather his thoughts and to determine what he could do next. More on edge than he had been before, Logan once again employed all his training to make his tracks as difficult to follow as he could. But there was no doubting that he was rattled. As if in response to his growing uncertainty over his own skills, Logan added a further layer of complexity to his route, finally arriving at the hotel an hour later than he otherwise would have.

The hotel, not far from the safe house in Saint-Denis, was a simple and functional building lacking any kind of elegance. Given its location it was used largely by people visiting the many local businesses rather than tourists, who stuck to the central areas.

Mackie had booked him a room under the name John Burrows. It was one of Logan's many cover identities. Each had a full range of identification: passport and driving licence at a minimum, with the same picture and date of birth, just differing names and nationalities. They were essential for keeping his trail clean.

'Good evening,' Logan said in French to the man at the front desk. 'I have a reservation for John Burrows.'

'Of course, Mr Burrows. Let me just check for you. Do you have your passport?'

Logan handed over a British passport for John Burrows.

'Ah yes, Mr Burrows,' the man said, typing away on the computer in front of him. 'We have you booked with us for three nights. I see your company has pre-paid.'

Three nights? Did they really expect him to be done and dusted in that time? Or maybe that was as long as Mackie had been able to buy for Logan from the JIA committee. He was under no illusion that they would be scrutinising his every move.

And they probably wouldn't be too impressed so far.

'How very kind of them,' Logan said.

'And we have their details already for any extras,' the man said, looking at his screen, 'so you don't need to worry about a thing. Here is your key. Your room is on the fourth floor. Number four-one-two.'

'Has my luggage arrived yet?' Logan asked.

He'd left the bag he brought from Vegas, with his limited belongings, at the safe house earlier in the day. Not that there was anything in it that he really wanted or needed, other than his toothbrush and a pair of clean boxers.

'Yes, it's in your room already, Mr Burrows.'

Logan thanked the receptionist and took the key from him, then headed for the small bank of lifts. He exited the lift on the fourth floor and found his door a few yards down the corridor. He reached out and put the key card into the slot and began to open the door. But when the door was open just a few inches, he noticed the lights in the room were already on.

Suddenly, thoughts went thrashing through his mind as to what that could mean. But his body didn't react and he continued to push the door open. It was only when he spotted a figure in the corner of the room that he finally responded.

His training taking over, Logan was already moving into a defensive stance, his hand pulling the Glock out of his trousers, when he realised the figure was Mackie.

'Jesus, Logan, put that thing away, will you!'

Mackie was sitting on an armchair next to the window holding a tumbler of what looked like Scotch or brandy.

Not for the first time in the day, Logan suddenly felt very foolish. But was that because he was pointing his gun at his boss? Or because of how long it had taken his mind and body to react to a potential threat? He'd got there eventually, but if it had been a real threat he would have been dead the second his head had poked around the door. No doubt about it.

This just wasn't him at all. Had he really lost it that much?

'What are you doing here?' Logan snapped, stuffing his gun away.

'I thought you might want some company,' Mackie said.

Logan closed the door, relieved that Mackie was seemingly ignoring his amateurish behaviour. For now at least.

'Plus, I've brought over some stuff for you.' Mackie nodded toward the bed, where there were four neat piles of clothes. In each was a pressed light-blue shirt, black linen trousers, black socks and black briefs.

'That's not my stuff,' Logan said, coming over to the bed and inspecting the clothes. 'Where's my bag?'

'Left it in the safe house. Sorry about that. Thought you might want something more appropriate. We couldn't have you running around Paris in that orange Hawaiian shirt, now, could we? The thought alone was giving me heart palpitations.'

'Well, you could have got me something a bit more stylish,' Logan said. 'I'm going to end up looking like you in these.'

'Ha bloody ha. Looks like you got your humour back then.'

'I wasn't being funny.'

'Do you want a drink?' Mackie said, shaking his glass. 'I'm paying.'

'Yeah, that's exactly what I need. What have we got?' Logan said, turning toward the unit that housed the mini-bar.

'Nothing good,' Mackie said. 'Blended whisky and cheap brandy.'

'Right now, anything that's strong is good enough for me.'

Logan poured himself a Scotch and took a sip, immediately feeling the pleasant burn as the alcohol slipped down his throat. He sat down on the bed and took another sip, relaxing into the situation, almost as if they were nothing more than two old friends sharing a drink after a hard day's work. It was, and always had been, clear to Logan that his and Mackie's relationship was one of subordinate and boss, and their moods and often clipped conversations with each other reflected that. But the two men had worked together so closely for the last eighteen years that they were also unreservedly comfortable in each other's company and with each other's ways. There was a mutual respect. A mutual affection. Logan didn't think it was friendship exactly, but something very close.

'So, Jean Vincent. What the hell happened?' Mackie said.

'Someone got to him.'

'That's bleeding obvious. But it wasn't what I was asking. What the hell were you doing charging through the hospital like that? Those places have cameras everywhere. I've had to pull some pretty big strings already to keep the police off your back.'

'I know. I'm sorry. I saw the man who did it. I thought I could get him.'

The expression on Mackie's face softened. 'You did? Anything we can work with?'

'Possibly. If you get the CCTV footage, I'll be able to pick him out for you.'

'Okay, leave it with me.'

'Is there anything more on Vincent?' Logan said, taking another drag of his whisky and hoping that his attempt at changing the subject would work.

Mackie smiled. 'There may be. We've followed a few leads on the phone records and a lot of them point to the same place. Or the same man, I should say.'

'So you agree now that Vincent was involved?'

'Well, there are certainly a lot of coincidences otherwise. The bigger question is, why the hell did someone trash his place and kill him?'

'Loose ends.'

'Maybe. But why him and why now?'

'Who knows? So what did you find on Vincent?'

'We've linked that phone number you found to a passport counterfeiter.'

'A counterfeiter? How does that fit into any of this?'

'It fits nicely into the police's theory that terrorists from outside of France are responsible. A reliable counterfeiter would be very useful, don't you think?'

'The terrorist link,' Logan groaned. The more he'd thought about the case, the less he was convinced that this was a terrorist attack. 'So we're all going with that now, are we? I'm sorry, but Jean Vincent didn't strike me as your usual Islamic extremist. Plus nearly all of the witnesses who said anything even remotely useful said the attackers were speaking English both to each other and to Modena.'

'Logan, everyone speaks English. I don't disagree with you but we can't rule out the link just like that. And it fits with the police's theory.'

'What does that mean?' Logan said, his tone more terse now. 'The French police think the kidnapping is something to do with terrorists, so we just follow their lead regardless?'

'I'm not following this line just because it fits with what the police think,' Mackie snapped. Logan's defensiveness had obviously got his back up. 'It's what I think too. And everyone else, for that matter. We need to take the leads that we have.'

'This is all weak as piss,' Logan responded. 'If terrorists wanted to make a big mark, do you not think they would just blow something up? Why go to all the effort of such an elaborate attack? The biggest question of all is still why was Modena targeted? If we think about what he could have that somebody out there could want, then that's going to lead us in the right direction.'

'So what have you got, Logan?' Mackie said, irritation clear in his voice. 'You tell me. What does Modena have that got him kidnapped?'

Logan stared daggers at his boss. He didn't like being challenged. But he knew it was a good question. And he didn't have an answer. 'Information, perhaps.'

'Like what?'

'Look, I don't know,' Logan conceded.

'Well,' Mackie said, 'until you do know, I suggest you go with what we've got. The lead with this counterfeiter is worth checking out. I think you'll see why when I tell you what we know.'

'I'm all ears.'

Mackie sighed. 'There's no easy way to tell you this, Logan. But I think you'll agree it gives a bit of weight to the link to Islamic extremists.'

Mackie paused.

'Go on,' Logan said.

'Two days ago Youssef Selim arrived in France. We think he might be behind this.'

Logan almost dropped his whisky.

Chapter 11

Johnny pushed the sleeve of his leather jacket up over his wrist to check the time on his watch. It was almost nine p.m. He'd been standing outside the Hotel Brittanique now for over two hours and there was still no sign of the mark. Having tortuously followed the man from the hospital back here, he was uncomfortable to now have him out of sight for so long. There was always the risk that he'd gone out of a back door or something. But then why would he have done that? Johnny was pretty sure the mark hadn't figured out he was being followed.

Though the guy was clearly more than just cautious. From what Johnny had seen he was highly trained in counter-surveillance. In fact, it was only through sheer luck that Johnny hadn't lost him. At one point the mark had vanished altogether for a good half hour, only for Johnny to stumble upon him again by chance, casually browsing in a clothing store. Or pretending to at least.

Johnny had clocked the guy as suspicious as soon as he'd laid eyes on him in the hospital corridor. The way he moved. The look on his face. And then the way the guy had charged down the corridor after coming out of Jean Vincent's room. He had to be some sort of police. Or intelligence.

Johnny's initial orders had been simple: kill Vincent. The guy had got greedy. Johnny could understand that, to some extent. Vincent wasn't being paid much; it wasn't like he had a big part to play. But the accident had been far worse than intended. The doctors had said Vincent may have never walked again. He was understandably pissed off and had threatened to go to the police if he didn't receive double.

Another ten thousand euros.

It was barely a drop in the ocean next to what Johnny knew Reggie would be taking. But Vincent chose the wrong people to blackmail. And he certainly wouldn't be walking again now. Johnny had carried out his orders no problem, exactly as Selim had suggested, though he had been unable to stop himself gagging at the sight of Vincent's neck opening up. He'd hurt people before, but it wasn't his route of choice to be so brutal, or to be so close. Killing with a knife was personal.

But after seeing the big guy in the corridor, Johnny knew something wasn't right. Why had he been there at all? There was no reason for Vincent to have been on the police's radar. Which worried Johnny. Because maybe it meant he'd missed something, made a mistake down the line. And the last thing he wanted was to have to admit that to Selim.

Johnny took out his phone to call Reggie. He wasn't looking forward to what he knew would be a heated conversation. He'd worked for Reggie on and off for over a year. The jobs he did paid by the day, which was good, and it was easy work, but it required Johnny to work for a man who was, quite frankly, uncontrollable. Their relationship constantly teetered on the brink of outright confrontation. And with the presence of Selim added to the mix, Johnny was beginning to seriously doubt his career choice. If he'd had another option for work, he would surely have taken it. But he didn't.

Reggie picked up the call on the second ring.

'What is it?' Reggie said in his booming voice.

'I'm still outside the hotel,' Johnny said. 'I haven't seen the mark for over two hours now. What do you want me to do?'

'Surely you know the answer to that? I want you to find out who he is. That's your job, isn't it?'

'Er, yeah, but I thought you just wanted me to follow him?'

'No, I want you to find out who he is. Didn't I just say that?!'

'And how am I supposed to do that?'

'For fuck's sake, how should I know? That's what I'm paying you for.'

'Okay, but how long do you want me to keep this up for? Is there someone else who can take over here for the night?'

'Johnny, is there something the matter with you? Are you trying to wind me up? We need to know if this guy is a threat. If he is then we need a plan to get rid of him. No loose ends, remember? But to know if he's a threat, I need to know who he is. And I need to know what he's doing here.'

'Okay,' Johnny cut in, hoping Reggie would stop. He didn't.

'Now I pay you to find out those things for me. So why are you asking me all these questions? Just do your fucking job and call me when you have something interesting to tell me. Got it?'

'Yeah. I got it.'

The line went dead. Johnny stuffed the phone back in his pocket. What was Reggie's problem anyway? It wasn't like he didn't know how to do this job. But that didn't mean he wanted to be stuck outside this hotel all night without any food or sleep.

He crossed the street toward the hotel entrance. Once inside, he headed toward the reception desk where a young lady was on duty.

'Bonsoir,' Johnny said as he approached the lady.

'Bonsoir, monsieur,' the receptionist said.

'I'm hoping you can help me,' Johnny said, still in French. He spoke the language fluently, and having lived in France for many years now, he'd pretty much lost his English twang. 'I'm looking for a man who checked in here about two hours ago. He's tall, over six feet, wearing jeans and a black jumper. Can you tell me if he's staying here?'

The lady scowled at him. 'I'm sorry, sir. That's not really something we would be able to tell you. We can't give away information like that about our guests.'

'Madame, this is very important. I'm really hoping you can help me,' Johnny said, pulling out his Interpol ID. His fake Interpol ID. He waved it in front of her face. 'My name is Detective Platt.'

Lord, thank you for Interpol, Johnny thought. How many people in this world would know what an Interpol ID looked like? Did Interpol detectives even carry IDs? Did Interpol have detectives? Johnny didn't have a clue, but he knew that his fake ID worked every time. Most people were gullible beyond comprehension.

'Detective, I'm sorry. I didn't realise. What exactly is the matter?'

'Nothing's the matter. I'm just trying to find this man as he's someone we need to speak to urgently. We believe he's staying here and that he checked in about two hours ago. Like I said, he's tall, about my height. Wearing jeans and a black jumper. He's got short brown hair and is in his mid-thirties. His face is pretty beaten up; I'm sure he'd stand out to whoever checked him in.'

'I wasn't on duty two hours ago. I can go and check with my colleague,' she said before scurrying off into the office behind the reception desk.

She came out two minutes later with a male colleague in tow who was looking worried.

'Detective, is there something wrong?' he said. 'Is this man dangerous?'

'No, no,' Johnny said, holding his hands up. 'There's nothing to worry about. I just need to talk to him. It's a very important matter, but I'm afraid I can't tell you any more than that. Can you please tell me if he's staying here?'

'Well, a man fitting that description checked in earlier tonight. An Englishman.' The man tapped away at a computer behind the desk. 'Mr Burrows. Mr John Burrows. Room four-one-two.'

'John Burrows? Do you have any details for him?'

'Er, yes, we always take a copy of the passports of our foreign guests. Do you need a copy?'

'Yes. That would be very helpful.'

The man hurried off and returned less than a minute later with a photocopy of John Burrows' passport. Johnny took it from him and quickly scanned the image before folding it and placing in the inside pocket of his jacket. It was definitely the right guy.

'Do you want us to contact him for you?' the male receptionist asked.

'No. That won't be necessary for now. Thank you for your help.'

Johnny turned and walked back toward the hotel entrance, away from the confused-looking receptionists. They were probably wondering why the Interpol detective was now leaving the hotel when he'd gone in there wanting to urgently speak to this John Burrows. But Johnny couldn't care less about that.

Once he was back in the street, he took his phone out of his pocket again and dialled his boss.

'Johnny, what is it now?' Reggie shouted.

'He's English,' Johnny said. 'He's called John Burrows. I've got a copy of his passport.'

There was silence on the other end of the line for a moment. Johnny took that as a small victory. It was about as close to vindication as he was likely to get from Reggie.

'John Burrows, hey? You've got a camera on your phone, right? Take a picture of the passport and send it over to me. I'll look into Burrows and find out what I can about him. You stay there until I call back.'

'Stay here? But, Reggie, I can't stay here all night ...' Johnny said, though the line was already dead. 'Bastard!' Johnny screamed at his phone.

He looked over at the hotel, seething with anger. He'd done exactly what had been asked of him. He'd killed Vincent without once questioning it. He'd spotted this Burrows guy and taken the initiative of following him. He'd been standing here doing nothing for hours. Had found out the mark's name, his room number. Had got a copy of his passport! And he was still being treated like some dumb skivvy by Reggie.

'You'd better be careful, John Burrows,' Johnny said out loud. 'Or you're going to end up just like that prick Vincent.'

Chapter 12

7th October

Logan tried his hardest to scream. But there was nothing left in his lungs now. The girl lay butchered in front of him. Lifeless. Her naked body almost completely black from the dried blood.

They grabbed him from behind and flung him to the ground. His face smashed on the hard concrete floor. A deep gash opened above his left eye. Warm, thick liquid gushed out over his face. They had him pinned to the ground: four men, each forcing their weight on one of his limbs, and a fifth man driving a knee into the small of his back.

He tried again to scream. Tried his best to struggle, to break free. But the days of endless torture and beatings had taken their toll. He could manage nothing more than a pathetic squirm as Youssef Selim, sword in hand, came into view, a look of quiet satisfaction on his bearded face. His blood-soaked clothes glowed in the electric light.

'This is it for you, my friend,' Selim said to him, in his almost surreally perfect English.

The blade of the sword glistened as he moved it through the air. The men began chanting in a language Logan didn't recognise. He tried again to scream. He wasn't sure whether anything came out. If it did, it wasn't enough to drown out the noise from the men.

Selim kneeled next to him. He placed the cold steel against Logan's neck. For a few seconds, the feeling of metal on skin was the only sensation that he was aware of. Gone was the pain. Gone was the chanting. Gone was the smell of blood, sweat and vomit. But it didn't last long. Seconds later, there was a whole new pain.

The sword began cutting into his neck. Slicing through his flesh. The cold metal moved back and forth, pushing its way deeper and deeper. He tried again to struggle, to shout. But his body lay silent and still as the life was cut from him.

Suddenly the silence was broken by a shriek of pure terror.

Logan opened his eyes and realised the scream was coming from his own lungs.

Selim was gone. And so were his men.

He lay still in his bed while his mind recovered from the nightmare. As always after the dream, his breaths were coming deep and fast and his skin was moist. He was lying on his side in the foetal position, his legs curled up to his chest as though that would protect him from the horrors. Instinctively he raised his left hand to his neck, where the cold steel had been sawing away just a few seconds earlier. His body was trembling and he fought back the urge to cry. It took a few minutes before he started to regain his composure.

The nightmare came every time he slept. But it had become worse recently, twisting reality into a whole new horror. He prayed for just one good night. So far, his prayers had not been answered.

Answered by whom? Logan wasn't a religious man, never had been. But the things he had seen, had been subjected to, had given even him the need to call upon a higher power to save him. It was nothing short of desperation.

As he regained his senses, Logan's thoughts went back to last night and the discussion with Mackie.

Youssef Selim.

Selim being in Paris had changed everything. When Mackie had left the hotel room, Logan's mind had been racing, thinking about what he was going to do if he came face to face with Selim again. No, not *if*, but *when*. A whole host of emotions had swept through him, from joy, at the unexpected prospect of defeating his foe, to pure dread. He'd hardly slept for most of the night, only nodding off in the last hours of darkness.

When Logan had arrived in Paris yesterday, his heart had still been in Vegas. His mind had still been focused on his recovery, on figuring out a way to get his life back together. Today, his heart was in Paris. He had unfinished business. And that business was now right here.

Mackie had been understandably wary about telling Logan about Selim. After all, he knew every last detail of what had happened on Logan's last mission. It was Mackie who had sent him after Selim in the first place. And it was Mackie who'd had to pick up the pieces afterwards.

'Why wasn't I told sooner?' Logan had said to Mackie, not attempting to hide the obvious anger in his voice.

'Why? Because we can't afford for you to lose your focus on this. Frank Modena is the goal here. Not Youssef Selim.'

'Then why did you tell me at all?'

'Because I had to have you engaged in this case. You were going to find out sooner or later. It's better you hear it from me now than from someone else at some point down the line. The police are putting all of their eggs into one basket on this. They're convinced Selim is involved.'

'How did he get into France?' Logan said. 'He's one of the most wanted men in the world.'

'He came in through Algeria. An Algerian passport in the name of Rabah Assad. It's a fake, obviously. We don't know how he got to Algeria, but it doesn't appear to be through any major airports. Our guess is that he was smuggled in. Some of those countries don't exactly have tip-top border control.'

'It doesn't make any sense,' Logan said, shaking his head. 'How did they let him through into France? Even on fake documents. It's Youssef Selim, for God's sake! He's one of the biggest arms dealers in the Middle East. He's linked to who knows how many extreme Islamic organisations. The man doesn't just recruit, he *trains* terrorists and insurgents. It's not like he isn't on the radar!'

'I don't know how they missed it,' Mackie said, staying calm, in contrast to the obvious emotion that Logan was feeling. 'There'll certainly be some heads rolling somewhere because of this, though. Not that that makes the situation any better.'

Mackie's calmness seemed to do the trick and Logan's anger, his exasperation, went down a notch.

'If they didn't know it was him when he arrived, then how the hell have they figured it out now?' Logan said.

'The answer's pretty simple. When Modena went missing the French police immediately suspected a foreign influence. What with Modena's speech about Gitmo and everything. Amongst God knows what else, they've trawled through the details of every Arab male who's landed in France in the past month. Eventually they came across Assad. They're certain it's Selim.'

'If Selim's here, I'll find him,' Logan said. The venom in his voice was clear.

'No,' Mackie responded, raising his voice. 'You have to remain focused. You find me Frank Modena. If this thing goes south, it's bigger than you and me. Just remember that. Remember what we're dealing with here. The JIA is not about personal vendettas.'

'You're right. It's about doing the right thing. Protecting innocent people from the likes of Selim.'

'No, Logan. It's about carrying out orders. And our orders are to find and rescue Frank Modena. If Selim gets in the way of that, then fine. But you are *not* here on a personal mission. You are not here for anything other than Modena. Have I made myself clear?'

'Crystal,' Logan said.

And that had been the end of it.

But that was last night. Today was a new day. And sitting on his bed now, Logan was having a hard time believing the assurances that he'd given to Mackie. This might be about Modena, but Selim being here changed everything for Logan. The memories of what happened on his last mission haunted him every day. And a day didn't go by without Logan contemplating what he would do when he came face to face with Selim again.

He wanted his revenge. He wanted Selim dead.

Selim was his.

And there was no way he would let that lie.

Chapter 13

Mackie slumped down on the dark-brown leather arm chair in his office. It was now almost ten a.m. He'd taken the train back to London from Paris first thing in the morning and he was tired. He'd barely slept and was still mulling over the conversation he'd had with Logan the night before. When Mackie had first heard about Selim being in France, he'd felt a strange sense of elation. Because he wanted to finally get that man almost as much as Logan did. Mackie had been tracking Selim for over ten years and had lost two good agents in the process. Logan had been closer than anyone else before to finally bringing that monster to justice. But then it had all gone wrong.

And Mackie knew he himself wasn't blameless for that.

Mackie had nearly sacrificed his agent just to further his own desires. He'd known Logan's cover had been blown, but he'd left him in there hoping – no, praying – that he could still get the job done.

But Logan's mission hadn't worked out like that. And Mackie's decision to not pull Logan out when he had known Selim was closing in had turned out to be one of the biggest regrets in his life. Because Logan wasn't just another agent to Mackie. Logan had worked for him for eighteen years. He was like the son he had never had. The son he wished he could have had.

And so it was only right that Mackie had been there to pick up the pieces in the aftermath of Logan's ill-fated mission. To try to get Logan back on his feet again. And to give him another shot when almost everyone else thought he was a spent force.

But Selim's involvement in Modena's kidnapping had been a truly unexpected twist. And Mackie had been dreading telling

Logan about it. He was desperate for Logan to prove himself on this case, and the last thing he wanted was for him to let his mind be further clouded by the need for revenge on Selim that now drove him.

Mackie stood up and walked over to his desk. He picked up the phone and began to dial the number for the conference call that had been arranged by the JIA committee. Lindegaard had requested the meeting, having been dissatisfied with the vague update that Mackie had requested Winter provide the previous night.

Mackie finished dialling and the call connected, but there was no-one else on the line yet. After a couple of minutes Mackie sat down at his desk, phone pressed to his ear, and fired up his desktop. It was unusual for the committee members to be late and he began to wonder whether maybe he'd got the time of the call wrong. It was, after all, another early start for the American duo.

He was just clicking through into his calendar when there was a knock on the door. Mackie opened his mouth to speak but before he could the door swung open and in strode Lindegaard.

'Good morning, Charles,' Lindegaard said merrily.

Mackie sat open-mouthed for a few seconds, unsure what to think.

'Jay, I … er, good morning,' Mackie said, placing the phone back down.

'Is something wrong?' Lindegaard said, sitting himself on a chair in front of Mackie's desk. He had on a tight-fitting light-grey suit that clung to his obviously muscular physique and matched almost perfectly his closely cropped grey hair. In his late forties, Lindegaard looked more like a movie star than a CIA agent and his confident swagger told the world that he knew it. His whole appearance was some sort of gimmick to make him seem more important, more special, than he really was. It made Mackie despise the man all the more.

'No, nothing wrong,' Mackie said, slowly regaining his composure.

'You were expecting me, weren't you?'

'Yes, of course. Sorry, I was just in the middle of something.'

Lindegaard didn't look convinced but he didn't push it.

Mackie was embarrassed but he hoped he'd managed to hide it. He wasn't sure where the lines had got crossed, but the last thing he had been expecting was for Lindegaard to be in his office. In fact, in Lindegaard's seven years in his role, Mackie wasn't sure the man had ever been in his office.

Mackie knew what this was about. Lindegaard's presence was intended to put extra pressure on Mackie. And he didn't like that.

'So I'm assuming he knows?' Lindegaard said.

'Who knows what?' Mackie said, deliberately feigning ignorance.

'Does Logan know about Selim?'

'Of course he does,' Mackie said, faking surprise at the question. 'Why would I keep something like that from the lead agent on the case?'

Lindegaard didn't look convinced but Mackie wasn't going to give him any wriggle room. Whatever his own thoughts were on the matter, he wouldn't delve into them with Lindegaard or the JIA committee, or anyone else.

'And how did he handle it?'

'How I would expect a lead agent to. He took it on board and I'm sure he'll be looking into the connection to Selim.'

'That's not what I meant. I think you know that.'

'Look,' said Mackie, leaning forward toward Lindegaard, his tone blunter now, 'I'm not entirely sure what you want me to say here. Logan knows. He was working the case before we found out about Selim. And he'll work the case the same now. There's nothing more to it. And, quite frankly, I'm getting just a little bit perturbed by your constant badgering.'

Lindegaard didn't respond to Mackie immediately. The two men stared at each other, as if competing as to who would look away first. Eventually Lindegaard did. He turned his head this way and that, looking around the room.

'It's a nice office you have, Charles,' Lindegaard said, his insincerity riling Mackie further. 'Very nice indeed. You've done well for yourself.'

'Thank you. That really means a lot to me.'

Lindegaard sighed. 'Charles, I'm going to be very frank with you. You know we weren't convinced by Logan being brought back for this case. And, well, that was even before we found out about Selim. And before Logan's little antics at Saint-Joseph. So surely you can understand that we're even more uncomfortable now?'

'Jesus wept. Logan's been in Paris for twenty-four hours. He's actually made good progress in that time. He –'

'Good progress?' Lindegaard interrupted. 'You mean him running around a busy hospital, making himself a person of interest in a murder inquiry?'

Mackie glared daggers at Lindegaard. 'The fact he was there at all was because of his own intuition,' he said, trying his best to defend what he knew had been an error by Logan.

'Yes, and I'm sure he's still got certain talents. And I'm sure, in his own way, he could get to the bottom of this mess. It's not like you can forget how to ride a bike. But you know, Charles, I've lost men before as well. Selim isn't just a big deal to you and Logan. Do you know how many agents we've lost going after him?'

Mackie assumed Lindegaard's 'we' was referring to the CIA. 'That's got nothing to do with me or Logan.'

'I'm just setting the scene here. I want this to work out right just as much as you do. But for that to happen, we have to run this case through properly. I've had to call it a day on many good agents who lost their way. Personal feelings shouldn't come into this. Logan is a loose cannon. God knows what damage he could cause us, you, in the process of getting the job done.'

'So what are you proposing?'

Lindegaard shifted in his seat, looking just a little nervous for the first time in the conversation. And Mackie knew that he wasn't going to like what was coming.

'I'm sorry, Charles. The decision has already been made. Logan's got twenty-four hours. And then we're sending in someone else.'

Chapter 14

Logan had left the hotel just before ten a.m. Mackie had given him the name and address of the passport counterfeiter, Thierry Djourou. Both the phone number Logan had found and the bar receipts linked Vincent to this man. And given his trade, it wasn't implausible that his skills had been used to help some of the attackers in their scheme. The fact that Djourou was also a Muslim and, according to the French police, had tenuous links to some extremist groups also hadn't gone unnoticed.

Djourou lived in Clichy-sous-Bois. Logan didn't know the area, had never been there, but he knew of its notoriety. It was one of the most poverty-stricken areas in Paris, a melting pot of unemployment and disadvantaged ethnic minorities. It had been the centre of riots in 2005 that made headline news around the globe. The riots had been sparked off after two local teenagers were accidently electrocuted as they hid from the police, who were allegedly pursuing them. Residents had long complained of police harassment and brutality. Friends of the boys claimed they had simply been playing football when they fled from a routine police patrol, fearing a confrontation with the officers.

Years later, tensions in the area remained on a constant high. Residents battled not only amongst themselves but with the police, who struggled to keep order. The majority of people living there were Muslims of Algerian and Moroccan descent. Djourou, though, was part of a growing population of immigrant Muslims from the Ivory Coast.

Logan had to get close to Djourou. He needed to find out what he knew about the attack on Modena. More importantly, he wanted to find out what he knew about Selim.

He sat in a rented Fiat, which he'd picked up near the hotel. Before him was Djourou's home: a ten-storey block of concrete, built in the sixties. It was decrepit, almost irretrievably it seemed. And yet it probably housed twice as many people as it was intended to, in conditions that many would have thought of as impossible in one of the most fashionable cities in the world.

But Logan had seen enough of the world to know that this was nothing out of the ordinary. Every major city had areas as bad, if not worse than this. Logan felt nothing but pity toward the majority of the residents of these ghettos. But he would never feel pity toward the likes of Djourou and the other criminals who lived amongst these communes, because they preyed on and exploited the vulnerability of their own people. And that was something that wasn't acceptable to anyone, from any race or religion, in any country.

He got out the car and started toward the apartment block. Bin liners, car parts and broken household furniture were strewn across the unkempt lawns in front of the building. The small group of kids kicking a ball around out front had taken to using the road as their playing field rather than the heavily littered grass. They probably weren't even as old as teenagers, but Logan kept his head down as he walked past them. There was no point in drawing attention to himself. It wouldn't be the first such place he'd been to where it was these young children who were the watchmen for the gang leaders. He was relieved that they didn't seem to take any notice as he went past them and up to the building entrance.

He was carrying a Beretta today, slipped into the back of his trousers. He was sure that Djourou would search him before he was willing to speak to him, but he'd kept the weapon on him deliberately. He hoped it would help to build trust with Djourou if Logan openly admitted to carrying it and handed it over to his host. That was the very reason he'd asked Mackie for a Beretta, which he'd been given at the hotel that morning, rather than the more usual Glock that he had carried yesterday. The Beretta had a safety catch, the Glock didn't. And if he was going to hand his gun over to Djourou, he at least wanted that little bit of extra comfort.

Logan walked into the open stairwell. He noticed a bank of lifts in the centre of the building, but he would get a better understanding of his surroundings by using the stairs, so he started up them. The stench of urine came and went as he made his way up the flights. The sound of TVs and stereos blaring, babies crying and couples fighting emanated from the nearby apartments as he approached each floor.

He reached the sixth floor and made his way toward apartment 609, walking down the exposed corridor which lined the front of the building. The door to this apartment was noticeably different to the others. It was made of metal, reinforced at the edges, and had a four-inch-wide square flap in the middle of it. Djourou was clearly a security-conscious man. Though it wasn't exactly discreet. He may as well have had a big sign on the door that read: *Criminal lives here*.

Logan knocked on the door three times and waited. Ten seconds later the flap opened and a man's face appeared in the hole. Logan couldn't see enough of the face to figure out whether or not it was Djourou, but he assumed it wouldn't be, given that he was the supposed boss of the counterfeiting operation and so was more likely to want to keep out of sight if he could.

'I need to speak to Djourou,' Logan said in English. 'I was told he could help me.'

'*Quoi?*'

There was a fair chance this guy didn't speak much English, but Logan had a role to play here. He wanted to appear to be a needy foreigner, someone who was in trouble and was desperate for Djourou's help. An easy ride for the African.

'I have money,' Logan said, waving his wallet in front of the open flap. Even this guy couldn't misunderstand that. 'I need a passport.'

The man slammed the flap shut without another word. Logan wasn't altogether surprised. He knew how these guys operated. Part of it was about being careful, but part of it was a show. They would never just let a stranger in straight off. But money talks, and they wouldn't want to turn away business. They wanted to know you were serious. And they wanted to know you were desperate. If you were both, then you were their ideal customer.

Logan waited a few seconds, then knocked again. The flap opened almost immediately.

'I need a passport. I have cash. Euro. I have euro.'

The man shouted something in quasi-French at Logan. He couldn't tell what it was, the accent was too strong. But he understood the sentiment.

'Jean Vincent told me to come here. He told me to ask for Djourou. Are you Djourou?'

The barrel of a gun poked out through the flap. A single-barrel shotgun from what Logan could tell. This was it: he was either going to get an invitation inside or he was about to get his head blown off. He wasn't sure whether to carry on talking, or even what more he could say. He thought of mentioning Selim. But even if Djourou and his cronies did know Selim, that may be a step too far. People didn't just go around bandying his name about.

'Please, you have to help me,' Logan said. 'I'm in trouble.'

He heard more voices inside but they were muffled and he couldn't pick out any of the words that were said. The gun barrel disappeared and the flap was shut. A few seconds later the door creaked open.

Two men stood in the doorway. One was only about five feet tall, in his late twenties, Logan guessed, and was holding the shotgun at shoulder height, pointing it directly at Logan. He saw now that it was a Remington 870, a twelve-gauge pump action shotgun – one of the most common shotgun types and one of the most reliable. The other man was taller and older, probably close to fifty. He wore a stained white vest that showed off his lean physique. He was of a similar height to Logan but probably a stone or two heavier. The extra weight was more or less pure muscle.

'What do you want?' the taller man said. His English was good but with a strong African twinge.

'I'm here to see Djourou. I was told he could help me.'

'I'm Djourou. Who are you?'

'I'm a friend. I know Jean Vincent. I was told you could help me.'

Logan saw the look of recognition in Djourou's eyes when he mentioned Vincent's name. He didn't know whether that was a good thing or not. He knew his pretence would come to an end sooner or later. It was just a question of when.

'I don't know this Jean Vincent,' Djourou said, less than convincingly.

'He knows you. And I have money,' Logan said, holding up his wallet again.

Djourou smiled broadly, exposing his nicotine-stained teeth, and said, 'Then come inside.'

He moved aside and Logan walked in. He stepped past the two men and stopped in the hallway of the apartment. The place was dark and dilapidated. The walls were scuffed and pockmarked, the carpets stained and worn. The smell of tobacco and marijuana was almost overpowering.

Djourou shut the door and the little guy came around in front of Logan, still holding the Remington, still pointing it at Logan. Another man appeared from the room at the far end of the corridor. He staggered through the doorway, probably stoned. He was of a similar size and build to Djourou, with the same muscular physique, but he was noticeably younger, probably in his thirties, and he was wearing only a pair of shorts. In his hand was a gleaming machete.

Logan looked from the machete to Djourou.

'If you're a cop, we'll kill you,' Djourou said with no hint of emotion in his voice. 'And it won't be with the gun.'

Logan got the picture. The man with the machete gave him a toothless smile and held the oversized knife up to Logan's face.

'Are you a cop?' Djourou said.

'Do I look like one?' Logan said.

'No. If you did, you wouldn't have made it inside.'

'Then why did you bother to ask the question then?'

'Because cops would know that,' Djourou said, smiling again, 'so would probably send someone who looked like you.'

Funny guy, Logan thought. 'Well, that makes sense. But no, I'm not a cop.'

'My friend here will pat you down. Please put your hands in the air.'

Logan did as he was told.

'Do you have a weapon?' Djourou said.

'Yes. A handgun. In my waistband.'

Djourou reached around Logan's waist and pulled out the Beretta.

'Nice,' Djourou said, twisting it in his hand before aiming it at Logan's head. 'Anything else?'

'No.'

Djourou nodded to the man with the machete, who handed his weapon to Djourou and proceeded to pat down Logan. It was a thorough search. These guys were being very careful – more careful than your average passport faker, Logan thought. Which meant they were probably up to something else in here as well. Drugs would be the obvious candidate, but it could be anything.

'Okay, please come through,' Djourou said.

He handed the machete back to the other man, then turned and walked toward the room at the far end of the corridor. There were four other doors that led off from the main corridor along the way: three open ones led into a kitchen, a bedroom and bathroom, and the final door was closed. Beyond was the room that would provide the answer of whatever else these guys were up to. But Logan wasn't here for that.

The room that he followed Djourou into was a lounge. It had two worn-out sofas and a small portable TV that looked like it was at least thirty years old. The single window in the room was covered with a makeshift brown drape. There was also a table and cluttered bookcase in the corner containing what must have been the tools of the counterfeiting trade. It didn't look like much. Without the guns and knives, Logan wouldn't have suspected Djourou of anything other than having an arts and crafts hobby.

Djourou sat down on one of the sofas and indicated for Logan to sit on the other. The two accomplices remained standing, one on either side of Logan. He was glad that they were both in front of him where he could keep an eye on them.

'Why do you think I can help you?' Djourou said.

'I told you, Jean Vincent said you could.'

'So you keep saying. Who is this Jean Vincent?'

'A friend.'

Djourou eyed Logan for a few moments before he spoke again. Logan could feel his heartbeat steadily getting faster from a mixture of adrenaline and anticipation.

'What is your name?'

'Ha, I'm not telling you that.'

Djourou laughed. 'Okay, well, what is the name you would like me to put on your passport?'

'John Burrows.'

'John Burrows. Very English. And you say Jean Vincent said you should come here?'

Logan's heart was now thudding in his chest, beating faster and faster in anticipation of what was to come. He had used the Jean Vincent ruse to get in, but he had never planned to leave with it still in place. And he knew that sooner or later events would head south. He just had to be ready.

'Yes. I told you that already,' Logan said. 'Look, are we going to talk about Jean Vincent all day, or are we going to do business? How much is this going to cost me?'

Djourou laughed again. Louder, more deliberate. 'How much will it cost? It will cost a lot. It's going to cost *you* a lot. You see, John Burrows, let me tell you how it is. Yes, I know Vincent. I met him through a friend. Vincent was a nobody. He was a courier. A dogsbody. He did whatever I wanted him to do for a little bit of money. And it didn't take much. He was a cheap man. But because I know the circumstances of how I met him, I seriously doubt he recommended me to you.'

Logan shifted in his seat. He had expected that this point would come. It had been the downfall of using Vincent's name to get in. But he hadn't had much else to go with.

'So,' Djourou said, cradling Logan's Beretta in his hand, 'you need to tell me, John Burrows. Why are you *really* here? And if you don't give me an answer I like –' Djourou nodded over to his accomplice with the machete '– well, you can use your imagination.'

Chapter 15

Logan remained silent. Tried to stay calm. At least on the outside. He didn't want to show any sign of weakness to these guys.

He looked over at the little man. Then at the one with the machete. They were both smiling at him. But neither was coming for him yet. They were waiting on Djourou to give them a signal.

But the initial ruse was over now. Everyone in the room knew that there would be no business transaction taking place today. Djourou smiled. His little accomplice began to laugh and Logan glared at him. But he just shrugged his shoulders and carried on laughing, the shotgun still held high.

'One chance, John Burrows,' Djourou said. 'Tell me who you are and how you found me, or I'll kill you myself. And please don't think that I'll make it a pleasant experience. We wouldn't be able to carry you all the way down those stairs in one piece. I'm sure you know what I mean.'

'I *could* tell you who I am,' Logan said, doing his best not to betray any emotion, 'but then I'd have to kill you.'

Logan cracked a smile.

The room went silent again. A deathly silence.

Djourou frowned, then smiled, then frowned again. He looked like he wasn't sure whether Logan was serious or not.

Logan carried on smiling back at him.

Djourou had placed Logan's gun on the sofa next to him. His right hand was caressing it. Logan could see that the safety was still on. He'd made sure of that before he'd handed it over and Djourou hadn't yet taken it off. No matter what was about to happen, that would at least give him a couple of seconds.

'All I want is information on who Vincent was working for,' Logan said. 'Who you are working for.'

Djourou shrugged, and Logan took the gesture as encouragement to carry on.

'Are you and your two commandos really sure you want to die over this?' Logan said. 'I'm just after some information, then I'll go. I'm not the police. You must have at least figured that out by now.'

Djourou's hand twitched. Then he made the move. His fingers reached around the butt of the Beretta and he cursed as he lifted it up off the sofa.

But Logan had already prepped himself for the moment. Long before Djourou had gone for the gun he'd shifted his weight so that he could spring into action at the right moment. He dived forward to the right, where the man with the shotgun was standing. The little guy was too slow to react and didn't even attempt to move out of the way as Logan tumbled into him. The gun went off as the two men fell to the floor. Pellets from the shot flew up into the ceiling.

The little man was no match for Logan's size and strength. With his foe still holding onto the gun, Logan manoeuvred the barrel. He pointed it toward the machete man, who was almost upon him, pulling back the blade in an almighty arc. Only a few seconds later and Logan would have been sliced in two. But as the machete came down toward Logan's head, he pumped on the shotgun, loading the barrel. He squeezed on the little man's trigger finger. The shot hit the machete man in the centre of his chest. A dozen or more holes opened up as he was propelled backward.

Logan heard Djourou pull on the trigger of the Beretta. But he hadn't released the safety and nothing happened. Logan was still on top of the little man. He elbowed him in the side of the skull. Once. Twice. Three times. The blows came in quick succession, knocking him out cold. The man loosened his grip on the shotgun enough for Logan to prise it away. Still on the ground, he pumped the barrel once more, loading another shot.

He pointed the gun at Djourou.

At the same time, he heard the click as Djourou unlatched the safety.

Taking out the two henchmen had taken just a few seconds. Not even enough time for Djourou to make a shot. The African could do nothing but look on at Logan, stunned.

But both men were now locked and loaded, their weapons pointed at their targets. It was a stalemate.

And neither man fired.

Djourou was wide-eyed. He looked scared. He obviously wasn't used to things not going his way. *Well, he'd better get used to it*, Logan thought.

He got to his feet, keeping the shotgun pointed toward Djourou.

'Who the hell *are* you?' Djourou said. '*Batard!*'

The machete man groaned. He was still alive. Just. But he had enough shot in him to make sure he would stay down at least for now, if not permanently. The little man was out for the count. But he'd come around eventually. Logan wouldn't forget about him just yet. Right now, though, his focus was on Djourou.

'You know, that gun's got a double-safety,' Logan said, bluffing. 'I don't think you've released it properly.'

Djourou laughed. He obviously wasn't completely stupid; Logan could tell that Djourou knew the claim was bullshit. But it didn't matter. With the thought put in his head, Djourou couldn't resist the momentary glance to double-check that he'd released the safety properly.

It was enough for Logan.

He dived to his left, firing as he fell. Djourou fired as well. But he hadn't counted on the moving target. Logan's shot caught Djourou just below his left knee. A dull thwack sounded as the ball bearings tore through muscle and bone. Djourou screamed in pain. He dropped his aim, clutching for his stricken limb with his free hand.

Logan was on his feet immediately. He lunged for Djourou's gun hand. It didn't take much to take back his Beretta. He took it in his right hand, pressing the barrel up against Djourou's forehead.

'So,' Logan said, smiling. 'Do you still want to know who I am?'

Djourou looked up at him. Beads of sweat were forming on his forehead. His nostrils flaring as he struggled to keep his breathing under control.

'I'll take that as a no,' Logan said. 'So let's start with you then. Tell me about Vincent. Who introduced you? And why?'

Djourou exhaled loudly through his nostrils and stared coldly into Logan's eyes. Logan knew he was trying to show that he wasn't scared. But Logan wasn't buying it. This guy was scared all right.

Logan nudged the barrel against Djourou's forehead, as if prompting him to speak. But Djourou remained silent. He wasn't going to give the information up easily. If he had been prepared to kill Logan over this, just like that, then chances were whoever he was protecting was someone big.

But Logan was sure he could persuade Djourou to tell him.

He pushed his knee against Djourou's injured leg, grinding it against the open wound. Djourou shrieked in pain. But Logan didn't let up. He kept the pressure on as Djourou's shrill scream got louder and louder. And saw the look of defeat slowly creep into the injured man's eyes.

'Just give me a name. I can make this much worse for you if you don't.'

'Okay!' Djourou yelled.

Logan took his knee away.

'I'll give you his name,' Djourou said, panting heavily as he talked. 'I never worked for him before. I was introduced through a mutual friend. Blakemore. Richard Blakemore. He's English, like you.'

'And who the hell is he?'

'Blakemore. That's his name.'

'Where can I find him?'

'I don't know! He came to me. But I think he's here. Somewhere near Paris.'

'What do you know about Rabah Assad? And Youssef Selim?'

'What?' Djourou said, shaking his head. The panic in his voice was growing further. 'I've never heard of them!'

He was lying. Everyone knew of Selim. But it didn't matter. Logan was done here. He had what he came for.

And he'd been here too long already. There'd been four shots fired. Even if the police didn't like coming to this part of town, Logan had to assume that they'd been called. And if that was the case, they'd be here sooner or later. He wanted to be long gone by the time they showed up.

'Richard Blakemore?' Logan said, putting the Beretta back into his waistband. 'Let's hope you're right about that.'

As he turned to walk out of the room, he saw the look of surprise on Djourou's face.

'Who *are* you?' Djourou shouted as Logan walked toward the front door.

He smiled. Djourou probably had no idea what had just happened to him. Logan knew exactly what he was thinking: Logan couldn't be a cop, otherwise why wasn't he being arrested? And if he wasn't a cop, then who the hell was he and why was he letting him live?

Logan stopped at the door, still smiling. 'Like I already said. I could tell you, but I'd have to kill you.'

He opened the door and left.

Chapter 16

When he left Djourou's apartment, Logan was on a high. More through relief than anything: relief that he'd made it out of there alive. But the high was also because it had been five months since he'd been in a situation anything like that. And for the first time in that five months, he felt alive again. Like he suddenly remembered what he'd been put on this earth to do. It had all come so naturally to him again. Unlike the skipping around Paris he'd been doing the day before to no avail.

It was only as he headed back to his car that he noticed his hands were trembling. At first he thought it was just from the adrenaline of the fight. But after a few minutes, he knew that wasn't the case. As the adrenaline wore off, the trembling didn't stop. It actually got worse. And it wasn't just the tremors in his hands. By the time he was back at his car, his legs felt like jelly, his head was in a spin, his stomach was churning, he felt like he was about to throw up. He was in shock. His body was reacting to what had just happened.

Logan had seen plenty of action in his time. He'd shot and killed people before – it was what he did. He was usually ready for anything. That was what he'd been trained for; that was what the JIA, his life, was all about. He'd remained calm while in the thick of it, confident that he would get out of Djourou's apartment alive. But he just hadn't been ready for that situation. Not mentally at least.

It had made him feel vulnerable.

It had made him feel scared.

It had made him remember the first time he'd seen a dead body.

It happened right before he'd met Mackie and joined the agency, when he was only seventeen years old. His childhood was a period he'd tried his best to forget, and over the years, with the training and the life that the JIA had given him, he'd been successful in that. He'd seen many more bodies since that day, and never felt anything like the intensity of emotion again. In fact, with each year that came and went, he'd felt less and less.

So why was it different today?

The answer was simple. From that day when he was seventeen up until a few months ago, as a result of his training, he'd spent his life on autopilot. He'd barely felt a thing; he'd become used to what he was, what he did and what he saw. But that had changed five months ago, when Youssef Selim had brought Logan back to the real world.

And after that fateful day had come the intensive physical and mental rehabilitation. That in itself had been almost as painful as his experience at the hands of Selim. At first, during his recovery, he'd felt liberated. He'd been glad to be alive. Like it was a new beginning. But then came the feelings of isolation, loneliness, guilt – a whole host of feelings that were alien to him. More than anything, hate was one of the emotions he'd now become used to. Hatred toward Selim: what he was, and what he'd done.

His heart rate built again as his mind went back to that dark period of recovery. He slammed his hands against the steering wheel to try to stop the memories. And to try to stop the trembling that had taken control of his hands. It worked, but only for a few seconds. Sweat was dripping down his forehead, but his body wasn't overheating. He opened the window to get some air and took several deep gulps. It helped to slow his heart rate back to normal. Finally, after a few more minutes trying his best to focus his mind away from Selim, away from Djourou and everything else that was clouding his thinking, the shaking in his hands began to subside.

This is why I needed a holiday, he thought, managing a wry smile.

He banged on the steering wheel with the palms of his hand again, angry that he'd let himself get this way. That he was being so weak.

Get a grip, man.

Why was he being so pathetic? This wasn't how Carl Logan acted. Carl Logan could handle anything.

Just get a grip.

Logan put the car into gear and drove off, fighting through the Parisian traffic back to Saint-Denis. By the time he arrived at the JIA safe house, the shaking in his hands had all but gone. But Logan was left with a feeling of betrayal. It felt like he'd betrayed who he really was by being this emotional wreck. Betrayed the life he'd led for eighteen years. Or was it the JIA that had betrayed him, for turning a seventeen-year-old boy into an emotionless killing machine? A boy who'd only really wanted protection from a world that had chewed him up and spat him out.

The Carl Logan of today was a different animal to that naive and deprived teenager. But in many ways, he was back at the beginning again. And right now, however hard it was to admit, perhaps he needed just as much emotional protection as he had back then.

Chapter 17

Johnny had only been following John Burrows for less than twenty-four hours and he already hated him. He was in a bad mood. A really bad mood. John Burrows had done a bunk on him about three hours ago. And yet, had Burrows even known he was being followed? This was all turning to shit right before Johnny's eyes. His boss, Reggie, was going to have a field day if he found out. And if Selim found out too? Well, Johnny didn't even want to think about what that might mean. Quite frankly, the man terrified Johnny. He wouldn't say it to anyone, but really he just wanted this whole job to be over and done with now.

But this wasn't the type of job you could just bail out of. At least, not if you wanted to keep your life. And all he could do now was wait by the hotel and hope for the best.

Burrows hadn't checked out, Johnny was sure of that. But three hours ago the guy had left the hotel and walked to a car rental shop not far away. Johnny hadn't been expecting that. And there was nothing he could do as he watched Burrows hop into a car and drive away from him. He didn't have time to hire a car himself. Burrows would have already been long gone by the time he'd sorted out all the paperwork. Burrows must have prearranged the car and prepaid for it, as he was in and out of there in less than a minute. They were never that quick in those places. And there were no taxis in this part of town that Johnny could have hailed. Nor were there any careless scooter owners or motorcyclists whom he could knock off their bikes while they sat at traffic lights. Not like in the movies, where they just appear from nowhere the second you need to follow someone.

So Johnny had been well and truly screwed. So now he just had to sit and wait. And hope that Burrows came back. Soon. It wasn't his fault, though. He *was* good at this. He'd been a policeman once. Had been a policeman for fifteen years, in fact. Until they'd booted him out. That was eight years ago. Even though his life had changed in many ways since then it still made him angry to think about it. He hadn't done anything wrong, really. Just taken a bit of coke out of evidence every now and then for personal use. It wasn't like he was out on the street selling it on.

That had been the key turning point in his life. Not long after that, his wife, Charlene, the bitch, had left him. It hadn't really been a surprise. She'd been running around with one of his colleagues for six months pretty much in front of his eyes. Still, the guy wasn't running around after he'd broken both of his legs in a freak accident not long after.

Johnny was better off without her anyway. And to be fair, he was better off out of the police. For the past six years he'd been working and living in Paris. He got paid almost twice as much as he had in the police. And the work was easier and more suited to his strengths. So it was their loss, really.

But it was days like these that brought back bad memories. Today he felt foolish, just like the day he'd found out his wife was screwing someone else. And just like back when he was still a street bobby, chasing rowdy drunken teenagers around fields. In his time in the police he'd dealt with drug dealers, with rapists, murderers even. But it was the drunk and stoned teenagers that caused him the biggest problems and the biggest embarrassments. Because there was just nothing you could do to them. They could hit you, spit on you, run rings around you, and you couldn't do a thing back to them. They thought they were untouchable. As far as the law was concerned they pretty much were. He'd always hated that, felt so useless. Like he was working with both arms tied behind his back.

Today felt just like that. Johnny knew what this job was about. He knew how to do it. But this John Burrows guy was starting to make him look stupid. And he hated him for that.

Johnny's phone began to vibrate in his pocket. He took it out and looked at the caller ID. It was Reggie. Johnny groaned before answering. This was the last thing he needed.

'Hi, Reggie.'

'Johnny, where the fuck are you?'

Shit. That wasn't what he wanted to hear. Should he tell the truth or lie? Lying might keep the boss at bay for now. But sooner or later it would come back to bite him.

'I'm at the hotel.'

That wasn't a lie. He didn't have to tell the whole truth and nothing but the truth. Not unless he was prompted.

'And where is our good friend John Burrows?'

Double shit.

'I don't know. I'm waiting for him to come back. He hired a car and went off this morning. I lost him.'

'You lost him? What the … You *lost* him? And how long ago was that?'

'Nine o'clock.'

'Fuck me sideways. Just tell me one thing, Johnny. At what point *were* you planning on telling me this?'

Johnny didn't know what to say. He was pretty sure Reggie already knew the answer: he hadn't been planning on telling him at all.

'I don't know,' Johnny said.

'Okay, this is going nowhere,' Reggie said. 'I already know you lost Burrows. Do you know how I know that?'

'No.'

'Because not long ago a very good friend of the man who's paying me, the man who's therefore paying *you*, was visited by one John Burrows.'

'What? Who?' Johnny felt himself lose a few inches. Maybe he really had fucked up this time.

'Thierry Djourou. And it wasn't a very nice visit. Djourou has been shot. His kid brother is dead. So I think we can definitely say that John Burrows is a threat!'

This was even worse than Johnny had imagined. For once, he had to hold his hands up: he'd messed up royally. John Burrows was going to pay for this.

'What do you want me to do?' Johnny asked. He knew there was no point in fighting this battle. He needed to make amends. It wasn't just his job on the line here. If he got on the wrong side of Selim, it was his life.

'Djourou is still at home,' Reggie said. 'I sent a doctor out to see to his shot leg. His brother was already a goner. The police don't know anything about this yet. Gunshots at Clichy-sous-Bois don't really get them too excited anymore. I want you to go over there and take care of Djourou.'

'Take care of him? You mean, like the doctor?'

'No, not like the fucking doctor! I mean *take care* of him, Johnny, you fucking retard.'

'But why?'

'Because he's talked. He says he hasn't but there's no way Burrows would've just walked away from there unless he had what he needed. You know, you're walking a very thin line here. I'm not sure how many cock-ups you think you're entitled to, but the answer now is none. Do Djourou, then go back to the hotel. I'm sending Lorik out to the hotel as well. Meet him there afterwards. Got it?'

'Lorik? That guy's a nut job!'

'Well, Burrows has brought it on himself. Are we on the same page now?'

'Yeah. How do you want it done? Djourou, I mean.'

'Just do it.'

'Whatever you say.'

'And Johnny. If you see Burrows, bring him to me. Alive. Selim's pissed. I'm pissed. Burrows is not going to get off this one easily.'

Reggie put the phone in his pocket. Johnny was just about on his last life. One more wrong move and he would have to cut that one loose.

'Problems with the troops?' said Selim, who was sitting on the beige sofa opposite Reggie. Richard Blakemore was sitting next to him.

And fuck you too, Reggie thought. Selim might be a big cheese, but that didn't mean he owned Reggie. And it certainly didn't mean that Reggie had to like him. Still, Blakemore was paying Reggie two million dollars for this. With any luck, Selim would soon be out of his life. So he would just have to bite his lip and put up with this crap for a few more days.

'No. No problems at all,' Reggie said. 'Nothing that can't be sorted, at least.'

'Well, let's hope it does get sorted,' Selim said. 'Your men don't seem to be doing too good a job so far.'

Selim was smiling at Reggie as he spoke. It made the big man feel uneasy.

'Johnny will sort it.'

'The point of having someone followed is to make sure they don't get in our way,' Blakemore piped up.

Blakemore was the man who had brought Reggie onto this job. He thought of himself as a businessman. By 'business' he basically meant anything that made him richer. The man had few morals. Reggie wasn't bothered by that, though. It was more the man's superior attitude that grated. To Reggie he was nothing more than a smarmy toff. The guy thought he was some sort of preppy model with his ridiculous clothes, rather than the pot-bellied forty-something that he really was. But he obviously had some talent in making money to be living the life he was.

'It's being taken care of,' Reggie said.

'Yes, well, it's just a pity that it's come to that,' Blakemore said, shaking his head. 'We're not too pleased about Djourou, you know. He's done some good work for me. And he was a good friend of Selim.'

Reggie looked over at Selim, who was staring at him. He nodded at Blakemore's words, then reached over to the coffee table to pick up his mug. Reggie doubted Selim fully understood the concept of *friend*. But the point had been made.

Djourou might have been considered a friend, but it was clear that no-one in the room was disputing his fate. He had it coming. He'd talked, and that meant that he had to go. Those were the rules. Though the ease with which the conclusion to kill Djourou had been reached made Reggie all the more nervous. Reggie had been central to planning and carrying out the attack on Modena's convoy. His military experience and training had been key. But what would it take for him to become just another loose end?

He banished the thought. If it came to it, he knew he was a fighter.

'Is it time for the show yet?' Reggie said, hoping the conversation could now move on.

Blakemore looked at his watch. 'Ah, you're right. 'Bout time too. I've been looking forward to this part. Where's Mohammed gone?'

'It's not Mohammed,' Selim said in a tone that was unusually terse for him. 'It's Mustafa.'

'Fine, Mustafa. Get him in here and let's get this show on the road.'

'He's already in the basement,' Reggie said.

Mustafa was a young guy that Selim had brought into the job. Initially Reggie had been unable to see the point in his involvement. Mustafa was barely out of his school years and didn't really seem to add anything to the mix. But then, as time had gone on, Reggie had begun to see his use. In fact, his complete lack of physical threat was the main thing going for him. He was the only one who was getting Modena to talk at all.

'Well, what are we waiting for then?' Blakemore said. He stood up and pulled on his balaclava, then held his hand out in the shape of a gun and fired an imaginary shot at Reggie. 'Gotcha,' he said.

What a twat, Reggie thought. He stood and picked his balaclava up off the table. Selim followed suit.

The three men headed toward the basement door. As Reggie stepped through the doorway, he pulled the wool over his head and started down the steps.

In the basement, Modena was on the chair, his head slumped. Mustafa was sitting next to him on the floor, talking.

'You two look like you're having fun,' Reggie boomed.

Modena looked up, terror in his eyes.

Yes, you little bastard, it's me again, Reggie thought.

'So, Frank,' he said, 'how're your acting skills?'

Chapter 18

The safe house had been empty when Logan arrived. Still lost in his thoughts about what had just happened to him, he'd simply sat down on the sofa in the lounge in silence. In contemplation. He wasn't even aware of how long he'd sat there. Maybe as long as an hour. He should have called Mackie. But his mind was too busy, going around in circles, trying to determine what it was he needed to do to get his life back on track.

Eventually Logan's phone chirped in his pocket, breaking his trance. He picked it out and answered.

'Logan, I've been wondering where you got to,' Mackie said. 'I tried calling you.'

Logan hadn't noticed any missed calls. 'I'm at the safe house. I thought you would be here?'

'I'm back in London,' Mackie declared without elaboration. 'Have you been to see Djourou?'

Logan sat up on the sofa. He was surprised that Mackie hadn't heard about the incident through his contacts. Maybe the police didn't know about Djourou yet. That would probably be of some benefit, keeping them a step away from getting under Logan's nose.

'Yeah, I paid him a visit.'

'And? Come on, the suspense is killing me. What have you got?'

'Well, I'm pretty sure we've got one dead and one with a serious gunshot wound to the leg.'

'Jesus, Logan,' Mackie said. 'Life's never simple with you, is it?'

'Never simple? At least I'm consistent,' Logan said, laughing. *Keep it up*, he told himself. *You may be an emotional wreck, but don't let on to anyone else.* 'And I'm confident no-one saw me coming or going,' he added, wanting to make it clear that his visit to Djourou hadn't resulted in his adding unwanted heat on himself following the previous day's exploits at the hospital.

'Wait. Please don't tell me you've gone and done Djourou?' Mackie said.

'Would it matter if I had? But no, it was one of his guards that I put down. Djourou will just have a bit of a limp from now on.'

'Just tell me what happened.'

'Well, Djourou's certainly involved somehow. As soon as I mentioned Vincent's name, his antennae went up. In fact, that very nearly got me killed.'

'Did he tell you anything?'

'A name: Richard Blakemore. A well-known client by all accounts. Oh, and Djourou said he was English. Nice to know we're playing close to home.'

'Richard Blakemore, hey?' Mackie said.

'Yep. Do you know him?'

'No. I don't think so. But we'll check him out. If he's anyone of interest, he'll be on our radar one way or another.'

'I also got the impression that Djourou is more than just your average passport counterfeiter. Judging by the level of security he had.'

'*Had* being the operative word.'

'I didn't get a chance to see what else he was operating from there, though. I was only in his place for a few minutes. Is there anything we know about what else it could be?'

'You tell me. If Djourou is as good as people say he is, then it wouldn't surprise me at all if the security you saw was just for his ID business. People will pay top dollar for a good fake.'

'Maybe so. But I'm even less convinced by the police's theory now,' Logan said.

'What, just because you've got the name of one English guy?' Mackie responded. 'The terrorist link is still pretty strong if you ask me.'

'I just think there's more to this than meets the eye,' Logan said, trying to keep hold of his irritation at Mackie summarily dismissing what he was saying. 'And it's not just one Englishman that's in the mix here. It's Blakemore plus Vincent, plus Djourou.'

Logan got up from the sofa and moved over to the lounge window, which looked out onto the street. It was quiet outside, with just the odd car and pedestrian passing by. The view onto the road and the ramshackle buildings on the opposite side was anything but alluring, and Logan couldn't help but think fleetingly of all the safe houses he'd been to over the years, nearly all of them in less than salubrious parts of the towns and cities in which they were located. As glamorous and thrilling as his secretive job may have seemed to young men and women on the outside world, he'd never himself bought into that false impression – it certainly didn't really match the reality. His job was about doing a duty, carrying out orders, not living a fantasy life.

'Did Djourou say anything about Selim?'

'I didn't really have time to stay around and ask too many questions. But it doesn't matter anyway. With Blakemore's name, we've got something to go on now.'

'Unless Djourou sold you a stinker.'

'I don't think so,' Logan said, offended. 'You didn't see the look in his eyes. Blakemore needs to be checked out.'

'Fine. Check him out.'

'How do you want to deal with Djourou? I just left him and his crew at his place.'

'Not much more we can do. Sooner or later it'll get called in to the police. We'll let them deal with it. As far as I know the police haven't yet made any link between Modena and Djourou, so we're a step ahead of them.'

'Are you going to tell them?'

'I will do, but we can't have them chasing the same leads as you. They'll just get in your way and slow you down. I'll pass on the Djourou information once we know if we've got anything to go on with Blakemore.'

'I'll get onto it now.'

'Okay, keep me in the loop,' Mackie said before ending the call.

Logan immediately dialled the number for Laura Anderson at the JIA office in London. Laura was a mid-level administrator. Probably the best one the JIA had, as far as Logan was concerned

– though he only knew a handful of the names and faces of the people at HQ. Although being a field agent may seem like the more desirable side of the intelligence business, they were somewhat segregated from everyone else. As a field agent, Logan didn't even have access to the HQ building – his role essentially saw him move from safe house to safe house, hotel to hotel, always following the action.

'Laura, its Carl. How are things?'

Logan wasn't one for idle chit chat – not with most people, at least. He made an exception for Laura. He'd never really figured why, other than the fact that she nearly always flirted with him.

'Good, thanks,' Laura said. 'I heard your holiday got cut short. What a bummer.'

'Tell me about it.'

'Well, at least you didn't have to spend too much time away from me.'

'That is a bonus, I guess.'

'Perhaps next time you should invite me. I've always wanted to go to Vegas.'

'I'll bear that in mind. I need to ask a favour.'

'Ouch, that was a quick change of subject. One day you'll take me up on my offers.'

'One day,' Logan said, well aware that both of them knew it was a lie.

Logan gave Laura the threadbare information he had about Blakemore. As he was doing so, his phone began to vibrate in his hand. He took it away from his ear and saw there was another call waiting.

'Carl, are you still there?' Laura said.

He let the call ring out. 'Yeah, I'm still here,' he said.

But seconds later his phone was vibrating again.

'Look, Laura, I've got to go,' Logan said. 'Call me as soon as you have anything at all on Blakemore.'

'Will do, sweetie.'

Logan couldn't help but smile at her words as he hung up and answered the incoming call.

It was Mackie again. And he didn't sound happy.

'We've had a development,' Mackie said.

Logan's first reaction at hearing the words was one of positivity. But that quickly dissipated as Mackie carried on.

'This might not be what you want to hear,' Mackie said, 'but I think the police's theory is looking a little more solid now.'

'What do you mean? Why?'

'The kidnappers have made contact.'

Chapter 19

It didn't take Logan long to find it. The kidnappers had posted the video on the internet. It was already going viral, being re-posted and commented on here, there and everywhere. TV and radio stations were playing it, reporting on it, and it would surely be all over the newspapers in the morning. Logan sat at the desk in the safe house office and watched the video on one of the laptops there. It brought back too many hard memories. At times he found himself close to tears, reliving in his mind what Modena was going through.

In the video, four armed men brandishing assault rifles stood either side of the forlorn figure of Frank Modena. They were wearing black clothing that looked like army fatigues and had balaclavas covering their heads.

Modena was kneeling on the ground, dressed in a bright orange jumpsuit. His hands were tied behind his back. He had almost certainly been beaten: his face was bloodied and swollen. With his clothes on, though, it was hard to tell the full extent of his injuries. Or what other kind of torture he'd had to endure.

One of the armed men opened the video, speaking in Arabic. After that, Modena introduced himself. He stated his name, the name of his wife and where he came from. He spoke slowly, clearly and without any obvious impediment. That at least suggested his physical and mental state weren't too far gone. But it wasn't really possible to confirm that just from the video.

Modena then proceeded with the demand of the kidnappers: for all Muslim prisoners of war held by the United States to be freed. He finished his address by stating that the kidnappers would kill him in three days if their demand was not met. After that, the video ended.

Logan sat in silence for a good five minutes once the video had finished.

'Jesus,' was all he eventually said.

He really didn't know what to think now. The video certainly looked genuine enough. But surely the involvement of Vincent and Blakemore meant something?

It wasn't long before Logan's phone was buzzing again. He picked it up and reluctantly answered.

'So, where does this leave us?' Mackie asked. 'What does this mean for your theory that Modena's kidnapping isn't simply a terrorist plot?'

Logan didn't know. If the video was legitimate, this would be one hell of a coup for whichever terrorist cell was responsible. They had kidnapped a prominent American and were parading him on the internet. There was nothing in the video that hadn't been done before with other victims, but the profile of Modena, and the fact he'd been taken not in a war-torn country but in Paris, made the nature of his disappearance all the more unique. And disturbing.

But the kidnappers were making a demand that was outrageous. They must have known it wouldn't be granted.

'It's just too obvious,' Logan said after a few moments' thought. Though he wasn't really sure why he was so reluctant to buy the whole charade anymore. What he wanted most in the world was for all of this to lead him to Selim. He was desperate for his revenge. But regardless of Selim's involvement, at the minute there were just too many elements which didn't add up.

'Meaning?' Mackie said, prompting Logan, who was still trying to convince himself of his own words.

'Meaning Islamic terrorists kidnapping a Westerner and parading him on the internet like that. It's not exactly original, is it?'

'That doesn't mean it's not true.'

'No, but I still don't like it,' Logan said. 'Why make such a stupid demand? They could have asked for ten million dollars. Twenty million. But no, they asked for something they won't ever get. Why bother?'

'I have to say,' Mackie said, 'as disturbing as that video is, I agree with you. Why bother making a demand at all? They could have just killed him straight off and made that their video. It certainly wouldn't be the first time a kidnapping by an extremist cell has ended that way.'

Logan felt his whole demeanour change at his boss's words. Finally it felt like they were on an even keel.

'It comes back to the same question then,' Logan said. 'Why Modena? What does he have that they want?'

'I don't know,' Mackie said.

'No. Me neither. But I'm going to find out.'

'Just be careful, Logan.'

It was almost a throw-away comment. Something Mackie had said to him more than once recently. But this time, Logan picked up there was more to it than that.

'What do you mean?'

Mackie didn't respond straight away. Logan was about to push him when he finally did.

'There're a lot of eyes on you, Logan. Just be careful.'

'This again? Is there something you're not telling me here?'

'Like what? I'm just concerned. I want to make sure you're okay. You know your psychologist told me you're suffering from post-traumatic stress. I mean, I guess I knew that, but –'

'She said that to you?' Logan interrupted. 'Isn't what happens in that room supposed to be between her and me?'

'That's not how it works. You're seeing her because I need to know if you're mentally fit to carry out your role. She has doubts that you are. I'm not so sure I agree with her, otherwise you wouldn't be here.'

'I'm fine,' Logan said. 'Just let me do my job.'

He ended the call before Mackie could say anything more, then stormed out of the safe house.

By the time Logan got back to his car, his hands were shaking again. This time he was pretty sure it was adrenaline, though. He was incensed by what Mackie had just said to him. And about what that stupid bitch of a psychologist had said to Mackie. Why did they care anyway? He did his job, he got results. So what did it matter whether he did that with a smile or a frown on his face?

And what the hell did post-traumatic stress mean anyway? What he had seen was traumatic. It was stressful. What they should have been worried about was the eighteen-year period before that during which he'd felt nothing about killing people and seeing people be killed. Surely that was the type of man who was a cause for concern. But no, the moment he reacted like a real human being, they tried to make out that he wasn't good enough to do his job.

He pulled away from the kerb, engine fully revved, tyres screeching. He only narrowly avoided hitting an oncoming car. The driver gave him the finger. Logan did his best to ignore it. He couldn't take his anger out on some random guy.

After a few minutes of driving, he started to calm again. The trembling in his hands stopped and the fog began to clear. Still, he was left with a sour taste in his mouth. Mackie was the person who had pulled Logan into this in the first place. Not just this case, but this entire life. If anyone was responsible for the direction Logan's life had taken, it was Mackie. Now he was talking to Logan like he was no longer the right man for the job. And that hurt him.

But he was sure he would prove Mackie wrong.

He had to.

Logan parked the car in an underground car park around the corner from the hotel. After paying at the ticket machine, he cautiously walked the short distance to where he was staying and went in through the front entrance. Logan glanced and noted the man on reception was looking in his direction. He kept his head down as he casually walked past toward the lifts.

'Er, Mr Burrows?' the man on reception called out.

Logan turned back to him and smiled though inside his mind was already racing as to why he was being collared. The man came from around the reception desk into the foyer and walked up to Logan.

'I just wanted to check that everything is okay with you, sir?'

What? Not another do-gooder, Logan thought. Perhaps he should start walking around with a sign on his head saying, I'm fine. Honest, I am.

'Yes, everything's okay, thanks. Why wouldn't it be?'

'Well, it's just after the Interpol detective was looking for you yesterday. I thought maybe something was wrong?'

Logan felt his body stiffen, his heart rate quicken. He knew immediately what the man's words meant: he didn't know how or why, but his cover had been blown. Someone was looking for him. And the chances were it wasn't Interpol. He thought back to the events of the last two days. He didn't think he had been followed at any point. In fact he had done everything he could to prevent it ... but he couldn't be sure. There was never any certainty with such things. And really he hadn't exactly been on top form recently. Perhaps Mackie had been right all along.

Logan knew it was time to leave. It wasn't worth the risk of going to his room. There was a good chance someone might be waiting on the other side of the door for him. And whoever they might be, it was a fight he didn't want to have, didn't need to have. Not now anyway. 'Know your enemy' was an age-old rule; walking into a blind ambush was not the way to do things. Mackie could send someone else to recover his things, amongst which the only items of any importance were his IDs. Right now he just had to get out of there.

Logan took a step toward the man, crowding his space, towering over him. It had the desired effect. The man shrank and looked scared, probably not knowing what to expect from a man that Interpol were supposedly after. He took a step back, looking left and right as if hoping someone might come to his aid.

Logan took another two steps forward, his face only inches from the man's.

'What was the detective's name?' he asked, his tone terse. 'The one who was asking about me.'

'I ... I, er, I don't know. I don't remember. He was English. It was my colleague who dealt with him.'

'What did he want?'

'I ... er ... he said he wanted to speak to you. He didn't say why.'

'He knew my name?'

'No ... that's what he wanted to know. He wanted to know your name. He said he needed to speak to you.'

'You gave him my name?' Logan sizzled. 'What did he look like?'

'I ... er, I don't know. Your size I guess, but older. He was just dressed like a normal guy. Not in a uniform, I mean.'

'Is that it?' Logan said, leaning closer toward the man. The receptionist cowered away even further, opening and closing his mouth but not saying anything. Logan could see people starting to take notice. As incensed as he was, he couldn't stand there all day questioning the guy. It was time to go. He turned and walked out of the hotel.

It was some comfort, at least, that whoever was looking for him didn't know who he really was. He'd used a cheap ruse to find out Logan's name. Or at least his cover name. The only thing he must have known before that was what he looked like. Which probably meant he'd been followed at some point. The description he'd got was pretty useless, but he couldn't do anything about that now.

He stepped out into the open and, as casually as he could, began to walk away from the hotel in the opposite direction of the garage. As Logan walked he recced the street outside the hotel as best as he could. There wasn't anyone who matched the receptionist's sparse description. But someone else caught his eye as a potential candidate: a man on the other side of the road, leaning against a lamppost and pretending to talk on his phone.

It wasn't the man the receptionist had referred to – this guy was squat, probably half a foot shorter than Logan. Even in his casual attire Logan could tell the guy was well-built. He had a shaved head and a mean-looking face with Slavic features. He looked like a fighter. A pit-bull terrier. But if this guy was the tracker, he'd also let himself be caught too easily, so surveillance probably wasn't his field of expertise. Logan's guess was he was a hired gun for someone.

But why would anyone be following me at all? Logan thought.

Logan carried on his walk away from the hotel, not looking behind him at all. At first he wasn't sure whether the Slav had followed him or not. After a few hundred yards Logan began to take a succession of quick turns, not trying to evade the guy, just testing him. Soon Logan was heading back toward the hotel.

Sure enough, Logan spotted the Slav once more, on the opposite side of the road. Trailing in the direction Logan had just come from. As they crossed paths, Logan looked up, over to the other side of the road. The Slav casually walked by, his head down. He didn't slow in his step or make to change course at all, despite Logan now back-tracking on himself. But Logan didn't buy it. This guy was definitely following him.

Now Logan just needed to decide what to do with him.

Chapter 20

Modena wasn't sure whether he had been awake or asleep, but the sound of the door closing startled his mind into clarity. He'd been thinking – or dreaming – about his wife, Lizzie. Their twenty-year marriage had been on the rocks for some time, largely due to his continuing infidelities and over-commitment to his work. But given the time to reflect and the shocking circumstances of his imprisonment, it was hard not to feel sentimental, which in turn was filling him with regret as to how he'd treated the woman he loved.

He looked up at the figure that had come into the room. It took him a moment to think why this time something felt different. And then it clicked. This man wasn't wearing a mask. Modena's immediate reaction was one of panic at this unexpected turn. Surely it couldn't be a good thing that they were now willing to show their faces? For a fleeting second, though, as the bearded man casually walked over to him, he wondered whether he might be one of the good guys, there to save him. But as the man's face came fully into view in the dim light, Modena saw the menacing grin and knew that wasn't to be the case.

But then something else struck him as well. Didn't the man's face look familiar? Where could Modena know him from?

The man kneeled down in front of Modena, who was once again tied and bound to the steel chair. His mouth had been taped over, restricting his breathing to his clogged and bloodied nose.

'That was a good performance you put in there, Frank,' the man said matter-of-factly in a snobbish English accent that surprised Modena.

The man reached out and ripped the tape off Modena's mouth. He let out a long groan at the sharp pain that rushed through his sore skin.

'Why?' Modena said through heavy breaths.

'Why what, my dear man?'

'Why the sham? That video. It's not what this is about. I already know that.'

'Who says it's not?' the man said, getting to his feet and walking over to the wooden bench off to Modena's right.

Modena watched nervously as the man unrolled what looked like a utility belt onto the table. There was something about this bearded man that worried him. He couldn't have been more different in his appearance, in his manner, to the oaf who had beaten him countless times now. Who had made the demands of him. And yet this man's demeanour, his voice, his presence were even more terrifying somehow.

'You could say,' the man said as he inspected the contents of the belt before rolling it back up, 'that you being here has a dual purpose.' He slowly walked back over to Modena, kneeling down once more. 'Do you know who I am?' the man asked.

'No,' Modena said, not entirely convincingly. He believed he knew the man's face, but he just couldn't think from where.

'Frank, I'm not a vain man, but you're disappointing me. I'm Youssef Selim. You know of me, right?'

Modena's eyes went wide as the man's appearance finally fell into place. Of course he knew all about Selim. Who didn't? And at the sudden realisation of what Selim's presence meant, Modena began to writhe in his seat, first shouting, then weeping.

'Shhh, come on now, calm down,' Selim said. 'There's no need to be like that.'

'What do you want from me?' Modena asked, his head bowed low, not wanting to look this man in the eyes.

'By *you*, do you mean just me? Or all of us? I can tell you what *they* want from you. But I think you already know that. The information you have is very valuable to them. There's a lot of money involved, and I'm sure a man like you can understand the lengths that people are prepared to go to for money.'

'I can't do it!' Modena shouted, the desperation clear in his voice. 'It's impossible!'

'Frank, Frank, come on now. You know that you can. And I know that you will. But you didn't let me finish. That's what they want from you. And honestly, part of their gain will be for me too. I like money as much as any other man.'

Selim reached out and, using just his forefinger, lifted Modena's head so that the two men were looking at one another again. Selim's dark eyes seemed entirely black in the low light, only adding to his menace. Above the stench of sweat, urine and faeces in the room, Modena was struck by the strong, sweet smell of the man's aftershave which seemed to clog up his nostrils with every pained breath.

'But there's something else that *I* want from you too. Something just for me.'

Selim stared into Modena's eyes, as if trying to burrow into his thoughts. Then the sides of his mouth crept up into a wicked smile.

'Frank, I want to see you suffer.'

Modena was unable to control his emotions and he cried out, tears rolling down his face.

'Please,' he begged as he watched Selim unroll the utility belt on the floor to reveal a set of gleaming metal tools.

'Oh, don't be starting with that,' Selim said. 'Surely you know that begging is demeaning. What will happen, will happen.'

Selim calmly caressed the top of each of the tools one at a time, as though they were precious jewels.

'Pain is subjective, you know,' he said. 'Like any other emotion or sensation, some people are more alert to it than others. Some people can train themselves to ignore pain completely. Can you imagine that? Being able to live entirely without pain? But doesn't that take away some of the life from you? If you feel pain, you know you are alive, and that is surely something to be thankful for. And completely blocking out pain is a very difficult thing to do, I imagine. I certainly can't. Unfortunately, Frank, I don't think you can either.'

'No, please don't do this!' Modena shouted, terrified by Selim's menace. 'I'm sorry, I'll try to help. Please!'

'I know you will, Frank, I know you will. You're a very honourable man. And I'm sure the others will be very pleased to hear that you're finally willing to co-operate.'

Selim unfolded a flap on the belt, took out a thick nail, two inches long, and turned it over in his fingers. With his other hand he pulled out a claw hammer, its head dented from previous use.

'But your sudden decision to help us is not going to make a difference for you now.'

'Please!' Modena shouted as loudly as he could.

Selim ignored him. 'This little trick is something I learned a long time ago. You see, the key to torture is to deliver maximum pain for minimum damage. There's no point in having your victim bleed out on you in just a few minutes. Where would the fun be in that?'

He chuckled to himself and held the nail up close to Modena's face.

'You take a nail like this, and you place it up against the fingertip.'

Modena's wrists were already bound to the chair, but Selim pressed his left arm down onto Modena's right forearm, pinning the arm and hand in place and allowing him to prise a finger open. He placed the tip of the nail at the edge of the finger where the fingernail ended.

'Then you take a hammer, like this, and ...'

Selim swung the hammer in a short, sharp arc, putting seemingly little effort into it, allowing the weight of the tool to do the work.

'... just give it a little tap to start.'

The hammer connected with the nail head, forcing the pointed tip into Modena's finger, between the flesh and the fingernail. Modena began to scream out, louder. Pain shot through his finger, up his arm.

'Once it's in, you can give it a bit more welly.'

Selim swung the hammer back and forth another two times, using more force now to drive the nail further up into Modena's finger. There was a sickly ripping noise as the fingernail rose off the flesh, and blood seeped out of all sides.

Modena writhed and coiled in the chair but he couldn't move. He screamed, he cried, he shouted, he spluttered.

Selim stood up, inspecting his handiwork: the nail protruding from Modena's forefinger and the small pool of blood forming underneath it.

'Now tell me, Frank, have you ever felt pain like that?'

Selim paused before kneeling back down to the belt to retrieve another nail.

'It's amazing, isn't it? How much pain can be caused by a seemingly innocuous wound. I always like to start off like this. It's a great opener.'

Selim lifted Modena's head up again, and held his face close. Modena squinted his eyes shut, not wanting to look, wanting to take himself someplace else. To his home. To his wife. But he didn't know how. All he could think about was the agony that he was now in. And about what more was to come.

'And I know what you're thinking, Frank,' Selim said, almost in a whisper, a wide grin on his face. 'You're trying your best to find some way to ignore the pain, hoping it will go away, hoping your body will get used to it. Hoping that this is as bad as it will get.'

Selim placed his arm back across Modena, pinning him in place, and then positioned another nail.

'But it's not, Frank. I'm sorry to tell you but this is only the start. I'm not going to stop. It's only going to get worse for you from here. So you'd better start praying.'

Modena was already screaming as Selim raised the hammer once more.

Chapter 21

Logan carried on walking, past the hotel. He didn't look back to check if the Slav was still there. He had to assume he was.

How had he not seen this guy before? Surely if this amateur had been following then Logan would have already spotted him? Which meant there was likely at least one more person involved in tailing him. Logan knew it was always much easier to track as a team.

So where were the others?

Then another thought struck. Had they somehow planted a tracker on Logan? It could be done with ease. As simple as brushing past someone in the street. But Logan was so used to such tricks himself he would surely have noticed if he'd fallen victim to a ploy like that.

Wouldn't he?

In a way it didn't matter. Right now he just needed to deal with the problem facing him. Logan still didn't know what his next move would be. The obvious route was to confront the man, but he didn't want to do that out in the open. If the situation turned nasty out in public, with witnesses, there would be far too much explaining to do.

He reached the entrance to the car park and walked down the stairs to his level. When he got there, he made his way over to his rented car, doing a recce of the area as he went. There was no sign of the man or anyone else having followed him in, which surprised Logan.

Where was he?

Logan got into his car. For the next five minutes he sat patiently at the wheel. But nothing happened. He wondered whether he may have been wrong. Maybe the Slav hadn't been following him. He certainly didn't seem to be the man the receptionist had referred to.

Logan nearly jumped out of his seat when his phone began to ring. He was on edge, but at least he knew his reactions were good. He took the phone out of his pocket. It was Laura.

'Hi, Laura.'

'Hi, Carl. I have some news for you.'

'On Blakemore?'

'Yep. Can you talk?'

'Go for it.'

'Well, as you would expect, there are quite a few Richard Blakemores in England. Though not many who look like they'd be of interest.'

'But there are some, right? That are of interest?'

'You got that right. Richard Blakemore, forty-one years old. His wealthy parents died twenty years ago in a car crash, leaving him a fancy townhouse in London. Looks as though he started mixing with a crowd of rebellious yuppies and soon wound up on drugs charges. Supplying class As, to be exact. Charges were dropped, but six months later he upped sticks to France, where he bought a big farmhouse about a hundred or so miles south of Paris.'

'Sounds like he could be our man, then. Anything since he's come to France?'

'Oh yeah, it gets better. For the past two years he's been on the radar of the French police and Interpol, on suspicion that he's peddling drugs from the Middle East and Africa into France. And peddling weapons back in the other direction. But so far they've never been able to get anything to stick on him.'

And there it was. The link to Vincent with his drug-dealing friends, certainly. To Djourou and Selim, possibly.

'Has to be our man,' Logan said. 'What's the address? Wait, just let me get a pen.'

Logan rummaged in the car for a pen and a scrap of paper. He opened up the glove box but all he could find was the car lease document. It would do.

As he looked up his heart jumped when he saw the outline of a figure move behind a pillar. His hand was already on his gun when the figure emerged on the other side. But it wasn't the Slav. Just a young woman on the way to her parked car. Logan breathed a sigh of relief.

'You okay, Logan?' Laura said.

'I'm fine, was just grabbing a pen. Give me the address.'

Laura gave him the address of the farm. It was in the French countryside, in the northern part of the Bourgogne region – an isolated position, miles from the nearest town. Perfect for holding a hostage, Logan thought.

'I'm going to head there now,' Logan said. 'Can you call Mackie for me?'

'Sure. Why?'

'Tell him I'm being followed,' Logan said. He really didn't want to be the bearer of bad news again. 'And ask him to get my stuff from the hotel. I don't think it's safe there for me.'

'You're being followed? Jesus, Carl, what's going on?'

'I don't know who it is yet, but I'm fine. Just let Mackie know.'

Logan put the phone back into his pocket and turned the key in the ignition. He took his gun out of his trousers and placed it on his lap. Just in case anyone was waiting for him on the outside. He pulled out of the parking space and turned left toward the ramp that led to the road.

He was about twenty-five yards away from the entrance when a man appeared, walking down the ramp toward him. At first, he was relieved when he saw it wasn't the Slav. But as Logan did a double-take, he realised that he'd seen the man before. Yesterday at the hospital. The big man with the brown leather jacket. The man who had killed Jean Vincent.

And Logan realised then that it was also the man the hotel receptionist had seen.

Logan's car slowed almost to a stop as he eased off the accelerator. He wasn't sure whether to keep on going or turn around. A second later, the man pulled a handgun out of his jacket. Almost at the same time, the Slav appeared behind him. He was holding a gun too, both hands around the grip. Whoever they were, these guys weren't here to talk.

Chapter 22

Without a second thought, Logan pushed his foot onto the accelerator and the tyres screeched as the car lurched forward toward the two men. It was the best option. Other than two stairwells, the ramp was the only way out, so he had to give it a shot. If he was fast, and lucky, he may get past them without either getting off any good shots.

As the Slav raised his gun, Logan was sure that he saw him give an evil smile. He opened fire, taking out Logan's windscreen in one shot. Logan reflexively took his right hand off the wheel to hold his arm up to his face. Shattered glass filled the air around him. He kept his foot on the accelerator and ducked his head down to protect himself. But it meant he could no longer see where he was going.

A succession of shots rang out. The car jolted as a tyre exploded. And Logan could do nothing as the car veered away to the left and smashed into a stationary vehicle.

He shot forward at the impact, the airbag deploying and smacking him in the face with the force of a heavyweight boxer. The seatbelt caught, propelling him back into his seat. For a second or two he saw stars. But although the car was badly damaged, Logan was more or less unscathed.

Logan wrestled with the airbag, punching and pushing it away from him. As he scrambled to get out of the car, he saw the two attackers were about ten yards away, on the other side of his car, still close to the exit ramp. He finally managed to open the door and dropped to the ground with his Beretta in hand.

More shots were fired as he hunched on the ground, his fuzzy head still recovering from the crash. But he knew that, within seconds, the attackers would be upon him if he didn't move. The stairwell that Logan had used to enter the car park was directly adjacent to the exit ramp. But there was another set of stairs at the far end of the car park, about forty yards away.

Crouching low, Logan began to move in that direction, moving between the parked cars. The whole place was completely deserted except for Logan and the two men. There was no sign of the woman Logan had seen earlier, and the sound of gunfire was probably keeping any other people away.

He heard another shot ring out and flinched as the bullet narrowly missed him, embedding in the body of a nearby car. He didn't risk looking behind to see where the attackers were. Using only instinct, he moved quickly to the other end of the car park, keeping low to try to stay covered. He heard voices as the two attackers gave each other orders. But they were too quiet for Logan to tell what they were saying – Logan assumed they were positioning themselves for their next attack.

Logan reached the far end of the car park and stopped behind a large Mercedes. All that stood between him and the stairwell was about six yards of open space. If he was quick, he could make it without getting shot. But if these guys were any good, they must have known that was where he was heading. And if they were ready, it would be an easy shot for them to take.

He sneaked a glance around the rear bumper of the Mercedes, looking out, back toward the exit ramp. He made out the figure of the leather jacket man about ten yards away, out in the open. The man was looking in Logan's direction, his gun held out in front of him at chest height. Logan pulled his head back in, expecting a shot.

But it didn't come. The man didn't fire. Even though he must have seen Logan.

What is he waiting for? Logan thought. *And the second man. Where is* he?

Logan's heart drummed in his chest as adrenaline surged through his body. There was no sign yet of the trembling that he'd experienced earlier. Not now. He was too focused. But he was running out of options.

He got down onto his belly to look underneath the Mercedes. He hoped to be able to see the feet of the Slav. But there was no sign of him anywhere.

And then the sound came. The gentlest rustle. Directly behind Logan.

Logan rolled, lying flat on his back, his gun pointed in the direction where the noise had come from. But he was aiming at thin air. And he was now staring down the barrel of the Slav's pistol. He was standing less than three yards away, with the same broad smile as when he'd first spotted Logan in the car.

They'd cornered him. And they knew it.

'Johnny. Come over here. I have him,' the Slav said. He spoke slowly with a thick Eastern European accent. Logan guessed he had been right about his facial features.

'Good work, Lorik,' Johnny said, coming into view.

This guy was English. *Are these Blakemore's men?* Logan wondered.

'Well, hello there, John Burrows,' Johnny said. 'Going somewhere, are we?'

'Was just doing some sightseeing,' Logan replied, trying to appear unfazed.

'Funny man,' Johnny said, not looking at all amused. 'Drop that weapon or we'll drop you.'

'You could have shot me already,' Logan mused. 'So could your friend. He sneaked right up behind me, but he didn't shoot. So I don't think you're going to shoot me *now* either.'

'We don't have to shoot to kill. I could stick one in a leg or even your bollocks. Drop your weapon or I *will* shoot you.'

Logan did as he was told, sliding the Beretta across the floor. Johnny stepped over and picked it up, placing it in his jacket pocket.

'I presume you're Blakemore's men,' Logan said.

Johnny didn't answer, but Logan saw the glint in his eye. Yep, these were Blakemore's men all right.

'Get to your feet, slowly, with your hands above your head,' Johnny said.

Logan again followed their command. They might have the upper hand for now, but he was sure they would give him an opportunity to turn the situation sooner or later.

'So are you taking me to see Blakemore?' Logan asked.

Johnny and Lorik ignored the question. Lorik still had his gun trained on Logan but Johnny was holding his down by his side. He was looking about the car park as if trying to determine their next move.

'What, you're not speaking to me now?' Logan said. 'By the way, how are you two going to get me out of here? Have you even got a car? Or were you planning to frogmarch me through the streets of Paris?'

Johnny sighed, turned to face Logan and threw a fist into his gut. Logan doubled over, the wind knocked out of him.

'Lorik, find us a car to take,' Johnny said.

The fist had hurt Logan. But with his head still hunched over, he couldn't help but smile. He'd been right. These two might have been good enough, or lucky enough, to have cornered him, but they hadn't exactly thought out their next move.

Lorik cursed in his native tongue. Logan straightened up. Lorik, gun still held high, now began to scan the area in front of him.

'There. We'll take that one,' Lorik said, nodding over to a silver Audi. It was parked three cars up from where they were. 'It's an old one. Will be easy.'

'Come on then, Burrows. Follow me,' Johnny said.

The two attackers began to move. Slowly and cautiously they edged forward, their guns trained on Logan the whole time. Logan followed the direction of their movement, one step after the other. Lorik was in front of him, Johnny was at his side. It was a wise choice on their part. If they'd gone opposite sides of Logan – one to the right and one to the left, or one in front, one behind – there was a big risk they'd end up shooting each other if Logan made a move. It wasn't rocket science, but plenty of people would have made that mistake.

They reached the Audi. It was an early nineties model. Johnny once again raised his gun to Logan's head. For the first time, Lorik dropped his aim as he moved toward the car, but he never once let his eye contact with Logan go. He side-stepped up to the driver's window. Still facing Logan, he delivered a single blow to the window with his right elbow. The glass shattered. Logan had expected an alarm to go, but nothing happened. It was an old model, but still, it was nothing more than bad luck that it hadn't had an alarm fitted. Lorik smiled at Logan again. He was probably thinking the exact same thing.

Lorik reached in through the broken window frame and unlatched the door. 'This will only take few seconds,' he said.

He opened the door and finally broke eye contact with Logan as he climbed into the car. Lorik ducked his head down, level with the steering wheel, as he hotwired the car. For the first time, Logan had only one attacker watching him. If he was to make a move, now was his chance.

He was still deciding on how to do it when there was a banging sound behind him as the door to the stairwell opened and shut. Johnny instinctively looked over to see what the noise was. It was all the invitation that Logan need. He dived forward, low, and rolled into Johnny's legs. He sent him straight up into the air. Johnny didn't even manage to get a shot off as he went up and then down, crashing onto the hard concrete floor.

Logan was up and onto him immediately, placing a knee firmly into the back of Johnny's neck. He picked up Johnny's gun, which had fallen to the floor next to him. Johnny squirmed and Logan applied more pressure to his neck, enough to subdue any attempted struggle.

Whoever had walked in on them must have had the shock of their life. Logan had heard a scream, and the door open and shut again as the unlucky person made a quick getaway.

Logan heard a putter as the Audi's engine came to life. He looked up at the car to see Lorik in the driver's seat, staring directly at him. No sign of that smile now.

The car lurched forward. Logan pulled up Johnny's gun. He fired two shots as he dived out of the way. Both bullets hit the Audi's windscreen. The glass cracked but didn't shatter.

Lorik didn't make any attempt to stop or change course as the car continued forward, rolling over Johnny, who let out a piercing scream. He only applied the brakes at the last second, narrowly avoiding a collision with the parked cars.

There was a crunching sound as Lorik rushed to change his gears. Logan readjusted his aim as the car began to reverse. He fired off two more shots. Both hit the vehicle, penetrating the metal exterior, but missing Lorik. Logan dived for cover again as the Audi swept past, rolling over the stricken body of Johnny for a second time. This time, there was no scream.

Logan, on one knee, fired the remaining bullets in his magazine as the Audi accelerated away from him, toward the exit. He hit with every shot. Both the back window and the windscreen shattered. But Lorik managed to keep his head down. All Logan could do was look on as the car went up the ramp and out of the car park.

Frustrated, he got to his feet. He desperately wanted to go after Lorik, but he had no chance of catching him. He hurled Johnny's gun away in anger. The magazine was empty anyway; he had no use for it now. He headed to the fallen Johnny and kneeled down beside his foe. He was lying on his side, his limbs twisted and bent awkwardly, his head turned with his face pointing up toward Logan. He looked in a bad way. But the small movements in his chest told Logan that he was breathing. They were short, shallow breaths, but he was definitely breathing.

Johnny didn't offer any resistance as Logan rolled him onto his back. Logan was no doctor, but Johnny didn't look good. The fact that the car had been travelling at low speed didn't make a difference. He'd been run over twice. Logan was sure the car had run straight over his chest the second time, and knew that Johnny had little chance of survival.

Logan waved his left hand in front of Johnny's eyes. They were open, but there was no response to Logan's hand. No movement, no dilation.

Not much point in wasting any more time here.

Logan reached into Johnny's pocket and retrieved his Beretta. He checked it over, pleased that the car didn't seem to have caught it at all. He then made to get to his feet. But he stopped in his tracks when he heard a voice coming from behind him. A female voice.

'Don't you move another inch,' the voice said.

Logan froze. Not out of fear, but surprise.

'FBI. Drop your weapon and slowly get to your feet.'

Chapter 23

Logan was facing away from where the woman's voice had come from. Ignoring the demand to drop his gun, he began to stand, turning as he did so to get a look at his new company.

'I said drop the weapon!' she shouted.

'Easy, I'm just standing up,' he said, not attempting to stop.

He completed his turn and took in the woman standing just a few yards away from him, holding her gun high, two hands around the butt. She was about six or maybe as much as nine inches shorter than Logan, and wearing a tight-fitting, deep-brown skirt suit with a white blouse underneath. Even if she hadn't already said so, ninety-nine times out a hundred he would have said she was FBI. The American accent together with the stuffy clothes and the gun stance gave her away. She was also attractive, with silky dark hair held back away from her face, tanned skin and deep brown eyes.

'You're a little far from home, aren't you?' Logan said.

'Just drop the weapon and step away from that man,' she said. 'Or I *will* shoot you.' Her voice was calm and assured.

'He's dead already,' Logan said, still not making any attempt to do as he was told. 'Or at least he will be soon enough. And I didn't do it.'

'Sure you didn't. Just drop the gun. Last chance now.'

She didn't appear fazed by the situation at all. He had no doubt that if he gave her a reason, she would fulfil her word and shoot him. He tossed the Beretta over to her. It skated along the floor, resting just a few inches from her feet. She didn't make any move to pick it up. Just carried on pointing her gun at him.

'Now what?' Logan said, taking a step toward her. 'Are you going to arrest me? You're a little out of your jurisdiction, aren't you?'

'Just stop there!' she snapped.

'Come on,' he said. 'What are you doing holding that gun at me? The man who killed this guy just sped off. Shouldn't you be off after him?'

'Who are you?' she said again.

'My name's Carl Logan.'

'Are you police?'

'No.'

'Intelligence?'

'About average.'

'Not what I meant.'

'The answer's no.'

'Really? So, you're just a concerned citizen?'

'I'd be less concerned if you stopped pointing that gun at me.'

'That would be a bit foolish of me, don'tcha think?'

'I guess. What are *you* doing here anyway? Were you following this guy?' Logan pointed to Johnny. 'Or the guy who did that to him?' He took another two steps toward her.

'I'm serious,' she said, ignoring his questions. 'One more step and the first bullet is going in your gut. Have you any idea how painful that is?'

'Maybe. Have you?'

'No. But I'm not the one who's going to get it.'

'I'm assuming you *were* following them. So who are you looking for? Blakemore?'

She didn't respond. She also didn't react at all to the name.

'Frank Modena then?'

Of course it was. It was amazing how often people's eyes gave them away without them having to say a word.

'You know, we're on the same team,' Logan said.

'And what team is it you think we're on?'

'I'm just out to get the bad guys too.'

She laughed sarcastically. 'If we're on the same team then you won't mind accompanying me to my command centre so we can check you out.'

'Well, actually I would mind that.'

'And why is that, Carl?'

'Because your command centre won't know who I am. And my boss would be very disappointed with me.'

'So you *are* intelligence?'

'I didn't say that.'

Logan heard several sets of footsteps moving fast, getting louder as they approached the car park entrance above.

'Police! Police!' came the shouts.

Just what I need, Logan thought.

'Looks like you're in a bit of a pickle, Carl.'

He turned around, looking back at the ramp. They weren't yet in the car park, but judging by the shouts, they must have been close. He didn't have long.

'Look, you can't let the police arrest me,' he said, speaking with a bit more urgency. 'I'm getting too close. You're here for Modena, right? The dead guy, he was working for the man who has Modena. I'm sure of it. You have to trust me.'

Her eyes practically lit up as he spoke about Modena. But without waiting for her to respond, he reached out, thrusting his hand around her gun. She squeezed on the trigger several times, but he'd pushed her aim away from him. The bullets sailed harmlessly into the air, lodging in the concrete roof of the car park. He twisted her arm around, moved himself forward and pulled her toward him until her back was pressed up against him. His right arm was now wrapped around her, smothering her gun arm.

'I've got to get out of here,' he said.

His superior size and strength had made it relatively easy for him to pull her into the position. He should have been able to prise the gun out of her hands without much effort. But maybe he'd misjudged her. She was an FBI agent, after all. He should have known that she would be trained for situations like this. And trained to deal with targets that were bigger and stronger than she was.

She let go of her gun, freeing her arm in the process, ducked down and threw her right heel into his groin, propelling herself away from him.

The move surprised Logan, but only for a second. His groin was on fire and the pain seemed to reach all the way up to his stomach, but he fought through it. He corrected his grip on her gun and aimed it at her. But in the intervening seconds, she had picked up his Beretta from the ground and was pointing it directly at him.

Stalemate. Again.

'I've been in this situation already today,' Logan said. 'The other guys didn't fare so well.'

'I'll take my chances,' she said. A picture of cool, still.

'I've got to get out of here,' Logan said. 'You can come with me if you want. All I want is Modena. Just trust me. Don't let the police arrest me.'

'Police!' came the shout again.

The steps were getting louder, but they were also slowing down. Logan glanced quickly to his left and saw the legs of half a dozen policemen appearing at the top of the ramp, creeping slowly down.

'Police. Stop or we'll shoot!'

Logan had no doubt that they would, too. Several shots had already been fired in the car park so the police knew their targets were armed.

'Come on, we've got to go,' Logan shouted as he moved toward the agent.

He lowered the gun and stepped past her to the stairwell. If she had wanted to, she could have shot him. But she didn't.

The French police weren't as forgiving, though. A gunshot rang out. The bullet hit only a couple of yards from Logan, lodging in the back wall of the car park as he ran for the exit. Logan and the agent both instinctively ducked.

But it wasn't enough to stop Logan. And as he reached the door, he couldn't help but smile when he glanced around to see the FBI agent following him out.

Chapter 24

Logan ran up the stairs, the FBI agent just a few steps behind him. They came up onto a quiet back street. There were few pedestrians around and little traffic, but they still both instinctively hid their weapons from view.

'This is a really bad idea, you know,' she said to him. 'How am I expected to explain this?'

'Look, I'm getting too close to spend the night in a cell,' Logan said. 'We need to get away from here. I'll explain everything afterwards. Do you have a car?'

'Yeah, it's this way,' she said, and ran off to the right.

There was a chance that she would lead him straight back to the police. But for now, Logan would trust her. He didn't have many other options. It would be easier to persuade a lone FBI agent that he was one of the good guys than it would a whole team of armed police.

Logan headed after her and she stopped at a blue Ford hatchback parked just down from where they'd come out of the car park. She clicked on her remote and got into the driver's seat. Logan moved around to the passenger side, put his hand on the handle. But it was locked. She looked at him through the window, as if contemplating whether or not to let him in. He gave her a pleading look. Finally she relented and unlocked the door for him.

'Very funny,' he said to her as he got into the car.

As he sat down in the passenger seat they exchanged their guns, which had been switched during the fracas, without saying a word to each other. She pulled away from the kerb and started off down the street at a leisurely pace, low revs, no burning rubber. Logan looked behind. There was no sign of any police following them, so he was content that going at a normal speed was the best option. It was less likely to draw attention.

She took her eyes off the road for a second and looked over at him, her dark eyes staring as though she was trying to read his mind. It made him feel uncomfortable, almost a little embarrassed.

'So what now?' she said to him. 'Why are you even running from the police? If we're on the same team, you should be working with them.'

'You're telling me the FBI like to share their cases?'

'No, we don't. But we disclose our presence when necessary.'

'Like you did in the car park just then?'

She didn't respond to that. He knew the FBI, the police, intelligence agencies, whoever, were all the same in that respect. They pretended to be helping each other when it suited them, but when it came down to it, no-one really had the slightest idea what the other was up to. And they all wanted to be the ones to get the credit for bringing the bad guys down.

Except in the case of the JIA: the only credit their agents were likely to get was internal. Few people in the outside world even knew the JIA existed.

'Just drive,' Logan said. 'Keep going until we're well away.'

'And then what?'

'Just keep going.'

Logan heard the sirens before he saw the flashing lights. As they came to a stop at the next set of lights, two police cars came into view about a hundred yards behind them.

'Go!' Logan shouted.

'Why are we even running? Why don't you just tell them what you've told me? That you claim to be on the *same team*.'

He didn't have time for this. Logan pulled out his gun and aimed it at her head, the barrel only inches from her face. 'I'm sorry. But just go. Now.'

She didn't move. Just stared at him, anger etched on her face. The police sirens got louder.

'You won't shoot,' she said, calling his bluff. 'Why would you shoot me? Whoever you are, that would just get you into a *really* big mess.'

She wasn't wrong. He had no intention of shooting her. But he wasn't going to let himself get caught by the police either. Even if

Mackie was able to pull the strings to get him free, it would surely be the end of his involvement on the case. Most likely it would be the end of his career with the JIA. The spotlight was well and truly on him, and the only outcome that he could contemplate was the one which saw him safely returning Modena. And felling Selim.

He opened his window, stuck his arm out and began firing at the fast-approaching police cars. His shots had been aimed to miss and they all did, sailing harmlessly into the tarmac. But they were enough to panic one of the drivers, who swerved, scraping into the other police car before mounting the pavement and crashing into a brick wall.

'What the hell is wrong with you?!' the FBI agent screamed.

The other police car, the driver probably spooked at being shot at, came to a stop in the middle of the road. Its occupants dived out, drawing their guns and hiding behind their open car doors for cover.

'Well, I guess they're probably going to be after both of us now,' Logan said, giving her a wry smile. 'It's not like they know who you are, either. I suggest we get going now.'

'Fuck you,' she said.

She opened her door and went to get out. But as she did so, a gunshot rang out, the bullet hitting somewhere on the back of their car. Both of them jumped at the unexpected attack from the police. The agent quickly retreated back inside, slamming shut her door. Pedestrians on the road around them screamed, some falling to the ground for cover, others aimlessly running to try to find safety.

'Like I said, looks like they're after both of us now,' Logan said. 'Let's just get out of here.'

With her face like a storm and without saying another word, the FBI agent relented and put the car into gear. The lights were still on red but she stepped on the accelerator, hard, and the car pulled forward, pushing them both back into their seats. A driver coming across the junction had to slam on the brakes of his car to avoid hitting them. But the FBI agent didn't even seem to notice. She just pushed down harder and the engine whirred and whined as the car accelerated away from the stationary police cars.

Within seconds they were approaching a heady speed for the cramped inner-city streets. Logan braced himself, clenching his fists as the needle on the speedometer edged past fifty, then sixty miles an hour. When they approached the next junction, the lights were on red. Logan thought that the agent was about to ease off the speed. But instead she pushed even harder on the accelerator.

The needle passed seventy as they raced through the red light. Logan saw why she had sped up when a police car came careening around the corner in front of them, lights flashing and siren wailing. It went hurtling past them before the driver realised that his target had already gone past. Logan could hear screeching tyres behind him as the police car driver attempted to turn around. For just a second, Logan thought they might make it through the junction unscathed. But as they went through the intersection, another police car came flying at them.

With no time to react, they were powerless as the police car side-swiped the speeding Ford, sending them into a relentless spin. Logan's head smacked off the passenger window. At one point it felt like the car was clean off the ground, floating through the air. The car then came to a sudden stop, crashing into another vehicle that had come to a skidding stop in the junction, snapping Logan back into his seat, sending a shock of pain down his neck and spine.

It took both Logan and the FBI agent a few seconds to recover from the impact, and to work out what had actually happened. And then a few more to figure out in which direction they were now facing.

The scene in front of them was one of carnage, with broken glass and mangled car parts – metal, glass and plastic – all over the road. At least half a dozen cars had been shunted or had shunted others as one by one they tried too late to avoid the pile-up. In many ways, Logan knew they'd been lucky, though. There had been only the slightest of contact with the police car, right on the back corner of their car. If it had been a full-on collision at that speed, no-one would have walked away from the crash.

'Just keep going!' Logan shouted.

This time, there was no hesitation. As soon as he spoke, they were moving again.

Logan looked behind him. The police car that had hit them was in the distance, at a stop. Steam rose from its crumpled bonnet. They were going nowhere like that. The level of damage couldn't have been from hitting the Ford, though, so it must have hit something else after it swiped them. And there was enough mangled wreckage on the intersection for it to be at least temporarily blocked.

For now, it looked like Logan and the FBI agent were home and dry.

Chapter 25

Angela Grainger was fuming. She'd given this guy, Carl Logan, the benefit of the doubt. She knew what she should have done. She should have stood her ground, waited for the police to arrive, and had the guy arrested. Whatever the result of her decision to do the opposite, there would be a hell of a lot of explaining to do. But she'd got caught up in the moment. He had said he was there to help. And Grainger knew she needed it.

That was before Logan had shot at the police, though. It was one thing running away from them. But shooting at them? How was that going to help anything?

'Just keep going this way,' Logan said. 'We're heading north, I think. We'll soon come to the turning for the motorway. If we take that, we'll be out of the city within minutes.'

Grainger didn't respond but did as he suggested. As much as what she really wanted to do was take him to the nearest police station, she still wanted to hear what he had to say. How it was that he was going to help her find Modena. And anyway, they were both unhurt and they were going to get away from the police. Considering the position they'd been in a few minutes ago, that was a pretty good result as far as she was concerned. And just like him, she really didn't want to be chasing down Modena with the police in tow.

'This is it here,' Logan said when they reached the turning for the A86 ring road which circumvented the centre of Paris. 'Head east. We'll go back around the city and then out to the south.'

She did as he said without questioning where they were going.

'Just keep going from here,' he said once they were on the motorway. 'I think we've definitely lost them, so just keep it steady.'

They sat for a few minutes in silence, steadily moving along the four-lane carriageway. When Grainger did finally speak, her voice was tinged with anger.

'Why did you do that? You could have killed those policemen.'

Logan looked at her. 'I did what I had to do,' he said. 'And I wasn't trying to hit them. I just wanted to get them to back off.'

'You might not have directly hit them but anything could have happened. They could have swerved off and knocked over someone – a child!'

'But they didn't. They weren't even going that fast. I'm sure they'll be fine.'

'But you don't know that.'

Logan didn't argue the point further, but Grainger could tell from the look in his eyes that he knew she was right.

A further silence followed. After a few minutes, the anger that Grainger was feeling started to subside. Whatever mess she had got herself into, it was done now. What she really needed was to figure out what she was going to do next. And what she was going to do with Logan.

'I'm sorry, okay?' Logan said, as if picking up on Grainger's more relaxed mood. 'But I wasn't banking on running into the police *or* the FBI. Those men in the car park are the bad guys. I'm simply trying to get the same thing as you: Frank Modena.'

'You've just assumed that I'm doing the same thing as you.'

'Aren't you?'

She paused. 'Yes, but I never told you that.'

'Maybe I've got a good sense for these things.'

She just hoped she did too.

The road they were travelling on was busy, but not yet congested. It was only three p.m. and rush hour wouldn't be in full swing for another hour. They were flanked either side by residential areas, mainly multi-storey tower blocks and townhouses. Outside of Logan's passenger window the centre of Paris, Eiffel Tower and all, was visible in the distance every now and then when the gaps in the apartment blocks allowed.

'Where are we going now?' Grainger said. 'Jesus, listen to me. Where are *we* going. *I* should be taking you to the nearest police station. *I* should be calling my team to tell them why I just ran away from the police after a shootout – the police, who we're actually supposed to be assisting.'

'Then why aren't you?'

She didn't answer the question. She couldn't. All she knew was that she had to do whatever it took to get to Modena. And if Logan really could help her to do that, then she would let him.

'What's your name?' Logan said. 'You haven't told me your name.'

'Special Agent Grainger.'

'Special Agent? That's a funny name.'

'Angela. My name's Angela Grainger.'

'Nice to meet you, Angela Grainger.'

'So come on then, *Carl*, who *do* you work for?'

'Does it matter?'

'Yes,' she said. 'It matters a lot. I'm an FBI agent. Fraternising with criminals isn't exactly a key part of our instruction manual.'

'You have an instruction manual?' Logan said, smiling.

Grainger tried her best not to, but she couldn't help but reciprocate the smile. Inside she cursed herself for letting her guard down so easily. But she knew why it was. His confidence and embattled appearance gave it away – Logan was an alpha male. Just like her father. Just like Tom, her ex-husband. She couldn't help but feel at ease with men like that. Even though she knew it rarely worked out in her favour.

'And anyway, I'm not a criminal,' Logan added.

'The police obviously think you are.'

'And they're always right? So how did the FBI get involved in this?'

'You avoided my question about who you work for,' she said. 'Again.'

Although she was pretty sure she knew the answer. She guessed he was an intelligence agent of some sort. What she didn't know was who he worked for or what his brief was. He said he was trying to find Modena. But there really wasn't any way yet to know whether she could trust him on that.

'And you avoided mine,' Logan said.

She'd had enough of this. If this was going to work, one of them had to start doing the talking.

'Fine. I'm an agent for the FBI. I'm working here in Paris on the authority of the French police – the Police nationale. Quite simple really. I'm here to help them find Frank Modena. I have full jurisdiction for carrying out law enforcement duties with identical powers to the local police. So I could actually just arrest you myself if I wanted to.'

'Well, you obviously don't want to then.'

'Maybe not,' she said. 'But that doesn't mean I wouldn't.'

'You don't want to because you know that I can help you just as much as you can help me.'

'Well, so far it seems I'm helping you. I'm still waiting for you to explain how you can help me.'

'You'll see.'

'Well come on then, I've told you about me. So what about you? What are you doing here?'

'I'm here to help the local police as well. It's just that they don't know it yet. Like I said, we're on the same team.'

'So you keep saying. Except apparently you think it's okay to shoot at people from your own team.'

Logan ignored her dig. Grainger glanced over at him then back at the road ahead. He was looking down at his hands, which were trembling. Out of the corner of her eye she saw him hold his hands up, turning them over, examining them, as though the answer to what was making it happen would suddenly appear to him.

'What's wrong?' Grainger asked, unconcerned about prying, her eyes still focused on the road.

'Nothing's wrong,' Logan snapped.

'Anxiety?' Grainger said.

'What?'

'Is it anxiety? Is that what's making your hands do that? I've seen it before. Used to happen to my dad all the time.'

'I'm not anxious,' Logan said defensively.

Grainger glanced back and forth at Logan as she drove, her intrigue growing. She watched as he pressed his hands down onto his thighs. The trembling stopped. But as soon as he lifted them up again it came back.

'How did he stop it?' Logan asked.

'My dad? Never did. Got worse and worse his whole life. Wasn't just the hands, though. It affected him in all sorts of ways. But the hands were always a tell-tale sign for me.'

She knew on the outside her face was calm. But even talking about her father briefly brought all of the painful emotions flooding back. Her dad. The one truly good thing she'd had in her life. And he'd been taken away from her so cruelly.

'Yeah, well,' Logan said, 'I'm not anxious. I've just had a rough day.'

'That's what *he* used to say.'

Logan turned away from her, looking out of the passenger window. She got the point. Something had happened to him, but despite her curiosity, she wasn't going to push it. Even if she did, why would he tell her anything? She had plenty of her own baggage that she had no intention of going into with a man she'd just met.

But his face now, the worry and pain in his eyes, was so different to the action man she'd met in the garage. And she couldn't help but feel empathy at his unexpected vulnerability. Perhaps she'd been wrong about him. Perhaps there was more to him than met the eye.

'So just how do you think you can help me, Carl?'

'I'm going to help you find Frank Modena.'

'And what makes you think I can't do that myself?'

'Maybe you could. But I'll get there first. Because I'm trying to find him using whatever means I can because that's what I do: the dirty work that you and the police can't do or won't do.'

She knew exactly what he meant by that. She'd come across his type before. And in a way his words made her feel more at ease. Because help from a man who wasn't constrained by the same rules, regulations and laws as the FBI was exactly what she needed. But his bravado on its own wasn't going to be enough.

'If you want me to trust you,' she said, taking her eyes off the road and looking over at him again for just a second, 'you're going to have to give me more than that. You need to tell me what you know. And what it is you're going to do next.'

He paused again but she could see he was mulling it over. And eventually he obliged.

'I've been in Paris for two days,' he said, looking out of his side window. 'This morning I went to see an African by the name of Thierry Djourou. When I asked him questions he didn't like, he and his men tried to kill me. They failed.'

Grainger noticed Logan turn to face her again.

'But I got a name,' he said. 'Richard Blakemore.'

Grainger held her breath, not wanting to show any reaction to the name.

'I got back to my hotel some time after that,' Logan carried on, 'and then two guys followed me to that car park. One English, called Johnny; the other Eastern European, I think, and called Lorik. They both pulled guns on me. Johnny ended up dead. Lorik drove off.

'Oh, and add into the mix a pretty well-known terrorist called Youssef Selim. Some way or other, this all links back to Modena. At least I think it does, but I'm not sure how yet.

'How does all that sound to you?'

'Djourou's dead,' Grainger said almost immediately after he'd finished his monologue. 'Don't worry,' she added, seeing the perplexed look on his face. 'I know you didn't do it. The man who is now lying dead in that car park paid a visit to Djourou not long after you left. It was pretty nasty, from what I've heard. He and his friend were both hacked up with a machete. The police weren't even sure which body parts belonged to which man. It was a bloodbath.'

'So you were keeping tabs on Djourou?' Logan said.

'Maybe. Maybe we were keeping tabs on you.'

'So what else do you know?' Logan asked. 'What do you know about Blakemore?'

Her brain whirred as she thought about how to answer the question. In the end she lied. 'I know his name because you just told me it. That's it.'

She could tell by the glare on his face that he didn't believe her answer, but he didn't press her on it.

'So who is he?' Grainger asked.

'I think Blakemore's either behind this or has a good idea who is,' Logan said.

'And why do you think that? There's a pretty convincing video that suggests otherwise.'

'It wasn't convincing to me.'

'Well, don't forget about Youssef Selim. You said yourself that he's involved in this. The video, Selim, a known terrorist – they all seem to point to the same thing to me.'

'You don't need to tell me about Selim,' Logan said.

The tone in his voice was enough to ward Grainger off asking why. And she didn't understand why she was arguing the point. She knew Blakemore was involved. What she didn't know was how or why Selim fitted into it. And that was what worried her most.

'So where exactly *are* you taking us?' Grainger asked.

'We're going to pay a visit to Richard Blakemore,' Logan said.

Chapter 26

The rain clouds that had covered Paris earlier in the day had now all but cleared, leaving behind a deep blue sky. Dusk would soon be upon them and the low autumn sun was casting long shadows over the buildings they passed.

They had left the A86 motorway ten minutes ago, moving onto narrower, more rural roads as they moved further away from the city. The further they drove, the more Grainger seemed to loosen up. But Logan wasn't yet sure how this was all going to work. He wasn't used to pairing up with people. And he didn't know if their agendas were even compatible. At least for now, though, they were in this together.

'I didn't know the FBI worked overseas,' Logan said, breaking the silence.

Grainger looked at him, her left eyebrow raised as though surprised at what he'd said.

'We do,' she said. 'More than you'd think.'

'Because you're asked to or because you force your way into things?' Logan said, being deliberately contentious. Though he'd said it with a smile on his face.

'Do you mean me personally or the FBI?'

'The FBI.'

'You think that's what we do? Force our way into things? What, because we're American?'

'Something like that.'

She shook her head and gave a tut but didn't rise to the bait.

'So do you buy the whole terrorist thing?' Logan said.

'Why wouldn't I? It's pretty cut and dry, isn't it?'

'If you say so.'

'Why are you so cynical?'

'It's just the way I am.'

'Modena was here talking about Gitmo, you know. You shouldn't underestimate just how much ill feeling there is toward America over that.'

'I thought he was one of those trying to get it closed down,' Logan said.

'Well, that's what he was saying, but it's not like they've been making much progress. It wouldn't surprise me if it took another five or ten years before the final prisoners leave that place.'

'Now who's the cynic?'

'It's hard not to be cynical,' Grainger retorted. 'Modena isn't that much different to any other politician really.'

The tone of her voice suggested this was a subject she had some strong feelings about. Logan wanted to probe that, whether to play devil's advocate or because he had strong feelings himself he wasn't sure.

'So you'd rather they just released all of those prisoners today?' Logan questioned. 'So they can go on their way and bomb the hell out of whatever they want?'

'Who says any of them are bombers? People are being held there without trial, without legal representation. No-one in the public knows why most of them are even there.'

'That's because most of them are there as a result of pretty top-secret intelligence,' Logan said. 'Intelligence that would cost lives if it were made public.'

'So who gets to decide whether that intelligence was good enough?' Grainger said, animated now. Logan had touched on something here. 'You? Me? The whole point about democracy, about a free society, is that everyone should be treated as equal. Everyone has the same rights. How would you like it if you were locked up for days, months, years without anyone ever telling you why you were there? Without there being any way for you to get out?'

'If I was a terrorist, then that would be nothing more than I deserved.'

'I don't think we're going to see eye to eye on this one,' she said, exasperated. 'How could someone like you understand? It's people like you who put those prisoners in there. You're probably used to taking actions just because you're told to. And without any kind of forethought as to why you're being asked to do it, or any kind of due process.'

'You seem to think you know a lot about me,' Logan said.

'Not you. But I know how these things work.'

'People like me, as you put it, serve a purpose,' Logan said.

The emotion in his voice was clear now. He had been trying to hit a nerve with her, but she had turned this around onto him in expert fashion.

'And what purpose is that?' she asked.

'In your rose-tinted world of due process, you think everyone gets a fair crack at the whip. But you ask me, not everyone in this world is equal. Some people don't deserve the same rights as everyone else. And that's their choice to have ended up like that. For those people I'm happy to do whatever I think is necessary to make them pay.'

'But where do you draw the line on who falls into that camp? And who gets to decide their fate? I don't see how there can be one set of rules for some and another for others.'

'I've never done anything that I didn't feel was justified,' Logan said. 'And for me, that's good enough.'

Though that wasn't strictly true. There was one incident where he wasn't sure he had done the right thing. The one that he still had nightmares about.

'Look, why don't we lighten the conversation a bit?' he suggested. 'This is all getting a bit heavy.'

She tutted again. But this time she was smiling.

'What a copout,' she said. 'How about the weather? We could talk about that. Isn't that what you British love to do?'

'You'd understand if you ever lived there,' Logan said, reciprocating the smile.

Despite their differing views, the debate seemed to have lifted the mood further. Logan wouldn't admit it, but he actually agreed with many of her points. But in the real world, things would never be as clear cut as she wanted them to be.

Logan looked over at Grainger, only turning his head slightly so as not to be too obvious. Without the anger that had clouded her earlier, there was a real softness to her features. And she was very pretty. He couldn't help but notice the white band of skin at the base of her wedding finger. She turned and saw him looking, reflexively covered it up and rubbed it with her other hand.

Neither of them said anything.

He got the idea. Whatever the story was, it was obviously a painful one and not one to be broached today.

'Why don't we stop in this next town?' Logan said. 'It's only a few minutes away. Let's see if we can get another car. We need to dump this one anyway. And I could do with some food. I'm famished.'

She laughed. 'Man, you guys are always the same.'

The town they stopped at was on the edge of the Paris commuter belt. It didn't seem to have anything to it other than dense housing and a few shops. It was now just after four in the afternoon and was still relatively quiet. Within a half hour or so the roads would probably be heaving as the commuters poured home.

They parked up outside a cafe at the end of a small row of shops and went inside, ordering their food and drink separately before taking it back to the car.

'I think it's funny you picked an American car,' Logan said, getting back into the Ford.

'Something wrong with that?'

'Just as well we didn't have to try too hard to outrun the police earlier.'

'Actually I didn't choose this, it was all they had. So you don't like American cars?'

'Some are all right. But in general I find them to be just like American people.'

She sat and waited for him to expand. When he didn't, she said, 'No, I'm lost. You're going to have to explain that one to me.'

'Overweight, slow, inefficient, unforgiving.'

'Wow, way to go, negatively stereotyping three hundred million people. And I'm not too happy you put me in that bracket.'

He could tell from the look on her face that she knew he was joking.

'Yeah, but tell me it's not true,' he quipped. 'Most of the time at least. Present company excluded, of course.'

'How about well-built, powerful, beautiful?' she said.

'Nah, I can't think of any like that. Are you sure you're not talking about the Germans?'

'Are we still talking about cars, or people?'

'Good question,' he said.

She gave him that smile again. What a smile.

'So, you got any other pearls of wisdom? Any other countries or races you want to insult today?'

'No. I'm good.'

They began to tuck into their food. Logan was still making his way through his sandwich and strong black coffee when his mobile rang. He put his food on the dashboard and took the phone out of his pocket. When he saw it was Mackie calling, he hesitated. The call rang out with Logan still staring at the screen. He couldn't face Mackie. Not yet. He knew he would be in a whole heap of shit for what had happened in the car park, not to mention the police chase afterwards. If Mackie had been unimpressed with Logan's antics at the hospital yesterday then he really was going to hit the roof now. But Logan was getting close. He could feel it.

'Your boss?' Grainger asked.

'Yep.'

'I know how you feel. I'm like that when mine calls sometimes. It's like they never trust you. Always checking up on you.'

'You can say that again.'

Logan put the phone back in his pocket and picked up his sandwich, deep in thought about the mess he had got himself into.

'Can I ask you a question, Angela?' he said, in between mouthfuls.

'Go for it.'

'What are you doing here? I mean, what are you really doing here?'

She looked put out by the question. 'Doing here with you, or doing here in Paris?'

'Both. Either. I don't know.'

'The same thing as you,' she said.

'Modena.'

'Exactly.'

Though for him, Selim was the real catch.

'We have to go and find Blakemore,' he said.

'We?' she questioned, sounding unsure.

He was unsure himself. He wasn't used to working as a team and he didn't really know enough about Grainger yet to trust her fully. But for some reason, he just did.

'Two heads are better than one,' he said, finishing his food and scrunching up the paper wrapper. 'And two guns.'

She laughed again. 'You got that right. Hey, if you're finished, would you mind putting the trash out?'

'Sure.'

He took her empty coffee cup and sandwich wrapper and then got out of the car and made his way to the bin just a couple of yards past where they had parked. He had just dropped the rubbish into the bin when he heard the Ford's engine purr into life. He turned on his heels and looked at Grainger through the windscreen. She was staring back at him. She had an apologetic look on her face as she mouthed something to him.

It looked like I'm sorry.

While his brain was still processing what she meant, the car pulled away from the kerb. Logan was stunned as she accelerated away, down the street and into the distance, leaving him stranded at the side of the road.

'Well, that was unexpected,' he said out loud.

Chapter 27

'Man, you should see some of the crap that's being spouted about this,' Reggie said. He and Blakemore were in the office of Blakemore's farmhouse, eyeing the latest internet news about Modena. 'It's insane. More hits than anything else at the moment.'

'Yeah, well, there are a lot of gullible people out there,' Blakemore said, who was sitting at the polished mahogany desk, Reggie standing behind him. 'And also a lot of people who like to make themselves feel better by reading about the misery of others.'

'Wow, man, that's like … really profound,' Reggie said with over-the-top sarcasm, rolling his eyes as he spoke.

'Don't irritate me, Reggie.'

'Sure thing, *boss.*'

The way Reggie said it made it clear that he didn't see Blakemore as such.

They'd been in Blakemore's lavish farmhouse for three days, and despite the beautiful surroundings, which even Reggie could admire, Blakemore was really starting to grate on him now.

When Reggie had first met Blakemore he had thought he was someone to aspire to. Blakemore had clearly made a good life for himself and had an eye for quality and style that Reggie could only dream of. Blakemore had spent vast amounts of money modernising his exquisite house with gizmos and technology, but he'd also gone for a much more traditional feel where it mattered, like in the kitchen where there was a hellishly expensive range cooker, classic walnut worktops and an oversized Belfast sink. It wouldn't have done the house, an eighteenth-century brick farmhouse, justice to have had it any other way.

But over the last few days, Reggie had lost almost all of his respect for Blakemore. While once he had wanted to be just like Blakemore, Reggie now knew that the two men were like chalk and cheese. They just didn't get along, and Reggie realised that the only part of Blakemore's life that he really had any desire for was the money. Reggie was quite content to be himself. He didn't want to be the posh boy gone wrong who thought he owned the world.

'Anyway, how much longer do we keep this up for?' Reggie said. 'I mean, don't you think it's possible that Modena just doesn't know what we're asking him?'

They'd been beating and torturing Modena for three days now and it seemed like they were getting nowhere.

'He knows,' Blakemore said, but Reggie could tell by the hesitant way he answered that he didn't fully believe his own words anymore.

And ever since Selim had been let loose on their captive, the goal had only seemed to drift further away. The guy was enjoying inflicting pain on Modena just that little bit too much. Reggie had no problem in hurting people and hurting them badly, but he didn't get off on it like Selim seemed to.

'Well, you'd just better hope that we get it out of him before it's too late,' Reggie said.

'Don't worry, big man, courtesy of our little diversion with that video, I'm sure we've still got plenty of time. Just stay cool.'

'But have you seen what Selim's done to him? It's Modena I'm worried about, not the police finding us.'

'Going soft on me now, Reggie?' Blakemore gibed.

'No, I just want to get my money before it's too late.'

Initially Reggie had been nervous at having Modena in Blakemore's home. But it was the obvious option, given the location and remoteness. And why would anyone make the link to Blakemore when the whole world believed that Selim, the enemy of the West, was the one behind the kidnapping? And there was also the contingency plan should anyone come knocking. A back-up should they need to move Modena quickly and quietly. But at the moment he felt like Selim's tactics were putting the entire operation in jeopardy. Modena would be too far gone before they got what they needed.

'He knows,' Blakemore said again, this time with more conviction. 'Otherwise we wouldn't be here. Otherwise I wouldn't be willing to pay to have *you* here.'

'Well, don't forget that. You'd *better* pay.'

'I will do. When you've finished your job.'

Oh please, let that be soon, Reggie thought. He couldn't wait, in fact. He was sick of having to listen to Blakemore's shit, day in, day out. The money for this job was going to set him up for a few years at least so it was surely worth it, but he was being pushed to breaking point here.

'Well, how do you suggest we go about getting what we need then?' Reggie said. 'Pretty soon there's not going to be anything left of Modena.'

Blakemore swivelled around in his chair and stood up, facing Reggie. His inferior height meant he had to crane his neck to look Reggie in the eye.

'I agree we need to rein Selim in,' Blakemore said, in an apologetic manner which told Reggie that the buck was being passed to him on that, 'but Mustafa's doing a good job in there. If he keeps that up, things might just work out – we might just get what we need. Reverse psychology, Reggie. Good cop, bad cop – whatever you want to call it. You should see Modena's eyes whenever Selim walks into that room. He's terrified of him. The same with you, in fact. It's not like you've been befriending him in there. But he doesn't talk to you. Because you don't talk to him. You just bully him and beat the crap out of him.'

Reggie felt a slither of pride at Blakemore's words. He knew he wasn't the brightest or most articulate person but he had his uses. And people like Blakemore needed him. It was Reggie, after all, who had planned the whole kidnapping using his tactical nous and combat training. Blakemore might have been a success with his millions in the bank and his fancy farmhouse with its vast wine cellar filled with bottles he would never drink, state-of-the-art gym, outdoor heated pool, and more bedrooms and bathrooms than he could ever need, but he still relied on people like Reggie. Blakemore was simply an organiser. Reggie was a doer. And Blakemore wouldn't be where he was without people like Reggie. Yet it was a fact that seemed lost on Blakemore, who pranced around like he was a queen bee.

'Well, I'm sorry if I forgot to take the course on how to be nice,' Reggie scoffed. 'And at least I'm not sticking nails in the poor bastard here, there and everywhere.'

'That wasn't my point. As long as Selim stays on side then I think we have it just right. Every time we bring in Mustafa for you or Selim, Frank must feel like he's just won the lottery. And vice versa. When he sees you or Selim coming, he's bricking it. Mustafa is the only one who talks to him and he's the only one who doesn't hurt him. We keep up this little tag team and we'll get what we want. My bet is that it'll be Mustafa he opens up to.'

Reggie agreed. He had come to the same conclusion himself. His phone began to vibrate in his pocket and he fished it out. It was Lorik. He left the office without saying another word to Blakemore and headed down the corridor to the vast kitchen.

'You have to be kidding me!' Reggie blasted as he listened to Lorik explaining the latest mess. 'You have got to be fucking kidding me!'

He sat down on one of the rustic oak dining chairs at the expansive dining table and looked out of the window of the kitchen. How many more fuck-ups was he going to need to sort out for this lot?

Reggie heard footsteps behind him and turned to see Blakemore entering the room.

'Just sort it out, Lorik,' Reggie bellowed at the top of his voice, his face like thunder. 'No more mistakes!'

Reggie ended the call and threw the phone down on the table.

'What is it?' Blakemore asked, sitting down on one of the chairs.

'Police. I think they're getting closer. Or at least this John Burrows fella is.'

'What!' Blakemore jumped up out of his seat.

'That was Lorik. Johnny's dead.'

'Dead? How?'

'They tried to bring in Burrows. But he's a tough one. Johnny's wound up dead. Had it coming, if you ask me. Never thought much of him.'

'So Burrows *escaped*?' Blakemore said, as though it was an impossible scenario.

Reggie had to agree. It should have been simple. All Johnny and Lorik had to do was grab him and bring him in. One man.

'For now, yeah,' Reggie said, trying to make the situation sound more under control than it really was. 'But we'll get him.'

'So you think he's police now?' Blakemore said. 'Thought you said earlier he wasn't?'

'We couldn't find any trace of the guy. But that doesn't mean he isn't police. Anyway, does it matter what he is? Either way we'll get him. Get *them.* Lorik is following one of them now. A woman.'

'Wait a sec. A woman? *Them*? Since when has there been a *them*?'

'First time we've seen her. She helped Burrows get away from Lorik.'

'But now she's alone?'

'Apparently, yeah. She dropped him off somewhere. Lorik stuck with the woman. Might not have been my choice, but that boy's got his needs. They're actually not far from here. About fifty miles or so.'

'What! She must be coming here! Fuck Lorik's *needs*. Just tell him to get rid of her!'

'Oh, don't you worry about that. I already did. As you can imagine, Lorik was itching to do it. She's about to get *way* more than she bargained for.'

Blakemore winced and Reggie couldn't help but smirk. He might not have had such sick tendencies as Lorik, but it also didn't bother him if he thought the victim had it coming. And this woman, whoever she was, certainly had it coming.

Chapter 28

Logan had only been stranded for a few minutes. In a bit of good fortune, the waitress from the cafe where they'd just bought their food had given him the number for a local taxi firm. The driver had taken him to the nearest car rental place, only a couple of miles away. Thankfully it had been a different company to the one from which he'd rented the now damaged and abandoned Fiat. He'd still got his John Burrows identification and enough loose Euros to rent a car for two days, which was the minimum term they would allow. Maybe this time he'd even get the chance to take it back.

Now he was on the road again, in his second rented Fiat of the day, his head churning as to why Grainger had run off from him.

He'd had doubts about tagging along with her and whether he could really trust her. But after she decided against handing him in to the police, he'd told her almost everything he knew about the case. It had never crossed his mind that she would then go and run away like that. He would have thought the logical option was for her to stick with him, to do this together, but she'd obviously had different ideas.

The biggest worry, though, was about what she was going to do next. He hadn't told her exactly where Blakemore was, but he'd told her the name and nearest town. Even if the police or FBI hadn't yet figured the connection, he'd effectively handed it to them now. It wouldn't be that hard for them to find out where Blakemore was and send a team in. In the grand scheme of things, that may not be a bad thing. It may well lead to Modena being recovered alive and well. But Logan didn't want the police or anyone else raining on his parade. Selim was his, and he couldn't bear the thought that someone else may get to him before he did.

That was assuming, of course, that Grainger was going to feed back the information on Blakemore to the police. Logan had to believe that she would and that Blakemore was, or very soon would be, a wanted man. And yet Logan still didn't know how or why Blakemore even fitted into this. More importantly, he still didn't know if Blakemore actually had Modena at all. The link was there, but Blakemore could just be another cog, rather than the mastermind.

There was only one way to find out. And Logan was now only twenty minutes from his destination.

Long gone now were the tall apartment and office blocks of the city, and the suburban tree-lined streets of the town where they had stopped. He was in an altogether more rural setting, with narrow, isolated roads twisting between undulating hills of brightly coloured crops, oilseed, poppies and sunflowers, whose dazzling yellow contrasted with and complemented the deep blue sky above to create a scene of pure beauty. It was a picture book setting – one which had been transferred to canvas by many famous artists, and it wasn't hard to see why.

Logan's phone buzzed and he picked it out of his pocket. It was Mackie again. This time he answered the call.

'So you're still alive, then?' Mackie said. It was clear he was in a bad mood.

'You sound surprised by that.'

'I am a little. You know, it would have helped if you'd called me to give me an update. You're a wanted man, Logan. The police are after you for four murders!'

Four murders? What was that all about? Logan thought. It only took him a few seconds to figure it out: the police must be pinning the deaths of Johnny, Djourou and his cronies on him. But how had Djourou's demise been linked to him? Had a witness seem him leaving Djourou's apartment? Or had Lorik and Johnny called it in to the police themselves to give Logan's description?

'You're causing me quite a shit storm with my superiors,' Mackie said. 'Not that I should be surprised by that. I ought to be used to your antics by now. But death by machete? What's that all about? That's a new one even for you.'

'That wasn't me, actually. I didn't kill Djourou.'

'Maybe not. But several policemen saw you running from the scene at the car park where there's a pretty mangled-up dead body. Saw you running away with a woman, I might add. Just what the hell is going on?'

'I didn't kill Djourou and his men *or* that guy in the car park. He was called Johnny; he was Blakemore's man. I think it was him that killed Djourou and Djourou's other accomplice. Then he was killed by his own colleague as he tried to get away from me.'

'Logan, you're making no sense whatsoever. Do you remember our little conversation earlier?'

Mackie paused. Logan wasn't sure whether he was supposed to answer the question or not.

'Well, do you?' Mackie asked eventually.

'Yes, sir.'

'Well, you'll remember then that some people, the JIA committee included, have quite big doubts about whether or not you should be out in the field at the moment –'

'There are no doubts from me, sir,' Logan said. 'And there weren't any doubts from you when you hauled me back in from Vegas.'

'*And*,' Mackie said, raising his voice, 'getting reports about you shooting at policemen and running away from a car crash where we've got fourteen people injured, some seriously, starts to raise some pretty big doubts in my mind about whether I've done the right thing in putting you on the case.'

'That's not how it was.'

'So you say. But you're not exactly being subtle so far. What happened to that? You need to keep your head down. You don't get nine lives on this. If you get nabbed, you know we can't bail you out. We're not supposed to be here. You're supposed to be a ghost.'

'I know all that. I'm getting close now, though. Closer than anyone else is, that's for sure.'

'And who's this woman you're running around with?'

'There's no woman,' Logan affirmed, quickly thinking about how he was going to bluff about Grainger's identity. 'She was just an unlucky bystander I carjacked. She's gone now.'

'You carjacked some poor woman? Logan, are you deliberately trying to ruin both our careers?'

'No, sir, I'm not. I'm trying to finish this. I'm heading to Blakemore's home now. I'll let you know what I find.'

Logan ended the call before Mackie could say another word. He knew he was making progress. But Mackie had a point. It was progress at what cost? And he knew Mackie would flip if he found out that Logan was in cahoots with an FBI agent. He was supposed to be running a covert mission. But Logan would do anything to get to the answers in the quickest possible way. He couldn't let Selim slip through his grip.

Logan brought his mind back to the job at hand. To find his way to Blakemore's he was using an old map that the car rental attendant had sold to him for five euros (he hadn't had enough cash to go for the GPS option). It looked from the map like the next turning should only be a few hundred yards up on his right, and he slowed a little to try to spot it. The turning, though, was well hidden on a corner, and with the lack of signposts and the overgrown hedges on both sides of the road he managed to go right past it.

With a quick glance in his mirror to check there was no-one behind him, he pressed his foot onto the brake and came to a stop a good fifty yards past where he needed to be. The road was barely wide enough to take two cars. A U-turn would require a number of back-and-forths. Rather than carry on and look for a turning spot further ahead, he put the car into reverse and made his way back to the junction. He hadn't seen another car on this road for at least five minutes and it would only take a few seconds to get back to the turning.

But he was about ten yards from the junction when a car appeared, coming toward him from around the blind corner. Logan felt his body stiffen and with the little time he had to react he was unable to do anything other than brake. The other driver, seeing Logan's stationary vehicle, slammed on his brakes, his tyres screeching and skidding on the worn-out asphalt. He shifted slightly to his right at the last second. It was enough to avoid a collision. The car came to a stop parallel with Logan's, but half up the verge on the right-hand side of the road.

Acknowledging his mistake, Logan smiled awkwardly at the driver who had wound down his window to hurl abuse. Logan didn't bother to get into an argument with the man. He just apologised and carried on reversing, eliciting several honks on the horn from the angry man before he carried on his journey.

Logan reached the junction and turned into the even narrower road. After a few hundred yards the road seemed to become narrower still and was barely wide enough for one car. A simple wire and wood fence on each side separated the road from the towering sunflowers in the surrounding fields.

As he approached a sharp left turn, he noticed what he thought was a slip road into the adjacent field. But as he got closer, he saw it actually appeared to be the scene of an accident. There were shattered headlight casings and skid marks on the road leading up to the fence, which had been torn from its position and lay haphazardly on the ground. On the other side of the broken fence, mown-down sunflowers created a neat trail that carried into the dark centre of the field.

Logan slowed as he approached the bend in the road. He stared into the heart of the field to see if there was any sign of the vehicle that had caused the destruction. There wasn't anything obvious. But with his attention on the field rather than the road, he didn't see the car parked just beyond the apex of the bend until the last second. Braking hard, yet again he only narrowly avoided a crash.

The other car, which looked more like it had been abandoned than parked, had its hazard lights flashing and the driver's door was wide open. There was no sign of any occupants. Even with the car tucked up against the right-hand verge, there was barely enough room to get past. But Logan wasn't about to even attempt it. He didn't like the look of this.

Logan turned off his engine and got out. As he walked up to the parked car he kept his right hand down by his side, only inches from his gun, in case he needed to draw it. He walked along the driver's side of the car, looking in through the back windows before stopping at the open door. The engine was off but the keys were still in the ignition. Other than the keys, there was nothing else in the car, no personal effects or other belongings.

He continued walking around to the front of the car, stopping when he saw the damage to the front left wing; the bumper was indented and the headlight smashed. There was similar damage across the rest of the front. The red streaks on the blue paintwork, if nothing else, gave away the colour of the unlucky object that had been hit.

Logan turned back to the trail leading into the field. All of the evidence – the keys in the ignition, the smashed headlights in the road, the damage to the front of the car – pointed to an accident. And it looked like it had taken place recently, given the way the car had been abandoned, keys still in the ignition.

His senses were heightened further when he heard a gunshot.

He stopped and instinctively ducked, though it had sounded quite distant. Whoever was shooting, he certainly hadn't been the target. But his mind was now in overdrive. Something was happening here. He needed to quickly decide whether he really wanted to be involved.

He stood up and carried on walking to the head of the trail that led into the field. Again he stopped in his tracks.

'Oh no,' he said in disbelief.

The decision about whether to get involved had just been made. This was going to be his fight after all.

The answer was right there, fifty yards in front of him, up the trail of flattened sunflowers.

It was Grainger's Ford.

Chapter 29

Grainger was here, and she was in trouble. He took out his Beretta and slowly walked up the trail, toward her vehicle, keeping low. No more gunshots came and there were no other noises to indicate where Grainger, or the driver from the other car, might be.

The smell from the sunflowers was almost overpowering. Logan had always suffered from hay fever and just the smell of some things – cut grass, barley – was enough to send his eyes streaming. He'd never been in a field of sunflowers before but he could feel his eyes itching, his nose starting to run. He tried his hardest to resist rubbing his eyes, not wanting to set off a reaction. Strange, the things you think about in a crisis.

When he reached the Ford, there was no sign of Grainger. The car was abandoned. Steam rose out of its bonnet, probably a result of the crash through the fence. From the damage to the back of the car, it looked like she'd been rammed off the road.

But by whom?

The driver's door was wide open, much like the other car. She'd made off in a hurry. But there was no indication of which direction she'd gone in. The car had flattened its way through the field and left a clear path. A human, though, could quite easily move through the gaps between the plants, leaving no obvious signs of their presence.

She could be anywhere. Any direction.

He didn't even know how long she'd been out there.

He guessed that given the time it took him to get his new Fiat, she could have been here as much as half an hour, forty minutes max, before him. Which meant she could be two miles or more away from here by now, if she'd kept on moving.

But that wouldn't have been his tactic. He would have stayed closer to the crash scene, doubling back on himself, trying to outflank his foe. Maybe Grainger would do the same.

Logan heard a rustling coming from his left. He spun around, sinking onto one knee. Gun drawn and ready.

A rabbit bounded out into the open, scrunched its nose at him and hopped back into the foliage. Logan dropped his head, relieved. That was when he saw what he was looking for. A human might not leave a trail of flattened sunflowers to indicate where they'd been, but they would leave footprints. Right in front of him, he could clearly make out two sets. Both entered the sunflowers where the rabbit had just appeared. Of course, they could have been there since who knows when and weren't necessarily from Grainger and her pursuer. But how many people go for a walk through seven-feet-high sunflowers?

Two sets. He would have much preferred to have only seen one.

He crept forward, entering the forest, the giant flowers making him feel like an ant walking through grass. The sunflowers were tightly packed and it was difficult to see more than a few yards in front before the view became obscured. Logan had never been claustrophobic but it was an uncomfortable feeling to be completely surrounded like this. In response, his heart rate had noticeably quickened.

He quite soon found himself deep into the field. Looking behind him, he could no longer make out Grainger's car at all. In fact, in every direction he looked the view was identical. Other than the trail of footprints, it was difficult to get any bearing at all.

No matter. Just follow the trail.

But after a few more yards, the footprints began to get shallower as the ground became drier. Pretty soon, they were all but gone.

Logan stopped and looked around. Still no signs of anyone. He guessed he'd moved about two hundred yards so far. He was pretty sure it had been more or less in a straight line but it was hard to tell.

More rustling from behind him. He turned quickly, not dropping down this time, but still aiming his gun toward where the sound had come from.

Nothing.

It was all quiet. No signs of any movement. No rabbit, no Grainger, no enemy.

More sounds came from his right. Logan spun on his heels, his finger twitching on the Beretta's trigger. Several sunflower stalks were swaying, just a few yards in front of him. But no indication of anything else.

Had it just been the wind?

There was another crunching sound from back in the opposite direction. Logan spun again. He was becoming disoriented. Nauseous almost. His eyes were streaming from the hay fever, his nose too. His hands were now clammy, his heart pounding in his chest. The pit of his stomach was churning. It felt like this forest of flowers that had been so picturesque from the outside was moving in on him, swallowing him up.

But that wasn't the hay fever. It was an altogether more unfamiliar feeling.

He would never admit to it, but the emotion he was feeling was fear.

Who or what was out there?

He spun around again. He didn't even know why this time. There hadn't been any sound in that direction. It had just been an instinctive reaction. But with all the twisting and turning, he now no longer had any idea which direction he'd come from.

The feeling of nausea was growing. The tell-tale hand tremors were also returning. But this time the shaking seemed to be going right through his body, all the way down to his toes.

He thought he saw movement up ahead. The outline of a person moving fast. His finger twitched on the trigger again. He had to concentrate hard to resist the temptation to shoot. It would have been a feat of desperation, giving away his position. And if he wasn't careful, it could well be Grainger he shot.

He was almost relieved when seconds later a gunshot rang out, loud and clear. He guessed it had come from no more than fifty or so yards away in the direction he was facing. It was something that he could at least focus his attention on, a target.

But the relief was short-lived. Not long after the shot came a shrill scream.

It sounded like a woman.

It had to be Grainger.

Chapter 30

Logan moved forward with more purpose, trying to move as quickly and quietly as he could. However disturbing the scream was, it had at least given him a sense of direction. Somewhere to aim for. The feeling of claustrophobia was diminishing, his focus returning.

He heard more screams, muffled now. They couldn't have been from more than ten yards away. He kept on moving.

But then came to a stop when he spotted them. Just in front of him, in a small clearing, were two writhing bodies.

Grainger.

And Lorik.

Her service pistol lay out of reach. The Slav was on top of her, a blade in one hand, held against her throat. Her tights were torn, exposing her bare legs, her skirt pushed up over her waist. The Slav's other hand was roaming free, pulling at her clothes, tearing at her blouse. She flailed at him with her arms but the struggle was half-hearted, the feeling of metal against her throat enough to keep her subdued.

That feeling. Logan knew that feeling.

Grainger's bloodshot eyes met Logan's. She gave him a pleading look.

But he couldn't move. He was frozen.

A rush of images flew through Logan's head. Selim. The young girl. The things Selim had done to her. The things he'd made Logan *watch* him do to her. Such a pretty face. Her soft, clear skin, forever stained red by her own blood as she lay butchered on the floor.

Logan was staring right into Grainger's eyes, but he wasn't seeing her at all. He was only seeing the girl.

Look at her. You did that. Not the hero anymore, are you?

Logan shook his head, trying to escape his nightmare. He felt his legs begin to twitch. Adrenaline surged through his body, readying him for action. Grainger's screams were no more than resigned moans now. She was still looking at him. Still pleading.

Her distraction caught the attention of Lorik. He turned, snarling like a dog, pure animal in his eyes. He half smiled through his gritted teeth when he saw Logan.

With the images of the girl still flying through his head, Logan was sure he heard a battle cry as he sprang into action. He couldn't be certain if it was in his head or if it had actually come from his lips. But he was no longer acting consciously. Something else was controlling him now. Something deep down inside him that had been waiting to come out.

Lorik, calm as anything, had just enough time to get to his feet before Logan barged into him.

But Logan had underestimated the pint-sized Slav, who almost caught Logan as he flew through the air at him. They both remained upright, grappling, trying to gain an advantage. Logan's gun flew out of his hand in the chaos. He tried his best to keep Lorik's knife at bay, his left hand tightly around Lorik's right wrist. But the Slav was strong. Far stronger than Logan had imagined. He knew he wouldn't be able to hold him in the position for long.

Lorik aimed a head-butt at Logan. It caught him on the base of the nose. A dull crack sounded out at the impact, but Logan felt no pain from the blow. He couldn't feel pain right now.

As Logan continued to focus on the knife hand, Lorik used the distraction to his advantage. Ducking and twisting his body, he hauled Logan to the floor. They landed with a thud, Lorik on top. But the knife had come out of his hand in the process.

It was now an even fight.

Lorik tried to pin Logan's arms. But as strong as he was, four men couldn't have held the rage inside Logan at bay. His right arm wrapped around Lorik's neck, pulling him into a headlock. He pushed upwards and outwards, swivelling them both around so that he was on top.

Logan had the advantage now.

But with him lying directly on top of Lorik, there was little room for either man to manoeuvre his arms to get any clear shots. Both men grappled, throwing fists at whatever flesh they could reach. But at close quarters none of the blows were strong enough to make a difference.

Time for a different approach. And some payback.

Logan lifted his head as high as he could, arcing it back until his neck strained, then brought it down onto Lorik's nose. He measured the head-butt poorly though. While it had the desired effect on Lorik, it also split the skin on Logan's forehead, just above his right eye. Not a bad cut, but a bloody cut. The blood began to pour, covering his face and filling his eyes. But the blow had still been enough to leave Lorik dazed.

Logan moved his body so that he was no longer lying on Lorik, but straddling him, his legs pinning Lorik's arms. He again threw his head into Lorik's. He felt his own wound open further, but also felt some more strength go from the Slav. Blood now covered both men. Logan couldn't be sure how much of it was his own and how much was Lorik's.

He hit his foe with another head-butt, then another. Each one sapped some more strength from the Slav. One more butt and Logan's world began to go dizzy.

But he was in charge now.

With him sitting upright, his arms had free rein. And Lorik wasn't providing much resistance now. Not anymore.

A right hook from Logan caught Lorik's jaw. Then a left to the cheek. Logan pounded him with his fists. A right to the Slav's other cheek. A left caught his right eye, the skin around it bursting open at impact.

Logan panted heavy breaths as his fists rained down on Lorik's head. One punch after the other. Hit after hit. No stopping him now. Nothing left to hold him back. The images of Selim, of the girl, returned to him. He pounded harder, trying to get the images out of his head. Harder and harder, pounding away.

'Logan. No.'

He barely heard Grainger's voice, just carried on. His fists were falling in a frenzied fury, the battle cry sounding out again. A left, then a right, then a left, his hands and arms moving in a steady rhythm almost like he was conducting an orchestra. Each shot was pushing further and further downwards, pushing right through Lorik now, it seemed. The surface beneath Logan's fists became softer and wetter with each punch.

'Logan, stop. Please!'

Grainger's pleading voice was weak. He'd heard it, but he couldn't stop. Didn't want to stop. He kept on going, kept on pounding. In his mind he saw the look on Selim's face. That ridiculous grin. Saw the look of terror in the girl's eyes.

He could have saved her.

Why hadn't he saved her!

'Logan! Stop!' Grainger screamed.

She thrust her arm around Logan's neck. Not an aggressive move, more consolatory.

Feeling her touch, Logan finally found the focus to stop. He was panting heavily, his chest heaving. His hands throbbed. His vision was blurred and red. The images of Selim and the girl disappeared.

He shut his eyes, not wanting to look at what he'd just done. Both of Grainger's arms were now wrapped around him. He put his hands on hers, fell back into her arms and fought back the tears.

'He's dead, Logan.'

He didn't move. Couldn't.

'Logan, it's okay. He's dead now. Come on, we have to get out of here.'

He opened his eyes but didn't say anything, just nodded his head.

'Come on,' she said. 'Let's get back to the car. We need to go. Before any others turn up.'

She stood, leaving a hand on his shoulder. He bowed his head and stood up with her. His legs felt like jelly, but the fog in his head was beginning to clear. With his senses returning, he was aware of the pain in his body for the first time. It was growing by the second; his nose, his head, his hands.

'My God, Logan,' Grainger said, putting a hand to her mouth in shock. 'Your face. We need to get you seen to.'

He kept his head down, not looking at her. He couldn't bring himself to. He felt ashamed. But he didn't know of what. What he had done to Lorik? Or what Lorik had done to her?

He stole a glance at her. As well as her ripped and dirtied clothes there were tears streaming down her face. Her bottom lip was cracked and bleeding, her left cheek swollen and red.

'Are you okay?' he said.

'Not really. But I'm more concerned about you. Look at the state of you.'

'I'm sorry.'

He wasn't sure what for, but he was. She didn't say anything to that.

They began walking, pulling each other along.

'Thank you,' she said, after a minute or two.

'For what?'

'You saved my life.'

He didn't respond. Right now, he certainly didn't feel like the hero.

Beyond the throbbing, he could still feel the tremors in his hands. He looked down at them. His knuckles had been rubbed raw. Opening and closing his fists was a struggle, but nothing seemed to be broken.

'You think those are bad, you should see your face,' Grainger said.

'Nothing a needle and thread won't solve,' Logan said.

'We're getting you to a doctor.'

'No!' he shouted, stopping. 'I'm not going to a doctor. We'll do it.'

'With what?'

'Just get us to a pharmacy.'

They carried on and reached her car. He didn't know how she'd found the way back. He wasn't sure he could have done that.

'Do you have a GPS?' he asked.

'Yeah.'

'Okay. Grab that. We'll take my car.'

Before they left, they moved Lorik's car into the field, behind Grainger's, so that both cars were more or less hidden from the road. They didn't want Lorik's friends finding the body. That would almost certainly make the kidnappers panic and run. And they would possibly kill Modena before they did so. Logan spent a few minutes propping the fence back up. He wasn't convinced it would hold for long. Hopefully they wouldn't need it to.

The GPS showed that there was a chemist's ten miles away. It was six o'clock, so with a bit of luck it would still be open. Grainger insisted on driving. They carried on down the road, past the sunflower fields. The scenery soon opened out once more.

Logan felt uncomfortable the whole way. He wasn't sure what he should be saying or doing. The way he'd been in the field, with Lorik, he'd never felt like that before. So disconnected from his own body.

What was she thinking about him now?

What he'd done hadn't just been about saving her. But how could he explain that to someone he'd only just met? He couldn't even explain it to himself. And now that it was over, it almost felt like *he* was the victim of something. It made him feel like a fraud that she was showing concern for him.

He wasn't the victim. *She* was.

He might have a few wounds, but they were more or less self-inflicted. She'd nearly been killed by that psycho. She would have been if he hadn't turned up. And he didn't even want to think about what else Lorik would have done to her.

She had suffered more than he had.

'Are you sure you're okay?' he said to her.

'No, Logan. I'm really not.'

Without taking her attention off the road, or breaking her grip on the steering wheel, she broke down in tears. She didn't even try to wipe them from her face as they cascaded down, falling from her chin onto her muddied and torn clothes.

'But thank you,' she said. 'I really mean that. God, look at me. How pathetic is this? I don't do crying.'

Finally she wiped at her eyes.

'Believe me, everyone does crying,' Logan said. He knew that better than most.

Chapter 31

'What are we going to do, Winter?' Mackie said.

He was sitting in his office, staring out of the window at the murky River Thames down below, his chair facing away from his desk at the other side of which Winter was sitting. He didn't often ask Winter for an opinion on anything, usually content that he knew the best course of action, but this time he really was at a loss. Mackie had been confident that Logan was up to the job, that it was the right time, or maybe he had just hoped that was the case; but with the unexpected involvement of Youssef Selim, the playing field had changed considerably.

Mackie had no doubt that Logan would still crack the case. That he would find Modena. But at what price? He would probably kill Selim and anyone else who stood in his way in the process. Could Mackie afford to let him do that? And Logan was drawing so much attention to himself with his reckless actions that it was becoming a full-time job just to keep the French authorities at bay, not to mention the JIA committee.

'Surely the best thing now is to pull Logan off,' Winter said.

Mackie was well aware that Winter had never been a fan of Logan, and vice versa. Winter would make a fine commander one day, but stripping away the confidence and arrogance he was a very different person to Mackie. Winter needed structure and rules and order. Mackie relied on gut instincts, as did Logan. It was easy to see, therefore, why Winter and Logan didn't gel.

Eighteen years ago Mackie's gut had told him that Logan was an ideal candidate to be a field agent, and he'd been right. In fact, Logan had been the best agent he'd ever had, and the best there was in the JIA. Until they'd gone after Selim, that was.

His gut instinct was that Logan could still be a successful field agent. But Mackie knew that his opinion was becoming harder and harder to defend.

'Take him off to save face for JIA or to help solve this case?' Mackie said.

'Both,' Winter answered, after thinking about the question for a moment. 'We already have the leads. Let someone else finish this off, before too much damage is done. This case could be the end of Logan. The way it's going, it could be the end of us.'

'No, however this pans out, it's on me and me alone.' Mackie didn't want Winter being drawn into a mess that was of his making.

'I don't think Lindegaard sees it that way,' Winter said. 'He's going after Logan, no doubt about it.'

'Certainly seems that way.'

'They've got previous history, you know, Lindegaard and Logan.'

Mackie raised an eyebrow and swivelled around to face Winter. He knew all about Lindegaard's history with Logan. But how did Winter know?

Winter must have picked up on the perplexed look on Mackie's face. 'You may not have known about it. I had to dig into Lindegaard's past to find the link. Twelve years ago he was working on a big case to crack a smuggling ring in central America. The CIA's case collapsed literally overnight. There was a lot of embarrassment for the Americans at the time because they'd invested heavily in it. The reason it crashed was because their lead informant disappeared. It was assumed his cover had been blown and he'd been taken out by the gang leaders. But actually Logan killed him as part of a JIA mission.'

'I remember it,' Mackie said. They'd only become party to the adjacent CIA case afterwards. Logan's instructions had been clear: tear the ring apart quickly and quietly. And that was exactly what he'd done. 'Lindegaard was running the CIA's lead agent on that case. Apparently it took him years to recover his reputation – they'd been working on it for months and then, in a matter of weeks, Logan brought the whole gang down. The CIA were expecting it to be a huge coup for them. As it was, the smuggling ring disintegrated once we became involved, taken to pieces one person at a time.'

'You knew about this?' Winter queried.

'I've worked on every case that Logan has ever been on. Of course I know.'

And Mackie also knew it wasn't the only time Lindegaard and Logan had crossed paths. But he wasn't going to go into that with Winter.

'I'm impressed with your digging,' Mackie said, turning his chair back around to look out onto the river, as he often did when pondering, 'and it clearly explains some of Lindegaard's behaviour. But I'm still at a loss as to what to do here.'

'Take Logan off the case. Limit the damage for all of us.'

It was the clear and obvious choice. But Mackie got the sense that even if he made that decision, Logan may still go after Selim. Would they not be better to stick with him so that the job was done properly?

'There must be another way,' Mackie mused.

'We could leave him on,' Winter suggested. 'I'm sure we'd get Modena if we did, and probably more quickly than using anyone else. But I'm thinking about how to do this while maintaining our own reputations too. Lindegaard is gunning for Logan. At least if we agree to take Logan off now, then we can insist on using one of our agents as a replacement. Much better that way than have Lindegaard force it on us down the line and throw someone else in.'

Mackie thought about what Winter had said. It was a valid point. Perhaps it was time to stop fighting.

'The least worst option,' Mackie said, thinking out loud.

'Exactly. And at least we get to keep control that way.'

'Control of what?' said an unexpected voice from the back of the room.

Mackie spun around in his chair to see Jay Lindegaard and John Sanderson standing in the doorway of his office. He hadn't heard them open the door.

'None of your goddamn business!' Mackie shouted, getting to his feet. 'This is my office and you bleeding well knock if you want to come in.'

'Sorry, Charles,' Sanderson said timidly as he shut the office door. 'But we need to speak. Urgently.'

Lindegaard turned to glare at Sanderson. 'There's no need to apologise,' he said, before turning his gaze back to Mackie. 'You're answerable to us and I asked you a very simple question. So what are you trying to keep control of, Charles?'

Mackie sat down on his chair. 'I said it's none of your business. Now what do you want?'

'What do you think?' Lindegaard said, no hint of pleasantness in his voice or demeanour. The two unwelcome visitors made their way toward the desk. 'We want to talk about your cock-up of an agent. This must be a record, surely, for one of our agents to be wanted for four civilian murders after less than three days on a case?'

'You don't know what you're talking about, Jay. You simply have no idea.'

'Then tell me how it is, please do.'

'Logan is out there doing a job that you or I never could. Have you any idea what it takes to put yourself, your life, on the line like that?'

'Yes, I'm sure he's very brave and we can all commend him for that. But he's in danger of making a fool of this entire organisation.'

'Oh, come off your high horse. I'm sure you've overseen much bigger messes than this,' Mackie said, glancing over at Winter, who shot his gaze downwards, clearly not wanting to get involved.

'What does that mean?' Lindegaard said, offended.

'And those *civilians*, as you put it,' Mackie said, 'are all people implicated in the kidnapping of Frank Modena.'

'This isn't some revenge mission where you kill your way to the end goal,' Sanderson said.

His intervention surprised Mackie. He'd thought it was only Lindegaard he was up against, but maybe not.

'Exactly,' Lindegaard added. 'I don't care how close Logan is, he's off this case. And that's it.'

The room suddenly fell silent as Mackie, Lindegaard and Sanderson paused for breath. Winter looked up at his boss and all eyes in the room were on Mackie.

'That's it?' Mackie said.

'The decision has already been made, Charles,' Sanderson said apologetically. 'We've reassigned the case.'

'Do you realise it's Frank Modena's life you're playing with here?' Winter piped up, to the surprise of everyone in the room. 'Any delay in getting to him could cost him his life.'

Lindegaard turned his stony scowl to Winter. Sanderson was open-mouthed. Mackie was beaming inside that his aide had jumped in to back him up. Not only to back Mackie up, but Logan too.

'And just who the hell asked for your opinion?' Lindegaard thundered.

'It's not an opinion,' Mackie said, banging his fist on the desk, redirecting Lindegaard's anger away from Winter. 'It's a fact. You put someone new on the case and all you're doing is delaying getting to Modena. And for what? So you can save us all a little bit of bad press?'

'You two are incredible,' Lindegaard said, shaking his head. 'Can you really not see the mess that Logan is causing here?'

'From where I'm sitting, he's doing exactly what's expected of him,' Mackie said. His defences were up now. Screw the least worst option. He wasn't going to back down to Lindegaard. He wasn't going to abandon Logan like everyone else was prepared to.

'I'm sorry, Charles,' Sanderson chimed in, 'it really is too late. The case has already been reassigned.'

Winter jumped in again. 'Then at least let us choose the new lead. Someone we know so we can make this as smooth as possible. Time isn't on our side here.'

'You must have misunderstood me,' Lindegaard said, a mocking smile creeping up his face. 'I said the case has been reassigned. Logan is off the case. And so are you two.'

Mackie shot up out of his chair.

'Get out of my office!' he yelled, gesticulating toward the door.

'Charles, come on –'

'Now!' Mackie boomed.

'Okay, we're done here,' Lindegaard said. 'I'll leave it up to you to inform Logan and to bring him back in. My man is on his way to France as we speak.'

Mackie spun his chair around as the two committee members got to their feet. They turned and walked out of the office, shutting the door behind them.

Mackie stood staring into space, embarrassed as much as he was angry.

'Sir, do you want me to call Logan?' Winter queried.

Mackie didn't respond. He walked around the desk, over to his office door, opened it, peered outside to make sure no-one was milling around and closed it again. He then went back to his seat at the desk.

'Sir?'

'No. Don't call Logan.'

'So you're going to call him?'

Mackie didn't answer straight away. His mind was whirring. He scratched at his goatee as he thought. This wasn't over. He wasn't giving up on Logan. Screw Lindegaard. There had to be another way.

'Winter, are you with me on this?'

Winter hesitated for only a second before saying, 'Of course.'

'Good. Then we're going to do everything we can to help Logan.'

'But … I mean –'

'You're with me, right?' Mackie said, halting Winter by holding up a hand.

'Yes.'

'Then let's bring this thing home. Logan stays out there until it's done.'

'Understood,' Winter confirmed, looking just a little wary. 'But aren't you worried about what that means for us?'

'We'll be just fine,' Mackie said with the faintest hint of a grin. 'I've got a good sense for these things.'

Winter had been right: Lindegaard was gunning for Logan. And the longer Mackie defied him, the more desperate he was going to get.

'So what do you want me to do?'

'I want you to keep close to Lindegaard, keep an eye on his every move. I want to know all there is to know about who he's put on this case and what their brief is. And keep digging into Lindegaard's past. See what you can find that might help us.'

Mackie knew that not only was Winter an excellent commander in the making, but he was also incredibly tech savvy. In his youth he'd been an amateur hacker – part of a ring of nerds who would hack large corporations and institutions just for the challenge and thrill of it. And both men understood what Mackie's instructions entailed.

'I'll get on it right away.'

'Good. We're going to have to clutch at whatever straws you can find. Because have no doubts that this is going to blow up in our faces. And when it does, we're going to need as much dirt on Lindegaard as we can get.'

Chapter 32

It was dark by the time they'd picked up the medical supplies. Although frustrated by the prospect, Logan had to concede that it would be better to get his wounds seen to before heading to Blakemore's. Plus both he and Grainger needed the rest. They ran the risk of Blakemore and the others involved being spooked by Lorik's disappearance, but the day's events had taken its toll on both of them. Even though Logan's wounds weren't completely debilitating, he was certainly not in good enough shape to be off confronting anyone else right now.

As well as the pharmacy, they'd also managed to find a shop where Grainger had bought them both clean clothes: some tennis shoes, jeans and a non-descript blue pullover for her and a similar outfit for Logan, albeit with a grey V-neck jumper.

They needed somewhere to stay, but overnight options in the area were limited. The only suitable place they could find was a modern, three-storey roadside lodge. It was cheap and functional but big enough to allow them to remain relatively inconspicuous. In a much smaller place they would have stuck out like a sore thumb.

As with the pharmacy and clothes shop, it was Grainger who went into the reception to get the rooms, while Logan waited in the car. She had now changed out of her damaged clothes but her fat lip and swollen cheek meant that she looked anything but discreet. Logan though, with gaping wounds in his face and covered in blood, looked a damn sight worse and would have certainly aroused suspicions.

Grainger came back from the hotel reception and they made their way toward the second floor.

'I got one room for us to share,' she said.

She looked up at him. Gone was that smile that had lit her face up so much earlier in the day. She looked in pain. Frightened as well.

'I don't want to be alone tonight,' she said. 'Not after what's happened. We don't even know whether there's still someone after us.'

His initial reaction to her words, before her clarification, had been that she wanted to be close to him for another reason. Was that what he wanted?

How could he even be thinking like that after what had just happened?

'It's okay,' he said. 'You don't need to explain. I agree with you. We're obviously the target of someone now. We need to stay close from here.'

'Twin beds, though,' she said. 'I'm not that easy.'

She tried a smile, but it didn't really work.

The room they had was basic. There were two single beds, a desk attached to the wall with a kettle on top, an old-fashioned portable TV and bathroom with shower, no bath.

'God, what are we even doing here?' she said. 'What am *I* doing here?'

'Well, I know it's not exactly the Ritz …' Logan said, trying to make light of the situation, but neither of them were really in the mood.

If she had even understood that he had been trying to be funny, she didn't let on.

'I meant here with you,' she said. 'I should be calling this in. Getting the police and the Feds down here.'

Even though in many ways she was right, that was the last thing he wanted, and he was certainly glad that she hadn't.

'Why haven't you?' he asked.

'I don't know. For starters, they'd want to know what happened to me and I'd have to explain why there's a dead man in that field. And why he's got no face left.'

Whether or not it had been her intention, her words stung him – the thought that perhaps she now thought less of him after the brutal way in which he'd killed Lorik. And he wasn't quite sure why that was. Why did he even care what she thought? But thinking about it, he knew the answer. As much as he was trying to push the feeling to the back of his head, he was attracted to her. There was just something about her. And he wanted her to like him back.

'But I know you wouldn't want me to do that,' she added.

'Thanks. I think.'

'And besides, if we really are going after the same thing then perhaps we should stick together.'

Then why did you leave me stranded earlier in the day? Logan thought. But it wouldn't have been right to question her about that now.

'The man who attacked me …'

She stopped and sat down on the bed.

Logan wasn't sure what she had wanted to say. He tried to fill in the blanks. 'His name was Lorik,' he said. 'He's one of the men who attacked me in the car park. The one who got away. I'm pretty sure he and Johnny worked for Blakemore.'

'He must have followed us from the car park in Paris. How did we not even notice him? Then, when I left you there …' She almost sounded ashamed of the fact. 'I was heading toward Blakemore's but I didn't know exactly where to go. I was trying to call in to my team but couldn't reach them. I was just driving along and he rammed me off the road. I didn't even see him coming. Next thing I knew I was stuck in the middle of that field. I didn't know what to do. I thought he was going to kill me.'

I'm pretty sure he would have done a lot more than that, Logan thought.

Grainger broke down in tears again. Logan thought about going over to her, trying to comfort her. In the end he didn't. As much as he wanted to, he wasn't sure it was the right thing to do.

'I'm sorry I left you,' she said. 'I was just … just confused. I know you're one of the good guys. But I have my orders. I'm trying to do things by the book.'

'I know. You don't have to explain that to me. We're both okay. That's the main thing.'

'Before you turned up, I was hiding,' she said. 'I didn't know where he was. Then I fired my gun in panic when I thought I heard him. Probably gave my position away. Next thing I knew he jumped me from behind.'

'You don't have to go through this with me,' he said. But was that to protect him or her?

'He spoke to me, before you arrived,' she carried on, ignoring him. 'He told me what he was going to do to me. I could tell he really wanted to as well.'

He knew that talking about it was helping her to cope with the trauma, but it was hard for him to listen. It was painful to hear her words, bringing back too many memories. Not just of what had happened today.

'I'm sorry,' she said. 'Listen to me, going on about myself like this. We need to get you seen to.'

'I'm fine. If you want to talk, you should.'

'No. I don't think I do want to. Not right now. Let's get you cleaned up.'

'Yeah, I guess. I'll take a shower first, get rid of the dried blood.'

He went to the bathroom and undressed out of his soiled clothes. He deliberately avoided looking at himself in the mirror. At first, the hot water in the shower made him wince as it washed over the wounds on his face. After a while, though, he became used to the sensation and started to feel it soothing him, calming him. His hands, which had stopped trembling, were still throbbing and aching. But the hot water was helping them too, creating a pleasant burning similar to having come into a warm house after being out in the cold for too long.

When he was finished he wrapped a towel around his waist. It only just fitted. He used a hand towel to mop at his face, which was still bleeding. Only then did he look into the mirror.

Not at his face, but at his scars.

He'd never seen them as a badge of honour. He hadn't flaunted them as a sign of his strength or superiority, even though to many women they'd made him appear to be some sort of battle-hardened warrior. In the past, he'd never held any emotions toward them at all.

But that was all different now. To the new Logan, they told the story of a lost soul. Of a lifetime of pain and suffering that was easier to ignore than to confront.

Since his encounter with Selim, he'd not shown his scars to anyone other than the doctors and carers who had rehabilitated him. He wasn't sure whether that was through embarrassment or fear or what. He just couldn't bring himself to do it.

But he felt different today. Like he wanted to share the emotions with someone else. With Grainger. Share his suffering with her.

Wasn't it about time he faced his fears?

What exactly was it that he feared anyway? Rejection? Ridicule?

He wasn't going to hide anymore. He had seen her at her most vulnerable, now it was his turn.

With just the towel wrapped around his waist, he headed back into the bedroom, stood in the doorway, waited for her reaction.

Grainger was still sitting on one of the beds. She looked up at him and her eyes inspected him for a few moments, but she didn't say a word.

He was almost disappointed.

'Come on then, let's do this,' she said.

She indicated for him to come over and he went and sat next to her on the bed.

After a long look at his face, she said, 'There're two cuts that need doing. One at the top of your nose and one above your right eye. Are you sure your nose isn't broken? It doesn't look quite right.'

'It's just swollen. It's been crooked for years. An old war wound.'

'You were in the army?' she said, sounding surprised.

'No, never. Just a figure of speech.'

He turned his gaze and caught her staring at his chest, at his scars. She averted her eyes quickly.

'Sorry,' she said.

'What for?' he asked. When she didn't answer, he said, 'Aren't you going to ask about them?'

'No. If you want to tell me, you will.'

He'd never talked to anyone about them properly. Not really. The psychologist had pried but he'd only told enough to keep her off his back. Other people had seen them, but he hadn't delved into the stories that lay behind them.

Dejected, he said, 'Put some of the alcohol on first.'

'I know. Are you ready?'

Before he could answer, she pressed the alcohol-soaked cotton wool against his eyebrow. He jolted with shock more than pain. It made her laugh, and for just a fleeting second her smile was back.

'Sorry,' she said. 'I couldn't resist that. It's like having a Band-Aid removed when you're a kid. One, two, *rip*. Take away the anticipation, take away the pain.'

'Are you sure you were never a nurse?' he joked.

'Very funny.'

She managed the threading without any issues; four stitches in his eyebrow, three in his nose. It hurt pretty badly, but he'd had a lot worse.

'What about your hands?' she said.

They were still throbbing and were about fifty per cent bigger than normal from the swelling.

'They'll be fine,' he answered. 'I just need some anti-inflammatories to ease the swelling.'

They'd bought both a gel and tablets. He would use both.

'They must hurt like hell,' she said.

Logan just shrugged.

'You're one tough guy, Carl.'

He wasn't sure whether she was being sarcastic or not. She collected together the rubbish and walked over to the bin by the desk.

'Can I ask you a question?' she said.

'Of course.'

'What were you thinking? Back in the field. I mean, what was going through your head? I've never seen anyone like that before. It was like you weren't even there.'

'I don't remember,' he lied. 'I just knew I had to save you. Me too, for that matter. He would have killed us both given half a chance.'

She didn't seem to buy the explanation, which hadn't really answered her question, but she didn't press the issue.

'I really am grateful, you know,' she said.

'I know. Thanks.'

'Have you, you know … Is that the first time you've –'

'Killed a man?' Logan said.

'Yes.'

'No, it's not.'

Grainger stared at him for a few seconds. Logan could see a whole world of emotions going through her mind.

'I never have,' she said, almost ashamedly.

'It's not something I brag about. It's just my job.'

'I didn't mean it like that. It's just hard to imagine what it must be like. I never even fired my gun in the line of duty before today.'

'They weren't good people, the ones I killed,' Logan asserted. 'And it was them or me. You saw that much today.'

'I guess,' Grainger said, getting to her feet. 'I should clean myself up.'

'Yeah.'

She headed to the bathroom. Logan dressed in the new clothes, tossing his soiled ones into the empty shopping bag.

He thought about calling Mackie, but decided against it. He didn't need to be babysat. As hard as Mackie might have fought it, Logan always strove to act independently, and in the past he had regularly gone without speaking to his boss for days at a time. Though the main reason for not calling this time was because he didn't want to have to explain what had happened today.

Grainger came back out of the bathroom a few minutes later, fully dressed but with a towel wrapped around her hair. Even after everything, and as hard as he tried not to think about it, she looked great.

'You hungry?' he said.

'Not really. You?'

'No. But we should try to eat something anyway.'

They'd bought some snack food earlier: crisps, nuts, chocolates, fizzy drinks. All they had found food wise was a convenience store, so it was the best they could get. Not surprisingly, they weren't really in the mood for eating out. There was nothing of real substance there, but it would keep them going. Logan began to tuck in. Eventually, Grainger relented and did the same.

They ate mostly in silence and it was nearly nine o'clock by the time they finished. Despite the sugary food, their energy levels were waning.

'You going to call your boss?' Logan asked.

'I don't have to, no. He can call me if there any developments. And like I said, it would be quite hard to explain to them what's happened today. Especially why I haven't come in after nearly being killed. And the whole thing with the police. God, what a mess.'

She put her head in her hands.

'You told him about the link to Blakemore, though, didn't you?'

'No,' she said, looking up at him.

He raised an eyebrow. That was a surprise. 'No? The police still don't know?'

'I don't know what the police know. I wanted to check it out myself first. Blakemore's place, I mean. And I'm here for the FBI, so it would be my boss there that I called in the first instance, not the French police. But I don't have to tell the Feds every time I tie my shoelace. I wanted to make sure this link was credible.'

So she really *had* doubted the link when he'd first told her about it. Well, she certainly didn't doubt it anymore. Despite himself, Logan couldn't help but feel vindicated by that. But he was also angry. They could have both been killed today, and the situation certainly hadn't been helped by her stranding him and running off after Blakemore alone.

'And how exactly were you going to determine if the link was credible?' Logan said, the irritation in his voice clear. 'Knock on his front door and ask him nicely?'

She frowned at him. 'Why, was that what you had planned, *action man*?'

He shrugged his shoulders, conceding the point. He hadn't needed to be facetious. It was hardly her fault that she had almost been raped and killed, even if she had been reckless.

'I just wanted to check it out first,' she added. 'See what I was dealing with before I brought anyone else in.'

'Okay, I'm sorry. And you're right. We should still do that. Check out his place, I mean. And soon.'

'Soon?'

'Let's get some rest now. We need it. We can't wait too long, though – just a couple of hours. It'll be harder to scope out the place in the dark, but at least it'll provide better cover for us than in the daytime.'

'Agreed.'

'Let's get some sleep now then.'

'So how do we do this?' she said.

'Do what?'

'Well, are you just getting into bed like that? Fully dressed?'

'I'll close my eyes if you're feeling a bit shy,' he said.

She blushed.

'It's not that, Logan. To be honest, I was actually regretting getting a room with two beds. It's kind of comforting having someone else close to you.'

Logan turned red as well. Her comment had been unexpected but she was understandably feeling vulnerable, and he felt a bit foolish about being so childish. It was just his way of dealing with an awkward situation.

'These are bigger than singles anyway,' Logan said, patting the bed that he was sitting on. 'We can both squeeze onto here.'

He lay down on the bed, fully clothed, flat on his back on top of the covers. She came and lay down next to him. After setting the alarm on the clock radio for midnight, he turned out the lights and shut his eyes.

Chapter 33

'Listen to me, Frank, those other two are loose cannons. They're uncontrollable. You should hear the things they're saying outside of this room. They want you dead, Frank. They honestly believe you can't help us and they want you dead. Because killing you is a much easier solution than just giving you back. You have to tell us what we need.'

Modena had his head down and his eyes closed. He could hear the words being spoken to him and recognised that they were from the slight man – the kind one – but his brain was a few seconds behind in processing them. The lack of food and water and the increasing physical and mental torture were quickly taking their toll. Sounds were more like echoes in his head. He was never quite sure whether he was awake or asleep. The one thing he was sure about was the pain. Each time the big man or Selim was in the room with him, the pain they inflicted was all too real.

Youssef Selim. Modena had long been aware of the man. His reputation. Not just as a terrorist but as a sadist. The stories of his victims were many and varied. He claimed to be a jihadist, but other than his religion and hatred for Westerners he shared little of the ideology of what most people would associate with Islamic extremists. He brokered arms deals. He trained terrorists for profit. He was, essentially, a capitalist. A capitalist with a penchant for inflicting pain and misery upon others.

Modena knew what they were asking of him. What he couldn't understand was why the information was of any interest to Selim. And that was what worried him most. Because Selim seemed intent on only one thing: hurting Modena. And so even if he was able to give the information they wanted, would that really stop Selim?

'Frank, are you listening to me?'

Modena groaned and tried to lift his head, but then hung it down again.

'Money,' he slurred. 'You can take it all. Just don't let him hurt me anymore.'

'It's not money they want from you, Frank. Don't you understand that? They're already getting money for this. That's why they're doing it. They'll get paid, but only if you give them what they want. That information is worth a lot of money. But if you don't give it to them then it's all over. All over for them. All over for you. All over for me.'

Modena shook his head. He wasn't sure how long it had been since Selim was last in the room with him, a few hours maybe, but the pain was still coursing through his entire body. At the tips of eight of his fingers the metal nails remained, dug deep into his flesh. The fingernails had been torn clean off the other two when Selim tried to hammer in the nail. Surprisingly, when Modena focused on them, those two seemed to be less painful than the others. But the throbbing in his hands was constant, and every few minutes a bout of drowsiness would wash over him as his body battled against the agony.

'Frank, you've only got a few minutes until Selim comes back in here. There's only one thing that's going to stop him. Just tell me what they need to know.'

'No. No more,' Modena garbled. 'Please. Don't let him hurt me anymore.'

Modena had mused about the fact that his captors were being so brazen about referring to Selim. None of the others had shown their faces or revealed their names. So why Selim? Modena could merely guess that it was because Selim was the only one who felt he had nothing to lose. The whole world already knew who and what he was. Modena knew that his capture was a major coup for Selim's so-called cause. And maybe there was something else too. They were banking on Selim's presence alone terrifying Modena into giving them the information they craved.

And Modena had to admit, if that was their plan, it was working.

A creaking noise came from behind the slight man. It took Modena a few seconds to process what it was. His heart had already started to pound when he realised that someone was coming in through the door. He pulled up his head and opened his eyes as much as the swelling would allow. It took a few more seconds for him to focus on the figure standing in the doorway, although he could already tell by the bulk of the man who it was. In a strange way, he felt a wave of relief. It wasn't Selim at least.

'Hello, Frank,' the big man bellowed. 'It's my turn now. Say bye-bye to Mr Nice Guy.'

As the big man moved further into the room, Modena spotted Selim coming in behind him. Modena's eyes met his and Selim gave him an evil smile.

Modena began moaning, his head shaking.

'No. No. No. Please, no more. Please!'

'This is it, Frank,' the slight man said. 'Please, just tell me. I'll make them go away, but you have to tell me!'

'Okay! Please, just … no more.'

'Wait!' the little man shouted. He held up his hand to the others, who stopped in their tracks. 'Just wait a second. Frank, what did you say? Talk to me?'

'I said okay,' Modena said. 'I can help you.'

'I don't believe it,' the big man spat. 'I don't effing believe it. I knew he had it. The little shit's been playing us all this time. Stringing us along, hoping he'd get rescued or something. What a hero, Frank. Well, don't you worry, there's still plenty of time for us to have some more fun with you.'

'I wasn't lying,' Modena pleaded. He panted and wheezed, trying to get his words out. 'I don't have the information you want. But … but I think I can get it.'

'Tell us how, Frank,' the slight man beamed. 'Just tell us how.'

Chapter 34

8th October

He tried to move toward her, but his body wouldn't react. It was like his feet were in quick sand. The more he struggled, the less he could move. The man held the knife high and then thrust it down into her chest. There was a sickening sound as the blade penetrated her flesh, but nothing more than a whimper escaped her lips.

She turned her head.

Grainger.

Those pleading eyes. Begging for it to stop. Begging for Logan to help.

He tried to reach out to her, but he couldn't move. His arms were numb and lifeless.

The man turned to him. Lorik. A grin on his face. His eyes red with rage. He drove the knife down into her body again and again, moaning as he did so, louder and louder.

Logan tried with all his might to move. But something was stopping him, holding him back. He looked down. There were arms around his waist, around his neck. Pulling on him, preventing him from moving, from speaking.

He looked up. Lorik stood right in front of him now, his eyes bleeding onto his face. The bloody knife in his hand was only inches from Logan's heart. Lorik lifted the blade, pushed it against Logan's chest. The knife broke through his skin. Slowly, assuredly, Lorik plunged it deeper. The blade tore through Logan's flesh with ease.

'Logan!'

Grainger was still alive! He had to save her. But how? Lorik was forcing the knife deeper and deeper, the smile still on his face. Logan felt the knife touching his heart, then piercing it.

With one last burst of energy, he tried to break free, but he couldn't. He wanted to save her. But it was too late now. He shut his eyes.

'Logan! Wake up!'

All of a sudden the arms that had been holding him back were gone. He found a burst of strength. At last he could move. He sprang into action.

He opened his eyes …

Confusion swept through him. He was upright, out of the bed. His body was clammy, his breathing heavy.

'Are you okay?' she said.

Grainger. She was okay. The images had gone now, and his confusion was dissipating. His mind wasn't completely with him yet, but he knew where he was. When he turned to look at her, he saw that she was upset. Then he remembered how he'd thrown the arms off him in his dream.

'Oh, no. I'm really sorry. Did I hurt you?'

'Kind of. I was trying to wake you, but you shoved me out of the way. I'm fine, though. Are you?'

'Yeah. It was just a bad dream.'

'Do you want to tell me about it?'

'No.'

'You were screaming.'

'I'm sorry.'

'Don't be. But you were really screaming. Screaming my name.'

Logan flinched. How embarrassing could you get? *Yeah, way to go, macho man*.

He looked at the clock. It was almost one in the morning. The alarm hadn't gone off. Maybe he hadn't set it right. He lay back down on the bed, next to her.

'Sorry for waking you,' he said. 'And for shoving you. You must think I'm insane.'

'Not really. My dad used to get the nightmares as well. I know what it's like. Well, I know what it's like to see it, anyway.'

'I'm just not sleeping well at the moment.'

'I know. The stress of the job, right? I understand.'

'No, it's not that. It's more than that.'

She put her hand on his shoulder.

'Talk to me about it,' she said. 'Let me help you.'

He shrugged her off, got up from the bed.

'I don't need help,' he snapped. 'I'm fine.'

She looked like she didn't believe him. *He* didn't believe him.

'I'm going for a shower,' he said. 'I need to try to clear my head a bit.'

He walked to the bathroom without waiting for a response.

He undressed and got into the shower. As the hot water coursed over him it seemed to relax not only his body but his mind too. By the time he turned the water off, all remnants of the nightmare had been banished.

After drying himself off he inspected his wounds in the mirror. Grainger had done a good job with the stitches. They were holding nicely and there was no sign of any infection. His hands were red raw on the knuckles, the skin completely gone, but the pain and the swelling had gone down some with the medicines he'd taken. He dressed and went back into the bedroom.

Grainger was still sitting up on the bed.

'I didn't mean to snap at you,' he said, taking a seat beside her. 'I just don't like talking about it.'

'You don't need to say anything more. I get it. You're a man: you don't do feelings.'

He had to laugh at that, even though she'd sounded a little hurt.

'Yeah. Something like that.'

'But I really do know what it's like,' she said. 'My dad had post-traumatic stress for five years. He used to get just like this.'

'You talk about him a lot.'

She looked a little put-out. 'Of course I do. He brought me up all on his own. He's the reason I am who I am.'

'He brought you up alone?'

'My mom died when I was a kid. Car accident. I don't really remember much about her – I was very young.'

'That must have been hard. For both of you. Is that what caused the stress?'

'No. Well, obviously for a while it did. But it was the job that caused him the most trouble. He saw some pretty terrible things.'

'What did your dad do? For a job, I mean.'

'Take a guess,' she said, looking up at him, a glint of pride in her eyes.

'FBI.'

'You got it.' She smiled. 'I joined the agency because of him. I always wanted to be just like him.'

'How did he get rid of it?' Logan asked. 'The stress, the tremors, the nightmares.'

'He never did,' she said, bowing her head. 'He died on the job.'

'I'm sorry.'

'Yeah, me too. So that's what you've got, is it? Post-traumatic stress?'

'Apparently.'

She fiddled with her hair, as though wanting to say more, but not sure whether she should.

'I can tell this is tough for you,' she said, 'but it really does help to talk. No pressure. But if you ever want to, just try me.'

'You'll be the first to know.'

And he really did mean that. There was something about her that comforted him. Perhaps it was that she seemed to understand what was happening to him. Perhaps it was because they'd both nearly died out in that field. Or perhaps it was just banal animal instinct, a physical attraction. But it felt like more than that.

He'd talked endlessly with the psychologist about his problems but he'd only ever said what she wanted to hear, not what he was really feeling. It was just easier to keep the issues locked in than to talk about them. But perhaps Grainger was right – maybe it was time to start opening up about what was happening to him. Even if just a little bit.

'I get nightmares all the time,' Logan said. 'More or less every night. I even get them when I'm awake sometimes. That's when it freaks me out the most. The dreams used to be real. I mean, they were the retelling of real events. Bad things that happened to me. But now they're different. More graphic. And more painful. The one I had just now, we were back in the field. Only this time I couldn't save you. Couldn't save either of us.'

'Yeah, but you *did* save us,' she said, shuffling closer to him. 'That's why we're still here.'

She leaned over and kissed him on the cheek. It sent a tingle all the way down the left side of his body. He thought about turning to face her and kissing her back.

But he waited too long and the moment passed.

'Why don't we get going?' he suggested. 'It's later than we planned and we're both awake now anyway.'

Without hesitation, she said, 'Yeah. Let's do it.'

Chapter 35

'Have we got it yet?' Reggie asked.

They were huddled in Blakemore's office. Habib, Selim's technical whizz, was at the computer. Blakemore was sitting next to him. Selim was standing behind them, leaning against a large wooden display cabinet and nonchalantly combing his hair. Reggie was hanging around by the door, his anxiety and irritation rising by the minute.

They'd had Modena for over three days now and Reggie thought he'd done well to stay relaxed during that period. It wasn't easy for him to keep his emotions, his anger, bottled up. He supposed the fact he'd let off a lot of steam pummelling Modena had helped. But he'd also been prepared for this taking some time. Now that the end goal was in sight, though, it was hard to keep his feet on the ground, and he felt like he was about to snap.

'It's getting there. Just give me a few more minutes,' Habib said.

Habib had arrived just a few hours ago. He was part of Selim's crew, along with Mustafa, who had been with them from the start, and two others who had been part of the attack on Modena's motorcade but who'd since taken a back seat in proceedings.

Reggie looked over at Selim. He seemed to be the only person in the room who was fully in control. Everyone else was edgy and nervous. Everything about Selim unsettled Reggie. It was like nothing at all moved him. Except hurting people.

Reggie knew that Blakemore had been doing business with Selim for over three years. He didn't get the impression that the two men were exactly friends, but then you don't have to like someone's personality to have a successful business relationship with them. Reggie had been involved in some of Blakemore's previous work with Selim, though this job was the first time either he or Blakemore had met the man in person.

He hoped it would be the last.

He could fully understand why Selim had been brought in, though. They needed a good cover story, something to send the authorities off at a tangent, and the extremist angle was ideal. Selim had been more than happy to play the role, given the amount of money involved for such a seemingly small piece of work. He'd even thrown in four of his men with the job to provide some much-needed skills, such as the techie Habib. Having Selim's men involved also gave more credence to the terrorist angle and Selim was more than happy to take the credit for Modena's kidnapping – it was a win–win situation.

But it hadn't been easy keeping Selim under control. Blakemore had made it clear that it was down to Reggie to rein Selim in after what he'd done to Modena. Reggie knew that Blakemore didn't have the balls to do that himself. And Reggie had been nervous at the prospect too. But ultimately, and to his surprise, Selim had obliged.

Money talks, Reggie supposed. Selim was, after all, a businessman. He knew that if they didn't get what they needed from Modena, he wouldn't be getting paid. None of them would.

'As soon as we get it, we should move out,' Reggie said. 'I haven't been able to get hold of Lorik since last night. Something's up. Wouldn't surprise me if the police had him.'

'I know, Reggie, you keep saying that,' Blakemore crowed, agitated, not taking his gaze off the computer screen. 'But all the equipment is here. We can't leave when we're this close – it could take us days to set up again.'

Reggie huffed. The longer they sat here, the more likely it was that they would get caught out. Wasn't Blakemore the one who had insisted on having the back-up plan to move Modena in the first place? And he was the one who had been the most worried when he'd heard about this John Burrows running amok.

'Your man, Lorik,' Selim said, looking over at Reggie, 'can he be trusted?'

'What do you mean?'

'If he's been caught, will he talk?'

'Hold on a minute,' Blakemore said. 'We don't know that he's been caught. He could be off with a whore somewhere. Or he could be lying in a pool of his own blood.'

'What!' Reggie scoffed. 'This is Lorik. I hardly think some lone woman would have felled him. You'd need a whole army to bring him down. He's either off having some fun somewhere, raping that poor bitch probably, or the police have got him.'

'That's my point,' Selim said. 'If the police have him, can he be trusted? Should we be worried?'

'He's unbreakable,' Reggie affirmed.

'Nobody is unbreakable,' Selim said, a stern look on his face. He stepped away from the cabinet, moving toward Reggie. 'Believe me. I've seen some tough cookies crumble.'

'It's the French national police we're talking about here,' Reggie retorted, nervousness clear in his voice. 'I hardly think they've taken the Torture 101 course. Lorik will hold out.'

Everyone else in the room had stopped to look in on the discussion. Reggie looked at Blakemore as if asking for assistance. None came.

'And what if it's not the police that have him?' Selim questioned, coming closer, his tone defiant. He was setting a challenge for Reggie. 'What if it's the CIA?'

'The CIA? Man, you've been watching too many movies,' Reggie said with an uneasy laugh. 'All I was saying was we should get out of here. No point in taking unnecessary risks.'

'Hang on a minute,' Blakemore chimed in. 'You think the CIA won't be interested that the Attorney General has been kidnapped by Islamic extremists?'

'Well, there's your answer,' Reggie said. 'They're out there looking for Islamic extremists. If the CIA were onto us, we'd know by now.'

We've got at least one Islamic extremist in the room with us right now, Reggie thought, but decided not to mention that fact. Given the look in Selim's eyes, he wasn't sure that he'd appreciate it.

'I don't think they exactly advertise when they're onto you,' Selim said. He was now within a hair's breadth of Reggie, who all of a sudden stood tall, puffing out his chest like a peacock displaying its feathers, as though his sheer size would get Selim to back off him.

'Habib, are we getting any closer?' Blakemore said, deflecting the attention away from a relieved Reggie. He really didn't know what had happened to Lorik. What he did know was that he wanted to get out of here as soon as possible.

'Just give me a few minutes!' Habib snapped.

This is hopeless, Reggie thought. Habib had been saying the same thing for over half an hour.

'You're looking a bit tense there,' Selim mocked, as though he didn't do tense. He reached out and squeezed Reggie's shoulder for effect. 'Everything okay?'

'I'm fine,' Reggie said, angrily shrugging Selim's hand off and moving away from him, over toward the computer. 'I just can't understand why this is taking so long.'

'Well, seeing as you're not really doing anything of use here,' Blakemore said, 'why don't you go and load up the vehicles so we're ready to move out.'

'Load up the vehicles with what?' Reggie asked.

'Well, for starters, with our prized asset.'

'Fine. I'll go and get Mustafa to help,' Reggie grumbled. 'Habib, how much longer do you need?'

'Please! I'm almost there. Just give me a few minutes.'

Reggie gritted his teeth and clenched his fists as hard as he could as he turned to head for the door. *If he says that one more time*, he thought, *I'm going to ram that keyboard down his goddamn throat.*

Chapter 36

Logan turned off the Fiat's headlights when they were about a mile away from Blakemore's farmhouse, wanting to remain as invisible as they could. It made the last part of the journey slow and awkward, particularly as there were no streetlights on the road. They arrived safe and sound nonetheless.

A few minutes before, they had passed the area where Grainger had been forced off the road the previous night. They'd both strained in the dark to see whether the two abandoned cars were still there. Sure enough, Lorik's car was still tucked up in the field where they had left it. There were no obvious signs of anyone having been there. The broken headlight pieces were still at the side of the road where they'd left them and the fence that they'd hastily re-erected was holding its position. Altogether it suggested there hadn't been any major clean-up of the area. With any luck, that meant the Slav's body hadn't yet been found by his accomplices.

They drove past the closed gates to Blakemore's property, turned and parked up a farm track a hundred yards away. The car would be hidden from the road at least while it remained dark outside.

In the bright moonlight they could make out Blakemore's farmhouse in the distance and what must have been a few acres of land, completely enclosed within a nine-foot-high white-painted wall, red tiles stacked on top. It was possible that some of the fields outside of the wall were his as well.

From the car they walked back toward the farmhouse through the adjacent field, which didn't seem to be anything more than a dust bowl. At least it hadn't rained recently, otherwise it would have been like a bog. Logan led the way, Grainger never more than two steps behind him. He turned every now and then to make sure she was still with him.

With the clear, star-filled skies above them, there was enough moonlight for them to find their way through the field. There was also plenty of light coming from inside the compound to light up the area around it. But the clear skies also meant there was a chill in the air: it was almost two a.m. and the nighttime temperature was somewhere close to zero. They didn't have a coat or a jacket between them and both shivered as they made their way toward the compound.

When they had passed in the car, they'd noted the arched wooden gates at the front of the property, twelve feet high at their peak. A keypad together with camera and infrared spotlight were the only obvious security. They had been unable to tell exactly where on the property the house was located. But as they approached from the side, they could now clearly make out the roof of the substantial house about sixty or so yards back from where the road was.

Logan slowed up as they neared the perimeter wall, senses on alert for any guards patrolling on foot outside, or other signs of security. There didn't appear to be anything. He signalled to Grainger with his hand, circling it in the air. She nodded and they carried on, doing a full circuit around the outside wall, scoping out the property. The wall housed two other standard-sized wooden doors, on opposite sides to each other, plus there was a large set of loading doors at the back, similar to the front gates, which led onto a farm track that carried away into the darkness. Each of the doors and the back gates had a camera and security keypad but nothing more sophisticated than that. And there were no spotlights like there were at the front.

The wall itself certainly wasn't impregnable. Blakemore had gone for looks as much as anything, with the wall's colour and styling fitting in well with the local architecture. It was, after all, supposed to be a private house and not fortified barracks, so that wasn't a surprise. The problem, though, was knowing whether or not there was more security on the inside. There would certainly be additional cameras and spotlights, but there could also be dogs, armed guards and whatever else depending on how safety conscious – or paranoid – Blakemore was.

'We should get ourselves inside,' Logan whispered.

'What? I thought we were just taking a look at the place?' Grainger whispered back, shivering. She cupped her hands to her mouth and breathed into them to try to give them some warmth.

'We are. But I want to look inside as well. Otherwise how do we know what we're dealing with? Thought you knew that?'

She seemed unsure, but then joked, 'Okay. Shall I knock or do you want to?'

Not laughing, Logan said, 'We should go over at the back corner. You'd typically have more security at the front of a property anyway. And even from our quick recce, the back end seems to be the darkest spot.'

It took them a few minutes to cautiously retrace their steps, Logan again taking the lead. From the back corner, because of the angle, it wasn't possible to see any of the house at all. There didn't appear to be any lights on in the grounds immediately inside the wall either. Logan knew there was every possibility a spotlight would be positioned somewhere near and would come on as soon as they went over the wall.

But they were here now, and there was only one way to find out.

'Can you take my weight?' Logan said. 'If you give me a bunk then I should be able to pull you up from the top. It's not that high. It'll be easier for you to push me than pull me.'

'Yeah, go for it.'

She held out her hands, clasped together at waist height. Logan put his right foot onto them, ready to hoist himself upwards.

'Ready?' he said.

'Yeah.'

He pushed as hard as he could, reaching up and grabbing the top of the wall. Grainger shifted on her feet, struggling to take his weight. Once he had managed to get both hands on the top of the wall he took the weight off her and hauled himself up.

The wall was only about six inches thick and it was hard for Logan to perch on the top. Particularly with the shape of the tiles, which were lying together to form an upside-down V, like a row of stacked cards.

'What can you see?' Grainger whispered up to him.

He did his best to shuffle round and get a look. Luckily no lights had focused on him and he didn't notice anything of concern nearby. He could clearly see some security lights attached to the back of the house, though, which was about fifty yards away.

There were numerous lights on inside the farmhouse. They provided enough illumination for him to make out the basic layout of the grounds at the back of the house. Other than the paved area directly behind the house, it seemed to be mostly lawn. Directly below him and all along that part of the wall were thick bushes. There were two vehicles parked near to the house: an SUV and a panel van.

Most importantly, though, there was no sign of any guards or guard dogs.

'I think we're good to go,' he said. 'Grab hold of my hand.'

She was able to reach his hand without jumping. He was surprised at how icy her skin was. He could feel the chill in the air, but it hadn't bothered him much. He'd learned a long time ago how to block out things like cold. Much of the technique was mind over matter.

Despite her being light, it was still a struggle to pull Grainger up, the awkward shape of the tiles meaning he had to keep one arm on the wall for balance. She made it to the top and adjusted herself. They gave each other a nod and pushed their bodies over the edge, holding on to the top of the wall with their arms outstretched. Their bodies dangled down on the inside of the compound, just a few feet off the ground. On the count of three, they dropped the short distance, managing to avoid getting tangled in the bushes.

They both crouched low behind the foliage, waiting to see if anything or anyone had been alerted by their arrival. Satisfied that they were in the clear, Logan stood up, surveying the area once more.

'I'm going to move forward, along the wall, toward the house,' he said.

'I'll follow you.'

'Okay, but keep your distance. Better to create two targets.'

'I'm not planning on being a target for anyone. But okay.'

They crept along the wall, a few steps apart, with Logan in front. Every few seconds he turned to make sure Grainger was still there. She was, though in the darkness he couldn't make out any detail, just that a figure of her size and shape was back there. Suddenly a spotlight came on at the back of the house. Its beam reached out to within three yards of where Logan was standing.

Had he done that?

He was only about fifteen yards from the house now. Although he wasn't directly in the beam, the glare from the light was enough for him to be partially lit up. Anybody coming out the back of the house would be able to see him if they were to glance in his direction. He turned around, looking back to where Grainger was. He could make out her shape and indicated for her move back, but because she was still in the darkness and he was unable to fully see her, he couldn't tell whether she had understood his signal.

Regardless, he began to creep back toward her, away from the light.

But then the back door to the house opened.

Logan turned his head toward the sound and froze. He had managed to move a few yards further away from the light. If he stayed still, he would hopefully remain out of sight.

He heard voices before he saw anyone. It was too distant to hear what they were saying, though. Two men emerged. The spotlight lit them up as well as if it had been daytime. Logan wondered whether they had turned the light on manually, rather than it having come on due to his presence. The men didn't seem to be spooked by it being on, so he guessed it was probably the former.

The man who came out first was short and slight, dark skinned and dressed in black. He looked young. The second man was much taller and wider, light skinned with a face like a prize fighter. He was holding onto a third man who was half walking, half being dragged. The third man's hands were tied together in front of him. There was a small brown sack over his head.

Modena, Logan thought. It had to be.

He risked a look back at Grainger. He almost jumped out of his skin when he saw her standing right behind him. She had crept up on him in absolute silence.

She sensed his surprise and put a finger to her lips. 'That has to be him,' she whispered.

He nodded, returned his gaze to the men. The short man opened the back doors of the van. It was parked with its rear facing the house and Logan couldn't see into the back of it at all. The larger man pulled Modena to the van and bundled him in. All three were now out of sight, inside the van. The men were talking loudly to each other, possibly arguing, though Logan still couldn't make out what they were saying. After a few seconds of banging, the bigger man came back into view and walked inside the house. A minute later he was followed by the short man.

'What now?' Grainger said. 'That has to be Modena in the van. We should go and get him. Get out of here.'

'Maybe. But not yet. We don't know how many men there are. Where they are. We need to be sure of what we're doing when we go in. Let's head to the side of the house. We'll be closer to the van and the spotlight doesn't reach into the corner at all.'

'Okay. But let's do it quickly. We don't want to be caught out in the light.'

They began to move forward, together this time, crouching low out of instinct. It wouldn't make any difference, though, if someone was actually looking in their direction.

And they were almost directly in the centre of the spotlight's beam, lit up for all to see, when the short man came back out of the door, assault rifle slung over his shoulder.

Chapter 37

Reggie was still on edge. This was taking too long now.

Come the hell on, he thought.

At least when this was done, they'd be more or less ready to go.

Reggie was back in the office. He had stuffed Modena in the van and had left Mustafa to collect up the weapons. Other than some of the computer equipment, there wasn't much else they'd be taking with them.

'Hey. Er, guys.' Habib stood up from his computer, grinning from ear to ear. 'I think this is it. We've got it!'

Reggie and Blakemore looked at each other, wide-eyed, then at Habib.

'Let me see,' Blakemore said, turning the screen toward him. 'I don't believe it. Son of a ...Would you look at that! The most expensive name in the world.'

'Told you I was close.'

'Here, let me sit there,' Blakemore said, nudging Habib out of the way so that he was at the keyboard. 'I need to get this sent straight away. I don't get paid until that name has gone. And neither do any of you.'

Blakemore began typing away. Reggie couldn't help but smile. This was it. The end was in sight now. He looked over at Selim, who was once again standing over by the cabinet, his face emotionless.

'When will the money arrive?' Selim said.

'It's been in escrow, waiting,' Blakemore said. 'Once I've sent this, it'll come through to me within the next few minutes. When it arrives, I'll have to give the go-ahead for the transfer to you. And

Reggie, for that matter. It's all set up, ready to go; it'll take no time at all. But we're better off doing it later, and getting away from here first.'

'Don't worry, Richie. I'm sure I can trust you,' Selim said. He smiled, but it wasn't a happy smile. Selim looked over to Reggie, and the smile faded away almost instantly.

Reggie turned his attention back to Blakemore.

'Okay, let's get this lot packed up,' Blakemore said after a couple of minutes. 'We're ready to move out of here.'

He got up and Habib began to dismantle the computer terminal.

'No need to bother with that, Habib,' Selim said. 'We've got what we need already. Better off travelling light from now on.'

'What do you mean?' Blakemore protested. 'We might need this stuff again.'

'I'm not going to need it. And why would you? You've got what you want. You've got your precious name and the money. And I've got Modena.'

'Sorry, what? *You've* got Modena? What the hell is that supposed to mean?'

'It means you've got what you wanted from this, now it's my turn to have some fun with him.'

Blakemore opened and closed his mouth but no words came out.

'What, you thought I was just doing this for a bit of money?' Selim sneered, the smile on his face showing that he was enjoying the moment. 'Don't be so naive, Richie. Don't forget who I am. Modena is worth a lot more to me than a couple of million dollars. Believe me, a *lot* more. Modena's mine now.'

Blakemore might have been slow to figure out what was happening, but Reggie wasn't. Selim had set them up. Used them. He was going to take the money *and* Modena. Satisfy all of his cravings. He reached around to his back and began to pull out the handgun that was stuffed in the waistband of his jeans.

But he stopped when he felt cold metal sticking into the back of his neck.

'Don't even think about it,' Mustafa said from behind him.

'Reggie? Oh dear,' Selim taunted, turning to face him. 'Did you think you'd get away with that? Please, hands in the air. Then come over here, away from the door.'

Reggie fumed, angered at himself as much as anything else, for letting himself be caught out. He put his hands up and Mustafa pushed the gun harder against his neck, indicating for him to move. He did so and felt Mustafa remove the handgun from his waistband as he edged forward.

When he'd walked three paces Mustafa tossed the handgun over to Selim, who caught it one-handed while still maintaining eye contact with Reggie.

Reggie could see Blakemore begin to inch toward the door. But Selim had seen it too. He lifted his right arm and fired. The bullet hit Blakemore in his left thigh and he screamed out in pain.

'Sit down, Richie.'

Selim reached out and pushed Blakemore back down into his seat. Then he turned the gun on Reggie.

Despite the turmoil inside, Reggie stood tall, defiant.

'Any last words?' Selim said.

Reggie didn't have anything. His mouth was shut tightly, his nostrils flaring. He wasn't going to beg. He wasn't going to try to bargain.

Another gunshot rang out. Reggie stumbled backward, falling onto one knee. He didn't feel the pain at first. But when it came, it came with a vengeance. Reggie winced, gritting his teeth. But he didn't cry out, not like Blakemore still was. He was determined to show no weakness.

He looked down at his wound, pushed his hand onto it. Blood was pouring out onto his shirt, seeping down to his jeans. Thoughts circled in his mind as to how he could turn the situation around. He wasn't finished. Not yet.

Mustafa calmly walked around to the front of Reggie, one of the AK-47s in his hands. Blakemore was still crying out; Selim had the handgun pointed at him, keeping him at bay. Reggie looked up at Mustafa, snarling, panting heavily. He would only get one chance.

Mustering as much strength as he could, he sprang to his feet, diving forward toward Mustafa. He caught the little man's temple with his elbow as he flew into him, immediately grappling to take control of the rifle. Reggie got it and another shot rang out. But it wasn't from the rifle.

Reggie released his grip on the gun and fell to the ground, lying flat on his back. There was a screaming pain in his chest.

'Phew. That was a close one,' Selim laughed. 'You almost had me panicking there, Reggie. I thought for a second you might make it.'

Mustafa wiped at the blood coming from the wound above his eye, then picked up the rifle from the floor, pushing the barrel against Reggie's head.

Reggie looked into Mustafa's eyes. The boy looked scared. Panicked. Reggie wished he could have finished that little prick off. But there was no fight left in him now. He tried to move but couldn't. His breaths were becoming slow and shallow, his vision blurry.

He blinked, then shut his eyes, but he opened them after a few seconds, trying to fight off the inevitable.

He could still hear Blakemore shouting. Screaming. Then he heard Selim's voice.

'Now, Richie, it's just you and me. I think it's about time we had a little talk. About my salary.'

Unable to hold on any longer, Reggie closed his eyes one last time.

Chapter 38

Sometimes things come down to nothing more than good luck. Logan and Grainger had been completely exposed when the man had come back outside. But he hadn't looked up at all as he walked over to the van. After putting the weapon in the front of the vehicle, on the passenger's side, he simply headed back into the house, not once glancing in the direction of Logan and Grainger.

Breathing a sigh of relief, they had both carried on the short distance to the corner of the house. Out of the light and out of sight.

Not long after, the shorter man had come out again, carrying two more rifles. He put those into the van too before returning to the house. It looked like they weren't planning on staying the night. And wherever they were going, they were certainly going to be well armed.

But Logan and Grainger's plans took an unexpected turn when they heard a gunshot inside the house. And two more not long after.

'What the hell was that?' Grainger said.

'Who knows? But at least it's not Modena they've shot.'

'There is that. But what else could it be? Each other?'

Logan shrugged. 'Well, I don't think there're any other visitors here. And if it's a police raid, it's the quietest one in history. My guess is it's each other they're shooting.'

'But why?' she said.

'Witnesses, most likely. Limiting the number of witnesses.'

Though quite who was in charge in there was hard to know. He just hoped Selim wasn't the one being disposed of. Logan had unfinished business with him.

'This is our chance,' Grainger said, moving away from Logan, toward the house. 'We should get Modena now. While they're still in there fighting each other.'

'No,' Logan said, grabbing her arm and holding her back. 'Modena's in that van because they're looking to make a getaway. Possibly any minute now. If we go over there, we could be running into them head on. And I don't fancy our chances against those weapons. There's another door here, at the side of the house. We'll go in this way and come up on them from the side or from behind.'

'We could just get Modena and get out of here. We don't have to face off to them at all. Let somebody else worry about them.'

Her suggestion was born of reason and sound judgement. Why bother walking into a fight when what they were after was right there in front of them?

But that was the problem. Modena wasn't really what Logan was after. He wanted to save him, of course. But getting Selim was way more important.

'No, we're here now,' Logan said. 'We can't let them get away.'

'I thought you said Modena was the goal?'

'He is, but I don't want to take the risk of us meeting whoever is in there as they come out. Come on, follow me.'

He didn't wait for her response but took off toward the side door, hoping that she would agree and follow him. The door was closed but it was a simple structure: wooden with six small, square glass panels in the top half and a single pin tumbler lock. It was possible the door was linked to some sort of security system, but Logan was prepared to take the chance.

As he reached the door, Grainger came up behind him. Logan took out his torsion wrench and a pick and within seconds had released the simple lock. He turned the door handle, pushed the door an inch and held his breath. No alarm.

Logan glanced back at Grainger. She had a look on her face somewhere between intrigue and admiration.

'Tools of the trade,' Logan said.

Then they both moved forward, into the house, guns drawn.

The door led into a pantry. The lights were off. But there was enough illumination from the open doorway off to the left, which led into the kitchen, to help them make out the layout of the room.

There was another door, closed, fifteen feet in front of them. They headed for it, Grainger walking behind Logan, who kept his eyes on the kitchen doorway, looking for any sign of movement.

'Are you okay?' Logan whispered as he neared the closed door at the far end.

He could sense Grainger's nerves. Her breathing was getting louder, her movements becoming stiff.

'Yeah, I'm fine,' she said, sounding offended that he'd asked. 'Are you sure you are?'

'Yeah.'

'Then what's with the hands?'

He looked down at his hands. The tremors were back. He hadn't even noticed. This was the first time it had happened before the action.

'Shit,' he said.

He wasn't going to let that get in his way now. Trying to ignore the involuntary movement, he put his left hand on the door handle and turned it slowly. When he felt the latch release, he inched the door open. The pantry opened out into a hallway with several more doors leading from it.

They'd heard nothing more since the three gunshots when they were outside. No more shooting, no voices. Logan began to wonder whether whoever had done the shooting had already left while he and Grainger were sneaking around the side.

But he realised that wasn't the case when there was a blood-curdling scream from somewhere further down the hallway, followed by muffled voices.

Logan looked at Grainger. The worry on her face now even more evident.

It was hard to tell which room the noises had come from. From the faint sound, it seemed unlikely to have been from the near side of the house.

There were five doors along the hallway: three on the left and two on the right. They walked past the first door on the left, which was another entrance to the kitchen, again looking in to make sure there was no sign of anybody. There wasn't.

They passed the next door, this one on the right, which was closed. There were no indications of what lay behind it, no light creeping out from underneath. There were also no sounds coming from the inside. They carried on.

As they got closer to what Logan had thought was the second door on the left, he realised it was actually another hallway, leading toward the back of the house. He could see the back door at the far end of it, the door that led outside to where the vehicles were parked. So they were now directly in the path of Selim, or Blakemore, or whoever it was that was planning their getaway. No better off than if they had just headed straight over to the van in the first place and got Modena out of there.

Logan resisted looking back at Grainger. He wasn't sure if the same thought had occurred to her. And if it had, he really didn't want to see her I told you so look.

Another scream. Not a scream of shock, but one of real terror and pain. It was followed by moaning. Whimpering. This time Logan could pinpoint the sounds. The last door on the right.

They passed another hallway leading off to the right, toward the front of the house. A cursory glance down the hall didn't reveal any obvious signs of life in that direction. They carried on toward the end of the corridor.

'Are you sure this is a good idea?' Grainger whispered. 'We could be seriously outnumbered here. Modena is right down there out the back. He's already in the van. Why not just go and get him?'

Logan didn't answer. A small part of him agreed with her, but he was trying his hardest to ignore it. He knew he was potentially putting her in harm's way. But he had other priorities right now. Selim was his immediate focus. And anyway, he was confident he could get himself and Grainger out of the house alive.

They reached the end of the corridor where the remaining two doors were set opposite each other. Logan crouched low as he peered into the lit room on the right, from where he was sure the sounds had come. He saw two men standing over a third. He quickly retracted his head. The tremors in his hands began to worsen. Even with the briefest of glimpses, Logan had seen enough to figure out what was happening in there.

'Logan?' Grainger whispered, almost inaudibly. 'What is it? What do you see?'

'It's Selim.'

Selim doing what he does best, he thought.

Torture.

Another scream. Even louder than it had been before. Logan closed his eyes at the sound. Having seen what was causing it, the sound now took on a whole new meaning to him.

'Logan, I don't like this. What do we do now?' She waited for a response. But he was dazed and confused. 'Logan!'

Come on, focus! he told himself. This is what you've been waiting for.

He tried his best to snap out of it. 'Okay,' he said. 'We go in.'

He was about to move when he heard footsteps behind them. He turned his head, looking past Grainger. There, coming around the corner, was the short man, the one who'd been loading the van earlier, a rifle over his shoulder.

'Shit! Move!' Logan said.

He grabbed hold of Grainger, pulling her with him as he headed for the other open doorway on the opposite side of the hall. But they couldn't shift quickly enough. The man had seen them.

With a shriek somewhere between surprise and anger, the man lifted his weapon and opened fire. A cloud of dust and plaster swept up as the bullets raked the wall next to them.

Hastily raising his gun as he and Grainger fell into the room, Logan fired back in the direction of the man, not looking as he did so. They rolled into the room in a tangled heap, immediately getting to their feet to look for cover. The room they stumbled into was a lounge. There were two big sofas adjacent to each other a few feet from where they stood. They dived over the top of the nearest one just as the short man reached the doorway, still firing.

But after a couple of short bursts, the shooting stopped. Logan and Grainger looked at each other, confused. Maybe he's reloading, Logan thought.

Then they heard voices. Shouting. Selim giving instructions, Logan realised.

He knew that the sofa would provide only temporary respite. If Selim's men opened fire with rifles at such a short distance, it would do little to stop the bullets. They were sitting ducks.

Logan looked at Grainger. She had her gun held up to her chest. She looked at him and he gave her a signal, nodding over to the door. With nowhere left to go, Logan knew they would have to fight back to have any chance now.

'When I go,' he whispered, 'just shoot.'

She shook her head, and he signalled again, more forcibly this time. She gave him a pleading look, but without another thought he leaped up and moved quickly across the room. He didn't look back but heard a cascade of gunshots coming from where he'd left Grainger. In between the shots, he heard the man cry out.

She'd got him.

Logan dived for the ground and rolled to a stop. For a moment, everything was silent again. He looked back toward Grainger, who was standing in her well-trained gun stance, and smiled at her. She crouched back down behind the sofa, not smiling back.

He wasn't sure where the little man had been hit, but he could see his legs sticking out through the open doorway. He was definitely down, but Logan knew this wasn't over yet. There were at least two more men – the ones he had seen in the other room. And one of them was Selim.

But where were they now?

Logan looked over at Grainger again. She was hunched behind the sofa, gun held tightly in both hands.

'Cover me,' he said.

This time Grainger nodded.

Logan moved quickly to the doorway, throwing himself up against the wall adjacent to the door. He looked down at the man Grainger had shot. The bullet had caught him in his gut. He wasn't moving, but Logan couldn't tell for sure if he was dead or not. Peering out into the room opposite, where Selim had been, he was surprised to see no signs of the other two men.

He looked back at Grainger and nodded his head, indicating for her to come forward. Then he headed out, pulling up against the doorway to the room across the hall.

Still no sign of Selim.

He stole a glance into the room. It was an office. There was a man on a chair, his hands tied to the chair's arms, his ankles bound to the legs. His face was bloodied. Logan didn't recognise him but his appearance matched what he knew of Blakemore. The small movements in his chest showed he was still breathing.

But Blakemore was alone in the room. So where was Selim? Logan heard the engine of the van starting.

'No!' he shouted.

He couldn't let Selim get away. Not again.

'Go!' Grainger yelled.

Logan didn't hesitate: he spun around and sprinted down the hall. He ran as fast as he could. So fast that when the right turn came, he almost skidded around the corner and had to put his arm out against the wall to keep upright. He bounded down the corridor. He could see Selim outside, climbing into the passenger seat of the van.

Selim glanced back at Logan. The two men, old foes, made eye contact. A look of recognition came to Selim's eyes. But it was also a knowing look.

He knew he was getting away.

Again.

'No!' Logan shouted, desperation now in his voice.

He opened fire but within a second Selim was safely inside the van. Logan held his nerve and resisted the urge to continue pulling the trigger. He couldn't risk hitting the back of the van where Modena was stashed. Logan ran forward, gun held out. But there was nothing he could do. He simply didn't have a shot.

The van sped away, through the open back gates and into the dark abyss that lay beyond. As it's taillights faded into the distance Logan felt a shock of emotion flow through him.

This day, that moment, had dominated his mind for the last five tortuous months. And he'd blown it.

He'd had Selim and he'd let him get away.

How could he have let that man, that monster, get away?!

Logan felt like collapsing to his knees. Then he noticed the other vehicle, the SUV, was still there, next to where the van had been. Feeling a sudden surge of hope he rushed over to it. He'd learned how to hotwire cars long before he'd joined the JIA. Although car technology had changed beyond recognition in all those years, many were still just as easy to start.

The driver's door was unlocked. He climbed in and had a quick look in the ignition and behind the sun-visor. No keys. Hurriedly he began to expose the wires underneath the steering column. If he was quick, he'd only be a few hundred yards behind

Selim's van. He would catch them up. They were in a worn-out panel van, versus this virtually new car. He would catch them up.

He had to.

The tremors in his hands were so bad now that he struggled to even grip the wires, let alone stick them together. He knew, though, that the shaking was as much anticipation and excitement as anxiety.

After what seemed like an eternity, it finally worked. The engine came to life. He couldn't help but smile. He reached out for the handle of the open door.

But then hesitated.

What about Grainger? Could he just leave her there alone? He'd been so hell-bent on getting Selim, he hadn't even thought about her.

But she would be fine, wouldn't she? She was with two subdued men. One had been tortured and was tied to a chair. The other had taken a slug in the gut. He was pretty sure she could handle those two.

But what if there was someone else in there? What if they'd deliberately tried to draw Grainger and Logan outside so they could go back and finish off Blakemore? Surely there were more than just four men in that house?

No, Grainger was a trained FBI agent – she could handle herself, Logan concluded. She would understand. He couldn't let Selim get away. Nor Modena. That was what this was about, after all.

Three gunshots rang out, loud and clear. They made Logan jump.

They'd come from back inside the house.

And that was enough to make up his mind.

He knew what he had to do. He shut down the engine and rushed back toward the house.

Chapter 39

Logan kept his weapon drawn as he re-entered the house. He'd heard three shots in total: two in quick succession, followed by a third moments later. It was hard to tell but he guessed all three shots had been from handguns. But he didn't know whether one or more guns had fired the shots. He could feel the pit of his stomach churning and realised it was out of concern for Grainger. He had no idea who had been shooting, or whether or not Grainger was in trouble.

Approaching the corner of the hallway, he paused, listening for any clues as to who or what might be around the corner. But other than the sound of the breeze coming through the open back door, there was complete silence.

He risked a peek. The man Grainger had shot minutes earlier was still sprawled on the floor, a pool of blood now stretching out underneath his lifeless body. Nothing unexpected there; a shot in the gut would result in a big loss of blood, enough to kill you by itself even if the bullet hadn't damaged any other organs. But what was strange was the neat, circular hole in his forehead, from which a line of blood was worming its way down the side of the man's face. And the handgun that lay on the floor, just inches from his right hand.

Slowly Logan moved toward the man and picked up the blood-soaked handgun. He wiped the gun clean with his jumper. It still had bullets in it, so unless it had somehow been flooded by the blood, it should still work. In any case he wasn't leaving it lying there for someone else to pick up.

Logan placed the pilfered weapon in the waistband of his trousers and trod around the blood pool to reach the office door.

Leaning against the wall, only inches from the doorway, he heard movement coming from inside the office.

It could be Grainger, but it could just as easily be someone else. He waited for it to go quiet, then, without looking, moved quickly into the doorway. He already knew the layout of the room and knew it would take just a split second to scope out a threat, if there was one there at all.

As he moved, his finger once again twitched on the trigger of the gun. Once again he held his nerve. Because although Logan found himself staring down the barrel of a handgun, it was Grainger on the other end. His pose mirrored hers, his gun just inches from her face.

'You're lucky I didn't just shoot you!' she shouted, lowering her weapon.

'Ditto,' he said, lowering his gun in return.

'I would have done too, without even thinking,' she said. 'But I guessed it might be you.'

'I heard shooting, I thought you were in trouble,' he said, moving away from her, further into the room. 'What happened?'

'He's dead.'

She walked up to Blakemore, who was still strapped to the chair. Logan only now noticed that he was covered in blood; he had a hole in his leg, shoulder and one in his chest. This wasn't good. Not at all. Blakemore would have been a key asset. May have known exactly where Selim was going with Modena.

'You were supposed to be keeping an eye on him!' Logan snapped, well aware that he hadn't actually told Grainger to do that, but unable to hide his frustration, as much with the situation as with her.

'Nice to know you're concerned for me.' She indicated to the man out in the corridor. 'He pulled a handgun from nowhere. He was probably shooting at me, not Blakemore,' she said. 'Luckily for me, the guy couldn't shoot straight, him being half dead and all. Still, he managed to get two shots off before I put him down for good.'

'What, you didn't check he was dead? And where's his rifle gone?'

'His rifle's right here,' she snapped, pointing over to the weapon, which was propped up against the wall next to the door. 'I didn't want anyone else getting it. And no, I didn't check he was dead. Did you?'

'No, I went to try to get Modena.'

'No. You went out for Selim,' she shouted, angrily pointing a finger at him. 'You left me here on my own.'

Logan turned away from her and moved over to Blakemore's dead body. He crouched down, inspecting the damage. There was a distressed, pleading stare etched onto the face of the corpse. Logan knew little about the man he had been, but he was sure he had suffered horribly before his death.

'I thought you could handle yourself,' Logan said.

'What, haven't you noticed? I can. Still here, aren't I?'

He didn't want to argue with her and knew that Blakemore being dead wasn't really her fault. It was just a bitter pill to swallow. They'd been so close to Selim, to Modena, to Blakemore. And they'd wound up losing all three of them. It was hard to take.

'Look, I'm sorry,' he said, getting back to his feet and stepping up to her. She didn't move from the spot, but turned her head away from him. 'It's just ...'

'No need to explain,' she said. 'I'm feeling the frustration just as much as you.'

Logan wasn't sure she was. That she could. For him, it was personal. For her, this was just her job. An assignment.

'I'm sorry,' he said again, reaching out and putting a conciliatory hand on her shoulder. 'I'm glad you're all right. You did good.'

His genuine apology seemed to lift her, and she turned her head back to look at him, giving a meek smile.

For the first time, Logan noticed a third body in a heap in the far corner of the office. The blotchy trail of blood that led to it, and the body's ungainly position, suggested the man had been killed by the door before his body had been dumped there. Logan moved over to him and turned him over. He recognised that it was the big man who had loaded Modena into the van earlier. Presumably one of Blakemore's men: the victim of the first gunshots they heard when they were still in the garden.

'Come on,' Logan said. 'We need to check this place out, make sure it's safe.'

'Agreed.'

They set off one after the other, guns drawn, and spent the next ten minutes searching the house, going into each of the many rooms. It was clear from the state of the bedrooms that Blakemore had been accommodating a whole host of people recently. But other than the three bodies downstairs, Logan and Grainger were now alone.

They also found the property's vast wine cellar, a closed-off portion of which it appeared had been used to house Modena. Logan stood staring for a couple of minutes at the solitary chair in the middle of the room. Unable to stop himself from imagining the horrors that had taken place there. Or from reimagining his own horrors at the hands of Selim.

As they headed back toward the office, Logan stopped and looked closely at the man Grainger had shot, the one out in the hallway. He must have been one of Selim's men. Logan saw for the first time just how young he was. He couldn't have been far out of his teens.

In a strange way, Logan felt some sympathy toward him. Their lives may not have been that different at one time. Selim and the other terrorist recruiters worked off a simple and well-oiled model: they took young, disillusioned males, indoctrinated them, radicalised them; gave them a sense of importance and something worth living and dying for. Cradling a dying friend in his arms at seventeen, Logan had been just about as lost and disillusioned as anyone could be, until Mackie had given him a reason to live: trained him to give his all for the cause, to die for his job and his country; taught him a sense of right and wrong, us versus them.

Was he really so different to this young man who had been recruited and trained by Selim?

Perhaps it was possible that Logan as a young, lost man could have been swayed by someone like Selim. But not anymore. He did at least believe in what the JIA stood for. What Selim stood for – advocating the murder of innocent people – Logan could never tolerate.

Logan walked back into the office. Grainger was standing by the desk, next to Blakemore's body.

'Did you get a chance to talk to him?' he said to Grainger, his voice calmer, less critical now. 'Did he say anything at all?'

'No. He didn't say a word. They'd tortured him pretty badly. Just look at him.'

She wasn't wrong. Selim had gone to town on Blakemore. He was missing both of his thumbs, cut off right at the knuckle. Both of his feet were bare and looked like they'd been smashed to pieces, holding little shape or sense of structure. And it was evident he'd taken quite a beating; his face was a big, red, swollen mess.

'Why would they do that to him?' Grainger said, clearly disgusted by the brutality in evidence in front of her.

Her tone suggested it was a rhetorical question and Logan didn't bother to answer. He'd seen worse, but he'd no doubt that Selim had only just got started when he'd been interrupted. This would just be foreplay for Selim.

'Do you think they were trying to get information out of him?' Grainger asked.

'Maybe. Or maybe Selim just wasn't happy not being in full control,' he said. 'So he took it back. The question is, why now? Why not yesterday, two days ago or in two days' time? There has to be a reason he did it now. They had Modena in the van, ready to move. Something happened here. Something we're not seeing.'

'There's a lot we're not seeing,' Grainger conceded.

'Selim must've only had minutes with Blakemore. The wounds are all fresh. We heard the gunshots that killed that guy over there and the one that's in Blakemore's leg. Selim wouldn't have worked so quickly unless he was after something. Blakemore had something he wanted. And he wanted it in a hurry.'

'Well, they already had Modena. He was safely in the van before we heard any shots.'

'You're right. So Blakemore had something else.'

'Like what?'

'Money,' Logan said. The look on Grainger's face suggested she didn't agree.

'Seems to fit if you ask me,' Logan stated. 'I think Selim crossed Blakemore. Not just because he wanted Modena for himself, but because he wanted to make sure he got Blakemore's cut as well.'

'It sounds good, but that's all dependent on Blakemore being behind Modena's kidnapping in the first place. How do you know it wasn't Selim leading it from the get go?'

Which brought Logan right back to where he'd started. The kidnapping. Because if Selim had wanted to snatch someone, he would have done it his way with his own men. He didn't need Blakemore or that big man, or Johnny or Lorik. Something else was at play. And Logan knew one thing that could bring all such men together was money.

So who was paying? And for what?

'We have to call this in,' Grainger said, taking out her phone. 'Get Forensics combing over this place. There must be some clues in here somewhere.'

Logan knew she was right; the house could be a goldmine of information. This was Blakemore's home and his place of business; it would all be here.

'Just give me a few minutes,' Logan said, putting his weapon away for the first time, and moving over toward Grainger and the desk. 'See if we can find anything in here. Diaries, address books – there might be something that can help us.'

'You'll get your prints everywhere,' Grainger said, frowning. 'How would I explain that?'

'Are you worried that I'll contaminate the scene or that you'll have to explain who the mystery man is?'

'The latter.'

'Doesn't matter. It's not like there's a public record of who I am. And I've already left my prints in plenty of other places here. I'll just go down as an unknown.'

'The same unknown who visited Djourou? Who was in the car park yesterday? Who was here tonight? I think that'll raise a few eyebrows, to say the least.'

'I don't see why. They'll mark it up as another one of Blakemore's men. Or Selim's. And anyway, it'll get sorted out in the end. My employers wouldn't let my prints stay on that file.'

'Why do I not doubt that?'

Logan moved over to the desk and started opening drawers and leafing through papers. He noticed that the tremors were still in his hands. They'd lasted longer this time than before. Seeing Selim had made them worse. They weren't just in his hands; he could feel them running through his whole body. There was also a feeling of failure, of dejection.

He found a notebook and flipped through it. Grainger had gone over to the cabinet and was pulling open doors and drawers. But it was too much to expect that there would be a smoking gun right there in front of them.

Logan was tempted to take away some of the documents and spend some more time going over the information. But he knew that could actually hamper the investigation. The key was having every last detail to work with. Some pieces of information, on their own, made no sense, were worthless. It was when they were combined with other information that they became key. Evidence analysis wasn't Logan's role, but he knew taking away something now could harm the whole process. He would have to just hope the police put the required time and effort into it.

Actually, no. What he hoped for was that he found Selim way before that.

Just give me one more chance, he thought.

'Okay, we're wasting time here,' Logan said. 'Let's make a move. Are you calling it in?'

'Yeah.'

'What are you going to tell them?'

'I assume that means you don't want me to tell them the truth? About you, I mean?'

'Can you do that for me?'

'I can try.'

'Thanks.'

He looked at his watch. It was not even three a.m. The sun wouldn't be up for a few hours. He was reluctant to leave, knowing that the key to the whole kidnapping, to Selim's whereabouts, could be right in front of him. But it was the only option.

'Why don't you make your call? I'll go back for the car and pick you up out front.'

Grainger nodded and took out her phone. With one last look at Blakemore, Logan walked out the room, dismay washing over him.

Just one more chance. That was all he wanted.

Chapter 40

Grainger knocked on the passenger window, making Logan jump. She could tell he'd been deep in his own thoughts. He put his hands onto the steering wheel, gripping it tightly, as if hoping the contact would be able to hide the fact that the tremors in his hands were now worse than ever.

She gave him a big smile when she entered the car.

'You done?' he said to her.

'Yep. I spoke to my boss. He wasn't too impressed at being woken up in the middle of the night. But he's sending a team in now. He wants me to wait for them here, contain the scene.'

She saw the deflated look on his face as she spoke.

'But I don't think anyone is coming back here,' she added, smiling again. 'Selim will be long gone by now. So screw it – the Feds will just have to write me up for it.'

Logan did his best to reciprocate her smile, then pulled away from Blakemore's gates and headed back in the direction they'd come from earlier.

Grainger could tell Logan wasn't in a good mood. Losing Selim had really shaken him. She didn't know the full story yet, but she could read him well enough to know that Selim was the big goal for him. They'd had the chance to get Modena out but Logan had opted to go after Selim instead. She'd gone along with it, hoping he was right – that they could bring Selim down and still get Modena out of there. After all, she knew what a monster Selim was and Logan had every right to want to quash him. But in the end he'd been wrong.

It hadn't all turned out bad, though. Blakemore wasn't going to be a problem anymore, that was for sure.

'So what *did* you tell your boss?' Logan asked.

'More or less the truth,' she said.

'More or less?'

'I told him exactly what happened. All except the part about me getting help from an MI6 spy.'

'MI6?' Logan said, managing a laugh. '*That's* what you think I am?'

'You're telling me you're not?' she responded, her smile broadening.

'I'm not telling you anything.'

'Well, regardless, he thinks I was acting alone.'

'He bought that?'

'Why wouldn't he? I'm good at this,' she said, although with no sense of genuine pride. She didn't like having to lie to people.

'We're not left with much to go on now, are we?' he said.

'No, we're not. But you never know when something's going to come around the corner.'

And she really did mean that. She wanted to help Logan. And she knew her own goal would be helped in the process. Selim, the man whom Logan craved, was holding Modena. And she knew she couldn't leave Modena out there with that madman. She had to save Modena; Logan could have Selim. And after that, the whole sorry saga could be put to bed.

She yawned, aware that her focus and strength were waning badly. Part of her wanted to keep going. To get to the end right there and then. But she also knew they'd both had a rough few hours – not just at Blakemore's, but before that as well.

'I guess we've got a bit of time to kill,' she said. 'Before anything else is likely to happen at Blakemore's place.'

'Yeah, I guess we do,' Logan said, looking over at her quizzically.

'It's not even four a.m. yet. And we don't have to check out at the hotel till one. Why not just crash out there? I could do with a rest anyway. You're a tiring guy to be around, Carl Logan.'

He mulled over the prospect for a bit too long. He was clearly torn, wanting to find some excuse to carry on. But where else could they go? What would they do?

'Okay, let's do that,' he said eventually.

It was still dark out when they reached the hotel and the temperature had dropped further. They both shivered as they made their way across the deserted car park, which was barely lit by a single overhead orange streetlight that cast an eerie glow over the cars below.

They made their way up to the second floor and Logan opened the door to their room. He headed in first and sat down on the unmade bed.

'I know you're disappointed, but we did good back there,' Grainger said, still standing by the doorway.

'You think?'

'Yeah, I do.' She closed the door, moved over toward him and stood over him at the side of the bed. 'No way were they expecting us to be so close. Just look at the way they scarpered when we turned up. We've got them on the run now.'

'True. But we may have just panicked them. Modena's chances of getting out of this alive are looking a lot slimmer now.'

'I don't believe that,' she said, not quite fully believing her own words. 'Selim knows we're onto him. He's a long way from home and that may just prove to be a deal-breaker for him. We may have them running scared.'

'I'm glad you were there with me, Grainger,' Logan said, looking up at her and taking her hand. His forward move shocked her initially but she didn't recoil. 'It's not how I normally do things, but I think we made a good team.'

'We did,' she said, squeezing his hand. 'I could never have done all that on my own. I would've called in a whole team of people to do what we just did. You've shown me a thing or two today.'

She truly was grateful for that. When she'd abandoned him the previous day she'd felt so alone. She'd taken it upon herself to finish this off on her own because it had seemed the only way. But whether because of what his job entailed or because his desire to fell Selim so closely aligned with her needs, she knew now that their being together was beneficial for them both. At least until Modena was safe.

But there was more to it than that. Twice in just a few hours Logan had shown himself to be courageous, a true warrior, and he had saved her life. Even though she knew it would only complicate everything, she couldn't help but feel an attraction to him. And it was strong.

The draw that he had on her was so different to what she'd felt for the last man she'd been with – her ex-husband, Tom. He'd been the perfect choice for her. He was tall, dark and handsome, came from a solid family, and was a fellow FBI officer. It was like they had been destined to be together. At least that was what everyone else thought, her dad included. In the end, it really hadn't been quite so perfect. It wasn't that she had never been attracted to Tom, but with him everything had been so easy. And plain.

'And that was the first time you've fired your weapon in the line of duty?' Logan said.

'Yeah. It was,' she said, taking her hand back and looking down at her feet as though embarrassed by the fact.

It wasn't just the first time she had used her gun, it was the first time she had killed someone. She had expected to be a bit more shaken up by it than she was. Maybe it would hit her later on that she had taken a life today. It could just be that she was still in denial about it.

'How are those stitches holding?'

She sat down next to him on the bed, close to him. Her hand reached out and gently touched the wounds on his face, making him flinch. She saw goose-bumps rise on his neck.

'They seem to be doing pretty good,' she said, feeling at the stitches above his eye. 'We can leave those in, I reckon.'

But he didn't seem to be listening. He was staring at her, his thoughts somewhere else. She looked into his eyes and guessed what he was thinking. It was lousy timing and probably completely the wrong move to make at that moment, but despite herself, she was thinking it too.

He gently cupped her face in his right hand and moved his face close to hers so that their lips were only inches apart. She didn't make an attempt to move away at all. She lowered her hand from his face and looked deep into his eyes.

'Carl, what are you doing?' she said.

'I don't know.'

And then she closed the gap completely, kissing him on the lips. Lightly at first, holding the position for a few seconds. Then, almost as if it were synchronised, they both parted their lips and allowed their tongues to dance. He pulled her closer to him and she gave a faint murmur.

They released from the kiss, looking longingly at each other, both waiting to see how the other would react next.

'You sure you're okay with this?' he said.

'Carl, know when to shut up.'

She reached down, took hold of her jumper and pulled it off over her head. He did the same, then drew her in again, kissing her even more passionately than before. After enjoying the kiss for a long period, she began to move away from him, standing up. He followed, their lips not parting.

They began to fumble at each other's trousers. As she reached inside his pants, Logan let out a gasp. She grabbed hold of him, instantly arousing him. With just one hand, he unhooked her bra, exposing her breasts, nipples erect. She pressed up against him, an incredible feeling of flesh on flesh. She murmured again, louder, as he lightly caressed the inside of her leg, moving his fingers slowly upwards, rubbing the outside of her cotton knickers.

They both removed what was left of their clothing, without ever halting their kiss, then fell back onto the bed, Grainger on top, her body draped over Logan as they made love.

Chapter 41

The racket caused by the phone vibrating on the bedside table shook Mackie rudely from his sleep. Rubbing his eyes with one hand, he reached out with the other to pick up the device, fumbling around in the dark before he finally grabbed it.

He didn't check the caller ID before he answered, but said, 'Hello,' with his eyes still half shut.

'Sir, it's me.'

'Winter.' Mackie sat up in bed drowsily and turned on the bedside lamp, then looked at the clock next to where the phone had been on the bedside table. It was five in the morning. 'What the hell is it? Do you know what time it is?'

Mackie's wife, Janet, stirred next to him.

'Sorry, but this is urgent,' said Winter. 'It's about Logan.'

'Shit,' Mackie said. 'Just give me a minute.'

He got up and walked through the dark room, then turned on the light in the en-suite bathroom before entering and shutting the door. He looked at his dishevelled appearance in the mirror, then rubbed his eyes again with his spare hand.

'What's he done now?' he said, trying his best to wake up.

He was guessing it was serious, given the tone of Winter's voice and the fact that he had dared call so early. He wondered whether Winter had been woken in the night too or whether he hadn't actually gone to bed yet. It certainly wouldn't be the first time his assistant had worked through the night.

'Richard Blakemore's dead. Killed in his own home. Two others dead at his house too.'

Mackie suddenly became alert. He cursed loudly, an instinctive reaction, then looked nervously over at the bathroom door, aware he had been too noisy.

Just what kind of chaos had Logan caused now?

'And Modena?'

'No sign of him. Apparently Selim escaped with Modena. But I've heard that Modena was still alive when he left the house.'

'You've spoken to Logan?'

'No, not at all. In fact, what I'm telling you got called in by an FBI agent, Angela Grainger.'

'So this isn't Logan's mess?' Mackie said, confused and also alarmed. How had the FBI got to Blakemore before Logan? Then he thought back to the reports that Logan had been seen exiting the car park in Paris with a woman. It was all starting to make a bit more sense.

'Well, depends how much you believe in coincidences,' Winter said. 'Logan was certainly heading to Blakemore's last time you spoke to him.'

Mackie cursed again. It wasn't hard to put the pieces together. Logan was in cahoots with the FBI agent. Just what the hell was he playing at?

'So what exactly did this FBI agent report?'

'Well, there's no mention of Logan, if that's what you mean.'

'But it does sound like his style,' Mackie said, referring to the growing body count that seemed to be following Logan's every move. 'We need to get hold of him. Now.'

'I've tried calling, but he's not answering. I've got no idea what he's up to now.'

'I've got a pretty good idea what he might be doing,' Mackie said, anger rising up inside him. He clenched his fist, trying his best to resist the urge to smash it against the marble counter.

Even for Logan, this was a step too far. Running around with an FBI agent? Was he really that naive? Or was he just so clouded by his vendetta against Selim that he'd lost all sense of how to carry out his job? Mackie had already resolved to ignore the demands of Sanderson and Lindegaard and keep Logan out in the field, though he'd had a hard time figuring out exactly what had led him to make that decision. He felt a duty toward Logan, there was no doubt about that. He also wanted to bring Selim down once and for all. And Lindegaard had got his back up and he was now intent on defying him regardless, even if Logan wasn't making that decision any easier to stand by.

But he'd also genuinely thought that Logan was about to finish the job off. With Selim escaping Logan's reach and taking Modena with him, maybe he'd been wrong. About everything.

'Is there anything at Blakemore's house to help us?'

'It's too early to tell. The French police are all over that place now. We can't send anyone from the JIA in. We'll just have to sit back and wait to see what they find.'

'Give me some good news. Who has Lindegaard sent out there? Is it someone we can trust?'

'I was coming to that. It's not quite as straightforward as you'd hope, though. It's Evans who's been sent out to Paris.'

Mackie knew of Evans. He was a slippery character, more of a tactician than a combatant. Very different to Logan. But he didn't overly worry Mackie. In fact, his brain might be a helping hand. If Mackie could get the chance to bring him onside.

'So what's not straightforward?' Mackie said, bemused.

He spun around, surprised, when there was a knock at the bathroom door.

'Honey? Is everything okay?'

He took the phone away from his ear and covered the receiver. 'Yes, dear,' he said to his wife. 'I'll be out in a minute. It's work.'

'Work! At this time! Jesus, Charles, do you never know when to stop?'

'Just go to bed! I'll be out in a minute.'

She huffed and muttered something he couldn't make out.

'You still there?' Mackie heard Winter say.

'Yeah, I'm here. You were saying?'

'I was saying I'm not sure if you're going to like this or not. I've managed to get into Lindegaard's phone. I've been tracking his calls and messages for the last few hours.'

'Good work,' Mackie said. He looked in the mirror and smiled. Winter was beginning to show himself to be a real asset.

'Well, it's good and it's bad. You said you wanted some dirt on Lindegaard?'

'Absolutely. What have you got?'

'It seems he's been in contact with a guy called Marko Dragovic. I've dug into him and he's a Serbian immigrant who lives in France.'

'Is this the good news or bad news?'

'Both. The good news is I think we've found some dirt. This Dragovic is a known bad guy. He works as an enforcer for a Serbian gang in Paris: they run prostitution, drugs, the usual kind of thing.'

'He could just be an informant, surely? Don't forget, Lindegaard still runs his own cases for the CIA.'

'Oh, absolutely, I'm pretty sure that's exactly how Lindegaard would know of him. Either directly as an informant or via someone else.'

'So what's the dirt then?'

'Well, that brings me on to the bad news. A couple of hours ago, Lindegaard sent over a picture of Logan to Dragovic and the address of a hotel not far from Blakemore's farmhouse. I think Logan is about to get a very unwelcome visit.'

Chapter 42

Logan and Grainger lay on the bed, naked, their bodies entwined.

'That was unexpected,' Logan said. The same words he had said to himself yesterday when she'd left him stranded by the side of the road, not long after they'd met. This time, though, he didn't feel foolish about it. Not at all. He was buzzing..

'Was it?' Grainger said.

'Unexpected? Yeah. Not that it hadn't crossed my mind the first time I saw you pointing that gun at me.'

She hit his arm playfully.

'You like that sort of thing, do you?' she said.

'I'll try everything once.'

He'd not felt this relaxed for a long time. Not just in the last five months, but in years. All of a sudden, lying there in the bed, all of his troubles seemed so much further away. Not gone entirely, but at least momentarily appeased.

What was it about Grainger? He sensed something about her, like she had gone through so much suffering, much like he had. Maybe physically she hadn't – the perfect skin which covered her entire body proved that much – but he could tell from the look in her eyes that she'd been hurt. And badly. And that meant there was a connection between them, a shared pain, a bond on a much deeper level than he'd felt before. He had noticed the pained look in her when she'd first mentioned her dad to him. Though he suspected her father's death was only part of the story.

'Well, I guess it was a little unexpected,' she said, snuggling her head into him. 'But in a good way.'

She was lying on her side. Her fingers running rings in the soft hairs in the centre of his otherwise smooth chest, her head resting on his shoulder. Her fingers moved to the scar below his right nipple that ran six inches down toward his bellybutton. He winced reflexively at first, not from physical pain, but from memory. With her light touch continuing to dance on his skin, he soon relaxed again.

'It's from a knife wound,' he said, as though having one were the most normal thing in the world. 'One of the oldest ones I have. Scars, I mean.'

'How?'

'From when I was a kid, a teenager. Let's just say I hung out with the wrong crowd quite a bit.'

'And the others?' she asked.

'Too many to tell.'

'Try me.'

Did he want to do this or not? Grainger wouldn't be the first woman he had told some of these stories to, but he had certainly never opened up to anyone about them on an emotional level. And the most recent scars, those that had come from his encounter with Selim, he had never spoken to anyone about.

But his scars, and the memories that went with them, told the story of who he was. They explained his life.

'A lot of them are actually from back then,' Logan began, taking the plunge, 'when I was still a kid. Some of the smaller ones are even older than that one. Cigarette burns, belt buckles, forks.'

'Forks?'

'Yeah. This one here,' he said, leaning forward and pointing to four small white circles on his back, 'this was from a fork. There was a good centimetre or so of it in there. I pulled it out myself. My parents used to beat me pretty badly. My foster parents. Or at least my foster dad did. Did all kinds of shit to me. Gwen, that was my foster mum, just used to watch and cry ... but she never tried to stop him.'

He'd always resented her for that, even though he knew she must have suffered at the man's hands just as much as Logan and the other kids had. Logan had spent five years with them, up until he was fifteen years old. By that time his foster dad no longer dared to touch him. In the end it was Logan who was shipped out for the protection of the others, after Logan took it upon himself to give the old man some comeuppance.

Grainger continued to work her hands around his body without saying a word. He didn't know whether he should carry on talking or not.

He did.

'That one there.' He pointed at a scar on his left thigh, close to his groin. It looked like a starfish, the skin having been pulled inwards at awkward angles during healing to create what looked like the creature's legs. 'That was the first time I got shot. I was twenty-two by that point, already on the job.'

'That must have hurt like hell.'

No shit. They all had.

He'd been on a mission in Russia, on the trail of one of the original oligarchs a few years after the break-up of the Soviet Union. Like many others, the man he was after had forced his way to the top through a heady mixture of violence and corruption. His mistake, though, was in trying to take his brand of business management into the western world. Logan had eventually got his man following an armed siege of one of the oligarch's properties, which had been more like a barracks than a home. Logan had been shot in the process of trying to flee the property with the captured oligarch, before ultimately taking him into the custody of the Americans.

'At the time, that was the most pain I'd ever felt,' he said. 'It took months for the limp to go. I've only been shot once since then, in my left arm.' She moved her hand up to that scar, which he'd received in Poland, where he'd been on the case of a human trafficking gang. 'That was even worse because of the bone damage. It took so long to recover that my arm was like a twig before I was finally able to use it again. The muscle had just disappeared through not being used. Since then I've tried to make sure I don't get shot. Never did like hospitals.'

'How old were you when you started this?' she said. 'Your job, I mean.'

'I was seventeen,' he said. The matter-of-fact tone of his voice may have suggested that he was nonchalant about it. But that couldn't have been further from the truth.

She raised her head, looking shocked.

'It was the best thing that could have happened for me,' he said. Though these days, he wasn't always sure he believed that anymore. 'I was going nowhere in life; had run away from home, was messing around with the wrong people. I was dealing drugs by the time I was sixteen. You've just seen the scars. You don't get many friends in that business. I probably wouldn't have lived past twenty if I hadn't come into this job.'

'And how do you come into it? What you've just described doesn't seem to be the sort of profile the intelligence agencies go for. No offence.'

'None taken. What, you thought they only accept people with solid degrees and a stable family background?'

'I guess so. Well, I don't know what I thought. I never really thought about it.'

'Actually lost souls make great agents. They've got nothing to lose. I had nothing to lose. MI5, MI6 and the likes might be full of university graduates and toffs, but that certainly doesn't fit the bill for what I do.'

'So you're really not MI6?

'No.'

'I guess it makes sense. So how did it happen? I'm assuming you didn't see an ad in the local newspaper.'

'When I was seventeen I got friendly with another dealer. He was quite a bit older than me but we used to cruise around together. His name was Pete. We'd been working together for months when he asked me to be his right-hand man. He said he wanted to take out the Yardies, the gang that ran one of the areas near where we lived. He was my friend, so I went along with it. I was young and stupid – what else was I going to do? Only problem was, the Yardies got wind of it, and when they confronted us, five against two, I got my first real scar. The one across my chest.'

She moved her hand up to it again, stroking over it with her fingers.

'You were lucky.'

He nodded. 'And not for the last time. But they hadn't wanted to kill me. If they had, they would have done. But Pete, he wasn't so lucky. He got knifed straight in the heart. He bled to death in my arms.'

The tone of Logan's voice betrayed that the death of his friend was still a source of pain and discomfort for him. That was the first time he had ever seen someone die. The first time he had ever seen a dead body. He still regarded it as the key turning point in his life.

'I thought I was a man back then,' he said. 'But I wasn't. I was a kid. I had been in scrapes before and had always come out on top. I thought I was invincible. Thought we were invincible. But you learn about these things the hard way.

'A few days later, when I was out of hospital, I was approached by a guy. He told me Pete was undercover, working for him.'

'And that was the agency?'

'Kind of. He said he wanted me to finish Pete's job for him. Finish off the Yardies.'

'My God – what, you killed them?'

'No, I told the guy to go fuck himself. Said if he ever came to me again I'd cut his balls off. I wasn't really in a good frame of mind at that moment.'

Grainger laughed. 'Wow, you've got some real good interview skills.'

'Yeah, well, he must have liked my response. He didn't go away. He started paying me odds and sods to do errands. Finding out info, spreading rumours. I never really asked questions about who he was or why he was getting me to do these things. I didn't have much else to do and he was giving me easy money. Not long after I started running those errands, the Yardies were dead. Murdered by another gang. He'd had me setting the bait without me even knowing it.'

'That's pretty sneaky.'

Logan nodded. 'This was all for some other agency at this point. A specialist unit dealing with organised crime. Not who I work for now. But it was the same guy. He moved up in the world and took me with him. When I started in that new role, when I was nineteen, they got me the training. How to fight, how to use knives, guns. They taught me just about everything I know. Turned me into a machine.'

The last words were said with bitterness, the only bitterness he'd shown in the whole retelling.

Grainger moved her fingers up to the long scar on his neck. 'What about this one?'

'No,' he said, taking her hand and pushing it back down to his chest. 'That's enough about me. What about you?'

She ignored the question and moved her hand back. 'That's the one, isn't it?'

'The one what?'

'The one that hurt the most.'

Yes, it was, he thought. But there was more than just his pain the night he'd received it.

'The one that's given you the anxiety,' she added.

His body was now tense again. The ease and relaxation he'd felt was quickly ebbing away. She caressed the area and he tried to remain calm, tried to keep his mind on her and not the pain.

'What happened?' she said.

He brushed her off and got up from the bed then walked toward the bathroom.

'I'm sorry. Just give me a minute.'

'It was Selim, wasn't it? Who did that to you.'

He didn't answer as he headed into the bathroom, closing the door behind him. He hung his head over the sink, unsure what to think. He was glad he had opened up to her. Talking to her about his life had given him a feeling of great power. But he wasn't yet ready to broach the subject of his history with Selim. The pain from that experience was still all too real, too vivid in his mind. And his business with Selim was unfinished. He wanted to tell Grainger about his experiences, what Selim had done to him, he really did. But not yet.

He washed his face in cold water that stung the wounds he'd received in his fight with Lorik and sent a shiver through his whole body. After drying his face he headed back out to the bedroom and stood in the doorway, looking at Grainger. She was sitting upright on the bed, the upper half of her body exposed, the lower half tangled in the soft bed sheet. She looked sensational. She gave him a smile. It wasn't a light-up-your-face smile. But it was enough. Being there with her made him feel stronger than he could ever remember.

'Thank you for telling me,' she said.

'Thank you for listening.'

'Try me, anytime.'

He walked over to the bed and lay back down next to her. Her body felt warm against his. He was about to lean in for a kiss when there was a knock at the door.

'Housekeeping,' said a male voice in French.

Logan and Grainger looked at each other, suspicions immediately aroused. But Grainger looked just a little scared too, Logan thought.

'You don't think ...'

She trailed off. She didn't need to finish the sentence. Logan was thinking the exact same thing. He threw his jeans on and creeped to the window. He wasn't about to put his face up to the spy hole on the door. He pulled the corner of the curtain just a quarter of an inch to look out. When he turned back to Grainger she was staring at him and the look on his face must have confirmed her fears. But he wasn't scared. Or even anxious. He was angry.

'Get your gun. Your clothes,' Logan said. 'Go to the bathroom and lock the door.'

Chapter 43

Grainger quickly shut and locked the bathroom door and began to throw on her clothes. Seconds later there was a crashing sound from the bedroom. Then banging. Muffled voices ... Then silence.

She finished dressing, grasped the gun in her hand, and put her ear to the door. But the only sound she could hear was the thudding of her heart in her chest.

She knew what was happening. Someone had come for them. Selim? The remnants of Blakemore's men?

Her head was in a spin. What the hell was she going to do?

A thought struck her. Did whoever was out there even know she was in the bathroom? If not, shouldn't she just keep quiet, keep herself hidden? That was surely why Logan had told her to go in there.

But then Logan had been willing to risk his life for hers. If he was in trouble, she had to try and help him.

Grainger jumped, her heart lurching in her chest, when there was a gentle tap on the door from the other side.

'We know you're in there, Agent Grainger,' the man said in an accent so thick the English was almost unintelligible.

Grainger gasped and lifted a hand to her mouth. A cold shiver swept across her. They knew her name?

'Please come out now. Or we'll cut his throat. And then we'll cut yours too.'

'Angela, come out,' Logan shouted. 'It's the only way.'

She heard a thumping sound and a groaning exhale from Logan. What choice did she have?

'Open the door, slide the gun, then step out.'

She did exactly as she was told. She pulled the door open just a few inches, slid the gun on the floor. It clattered to a stop next to a pair of thick black boots.

Grainger took a step forward, caught just a glimpse of the man the boots belonged to - a garish Frankenstein mask covering his face - before he grabbed her and pulled her into him, spinning her around.

Frankenstein was big, as wide as he was tall. His thick arm wrapped around Grainger's neck like a boa as he held her close up against his body, squeezing her tight. As she looked over toward the splintered bedroom door, she saw Logan on his knees. Another man, dressed similarly to the first in dark clothes but with a nightmarish Clown mask, was standing behind him, a baseball bat held tightly across Logan's neck.

Logan looked into her eyes. No pain, or fear. Just pure rage.

With his thick arm wrapped around her, Grainger could sense the muscular bulk of Frankenstein, hear and feel his breath on her neck. He smelled of stale sweat and cigarettes and a sickly sweet aftershave; the combination made her gag.

Frankenstein squeezed harder on her neck and Grainger writhed and scraped at his arm, trying to get him to loosen his grip.

Logan began to laugh. The Clown pulled harder on the baseball bat. Logan winced as he did so, but he didn't stop laughing.

'You really don't want to do that to her,' Logan wheezed.

'No?' said Frankenstein. He squeezed her neck even harder, and Grainger thought her head might actually explode.

Her mind was going into a panic. It felt like the man was crushing the life from her. She stared deep into Logan's eyes, not sure what he was doing, not sure what he was expecting her to do.

'Believe me,' Logan strained to say. His face was red, his eyes bursting out of his head. 'I've been there before.'

Grainger didn't need a second invitation. She now knew exactly what Logan meant. She mustered all the power she could as she raised her right leg and threw her foot back and up, aiming for Frankenstein's groin. The connection was solid and the man let out a loud groan, weakening his grip on her neck just enough. She immediately took a deep gulp of air.

There was a commotion over where Logan was being held, but she was too engrossed to pay attention to what was happening. She had to assume he was making his move too.

Before Frankenstein had a chance to recover, Grainger thrust back an elbow, aiming for the point just around his waistband where his bladder was. The elbow dug deep and his legs kicked out involuntarily as she'd known they would, causing him to stumble backward. He took her with him, but his grip around her neck was now almost gone entirely.

She grabbed at Frankenstein's arm, pulling it down, then swivelled her body around. Now at his side, she delivered a double-blow: she aimed a fist downward, making contact at the side of his leg, just above the knee, causing it to buckle inward, and almost immediately she smacked him with an open palm up against the base of his neck. Frankenstein fell into a heap on the floor. Before he could move an inch, she delivered another blow to the back of his neck, and he was out cold.

Four strikes was all it had taken to fell a man more than twice her size. She'd aimed for pressure points that she knew would make a difference. Tricks her dad had taught her when she was just a skin-and-bone teenager.

Only when she was content that the man was no longer a threat did she look over to where Logan had been. He was now sitting on top of the Clown, whose arms were pinned down by Logan's knees. Logan's face was snarling but he was otherwise restrained. Not at all like he had been with Lorik.

'Nice moves,' he said, looking up at her and winking.

'Not so bad yourself,' she said.

Logan pulled the mask off the man he'd felled. Grainger didn't recognise him. His eyes were rolling, his head lolling from side to side. He was conscious, but completely dazed.

'Who sent you?' Logan snapped, the anger in his voice clear. The man murmured a sound but no words came out. Grainger moved over and grabbed her gun, checked the chamber. A habit.

Logan jumped up, went over and grabbed his gun too, then returned to the man. He kneeled down on him and stuffed the barrel of the gun into his mouth.

'Logan, no!' Grainger shouted.

The man began to moan and writhe. Logan took the gun out of his mouth.

'Who sent you?!' Logan spat.

The man again murmured but whatever he tried to say was indecipherable. Logan grabbed the barrel with his other hand and, with a backhanded swipe, he smacked the butt against the man's jaw. Blood and teeth spluttered out of his mouth.

'Who sent you?!' Logan screamed.

He grabbed the man by the scruff of his neck, lifted his head up into the air, then smacked it off the floor. Once. Twice. A third time. His body squirmed for just a second. After that, he went still.

'Stop it!' Grainger screamed. 'What the hell is wrong with you?'

She shook her head. She was just as angry as Logan that they had been attacked, and just as confused as to who the two men were, but the brutality of Logan's methods, which seemed to come so naturally to him, shocked her.

She was also scared. Just who was after them? All she wanted to do now was to go, as fast and as far away as they could.

'We have to go, Logan. We don't know who else is out there.'

'Shit,' he said, sitting back.

Moving to the side, he quickly rifled through the man's pockets, but other than a set of car keys there was nothing there. He stood up and marched toward the bathroom where Frankenstein lay slumped near the doorway. Grainger held out a hand to him but Logan brushed past and crouched down next to the man.

'Logan, I'm going,' she said, turning away from him and making toward the door. 'We don't have time for this.'

She wasn't sure whether she really meant it, whether she really would have walked away and left him there with the two men. But in the end it didn't matter. As she reached the bedroom door, she heard his voice from behind her.

'Okay, there's nothing more we can do here. I'm coming with you.'

Chapter 44

Logan and Grainger jumped into the Fiat and sped out of the hotel car park. They hadn't spoken to each other since leaving their room, even though they'd moved in unison like two long-time partners, scanning and scoping out the area as they'd made their way to the car. There had been nothing out of the ordinary. No signs of anyone else after them.

Logan was again driving the car. There was only one place he knew to go to now. The JIA safe house. Although he was somewhat reticent to do that, knowing that if Mackie were there he would surely only be walking into a confrontation that he didn't want to have, it had to be the safest option.

'Who do you think they were?' Granger asked after they'd been driving for more than ten minutes.

'I don't know. I was trying to find out.'

Grainger tutted. 'There's no need to be like that with me.'

She was right, but he didn't feel like apologising. He could still feel the rage boiling up inside him. Yet another emotion that he was so inept at keeping under control.

'Where are we going anyway?'

'I'm going back to Paris.'

Grainger didn't respond initially. 'Why?' she said eventually.

'I don't know,' he said. 'Where else would we go? It's the only place that I'm sure is safe.'

'Do you think it would be better if I stayed around here? I'd be out of harm's way with the police team. I could help with the work going on at Blakemore's. There's nothing in Paris for me.'

They reached a T-junction and Logan stopped the car and looked over at her. She seemed upset. Let down, even.

He was still seething inside. Not with Grainger, but with the situation. He wanted to know who those men were. He wanted to make whoever had sent them after him pay. But he also knew the special moment he'd been having with Grainger had been ruined. Which only made him all the more angry. It was pointless to take it out on her, though.

'I'm sorry,' he said.

'For what?'

'For our time together having been spoilt like that.'

'It's not your fault,' she said, putting a hand on his thigh and giving it a squeeze.

Her touch made just a sliver of anger dissipate. He turned to the right when the road was clear, then glanced over at Grainger again. He didn't like the prospect of leaving her behind, but at the moment they were stuck. Until there was another lead to follow, he simply had no idea what to do next. He guessed her being at Blakemore's house had to be the best way to keep on top of the case. She'd surely be safe with the police and FBI team there. And he was content that he could handle himself if anyone were to follow him and confront him.

'Are you sure you'd be okay if I left you?'

'You really don't think yet that I can take care of myself?' she said, smiling at him.

It was true, she certainly had a few good moves.

'Okay, where shall I drop you off?' he said.

'Just take me near to where we stopped in the night. I'll walk from there.'

Logan didn't say anything more. He pulled the car over to the side of the road and then waited for the right moment to turn around. It would only take thirty minutes to retrace their way back to Blakemore's house.

After heading a few miles back the way they'd just come, Logan's phone began to ring. He knew it would be Mackie. He and Winter had been calling on and off for hours. Logan had not been deliberately ignoring them. There'd just been no opportune time to answer.

'Go on, take it,' Grainger said.

He only hesitated for another second.

'At least I now know you're still alive, I suppose,' Mackie said without any pleasantries.

'Why, were you not expecting me to be?'

'Well, funny you should ask that, but this time I wasn't sure. You're making a lot of enemies on your little mission.'

Logan gritted his teeth. Did Mackie know about the two men at the hotel? How could he?

'Who were they?' Logan snapped.

'I can't explain now,' Mackie said, all but confirming Logan's suspicion. 'What happened?'

'Two grunts paid a visit to our hotel room. They shouldn't have bothered.'

'Are they still alive?'

'Does it matter?'

'I'm trying to help you here, Logan.'

'I'm struggling to see how. But to answer your question, yes, they're alive.'

'Good. I'll get the local police down there straight away. See if we can get hold of the two attackers.'

'Who were they?' Logan asked again.

'You need to come in,' Mackie said, his disregard for the question only riling Logan further. 'I can help you, Logan, but you have to come in first.'

'I'm on my way.'

'So is she still with you?' Mackie said. Not shouting exactly, but the irritation and anger in his voice was evident.

'Is who with me?'

'You know who: the FBI agent you've been running around with. Is she still with you?'

There was no point in lying anymore. Logan wondered for a brief moment how Mackie had found out. But it wasn't hard. Logan had told Mackie he was going to Blakemore's and then a few hours later Grainger made the call to her colleagues about what went down there. Even though she hadn't mentioned Logan at all, it wasn't hard for Mackie to link the two. By now, he would know everything there was to know about Grainger.

'Yeah, she is.'

'Did you think I wasn't going to find out about her? Do you know what covert means? For fuck's sake, Logan. Co. Vert. I got a call at five a.m. saying they're sending a team of crime scene investigators to Blakemore's place. *Three* more dead bodies. What, you've got shares in an undertaker's now?'

This was just the ear-bashing Logan had been expecting. The only way to get through this was to ride over the top of it. Which, given Logan's bad mood, was easier than it sounded.

'You always assume the worst about me, don't you?' Logan said, barely trying to hide his own irritation. 'Have you ever considered getting my side to the story before jumping to your baseless conclusions?'

'It's no assumption,' Mackie said. 'You're always kind enough to leave a trail of destruction, so it's pretty fucking obvious really. Why exactly *are* you with her anyway?'

'Because it was the only way I was going to get away from the police. Who think I'm a murderer. It's a far better option than getting myself nabbed. Besides, if you ask me, it's not worked out too bad so far.'

'Well no, not if your aim is to achieve a good body count. But it's not. The aim is, and always has been, to rescue Modena.'

'And find those responsible.'

'You should just be glad that your little friend decided not to tell *her* superiors that she's with you. That would *not* have gone down well. For either of you. Let me ask you this, Logan. If *she* was a *he*, would you still be running around as a twosome?'

'What's that supposed to mean?' Logan said, offended. Though he knew that the answer was a clear 'no'. Not a chance. But that didn't mean that it wasn't beneficial to have teamed up with Grainger.

'I'll take that as a no,' Mackie concluded. 'And what it means is that I don't want this investigation and our involvement in it compromised because you felt like having a little bit of action along the way. You're not James Bond.'

'Nothing's compromised. We almost had them, Mackie. I'm not kidding, we really almost had them. Modena was right there. And Selim …'

Mackie must have heard the dismay in Logan's voice.

'Okay, okay,' he said. 'Look, the police have turned that place over and they might have some stuff that will help you. I want you to come back to the safe house straight away so we can figure out where to go from here. Got it?'

'Yeah. I'm on my way anyway.'

'Good. And Agent Grainger?'

'I'm dropping her off at Blakemore's house,' Logan said, glancing over at her.

'I'm glad to hear it. And I'm glad you're both safe. You've got two hours.'

Chapter 45

Mackie ended the call with Logan and looked up at Winter, who was standing on the other side of the desk.

'So he's okay then,' Winter said; a statement rather than a question. He'd been listening in to the call.

'Seems to be. We can at least be sure he's alive,' Mackie said. And he was genuinely relieved about that. 'I think it's about time we had a little chat with our friend, don't you?'

Winter smiled. 'I'll go and get him.'

Winter headed over to the door of Mackie's office, then unlatched the bolt before opening it. After their last intrusion from Lindegaard, Mackie was taking measures to ensure they wouldn't be disturbed again. Requesting a meeting with Lindegaard had been the first thing he'd done that morning. He'd arrived at the office before seven a.m., unable to get back to sleep after the earlier call he'd taken from Winter. Since then, he and Winter had been planning exactly how to handle Lindegaard.

During that time it'd become apparent to Mackie that Winter had in fact been working through the night. He'd now been on shift for over twenty-four hours. Although he still claimed to be alert and raring to go, Mackie could tell that his concentration was quickly fading. They just needed to get through this next meeting, for which they were now ten minutes late, before Mackie was going to pack him off home for some much needed rest.

Since last speaking to Lindegaard, Mackie had also brought Evans into the fold. He was the agent Lindegaard had brought in to replace Logan. But the playing field had changed quite considerably in Mackie's favour now. As it was, Evans was on his way to the safe house in Paris where he would await further instructions from Mackie.

It had also been a nervous few hours, though. Mackie had experienced conflicting emotions when he'd heard about Dragovic. On the one hand, he had felt satisfaction that his hunch about pushing Lindegaard had been right. But then, even though he knew Logan was more than adept at taking care of himself, he'd felt anxious about what was going to happen to him. Both Mackie and Winter had been trying desperately to get hold of Logan to warn him. They couldn't tell him exactly what the problem was; he did not need to know what was happening with Lindegaard, not yet. But they had at least wanted him to be prepared for whatever attack was coming. They'd been too late, though. The strike had already come. Thankfully Logan was skilled enough, or perhaps just lucky enough, to have dealt with it.

Now it was time to turn Lindegaard's underhanded approach on its head.

'Good morning,' Mackie said with a beaming smile as Lindegaard was ushered into the office by Winter. He had deliberately tried to sound over-the-top upbeat. The sour look that Lindegaard gave him suggested it had done the job of irritating him.

'What's this about, Charles?' Lindegaard said, walking over to the desk but not sitting down. He stood with his arms folded, a constant glare on his face.

'What do you think it's about?' Mackie said, waving his arms about theatrically. 'It's about our favourite agent.'

'So where the hell is he?' Lindegaard said. 'I expected him to be back home by now.'

'Are you sure about that?' Winter asked, coming over and sitting down at the desk.

Lindegaard looked down at him and huffed but didn't respond.

'That was quite some mess he caused last night,' Lindegaard barked. 'Three more dead bodies? Logan is no longer on this case. I thought that had been made perfectly clear. So why the hell is he still running around out there causing me problems? You know, I should sanction all three of you for this. Disobeying a very direct and very clear order.'

'Oh, Jay, I really don't think you want to do that,' Mackie stated, unfazed.

'Tell us about Marko Dragovic,' Winter said. 'He lives in Paris, right? So how do you know him?'

Again Lindegaard didn't respond to Winter's question, but for the first time the confidence and arrogance behind his eyes seemed to fade.

'Let's not play any more games here,' Mackie said, the false pleasantness now removed from his tone. 'We know what you did. We know about Dragovic.'

'And the two men who were sent to Logan's hotel are now in police custody,' Winter added. 'I wonder what we'll find out from them. Did you really think this would turn out in your favour?'

'You little piece of –'

'Ah, ah, don't take it out on Winter. You've brought this on yourself.'

Lindegaard unfolded his arms and sat down, as though for the first time willing to take the conversation seriously.

'What do you want?' he said. 'I could report both of you for this. There's only one way you could know about Dragovic. Are you aware you've both committed a crime?'

Mackie laughed and shook his head. 'Really? You're going down that route?'

He knew that Lindegaard was at least partially right. They'd had no approval to hack Lindegaard's phone and messages. It wasn't a crime exactly – the relationship between the actions of the JIA and the law were somewhat murky. The way they had gone about it, though, was certainly against the JIA's own procedures. But then, so was what Lindegaard had done. And the way Mackie saw it, his adversary had a lot more to lose.

'So what do you want?' Lindegaard repeated, the colour in his face dwindling as the reality of the situation dawned on him.

Mackie pondered the question for a good while, though he knew what the answer was. 'You call off the dogs. Logan stays on the case. Me and Winter too.'

'That's it?' Lindegaard said, laughing nervously, as if surprised that he was getting let off so lightly.

Mackie was aware that was the case. If he wanted to, he could take what he knew to the other committee members. With what

Lindegaard had done, they might even be able to get him removed from his position at the JIA altogether. But this wasn't a boardroom scuffle where Mackie was going for some power play. This was the world of the secret intelligence services. In the long run, having this card in his deck, this dirt on Lindegaard, would be much more valuable. Plus it meant that he could keep his and Winter's tactics, and Winter's technical nous, under wraps should they find themselves in a corner again in the future.

'That's it,' Mackie said.

Lindegaard shifted in his seat as though unsure what to think about Mackie's proposition. Eventually, without saying another word, he got to his feet and began to make his way toward the door.

'Oh, actually, Jay,' Mackie said, getting to his feet, 'there is one more thing.'

Lindegaard turned around to face Mackie.

'Logan doesn't yet know about what you did. And it'll stay that way as long as you keep off our backs. That man really has a penchant for revenge, if you know what I mean.'

Mackie smiled as his words sank in and Lindegaard's complexion turned a ghostly white. Without another word, Lindegaard spun around and walked out of the room.

Chapter 46

Before dropping Grainger off, Logan had swapped phone numbers with her and they'd made a clear commitment to be in touch later in the day. Logan had then made the journey back to Paris and arrived at the safe house ten minutes outside the two-hour limit that Mackie had given him. Inside, he walked casually into the lounge, expecting to see Mackie there, so he was shocked to see a man he didn't recognise sitting at the desk, facing the door. Logan guessed the man was a few years younger than himself. He was fresh-faced and dressed in an open-necked shirt with a blue blazer.

Logan stopped in the doorway, alarmed by the unexpected presence, and his hand instinctively reached toward the butt of the handgun stuffed in his trousers.

The man looked up and met Logan's eyes. 'He's here,' he said.

'Logan? You're there?' said Mackie, over the conference phone.

Logan sighed and carried on walking over to the desk, eyeing the young man suspiciously.

'I'm here,' he said.

'Good. Well, take a seat.'

'I thought you would be here too.' The tone of his voice showed Logan wasn't pleased by the surprise.

'Well, I would have been if you hadn't left me with such a shitstorm to deal with back here. Things are getting complicated, Logan, very complicated.'

'And who is this?' Logan said, sneering at the man behind the desk, who reciprocated Logan's less-than-impressed look.

'This is Paul Evans.'

Evans nodded on cue.

'My replacement,' Logan concluded, starting to put the pieces together.

'Well, in a way, yes,' Mackie said. 'But I think we can all come to a compromise on that. I don't think you realise just how hard I'm working to keep you on this case, Logan. Evans has been drafted in to replace you, against my say-so, but luckily for you he's willing to help us both out here. For some reason, I still trust that with you on board we can get to the bottom of Modena's disappearance more quickly than we can without you.'

'Is that so,' Logan said, looking Evans in the eye. The young agent held Logan's stare, a stoic expression on his face.

It didn't surprise Logan that he hadn't recognised the face of Evans, a fellow agent. Unless he'd worked with someone directly then there was no reason for him to know their face or their name.

'And whose decision was it to replace me?' Logan questioned.

'It was the committee's decision. Nothing I could do about that.'

'Lindegaard,' Logan stated.

'It's not important right now,' Mackie said. 'What's important is that you keep out there, keep on after Modena. Let me handle the politics.'

Logan didn't push the subject, but he knew it would be Lindegaard behind the decision to remove him from the case. He'd never seen eye to eye with the man. Although they rarely had direct dealings, their paths had crossed numerous times in the past. Most recently, and most regrettably, had been when Logan had slept with the man's sister. He hadn't known that fact beforehand; it was just one of life's coincidences. After a fractious relationship, in which Logan had only been interested for a couple of weeks, he'd had a tough time rebuking her many subsequent advances. Ultimately that had incurred the significant wrath of her older brother, to whom she'd been mouthing off about the nasty man who'd been treating her like dirt.

That was all in the past, as were all their other run-ins, but Lindegaard was a man who held a grudge. Logan guessed that in that respect, the two men were very alike.

'So what are we doing here?' Logan said, looking at Evans as he spoke but talking to Mackie.

'Tell me what happened at Blakemore's house,' Mackie said. 'Why is he dead?'

'Isn't it in the police file?' Logan said.

'The one that conveniently omits the presence of a certain super-spy?'

'Thanks for the accolade. Yeah, that file.'

'Well, it gives me some of it, but I want to hear it from the horse's mouth, so to speak.'

'We can safely say that the link to Blakemore was good. We saw Modena being dragged to a van at the back of the house.'

'Did you actually see Modena's face?' Evans said.

'No,' Logan sighed, raising an eyebrow. He did not like being challenged by the young agent, whose stuffy accent suggested to Logan that he was likely to have come from a well-to-do family. Exactly the kind of agent Logan had come across time and time again in his days, who thought he was the next big thing but ultimately ended up taking a desk job after finding fieldwork just that bit too, well, real.

'But you're sure it was him?' Evans queried.

'Unless Selim and Blakemore have kidnapped someone else recently then yeah, I'm sure.'

'Any idea what was happening out there?' Mackie said.

'I think that Blakemore has to be key to the kidnapping. That's the only explanation that works for me. Whatever this is about, Blakemore was the key organiser. Has to be that way. He recruited Selim into this.'

'You don't think it was the other way around?'

'No chance. If this was Selim's deal then he wouldn't have bothered with Blakemore in the first place. He didn't need him. Blakemore brought in Selim to help out. Provide them with the terrorism link to keep us all guessing. They probably knew each other through business deals. Drugs and weapons and the like. We should check out that connection.'

It was a connection they should have found when they were investigating Selim before. It might have prevented Modena's kidnapping happening in the first place if Blakemore had already been locked up.

'That's already underway,' Mackie confirmed. 'With a bit of hard negotiation we've got direct access to what's coming out of

Blakemore's house and all of his personal records. We're looking over every financial transaction that Blakemore has been a party to in the past five years.'

Logan nodded. 'What I want to know is how and why Blakemore got involved in the first place.'

'Money would be my guess,' Mackie said.

'That's where I'm going too,' Evans chipped in.

Logan again gave him the raised eyebrow, this time for the unexpected interjection.

'What? You might have a couple of days' head start, but this sort of puzzle is exactly what I'm good for,' Evans explained. 'The way I see it, Blakemore hired Selim to provide the front for the operation, muddy the water a bit.'

Logan had to admit, he was pleasantly surprised by Evans's comment. Finally someone else who was on his wavelength. Not that it made the man's presence any more welcome for Logan. He had no intention of working out in the field with him.

'But Selim must have planned to cross Blakemore all along,' Evans said, looking at Logan. 'He probably got paid handsomely by Blakemore for his part, knowing all the time that he was going to kill the guy and run off with Modena. For Selim, it's all win-win. What we still don't know is who paid Blakemore in the first place. Or why Modena was kidnapped.'

'Well, I'm not sure that's the biggest concern right now,' Mackie argued. 'The most important thing is still to rescue Modena. The whys and wherefores of Blakemore won't help us to locate Selim. Or Modena.'

Logan had to agree with that. Knowing who had hired Blakemore and why was all very interesting, but it didn't help get Modena back. And it didn't help get to Selim, which, for Logan, was still the main event. But then …

'If Modena was snatched for a reason,' Logan mused, a thought hitting him, 'that reason could still be important. What if Modena was kidnapped because he's got some priceless information that's worth a lot of money to someone?'

'Like what?' Mackie said.

'I've no idea. But surely it's important that we find out? If they were after information, and Selim and his cronies now have it, what further damage could there still be to come?'

'It still doesn't help us actually *find* Selim,' Mackie said. 'I'm not denying that I'm dying to find out who hired Blakemore and why, but that's got to go on the back burner. At least, for you it has. We've got a team already going over Blakemore's life: his bank accounts, credit cards, business dealings, phone records. As well as helping you, Evans will lead that side of the investigation. Sooner or later, we'll find out who hired Blakemore and why. But right now, you concentrate on getting Modena back. Find Selim.'

Logan mulled over Mackie's words. It should have been what he wanted to hear: an order to go after Selim. That's what he had wanted from the start. Much more than he had wanted to rescue Modena. But now, he felt like there was still a big piece of the jigsaw missing. Like there was much more to Modena's kidnapping than met the eye. It was an uncomfortable feeling.

'Is there anything at all that the police have found so far that could help us locate Selim?' Logan said.

'It's going to take them a long time to process,' Mackie admitted. 'Evans can give you the low-down when we're finished on this call.'

Another thought suddenly came to Logan. 'When we arrived, they were already loading up the van to go. That was before we heard any gunfire. And given Blakemore's state when we found him, I think Selim's ambush had only just started.'

'Blakemore's state? You're making it sound like he was drunk and disorderly. He was a complete mess!'

'I know he was. But it was nothing that couldn't have been done in five minutes. And the van was being loaded up by one of Blakemore's guys. It wasn't just Selim's man. That to me suggests that Blakemore thought they were getting out of there. They had a plan to go somewhere else. Maybe it was because of the heat on them, or maybe they had planned to move out all along. Either way, the key to where they were going will be in that house somewhere.'

'And you think Selim will go there still? The same place Blakemore had planned for them?'

'It's got to be worth a shot. We know Selim's only been in France for a few days. It would have made more sense for him to let Blakemore arrange all those details. Then all Selim had to do was kill him and he already had everything he needed planned and in place for him.'

'I agree,' Evans said, catching Logan's eye, who nodded in response. 'It's definitely worth checking it out.'

'Okay, we'll keep that in mind. How are you doing for supplies?' Mackie asked.

'I need some more magazines,' Logan said.

'Okay, there's fresh equipment in the cupboard in the bedroom next to you. Anything else?'

'Did you get my IDs?'

'Yeah. Why, you planning on going somewhere?'

'Not yet, but it's about time I swapped over. Burrows has been all over the place for the past couple of days. And he very nearly got me into trouble.'

'Well, just keep your eye out. Don't assume they're not still after you.'

'Who's not still after me?' Logan said, agitated that Mackie hadn't yet said anything more about the two attackers back at the hotel.

'I can't explain just now. Like I said before, you're making a lot of enemies out there.'

Logan sensed he wasn't going to get any more information than that. He didn't know why Mackie was being so cagey, but what could he do? If Mackie had thought it would help, he would have answered Logan's question. All he could do was remain vigilant, as Mackie had suggested.

'Is there anything else?' Logan asked.

'Just keep me in the loop, please,' Mackie said. 'Both of you.'

'Of course,' Evans responded.

They ended the call. Logan and Evans stayed sitting, an uncomfortable air still between them, though Logan was pleased that Evans seemed to be well on his side.

'So what now?' Evans said.

'Well, it seems that you're already up to speed.'

'Yeah.'

'I'm off then.' Logan got up to leave.

'What? Where are you going?'

'I don't know yet.'

'We're supposed to be working together now,' Evans said, getting to his feet, frustration in his voice. 'I'm helping you out here, don't forget.'

'I'm very grateful,' Logan said without any real sincerity. He picked up a pen off the desk and a piece of paper and scribbled out his phone number. 'When you find out something that can help me, give me a call.'

Logan put the pen down and handed the paper to Evans, who snatched it off him.

'Oh, well, yeah, thanks a lot,' Evans grumbled.

Logan ignored the sarcastic comment, turned on his heel and walked toward the door.

Chapter 47

Logan headed back to the car. He was very conscious that there may well still be people after him, and he would much rather keep on the move, keep them guessing, than stick around the safe house with Evans, a man he had never worked with before and knew nothing about.

He was more than a little perturbed by the way Evans's involvement had been revealed. He trusted that Mackie was fighting for him, but Evans being sprung on him like that seemed to just be rubbing salt into his wounds, almost as if Mackie were making it clear that even he thought Logan needed assistance. Evans may well be a great guy and a good agent to boot, but that didn't mean Logan wanted or needed to work with him.

As he drove aimlessly through the busy central Paris traffic, Logan couldn't rid himself of the feeling of frustration. All of a sudden it felt like his role in the investigation had ground to a screeching halt.

He had to figure a way to get things moving again.

With only limited next steps at his disposable, he went for some food, not only to pass the time, but because he hadn't had a meal of any substance for some while. Add on the lack of sleep and the fighting that he'd been involved in and the result was that his energy levels were seriously depleted.

Logan was no health freak. Although he worked out during downtime, even more so during his period of rehabilitation, he didn't really pay attention to his diet at all. He guessed he was still relatively healthy, though. He didn't overindulge in any particular thing, but that wasn't a conscious decision, more down to the fact that he liked most types of food so he ended up eating a large variety: high fat, low fat, high carb, low carb. A balanced diet. But today was different. Today he needed something specific. He was eating for energy.

He was in central Paris, famed for its haute cuisine, its endless pavement cafes and the like, but it didn't take long to find what he was after: an Italian restaurant. It was like it had been cut and pasted straight out of an Italy guidebook, together with fake vines on the ceiling, wood panelling, empty wine bottle displays everywhere and red-and-white-checked tablecloths. The food was simple but it did the job. Pasta, meatballs, fresh bread. It had just about everything he needed: protein for strength, fat for slow-burning energy, carbs for the immediate burst. He also had a glass of red wine, just for the hell of it.

He'd finished refuelling when Grainger called him. A welcome surprise.

'Carl, are you busy?'

'Not particularly,' he said, downing the last of his wine.

'Right, we need to meet up then. I need to talk to you. Where are you?'

'In the city.'

'I've just left Blakemore's. Meet me halfway. Where we stopped for coffee yesterday?'

'*That* place? You mean where you dumped me?'

She laughed. 'That's the one.'

'Okay.'

'I'm heading there now,' she said.

'Me too.'

She hung up.

He decided against another wine and left cash on the table before he walked out and headed toward the car. After fighting through the traffic toward the motorway, he had an untroubled journey back to the town where he and Grainger had eaten the day before. As it had been the previous day, the sky was clear and blue and there was a warmth that belied the time of year. That, and the prospect of meeting up with Grainger again, lifted his spirits considerably.

Grainger was already waiting for him when he arrived, standing on the pavement, leaning against a Ford – the same model but a different colour to the last one she'd had. She'd changed clothes since he last saw her too: another tight-fitting suit, dark grey; standard Feds uniform, obviously. As he pulled in at the kerb, she gave him a broad smile. He parked two cars down from where she was. She didn't wait for him to get out, but walked over to his passenger door.

'Everything okay?' he said, giving her a beaming smile as she got in.

Should he try to kiss her? No. *Just play it cool*, he told himself. This really wasn't something he was used to having to deal with. He'd felt lust before. Who hadn't? But this? What *was* this?

'Yeah, fine. It's good to see you,' she said. Her expression didn't agree with her words. It seemed to Logan that some of her troubles were back. 'I kinda missed you,' she added.

Despite the hesitation in her face, he felt a wave of relief at her words. It had only been a few hours since they'd seen each other, but he'd missed her as well.

Was this really him? Where had these feelings come from?

He smiled and put his hand on her leg, giving it a gentle squeeze, but resisted going in for a kiss.

'So you didn't take my advice on the cars then?' he said.

'What?' she said. 'Oh, that. No. Is your boss okay with you then?' she asked.

'Yeah. Wasn't happy at first, but I think he sees that you and I working together has helped out so far. You can't really argue with that. We very nearly closed this thing off earlier.'

Logan deliberately didn't bring Evans's involvement into the conversation. There was no need to complicate matters unless absolutely necessary.

'That's good. That your boss is okay with you, I mean. The police are pretty suspicious down at Blakemore's, though. There are quite a few slugs from your gun. When they put them together with your prints, they'll soon realise they belong to someone who's missing. Perhaps they'll pin you as one of Selim's men who got away.'

'Doesn't matter. We'll have this cracked by then. Once it's all over, there's no need to hide my involvement anymore.'

'Wouldn't that blow your … you know … cover?'

'Well, they won't actually name and shame me or post a picture in the paper, but exactly what happened will be explained to the police, high up the chain at least. Who their missing link was. Me, that is.'

'Oh, right.'

'What about you? Any other signs of trouble for you?' he asked.

'For me? No. Why? Should there be?'

Logan frowned; she really wasn't with it. Something was troubling her.

'Are you going to tell me what's up here?' he said. 'What's happened?'

'Nothing,' she said bluntly. 'Nothing's happened.'

'Then what the hell is the matter?'

She started fidgeting, reluctant at first to answer the question. Then she smiled meekly and said, 'You don't realise how similar we are, Carl. Remember what I told you about my dad?'

'Yeah,' Logan said, utterly confused. 'You joined the FBI because of him.'

'What I didn't tell you was that it was my fault he got killed.'

'What?'

'The man who killed him, I knew him. Not in a personal sense, but I knew who he was. And I had the chance to stop him. But I didn't take it. I could have saved my own father's life, but because of my inaction, he was murdered.'

She'd only spoken for a few seconds but already there were tears streaming down her cheeks. Her voice, though, remained calm and unwavering.

Logan suddenly had a strange feeling in the pit of his stomach. He had sensed her pain, had sensed it from the moment he met her, but this was the first time she'd shared it with him.

'Why are you telling me this now?' Logan said, sounding sympathetic, but also aware of the growing anxiousness that he was feeling at her unusual behaviour.

'Because the man who killed my father is still running free. Just like Selim.'

It was then that Logan started to understand.

'I saw the way you were at Blakemore's when you knew you'd missed the chance to get Selim. Not just then, actually – the signs are there for all to see. I don't know what Selim did to you, but I can see the look in your eyes. The need for revenge. For redemption.'

She could read him like a book. He gripped hold of the steering wheel tightly and looked down, feeling almost ashamed. Ashamed because he'd had the chance to let her in, to tell her about Selim, and had blown it due to his own insecurities. And now here she was, doing what he couldn't.

'And I know how you feel,' she said. 'It hurts. Every time I think about it. Every time something reminds me of my dad's death. About the man who did it. Every day I think about what it would be like to find him, to come face to face with him, to make him pay for what he did to my dad.'

'Then I guess we really are the same,' he said.

And finally Logan saw why their attraction to each other was so strong: theirs was a bond built on shared grievances, on pain and suffering, but also on an unrelenting need for revenge. It was the strongest bond that Logan had ever felt with another person. His instincts about Grainger had been right. There was a connection, something solid.

But there was one thing that she still hadn't explained. Why was she telling him this now?

'I know what you're thinking,' she said, as though reading his mind. 'I want to help you, Carl. That's why I'm telling you this. I just want you to know what I'm doing … what I'm doing here. I'm taking a big risk being here.'

She was sounding very unsure. Her hand played with her hair, pushing it back behind her ear, then pulling it forward again. She was doing her best to avoid making any eye contact with him.

'What is it?'

'Look. This could land me in big trouble,' she said. 'Hell, I'm already in big trouble. I've just been lying to an FBI director and a lead investigator of the French police for the past few hours. But what I'm about to do, you understand, this …'

'What?' he said, more agitated than intrigued now.

'This is something else. And I'm telling you because I really trust you, Carl. And I know you'll do the right thing here.'

'Angie, just tell me!'

She opened her jacket, took out a folded piece of paper and handed it to Logan, who sat there, bemused.

'Look at it,' she said.

He unfolded it and stared at the handwritten scribbles.

'What is it?' he said. But he hoped he already knew the answer.

'It's an address. Carl, I think I know where Selim is.'

Chapter 48

The piece of paper Grainger had given Logan looked like it had been torn from a notepad, the corners on the left-hand side frayed and torn. There were numerous unintelligible scribbles on both sides of the page, tit-bits that wouldn't mean much to anyone other than the original scribe. But quite clearly, in the bottom right of the paper, squared out and doodled over, there was an address.

'Where'd you get this?' Logan said, with a hint of suspicion in his voice. He looked over at Grainger and saw that her nervousness was still there.

'Where do you think?' she said. 'Blakemore's office.'

'You think Selim is there?'

'I do. That has to be the address Blakemore had as a back-up. There was some other stuff as well: a lease document in Reggie Graham's name – he was the big guy slumped in the corner of the office – and an invoice for ground rent. I destroyed those. Just kept the address.'

She bowed her head as she finished, as though ashamed by what she had done.

'You destroyed them? Why?'

Her face creased. She looked upset by his question.

'If I'd just given you the address, the police would have found the other stuff and come to the same conclusion that I've come to: that Selim is there. I thought you'd want the chance to do this without the police getting in the way. I thought you'd want to get Selim. I did it for you!'

He was completely gobsmacked. He wasn't disappointed or angered by what she had done, more concerned at what the ramifications for her would be. She had taken a massive risk for him, may have just gambled her entire career for him. Nonetheless, he was delighted that she had. Selim was his, no-one else's.

Every day I think about what it would be like to find him, to come face to face with him.

They were her words. But they meant so much to him.

'Angie, thank you. I really mean that.'

And with his words, she seemed to grow a little, some colour returning, her eyes lighting up, shoulders relaxing. Finally she looked more like her normal, glowing self again.

'I just hope you're worth it, Carl Logan.'

'Me too.'

'And anyway, where'd this Angie thing come from? That's twice you've called me that.'

'Sorry. Don't you like it?'

'That's what my husband called me. My ex-husband I mean.'

She rubbed her wedding ring finger again, as she often did.

'Wow, way to go, putting my foot in it,' Logan said.

'It's okay. I didn't mean I didn't want you to, just that no-one else does.'

'That's the first time you've ever mentioned your ex to me. Was it recent?'

'It'd been on the cards for years. Don't worry, he's out of my life one hundred percent. It just took me a while to convince myself of that.' There was a certain sadness to her words, but she didn't have the same look of pain as when she'd recounted the story of her father. The breakup had obviously caused her some hurt, but nothing on the same level as her father's loss.

'Falling out of love with someone is the hardest thing in the world to do,' she said. 'Falling in love is much easier ... and more fun too.'

He guessed he didn't really have experience of either. Though the way she'd said the last sentence made him shiver. In a good way.

She leaned over and kissed him on the cheek. When she moved back he said, 'So what do you want me to call you then?'

She laughed, 'Carl, you can call me whatever the hell you like. Actually, I quite like it when you call me Grainger. Feels kinda kinky the way you say it.'

He laughed too. 'How about Agent Grainger.'

'Phew!' She wiped her brow theatrically. 'Special Agent Grainger would work even better.'

'So, Special Agent Grainger. Are we ready to go?'

She looked at him blankly. He held up the piece of paper.

'No way, Carl,' she said. 'Giving you the address is one thing, but I can't get caught up in this. My career could well be over now and it's not going to help matters one bit if I actually go there with you. I could even end up in jail over this!'

'But you already are caught up in this,' Logan said. He didn't want to appear unsympathetic, but he was determined to have her with him. 'Plus, it was you who got me caught up by bringing me the address,' he added.

She looked hesitant. But he wasn't going to let her say no. She'd already shown herself to be capable, and he would much rather have her help than not. And not just because he couldn't get enough of her.

'We're in this together now,' he said. 'Let's finish it together. It could even save your career if you're there to walk Modena out.'

'I already said it: no.'

'Do you have your piece?'

'Yeah.'

'Then we're ready to go.'

She didn't say another word, and Logan took that as a sign of compliance. He started the engine and pulled away from the kerb.

Chapter 49

The vehicle came to a sudden stop. With his hands cuffed together behind him, Modena struggled to keep his balance and he fell sideways, smacking his shoulder off what he guessed was the side of the van. The engine shut down, the constant reverberation that had been coursing through his body for hours and making him feel queasy finally coming to an end. The men in the van began to talk in a language he didn't understand but which he assumed was Arabic, then he heard the doors of the van being opened.

Someone grabbed his arm and pulled Modena toward him. He kicked out with his legs, trying to keep his feet on the floor of the van, but failed. His body fell out of the vehicle and crumpled to the ground. The man still had hold of his arm and it twisted around painfully as he fell, causing Modena to shout out.

'Get up!' shouted a voice. The man was still pulling hard on his arm, then he felt a dull whack as a strike, from what felt like a fist, landed hard on his back.

'Get up!' shouted the voice again.

Modena struggled as best as he could to get to his feet. A second man grabbed hold of his other arm, giving him the help he needed, and they escorted him along. His feet were bare, and although he was struggling to focus on the feeling in them because of the pain still flowing through his body from his ordeal, it felt like they were walking on soft, wet ground. After a few pained strides he was ushered up two cold, hard steps and then the ground became warmer. He assumed he was now inside.

'Sit,' one of the men said, pushing Modena down to the floor after he'd been marshalled to a stopping point.

Modena dropped to the floor, his backside smacking off the hard surface, causing it to go numb for a few seconds.

He heard the two men walk away. For a while after that there was almost complete silence. No more voices. No sounds of footsteps or other movements. Just a low-pitched electric hum – which Modena guessed was from either lighting or heating – and the sound of his own breathing telling him he was still alive.

Modena wondered what was happening. His hands were tied together but his legs were free. He could get up and walk if he wanted. He could reach up and pull the sack off his head.

He could try to escape?

In the end he didn't move. He just sat there on the floor, his mind wandering in and out of reality.

Finally, after what seemed like an age, during which time Modena was not sure whether or not he had drifted off to sleep, he heard the sound of footsteps coming toward him. He lifted his head. Seconds later, he recoiled when he felt fingers around his neck. At first he thought someone was going to choke him, but he soon realised they were loosening the sack on his head.

When the cloth bag was removed from his face it took Modena's brain a few seconds to recalibrate his sight and decipher what his eyes were seeing. And when the man kneeling down in front of him finally came into focus Modena gasped, then moaned.

'Hello, Frank,' said Selim. 'I hope you enjoyed the ride.'

Modena didn't say anything. There was still the same disconcerting calmness in the way that Selim spoke, but Modena detected something else in the man's gaze that hadn't been there before. Not worry, but something close to it. He didn't know what had happened at the previous place they'd been keeping him, but he'd heard the shouting and the gunshots. He'd hoped against all hope that the commotion was a rescue mission, but the hope hadn't yet come to fruition.

'Oh, Frank, come on now, don't give me the silent treatment.'

'Where are we?' Modena mumbled, curiosity getting the better of him.

Selim got to his feet, smiling. He waved his arms in the air as he spoke. 'This is where you give your swansong.'

Modena shook his head, barely feeling anything at Selim's words, resigned to his own fate now. He knew there was nothing he could do to save himself. No amount of begging would make a difference. He just had to pray that someone else would rescue him.

He looked around the room they were in. It was dank and dark and in disrepair. He was sitting on a bare wooden floor from which some of the boards were missing. The walls were a dirty white, small holes marking where clumps of plaster had fallen off. At the large bay window long drapes, stained and worn, closed off whatever view lay outside, but Modena could tell from the light behind them that it was still daytime.

'You remember the little video that you helped us to prepare?' Selim said, sitting down right next to Modena, their shoulders brushing. 'Well, I'd like you to take part in another one for me.'

Selim moved forward onto his knees and swivelled around theatrically so that he was in front of Modena again, his face only inches away.

'I'm sure you can imagine the type of video this is going to be. You've seen them, heard them being talked about before, haven't you? Only this one is going to be bigger, bolder. I've been waiting for someone like you for a long time, Frank. And the whole world will be in suspense to find out what I do to you.'

Selim leaned right in, his nose touching Modena's. He grinned, then spoke almost in a whisper. 'And, Frank, with what I've got planned for you, I'm not going to disappoint them.'

Chapter 50

Grainger sat for a few minutes not speaking to Logan, her face screwed up, trying to look angry, but she didn't raise any more objections. She'd guessed Logan would want to take her with him; it was the assuming manner in which he'd gone about it that had irked her. The ideal would have been for him to go after Selim alone. But it was important for her to do everything she could to get Modena back safely. Ultimately she knew that they both still needed each other.

Plus, she genuinely wanted to spend more time with Logan. There was no denying that the feelings she had for him were strong. Stronger than she had ever expected they would be.

She rubbed the band of white flesh on her wedding finger, from instinct more than anything, then quickly stopped when she saw Logan looking. He didn't say anything but she couldn't help but blush.

What would Tom think about what she was doing now? With Logan? And what would her dad think, for that matter?

It wasn't hard to answer. She knew exactly what they would both think.

She tried to push the thoughts out of her head. Everything in her life she had done to try to please other people. Perhaps it was time she started to do things for herself for a change.

Which was exactly the reason she wanted to help Logan.

The address they were heading to was in Dunkirk, the port town in the far north of France. It would be simple enough to get to the town, but after that they were going to need help.

'You could have just taken my GPS,' Grainger said. 'It was in the car. It would have been a lot easier than trying to find our way there through guesswork.'

'Yeah, but that would have given you an excuse to get out of my car. You might not have come back.'

Grainger huffed, more for effect than anything.

Factoring in the time to get around and out of Paris, plus the mileage displayed on the road signs, Grainger estimated the drive would take about three hours. It had been close to dusk when they set off, which meant they would again be arriving at their destination at night.

'There's no guarantee Selim and Modena are there, of course,' Grainger said, shuffling in her seat. 'But from talking to the other officers and from everything I looked at myself – and I looked at a lot – it was the only thing that even *hinted* at where they could be.'

'That's good enough for me,' Logan said. 'Like you said, there isn't anywhere else where we think he might be, so we have to check this out.'

'Do you think Modena is still alive?'

'I hope so. Having been so close to getting him, I feel like we owe him one. And knowing what Selim might be doing to him ...'

'Yeah, best not to think about that.'

'But I think he is alive,' Logan said with confidence. 'Selim wouldn't have gone to all the trouble of crossing Blakemore like that if he was just going to kill Modena straight off. He could have just shot him in the head back at the farmhouse if that was the case.'

'Yeah. Good point.'

'I'm really glad you did this for me,' Logan said, turning to Grainger.

'Just what did he do to you?' she asked, her intrigue getting the better of her.

Logan took his eyes off her, facing the road again, and didn't answer for a good while.

'You really want to know?' he said, his eyes still fixed on the road ahead.

'Yes.'

He let out a long sigh but eventually gave in.

'The aim was to break up a network of terrorist training camps,' he began. 'We wanted to find and capture the ring leaders and those who were financing the operations. This was a big deal. Not just my agency, but every major intelligence agency around had a finger in the pie somewhere. There was one guy I was trying to find. He seemed to be the key to much of what was happening. But he was like a ghost. I didn't even know it was Selim I was after until it was too late.'

Her stare was focused on him the entire time he spoke but he didn't look over at her. She didn't say a word. Just let him carry on.

'Selim caught me just as I was starting to put the pieces together. I thought I was going to meet with someone who had been a trusted informant for me for months. But it was a set-up. They ambushed me. Selim held me prisoner, tried to break me, tried to find out what we knew and who knew it. But it was personal for him too. He wanted to get his own back. I'd already caused him so much trouble – a number of his close allies had already been captured or killed because of my work. He said he wanted to show me how vengeful he could be.'

Grainger watched as a tear rolled out of Logan's eye and down his cheek. He seemed oblivious, almost in a trance, as he recounted the story.

'This girl ... I didn't even know her – she was just some girl he'd picked up. But the things he did to this girl, right in front of my eyes ...'

He tailed off, finally dabbing at the tears rolling down his face. Grainger still didn't say a word.

'And do you know why he did it?' Logan said.

Grainger didn't know whether he expected a response or not. In the end he carried on.

'Because he could. He just wanted to show me that he could. That he was in control. Her life was nothing to him. Just like mine. I begged him to leave her alone, to hurt me. But that just made him more determined.

'You can be trained to deal with pain. Trained not to break under torture. I was. And it worked. Would I have broken eventually? Probably. Your mind and body can only protect you for so long. But he knew that *she* would suffer more under torture than I would. He knew that he could cause even more suffering to her than he could to me. And that it would damage me in the process. He wasn't after information from her; she didn't need to be cognisant. So there were no limits to the things that he could do. To the things that he *did* do to her.

'They never train you for that. To see someone else suffering so badly? Someone as defenceless as she was? And to know that it was my fault – that caused me more pain than I have ever felt.'

Grainger reached out and put her hand on his shoulder, wishing she could do more to comfort him.

'Carl, that's what makes you human, feeling like that.'

He shoved her off.

'But don't you get it?' he said, his bleary eyes looking at hers for just a second before returning to focus on the road. 'I felt it, but I didn't do anything. I never broke. I stayed true to my country, or whatever the fuck my loyalty was to. To my job. But I never broke once. I didn't tell Selim a single damn thing! I could have made him stop if I'd told him what he wanted to know. If I'd told him what we knew. If I'd told him *anything*. I could have given him the names of other agents, of people in his own camp who had turned against him. But I never did. I didn't tell him a thing. I just watched for days as he slowly butchered a defenceless girl. You could see it in her eyes. Pleading with me to say something to make him stop. But I didn't do a thing. I could tell from the way she looked at me that she knew all of her suffering was my fault. And she was right. You think that makes me a good man?'

'Yes, I do. How many other people, other agents, informants, would have suffered if you'd talked? And you all get to carry on. Carry on bringing down the likes of Selim.'

'Are their lives worth more than that girl's?'

'Maybe not, but they're worth just as much. One life to save many.'

'It shouldn't have been her life, though. It should have been mine.'

'But you *are* still alive. And you *will* get him.'

And she was going to do everything she could to help him do it. Because she knew what it meant to want revenge so badly that it clouded your every thought, your every move.

'I'm alive,' he said, 'but it was nothing to do with me. It's a strange feeling to know that you're only alive because of someone else's actions. To know that without them you'd be dead. That you have no control over your own existence.'

'Don't forget, I do know that. *You* saved *my* life.'

'Selim was going to cut my head off,' Logan said, almost offhand. 'I don't know if he was just tired of me or if he was getting scared that we were on to him, that his days were numbered. He was only seconds away from doing it as well. It was only by a miracle, or really bad luck on his part, that he didn't succeed in killing me.

'Special forces troops rescued me. They stormed the place, but Selim got away. I was left with a gaping wound in my neck that should on its own have killed me. But somehow I made it. No-one could explain to me how. The doctors just kept telling me how lucky I was. Yeah, really fucking lucky. Fit to fight another day.'

They both fell into silence for a while. Grainger wasn't sure at first whether or not he had finished his retelling. She couldn't help but feel a tiny bit of elation inside that he had opened up to her like that, even though it was an ordeal for him. Not just because she now saw exactly why her attraction to him was so strong – because of the painful experiences that they both shared – but because she knew that Logan was going to stop at nothing to get his man. And with his help, she was soon going to be able to finish this thing once and for all.

'Thank you for telling me,' she said. 'I know it must have been hard. Most people would have given up after what happened to you. But you didn't. You're back, you're still fighting. There aren't many people who could do that.'

'Thanks. For listening to me. For trying to understand.'

'And what you said before,' Grainger said, 'about us being the same? I see it now. Both of us had the chance to save someone's life. And we both failed. And both of us have paid the price.'

'Maybe,' he said, wiping away the remaining tears from his face, a resolute look returning to his eyes. 'But now it's time to make it right.'

Grainger smiled to herself. *You're right, Carl*, she thought. *Now is the time indeed.*

Chapter 51

The roads had been busy initially as they fought their way through the Paris commuter traffic, but as they drove further north the motorway became quieter and they reached the town of Dunkirk not far short of nine o'clock in the evening.

'Are we going to go straight there?' Grainger asked. 'Or shall we rest up first?'

Resting was certainly a welcoming option. They were both tired, having had little sleep over the last forty-eight hours. The pasta Logan had eaten in the afternoon had all but been digested. It would certainly be nice to eat and sleep.

But they were here now. So close.

'No, we should get this done,' Logan said. 'There'll be plenty of time for resting afterwards.'

'We could grab a motel room again. Just sleep for a few hours. Go out in the early hours like yesterday. We'd be a lot fresher that way.'

He had to admit, it was a tempting offer. Plus, he knew *exactly* what they would end up doing if they did go to a hotel. But he didn't want to be swayed on this.

'No. Not this time,' he said, trying his best not to let the lingering thoughts of the night before cloud his judgement. 'Every second counts now. Selim has Modena to himself now and God only knows what he could do to him in those few hours.'

Logan looked over and noticed that Grainger's cheeks had turned red. She was clearly embarrassed at having put her own needs and desires first, despite the grave situation.

'You're right,' she said. 'Let's find out where this place is then.'

They pulled in to a petrol station. They were the only customers there. While Logan filled up the tank, Grainger got directions to the street they were looking for from the cashier. 'It's only a mile or two from here,' Grainger said, returning to the car. 'We're more or less on the right road, just a couple of turns.'

Logan felt his stomach moving, the first signs of butterflies for what lay ahead. They were nearly there now.

This time he had to make it count.

They continued on their way through the centre of the town to their destination. Much ravaged during the Second World War, Dunkirk's centre was nonetheless a place full of historic architecture. It had a number of attractions, not least its wide beaches and pleasant promenades. But at its heart was industry; it had one of the largest and busiest ports in France. As with many places with a traditionally industrial heritage, parts of it had, in more modern times, fallen into dereliction. A few minutes later, it was in one of those parts that they found the address they were looking for.

It was a residential street consisting of a row of rundown terraced houses, built one next to the other, but of all different shapes and sizes. The terraces ranged from two to four storeys high and up to four houses wide. Number fifty-seven was toward the far end of the street. There were no houses on the opposite side of the street here, and only a few more houses beyond it before residences gave way to what appeared to be derelict wasteland.

The building they were looking for was a simple two-storey structure. There were four steps up to the front door, which was at the same level as those of the neighbouring houses, the street descending away to its right. Curtains were drawn in all three of the windows at the front of the house. An orange glow showed that lights were on in the downstairs front room and in one of the rooms upstairs.

'Looks like someone's home,' Logan said.

'Yeah, though there's no sign of the truck that they took off in.'

'Let's drive around, see if there's a back way in. Maybe the van is around there somewhere.'

There was a narrow back lane behind the properties, running the full length of the road. Each of the houses had a fence or wall backing onto it. To the other side of the lane there seemed to be more wasteland, though in the darkness it was hard to tell how far into the distance it went.

Number fifty-seven had a simple wire fence and gate enclosing its unkempt yard. And through the fence, Logan could clearly see a van parked up inside. The same van in which Selim had escaped from the farmhouse.

Logan felt his heart skip a beat.

'They're here,' he said, stating the obvious, feeling both relieved and nervous.

'There's no-one else parked on this lane; it's too narrow,' Grainger said. 'Let's park back on the street, where we're less obvious. If they make a run for it, they'll hardly be making a quick getaway in that thing. And it doesn't matter which way they go in the van, they've got to come back to the front street.'

'Okay. Let's get around to the front so we can dump the car.'

There were only a few other cars on the street. A number of the properties appeared to be empty and, judging by the size and condition of the buildings, Logan guessed even those that weren't empty probably had occupants who couldn't afford a car. They parked twenty yards down from the house, away from the other cars, so that there was nothing to obstruct them either in front or behind should they need to move on quickly.

'Isn't it a bit strange that they'd bring him here?' Grainger said. 'To a street full of other houses? Lots of witnesses around, which means they have to be careful, not just about being seen but about noise as well.'

'It's a good tactic. They're banking on people thinking that, assuming that they'd go somewhere out in the middle of nowhere. To stay hidden, you're better off going where you're least expected, even if it's right under the noses of those who are looking for you.'

This he knew from experience. He'd once trailed around Eastern Europe for almost a month, following numerous false leads while looking for a man who had got away from him. In the end, it turned out the guy had been holed up the entire time in another apartment in the same block where he lived, and where Logan had first encountered him.

He also knew that being in a port town like Dunkirk gave Selim options for getting out of France. It would be far easier to move on by boat than it would be to try to leave France by car or plane. And from Dunkirk, Selim could move easily into eastern Europe and beyond, or even trail around France, Portugal and down into Africa.

'In a way I'm glad it *is* here rather than in the middle of nowhere,' Grainger said. 'They'd have to at least be conscious of the noise they're making.'

Logan understood what she meant, but he wasn't sure that would stop Selim doing whatever the hell he wanted to do to Modena. This wasn't exactly middle-class suburbia and Logan wasn't sure that noisy neighbours really got people's juices flowing around here.

'How are we going to get inside?' Grainger asked.

'It doesn't look like security is going to be a hindrance,' Logan said.

'So how about we just knock on the door?'

Logan scoffed, 'You're kidding, right?'

'No.'

'And *then* what? Wait for them to shoot us down?'

Grainger looked offended. 'I could pretend to be a lost motorist or something. There's more chance of them opening the door to a lone lady than to you. Plus, Selim knows you. Me coming to their door will still raise their suspicions, but at least it should draw their attention away. You go around and in the back way. Hopefully unopposed.'

'You're going to use yourself as human bait?'

'I wasn't planning to, no. Just keep them talking for a few seconds, that's all.'

Logan still looked unsure.

'Are you happy with that?' she asked.

'Yeah, fine,' he said without conviction. He didn't like that she was putting herself in harm's way, but he knew that the plan was as sound as any he could come up with. As long as they timed it right, he'd be in the house and on to whoever was inside before there was any chance of Grainger getting hurt.

'I'll just ask them for some directions, then leave,' she said. 'So try to be quick.'

'I will. I'll get out of the car here. You should park up right outside their house. It'll help with your story. Wait till I get around the back. I'll call you when I'm ready. No need to answer the phone – I'll just let it ring a couple of times.'

'Okay. Good luck.'

'You too,' he said. 'This'll all be over in a few minutes. *Then* we get to a hotel.'

'Can't wait,' she said, giving him a smile.

He opened the door and was almost out when she said, 'Oh, and Logan? What will you do to him? Selim? I mean, are you going to kill him?'

'I don't know yet,' Logan said. 'That's entirely up to him.'

He just hoped Selim would give him no choice.

Chapter 52

There was no easy way to do this. Logan knew that both the stakes and the risks were sky high. They could quite easily be walking into a literal death trap. With only two of them, they couldn't go for an all-guns-blazing armed siege. He knew that the safest course of action was to call in for support: Evans, the FBI, the French police, whoever. But that was never going to happen. This was his moment. Logan was determined to rescue Modena and finish off Selim here and now, not with the help of a tactical response team.

It had to be expected that Selim and his men would be on edge. A knock on the front door was going to send them into a mild panic. They would surely reach for their weapons. Maybe they would even answer the door by pushing a gun into Grainger's face. Whatever happened, Logan was going in after them.

When he reached the back yard, he swung open the wire gate just enough for him to creep in, entered and then shut it behind him. The yard was in almost complete darkness, the only illumination coming from the crescent moon. There were no streetlights on the lane and none of the lights in the back of the house were on.

Moving cautiously in the dim light, Logan crept past the van and over toward the back door of the house. It was a bog-standard wooden door with one Yale lock and one deadbolt lock. He was hoping it was unlocked, but if it wasn't, he was sure he could simply crash through it.

As he took out his phone, he could feel the anticipation building. A wave of goose pimples washed over him as the adrenaline began to surge, readying him for what was to come. He dialled Grainger's number to send the signal, then stood listening for the response. He heard the faint noise of a car door closing. A few seconds later he heard Grainger knocking at the front door of the house.

Immediately, there were voices inside. Debating. Arguing. They were definitely panicked. The voices got louder and lights came on at the back of the house. Logan jumped a yard to the left, away from the door, out of the way of the window. The voices died down, but he could still hear movement coming from the other side of the door.

Seconds later, the back door suddenly opened and a man came rushing out, heading over to the van. Logan felt himself jerk in surprise. But the man, in his haste, hadn't spotted Logan.

The man was tall and skinny. Logan didn't recognise him. He was opening the van door when Logan, moving almost without a sound, rushed him from behind. With one swipe, he smashed the butt of his gun against the side of the man's head. Logan winced at the cracking sound as metal made contact with the man's skull. The man was out cold before he'd even known Logan was there. He did his best to catch the man in mid-air as he plummeted toward the ground, not wanting the fall to make too much sound.

Logan rested the limp body down, then turned and walked quickly toward the open back door, approaching it from the side so as to stay out of sight. He reached the door and peered his head around. The doorway opened into a corridor. It ran the full length of the poky house, all the way to the front door which was still shut. There was no sign of anyone in the hallway. Logan wondered whether Grainger was still there, on the other side of the door, or whether she'd already retreated to the car.

His question was answered when he heard another knock. Then more voices, coming from one of the downstairs rooms, but quieter now. A man came out of the front room, facing away from Logan. He had a handgun in his right hand, which he was holding behind his back. He walked up to the door and looked through the spy hole. It seemed like he was debating whether to open the door or not.

In the end, he didn't.

But as he turned back around, his eyes met Logan's. A look of confusion was still etched on his face when Logan's bullet hit him square between the eyes. He fell to the ground, body slumping half inside the doorway of the room he'd just come from.

That was it. There was no element of surprise now. Now it was just a straight-out fight.

From the voices he'd just heard, Logan knew there was at least one more man in the front room. He moved forward, cautiously, gun held out at the ready.

'Armed police! Come out now! Hands above your head!'

Nothing. He crept further forward.

'We've got this place surrounded. There's nowhere for you to go.'

Still nothing. It had been worth a shot, Logan thought.

He heard footsteps coming from the room, then the sound of glass smashing.

'Shit! Logan!' Grainger shouted from the other side of the front door.

Someone must have been trying to escape through the front window. Logan rushed forward, past the wooden staircase on his left, running into the front room without even hesitating. It was a potentially suicidal move but he did it without even thinking – an instinctive reaction to hearing Grainger's panicked voice.

But in his haste, Logan hadn't anticipated the threat from the staircase on the other side of the hall. As he reached the room, in time to see a pair of legs disappear out of the smashed window, there was a chorus of gunfire from both within and outside the house. Chips of wood and plaster filled the air as several rounds hit the wall and door frame next to Logan. Realising that the shots must have come from someone on the stairs, he flung himself to the ground, rolling into the front room for safety.

He heard more shots coming from outside. Then Grainger's voice, loud and clear: 'Stay down or the next one is in your balls!'

Whom did she have? Was it Selim? If so then it was game over, but Logan half hoped that wasn't the case. Selim was *his* to take down.

He heard the unseen attacker coming down the stairs. Another two rounds were fired into the room, but they didn't come close to Logan, who was pressed up against the wall adjacent to the doorway and, for now, under cover.

He kept his cool – didn't fire in haste, like he had done yesterday. He checked his gun, made sure it was ready to go.

It was only then that he spotted the forlorn figure in the corner of the room.

Modena.

He was lying on the floor, hands cuffed to a radiator. Gaffer tape around his face secured a rag that was stuffed in his mouth.

His chest was moving. He was alive.

'Frank, you're going to get through this,' Logan said. 'Just hang in there.'

Another gunshot came from out in the street, followed by a long moan.

Grainger obviously kept true to her word, Logan thought with a wry smile.

But soon it was Logan who was screaming when he heard the front door opening. He moved over, peering out of the bay window to see Grainger walking in through the now open door.

'Angela! No! Get down!'

She responded just as the first shots were fired at her, flinging herself to cascade down the front steps.

Logan rushed back to the doorway of the front room and fired two shots toward the staircase, aiming at an enemy he could hear but not see, hoping that it would at least halt the progress of the attacker. It was an instinctive action, born of selflessness, trying to save Grainger with complete disregard for his own position.

But it was a rushed move. This wasn't a situation he was used to dealing with. On his own, it was all about him and them. With a partner, he had two people to protect. And that could be a big hindrance. In his rush to protect Grainger, he'd made a big mistake. As he moved out into the hall, he spotted something out of the corner of his eye. He turned to the left and found himself staring down the muzzle of an AK-47 assault rifle.

Standing behind, holding the weapon, was Youssef Selim.

Chapter 53

Logan froze. His eyes met Selim's. As before at the farmhouse, there was a brief moment of recognition.

'You again,' Selim said nonchalantly. 'We really should stop meeting like this.'

'Don't you worry. It won't happen again,' Logan said, his voice calm and collected, betraying the turmoil he was really feeling inside.

'Throw down your weapon, please.'

Logan did as he was told, flinging his gun into the front room.

Something behind Logan caught Selim's eye and he smiled. 'Now please turn around, toward the door.'

Logan turned, feeling the constant pressure of the rifle's muzzle against his head as he did so. When he was facing the front door, he saw what Selim was smirking about. Standing in front of him was Grainger. There was a gun pressed up against the back of her head. The man holding it had dark skin and was wearing a pair of khaki trousers and a brown woollen jumper. He was tall and skinny and had blood pouring down his face from a wound on the side of his head.

The man Logan had knocked unconscious at the back of the house.

If only he'd killed him when he had the chance.

The skinny man shoved Grainger and she cried out as she skidded across the wooden floor. She landed in a heap at Logan's feet. The man shut the front door, then made his way over to them.

'Both of you, on your knees,' Selim said.

The skinny man smacked Grainger across her face with the back of his hand, then pulled her up into a kneeling position.

Logan twisted at the sight of the man striking Grainger but otherwise didn't respond. Without waiting to be prompted, he lowered himself to his knees too.

'I'm in two minds here, Mr Logan,' Selim said. 'That is your name, isn't it?'

Logan remained silent. He turned his head toward Grainger. She looked terrified. The skinny man was once again pushing the barrel of his gun into the back of her head. As he was looking, Logan too felt pressure as Selim placed the rifle's barrel against his skull.

'You see,' Selim said. 'On the one hand, I'd really like you to be part of this. Part of Frank Modena's spectacular finale. You've got good experience – you'd be a natural to take a supporting role.'

Selim paused. Logan was listening to him, but he wasn't paying attention to the words. He was only thinking about what moves he could make, calculating the risks of each. The big problem, though, was that any move he made would be a complete gamble. And with not just his own but Grainger's life at stake, he wasn't sure he could afford to take that risk.

'But then I think I'd get a quiet satisfaction from just killing you now, getting it over and done with. I mean, how many more times are you going to come to spoil my party? It's getting just a little bit repetitive.'

Logan had no choice. They were out-positioned and out-gunned. Selim wasn't bluffing. If Selim didn't put a bullet in their heads here and now, he would only draw out their deaths agonisingly. Logan couldn't bear the thought of that. He'd been too close to it before. He wasn't going to go through it again. And there was no way he could put Grainger through that.

He had to give it a go.

He waited for Selim to start speaking again, knowing that any distraction at all would be helpful.

'But a leopard doesn't change its spots,' Selim said. 'I am what I am. And there's a few new tricks I'd like to try on you two. Kind of like –'

Selim didn't finish his sentence. Logan reached up behind him and grabbed the barrel of the rifle, pushing it away from his head. He was banking on Selim pulling the trigger, which was exactly what he did. Bullets sprayed out of the muzzle, hitting the floor and the wall opposite. The din was deafening, making Logan's head spin. He tried his best to force the barrel of the gun up, away from himself and Grainger, toward the skinny man. Selim didn't have the strength in his arms to stop it and there was a cry as the skinny man was hit. Logan had to assume that Grainger would take care of him from there.

Logan swivelled himself around, then put his body's weight from his knees back onto his feet. Selim was still holding on to the rifle, still struggling to regain control. But Logan wasn't going to let him. He yanked down on the gun, at the same time reaching up and grabbing Selim behind the shoulder. He kicked his leg out and pulled down hard on the weapon and on Selim. The momentum threw Selim over Logan's outstretched leg and into a heap on the floor.

Selim's arm twisted around awkwardly as he fell and he let out a shrill scream. But he had kept a finger on the trigger. And when he fired a single shot, it caught Logan, tearing into his shoulder. The bullet went right through him and a spray of blood projected out behind him.

The shot knocked Logan off balance and he stumbled backward, falling to the floor. Out of the corner of his eye he spotted Grainger and the skinny man. The two of them were wrestling on the floor. The man had been shot in the arm. His gun was nowhere in sight. Logan guessed it had fallen from his grasp in the melee. He wanted to help Grainger, but he knew Selim, who was still armed, had to be his priority.

Logan did his best to fight off the pain in his shoulder. Just in front of him, Selim was getting to his feet. He was disoriented, but still holding on to the rifle. As he began to raise it, there was only one thing Logan could do. He lunged forward and his body crashed into Selim's, slamming him against the wall. They both hit the deck.

At such close quarters, Selim's rifle was now useless. Logan knew his injured shoulder was debilitating; he just hoped the adrenaline coursing through him would be enough to keep him going. Unlike in the fight with Lorik, Selim should be no match for Logan's size and strength.

He arced back and crashed his forehead down onto Selim's nose, then began to prise the rifle out of his weakening grip. He hurled his right knee upwards into Selim's groin. Selim let out a long groan. Logan balled his left fist and sent a hook onto the temple of Selim's head. He put his whole body weight behind it, punching right through to the target. Selim's head rolled and his body flopped.

The quick succession of hits had been enough to turn the tide in Logan's favour. Selim was out for the count.

A second later Logan was on his feet. He looked over to Grainger, expecting to see the two bodies on the ground. But what he saw was Grainger disappearing down the front steps, shouting after the skinny man. He smiled to himself, knowing she wouldn't let her man get away. He kicked the rifle out of the reach of Selim then walked into the front room to reclaim his gun. Checking the chamber he walked back to Selim, who lay on the floor. He was starting to come around but was clearly dazed and confused.

This really was it now. Logan had his man at long last. It was the moment he'd been waiting for. So why did the whole situation leave a sour taste? He should have been on top of the world.

Logan knew why: Selim was still alive. And the police wouldn't be far behind. This time tomorrow, Selim would be waking up in a prison cell in France that would knock spots off the torturous hell hole that he deserved. And then what? For years Selim would fight extradition charges with every bogus story he and his lawyer team could come up with, all the while evading justice.

No, that wasn't going to be Selim's fate. Logan would not let that happen.

He knew first-hand what this man was capable of. He had seen what he could do to other, defenceless humans. Jail time just wasn't going to cut it. Logan wanted to skin him alive! He wanted Selim to suffer in the same way that he had made so many others suffer. A slow and painful death, that was what Selim deserved.

But Logan knew he could never do that and live with himself. He couldn't bring himself down to that level. He wasn't a sadist.

But he *was* a realist.

Logan raised his gun, aiming at the spot between Selim's eyes. His hand was shaking so badly that it was almost impossible to keep his aim. He wasn't even sure he would be able to hit his target, despite the short distance. He pulled his left hand around to steady the grip as best as he could.

Selim, his head still lolling, made eye contact with Logan. There was no pleading, no look of resignation or fear. Logan hated him even more for that.

In fact, Logan thought that Selim actually looked amused: the corners of his mouth were turned upwards, as though he was mocking the predicament that Logan found himself in. Like this was all his making and was what he wanted.

'This ends here,' Logan said.

Selim began to laugh. 'What ends here?' he said. 'Do you even know why Modena was taken? What I was being paid for?'

'What?' Logan said. Despite himself, he couldn't help but be intrigued by Selim's words.

'Eight million dollars,' Selim taunted. 'That's a lot of money for a name.'

Selim opened his mouth to say something else. But he never got the chance. Logan wasn't going to pass up this opportunity.

He fired his gun. The bullet tore into Selim's face, just above his left eye. Then he fired again and the glimmer of a smile was gone for good.

Logan lowered his gun and bowed his head. A rush of feelings coursed through him. Relief was the predominant one. But also confusion as to the meaning of Selim's dying words.

It only took a few seconds before the adrenaline surge that had helped him through the fight dissipated. And it was only then that Logan really felt the searing pain in his shoulder. He looked at his wound, but as he did so caught a glimpse of a shadow, a person standing in the open doorway off to his right.

Logan's world was going into a blur. The pain in his shoulder was immense, sending shock waves all the way down the right side of his body. He slumped to his knees.

'Carl. Are you okay? Carl!'

It was Grainger. She rushed over to him.

'I'm okay,' he said, fending her off. 'I'll be okay. Check Modena.'

Reluctantly she stood up and turned.

'Oh no. Logan … He's hit. Modena's been hit!'

She ran into the front room. Logan followed, fighting off the pain and the spinning in his head, and looked at the crumpled figure of Modena hanging from the radiator. His eyes were shut. Blood was trickling down from his gagged mouth and on his chest a large patch of red on the shirt he was wearing was widening by the second. He must have been shot by one of Selim's stray bullets.

'Frank? Frank! Can you hear me?' Grainger said, kneeling down by him.

Logan fell to the floor next to Modena, wincing in pain as he did so. Grainger lifted up Modena's head and untied the rag around his mouth. A rush of pooled blood escaped and ran down his chin.

'Frank! You're safe now,' she said. 'You hear me? We've got you now. Just hang in there.'

Modena murmured, a gargling noise; he tried to speak.

'Frank, you listen to me. Just hang in there!'

Grainger lifted up Modena's shirt. The bullet had hit him low in his chest. It had avoided his heart, but it was a bad wound. He was losing a lot of blood, which was coming out of the hole in big gulps with each beat of his heart. And with his hands cuffed to the radiator, it was impossible to move him into a position to tend to him properly. Grainger put a hand on the wound, trying to stem the flow of blood. Frank's swollen eyes opened wide at the touch, looking like they might pop right out of his head. Her touch would be painful, but it might help him survive.

Everything around Logan was spinning. He knew he needed treatment, fast. But Modena was dying. And Logan couldn't let that happen. He pulled himself up next to Modena and held the man in his arms. Modena wasn't his friend; there was no emotional attachment. He had never met the man before in his life. But he felt a duty toward him. A duty to save him.

'Go and get help,' Logan spluttered.

Grainger didn't hesitate. She released her hand from Modena's chest and got to her feet. Logan pushed his own hand onto Modena's wound, pressing as hard as he could. The soaked skin squelched and bubbled as the blood tried to find its way through. Grainger rushed out into the hall, talking hurriedly into her phone.

Modena tried to speak again. This time he got his words out, so faint that they were almost a whisper.

'Lucky. It was …'

'What was that?' Logan said. 'Frank, what did you say?'

'It was … lucky. Lucky that …'

'Yes, Frank. It was lucky. *You* are lucky. You're going to be fine, though. Just hold on.'

Modena opened and closed his mouth again and again, but no more words came out.

'Frank, just stay with me,' Logan shouted. He could sense that he was losing Modena. But he was also on the brink himself. Everything around him was hazy.

Logan opened and closed his eyes, struggling to stay alert, struggling to stay conscious.

Then he felt the pressure underneath his hand lighten and his focus seemed to return.

'Frank! Stay with me.'

But no response came from Modena this time. Logan took his hand away from the wound. The blood was no longer gushing. Just a constant, slow trickle.

'Frank!'

But there was no response.

Modena's heart had stopped beating.

'Carl?'

It was Grainger. He turned to face her. She stood in the doorway, tears rolling down her cheeks. The look on her face said it all.

Logan simply shook his head, then closed his eyes.

Chapter 54

There would be no needle and thread in a hotel bedroom this time. Logan needed professional treatment. But regardless of his needs, he and Grainger had another priority. The man they had both been looking for, both trying to save, was on the brink of death. His heart had stopped beating. And until further help arrived, they had to do everything and anything they could to keep him alive.

First they needed to release Modena from the radiator to make it easier to tend to him. Grainger held the barrel of her handgun up against the chain that connected Modena's handcuffs together and fired. At such close quarters the shot caused a fair bit of damage to the skin on Modena's hands in the process, but if he made it through this, they were sure he would forgive them. With his arms freed, they both helped to move Modena so that he was lying flat. Grainger then tried her best to resuscitate the dying man.

Logan had plenty of training in first aid, but it wasn't quite as simple to perform when you had a gaping hole in your shoulder. With the blood that Logan himself was losing, it was a struggle just to stay conscious.

An ambulance and a local police car were first on the scene. The paramedics promptly whisked Modena off, reluctantly leaving behind the injured Logan; they assured him they would send another ambulance for him. In lieu of proper medical attention, Grainger had hastily tied a makeshift tourniquet around Logan's injured shoulder.

The two local cops had quickly subdued the last of Selim's men who was still alive: the skinny man whom Grainger had fled into the street after, and whom she had shot in the leg to add to the wounds he already had in his arm and to his head. With all loose ends apparently taken care of, the two policemen were left scratching their heads and struggling to do anything else useful.

Logan and Grainger were left to contemplate what had just happened while they awaited the cavalry.

'There's still time if you want me to take you away from here,' she said to Logan. 'We don't have to wait for the others to arrive. Don't you want to get away before they do?'

'I think the moment for caring about that has passed,' Logan said. 'Everyone already knows we were both here. It wouldn't make any difference now. Dead or alive, we have Modena. And Selim is dead. There's no need to run now.'

His relief when he spoke Selim's name was obvious. The first time he had ever spoken the name in that way.

But he was also troubled by Selim's parting words. A name. Eight million dollars for a name. It was what Logan had suspected: that Blakemore and the others were being paid to extract information from Modena. So why was someone paying eight million dollars for a name?

'How's that shoulder?' Grainger said, shaking Logan from his thoughts.

'I'm sure I'll live.'

He was still slouched on the floor, next to the large pool of blood where Modena had been. It was all smudged and smeared and there were bloody footprints trailing all around the room and out of the house – a combination of Logan's, Grainger's and the paramedics who had escorted Modena out. Much of the blood was from Logan's own wound.

The tourniquet had so far been successful in stemming the blood flow, but it couldn't stop the pain. Logan was feeling drowsy from its persistence.

'Did Modena say anything to you?' Grainger asked. 'While I was on the phone before?'

'No. He could barely speak,' Logan said. His speech was becoming more laboured by the minute. 'Just something about him being lucky. Poor guy.'

Logan noticed a twinkle in Grainger's eye at his words. The briefest flash of recognition at what he had said – at what Modena had said to him. But just like that, the look was gone again.

'Let's hope he was right,' she said.

'Wait,' Logan interjected. 'Does that mean something to you? What he said to me? About him being lucky?'

'What? No ... not at all. Why would it?'

Perhaps he'd just imagined it. He was hardly on top of his game.

An armed response team from the French police arrived a few minutes later. Too little, too late: they'd already missed all the action. But, determined to leave their mark, they made plenty of noise as they stormed through each room in the house, securing an already secured area.

Next came a small team of FBI agents, some detectives from Paris, crime scene investigators and, finally, Mackie, who'd rushed over from London on the Eurostar.

By that point, Logan was the subject of some heated debate between the Feds and the police. Half of them were contemplating arresting him despite Grainger's protests.

Things were quickly squared off once Mackie had arrived, though. After that, Logan was left to deal with only the persistent stares and sneers of the various law enforcement teams.

He could handle that.

Three further ambulances had arrived in between all of the squabbling. A young female paramedic tended to Logan. She gave him some morphine and stitched up the wound on both the front and back of his shoulder. As ever, he resisted being taken to a hospital and had persuaded the paramedic to let him stay on the scene, albeit inside the ambulance. He didn't yet know what kind of damage had been done to the bone and muscle, but right now it didn't really matter to him.

Only two things did: Modena and Grainger.

Grainger was busy being debriefed by her bosses. It was hard to know what kind of trouble she would be in now. She could be fired for what she'd done. Maybe more than that. On top of lying to her superiors, she'd destroyed evidence, helped a suspect escape a police chase and had been involved in the deaths of a number of people. The list went on. Yes, she'd helped to get Modena back. But for her, for the police and for the Feds, rules were everything. And she'd broken just about every one.

Mackie put his head around the ambulance door.

'I suppose we should just be grateful that Modena is at least still alive,' he said, barely able to hide his annoyance.

Despite Mackie's tone, Logan perked up. He hadn't known that Modena was still alive. When he had been carted off his heartbeat had been so faint it was almost not there. 'He is?'

'Just about, yeah. Too early to tell what's going to happen to him. His heart stopped twice more on the way to the hospital. But he is technically alive. Whether or not he'll recover, I don't know.'

Modena was alive. And as long as that was the case, there was a chance he would recover. It was something, at least.

'As you can imagine, you haven't got many friends out there at the moment,' Mackie said. 'You've caused a lot of people a lot of problems. And not just tonight.'

'And I've also potentially helped to save Modena's life.'

'Well, if he doesn't live, I think people will probably point the finger at you, so don't count your chickens just yet. And you've done it all in a completely gung-ho way right under the noses of regular law enforcement. I'm going to have to pull some pretty big strings to keep the wolves at bay. You and that friend of yours are prime targets for the role of scapegoat in this whole mess.'

What mess? Logan thought, but he decided not to say it. All of the kidnappers were dead or in custody and Modena had a fighting chance of survival. It was better than many of the other possible outcomes. But Logan knew not everyone would see that. And whatever came next, Logan would just have to live with it.

What really worried him, though, was what would happen to Grainger.

'It's not Grainger's fault,' Logan said. 'I insisted on her coming.'

'You may have done, but how did you know that Selim would be here in the first place?' Mackie asked.

Logan didn't answer.

'I think I know what that means. Agent Grainger's got herself into a lot of trouble and there's nothing you or I can do to help her now.'

Mackie sighed and put his hands on his hips. Logan sensed that he was calming down.

'Look,' he said. 'As far as I'm concerned, you've done exactly what I would expect you to. And that's why I brought you into this.

Just don't let me hear you passing that on to this lot. They don't see the world the same way as you and I do.'

Logan had to smile at that. Mackie knew better than anyone how this job worked. He was the one who'd trained Logan, after all. It certainly wouldn't go down as Logan's most successful mission – he was well aware of the chaos that seemed to have followed him around for the last few days. But he'd got there now. It was all over.

Except that wasn't quite true. Logan thought again about Selim's dying words.

'This isn't over, Mackie,' Logan said.

'What do you mean?'

'We still need to find who was behind this, behind Modena's kidnapping.'

'Logan, they're all dead. Everyone is dead! Just who do you think is still out there?'

'Someone who would pay a lot of money for a name that Modena had.'

'What? Where'd all this come from?'

'Selim.'

'You're taking advice from a madman now?'

'It all makes sense,' Logan said, his tone not hiding his offence at Mackie's having so brazenly dismissed what he was saying. 'Someone paid them to kidnap Modena. Someone who had a lot to gain from information that Modena had.'

'Okay, okay. I'll mention it to Evans. They're still piecing together Blakemore's life. If there's anything out there, sooner or later we'll find it.'

'Let me help. I need to finish this.'

'Not yet.' Mackie put a hand on Logan's good shoulder. 'I've arranged for you to stay at a private clinic for a couple of days while they check out your arm. You need to rest and build your strength back up.'

'And then what?'

'And then we'll see.'

'Thanks.'

'For what?'

'For everything.'

Mackie looked embarrassed by Logan's comment. 'I'll speak to you tomorrow,' he said. 'Get some rest. Fagan here will take you to the clinic, keep an eye on you.'

On cue, a brutish-looking man, a good couple of inches taller than Logan and dressed in a smart dark-blue suit, walked into view. He may have been another of Mackie's agents, or perhaps he was just some hired muscle. Logan hadn't seen or heard of him before.

'What, you got me another babysitter?' Logan said, eyeing up his competition. 'Thanks a lot.'

Fagan looked insulted, but didn't say anything.

'Just play nicely, you two,' Mackie said. 'You're on the same team.'

Mackie left them to it without another word.

'I don't like it any more than you do,' Fagan said. 'Come on, let's go. The car's waiting.'

Logan stood up off the gurney, took a second to steady himself in his drugged-up state, then headed off with Fagan to the waiting car. He spotted Grainger, tail between her legs, talking to two suited men. Her eyes caught his and he smiled at her. But she just looked away, down at her feet, not showing any reaction to having seen him.

He walked on to the car.

Yes, Selim was dead. But, to his surprise, he was finding it hard to feel any joy at the current situation. What would happen to Grainger? What would be the consequences for her FBI career? Was Modena going to survive? And just what information had Modena given away that had cost someone eight million dollars?

More than anything, whatever the answers to those questions, Logan just hoped against hope that he'd get the chance to see Grainger again.

Chapter 55

When Logan opened his eyes, the world in front of him was blurred and swirling. He squinted to try to bring it into focus.

He was lying in a bed. The room was not one he immediately recognised and it took a few seconds to recall what had happened and where he was.

'Welcome back.'

A woman's voice. At first he couldn't place it. The drugs were making his brain cloudy and confused. But then he remembered where he knew the voice from. He'd been dreaming about her.

Not a nightmare. A real dream.

As his senses returned, he saw he was lying on a hospital bed, white sheets draped over him. To his side were various machines and monitors, none of which seemed to be turned on. A drip bag was attached by a tube to a cannula in his hand. Other than that, a sink and a closed white cabinet, the room was bare.

He tried to sit up, pushing on the bed with his elbows. But he had forgotten about his injured shoulder and he cried out as pain sliced through him.

'How did you find me?' he said, after waiting for the shooting pain to subside.

'I asked your boss,' said Grainger.

'He told you?'

'Yeah. Are you surprised at that?'

'Very. I'm surprised he even spoke to you.'

'Yeah, well, don't underestimate him.'

Logan never had.

'Do you think you could get me some water?' he said.

'Yeah, sure. God, where are my manners? I should have asked.'

She wandered over to the sink and came back with a paper cup full of chilled water. The liquid was so cold it made Logan's teeth hurt, but it perked him up a little.

'What time is it?' he asked.

'It's about five o'clock in the afternoon. You've been asleep for almost two days. They've had you pretty drugged up.'

'That's their ploy to keep me here.'

'How are you feeling?'

'Like crap. My head feels like a balloon. My arm feels like there're razor blades in it. I'm hungry. And thirsty. But other than that, I'm fine. In fact, I'm ready to get out of here. I hadn't planned on staying this long.'

'Your personal security guard might have something to say about that.'

She indicated to the door. Logan could see Fagan through the glass, standing outside the door with his arms folded.

'Oh, him. Don't worry about him. So what's happened to you? Are you still in a job?'

She fiddled with her hair, rubbed her cheek. Signs of tension.

'Officially I'm suspended. But that's not bad, all things considered. They could have thrown me out straight off. But my boss recognised how well we'd moved things forward. Everyone believes that Selim would have tortured and killed Modena. I'm not saying anyone is happy with how this has turned out, but I think they're at least realistic that things could have been much worse.'

'And we got Selim. That's got to count for something.'

'Actually it seems that's being played down. There's a lot of embarrassment and uncertainty over how he became involved in the first place. The French are desperate to keep quiet the fact that one of the world's most wanted men smuggled himself into their country. Plus both the French and the Feds are a little uneasy about how he died.'

'What do you mean?'

She rubbed at her neck again.

'Well, you know.'

'Not really. Spit it out.'

'You killed an unarmed man, Carl. A defenceless, unarmed man.'

'He wasn't defenceless when he shot me through the shoulder.'

'Logan, I know that. But you know how these things get portrayed. A story's a story. People are saying it was an execution.'

Logan shifted on the bed, anger immediately boiling up inside him. He knew questions would be asked about the manner of Selim's death, but to hear it from Grainger's mouth was hard to take.

'Well, it's not like you tried to stop me,' Logan snapped. 'I saw you standing there, watching.'

Grainger's cheeks turned red and she bowed her head. Logan thought he could see tears welling in her eyes and immediately he felt bad. He and he alone had made the decision to kill Selim. He couldn't try to pin the blame on anyone else.

'I'm sorry,' he said. 'It's just hard to hear how people can twist things.'

'Look, I know why you did it and I know he deserved it,' Grainger said. 'But not everyone sees the world like you do. But that's why everyone is trying to downplay Selim's death. The authorities don't want or need the heat. And I'm sure you don't.'

'I can handle it. It wouldn't be the first time. Anyway, how's Modena?'

'He's in a coma. But he's alive. He may or may not recover, but we saved him.'

Logan felt tangible relief at that.

'And if we hadn't got to him when we did,' he said, 'well, I guess it could have been much worse.'

Logan winced at his own words. It was like he was trying his hardest to justify the outcome to himself. And that made him angry. It wasn't usual for him to feel awkward in Grainger's presence, but right now he felt like a failure. Yes, he'd got Selim, but at what cost? Modena may be alive, but what if he was nothing more than a vegetable? And it was clear that not everyone was going to be congratulatory over the nature of Selim's demise.

What if he had just taken the chance when they were at Blakemore's and gone for Modena rather than the bad guys? Just like Grainger had said they should. It was *him* who had insisted on doing it his way. He was responsible for how things had turned out.

'It's not your fault, Logan. None of this is,' Grainger said. Perhaps she had recognised the look of discontent on his face. 'You didn't notice it, did you?' she added.

'Notice what?'

'When we were at that house. Before you went in, and even after the fighting had stopped, I was looking at your hands. There were no tremors. Nothing at all.'

He thought back to the fight. He hadn't noticed that. When he had been pointing the gun at Selim, his hands had been shaking so hard it had been difficult to focus. But, thinking about it now, he hadn't noticed tremors at all at any other time. Maybe she was right. Maybe it had only been the adrenaline and anticipation causing the shaking when he confronted Selim.

Either way, it meant a lot to him that she had noticed.

'And you can't tell me that it wasn't a stressful situation,' she added. 'So while you might not be happy with how things are right now, your hands are telling me a different story. We've already saved Modena. Selim is dead. And your body is telling me that you and your head might be on the road to recovery. And I think, deep down, you *know* that's the case.'

She could read him better than he could read himself. Selim being dead made a huge difference to his life. But there was more than that. A big part of his recent recovery was also down to her.

'You might be right,' he said. 'But I have to finish this first.'

'Finish what?' Grainger said, surprised.

'I need to find out who paid Blakemore and Selim in the first place. What it was they kidnapped Modena for.'

'You still think that's the case? That there was someone else behind this?'

'I'm convinced.'

'I'm not sure the Feds are. Our investigation has been closed down. As far as we're concerned, it's all over.'

Logan raised an eyebrow at that. It wasn't what he had expected at all. Was that really true? Or now that Modena had been rescued had Grainger reverted to type and this was now her speaking with her formal FBI hat on, not wanting to give the game away?

'So what are you going to do next?' he said.

'I have to stick around here for a few days. They're bringing some of the bigwigs over from America. Debriefing this one is going to be a long haul. We're talking days rather than hours.'

'And the suspension? What does that mean?'

'That I'm on leave until they say otherwise. But that doesn't mean I won't be needed. I think they'll be picking my brains a fair bit.'

'By the way, where are we?' he asked.

The last thing he remembered was being in the car leaving the scene at Dunkirk. Soon after that, the drugs they'd given him, more morphine and a sedative he'd not heard of, had knocked him out and he'd no idea what had happened to him since.

'Now? We're in Paris again. Montparnasse.'

'You're staying in Paris still?'

'Yeah.'

'Great. Then why don't we get out of here?' he said.

'Are you sure you're up to it?'

'Just try to stop me.'

He threw the covers off himself and got to his feet. He had to hold his arms out to balance while his brain got to grips with what he was doing. The sedatives they had given him were certainly still in his system.

Grainger burst out laughing. At him.

'What's so funny?' he said, offended.

'You look like one of those wobbly baby deer or something. And I can see your big red baboon ass sticking out.'

He looked down. He was wearing a light-blue hospital gown. It stopped at the waist at the back, exposing his rear.

'Where the hell are my clothes?' he said, unable to hide his embarrassment. Even Fagan, on the other side of the door, who had turned his attention to them in the commotion, struggled not to break his usual deadpan stare.

'I'll go check.'

She carried on laughing as she went out of the room.

Wiping the smirk from his face, Fagan came into the room just as she left.

'Logan, you're not supposed to leave this place until I've heard from Mackie.'

'You going to stop me?' Logan said.

Fagan shrugged, unfazed. 'No. I couldn't care less. But I'll call it straight in if you go.'

'That's hardly going to make a difference to me, is it?'

'It really doesn't bother me. I'm here to look out for you. If you don't want my help then it's on you.'

'You'd better call Mackie, then. Tell him I'll come and see him later.'

Fagan shrugged again and left the room.

Grainger returned a minute later with a pile of crisp new clothes: linen trousers and a light blue shirt. Mackie's choice, no doubt.

It took Logan a while to get dressed. Having one arm that was more or less immobile made everything ten times as hard as normal. He had got used to it years ago when he'd been shot in the arm, but it wasn't really something he'd carried on practising once that wound had healed.

Grainger offered to help but, stubborn as ever, he refused.

Finally, he was ready to go.

As Logan walked out of the room, Fagan came back up to him. 'I spoke to Mackie. He says he wants you at the safe house at nine a.m. tomorrow.'

'Fine,' Logan said.

'Oh, and he said to bring along your passport.'

'Which one? And what for?'

'Dunno. He just said you'd be going to America.'

Chapter 56

12th October

After leaving the clinic with a suite of medical supplies that would hopefully keep Logan mobile, they had initially thought about heading to Grainger's hotel, on the other side of town. But the fact that her FBI colleagues were also staying there had persuaded them otherwise. Instead, they had found a low-budget option nearby. And after heading out for some much needed food they'd spent the rest of that evening in bed together, only going to sleep in the early hours of the morning. The next day, too, had come and gone with them barely leaving the bed. Logan had called in to Mackie, rather than heading to the safe house as requested, and his boss, although hesitant, had okayed a further twenty-four hours' rest. Not that Logan or Grainger had rested much.

It had been an amazing two nights. Grainger couldn't believe just how relaxed they had both become in each other's company. And how Logan seemed to be almost a changed man from the complex mess she'd met just five days ago.

But this morning, Grainger felt altogether different. And not just about the prospect of Logan leaving for America. What was bothering her most, and what really shocked her, was that she couldn't bear the thought that after this morning she may never see Carl Logan again.

They'd briefly broached the subject of when they'd next see each other the night before, but neither had wanted to spoil the atmosphere then and the conversation had quickly moved on without resolution. But it was now playing on Grainger's mind again. Plus she could feel the pressure beginning to build now for what lay ahead for her. Logan had been a convenient distraction for the past two days but she still had work to do.

Having set the alarm to ensure he wasn't late for Mackie, Logan had got out of bed at six. He left Grainger in bed and headed out to a café to get coffee and some pastries for breakfast. When he got back to the hotel room twenty minutes later, Grainger was already up and dressed.

'Oh, I thought you were still sleeping. I just went out to get breakfast,' he said, holding up the purchases with his one useful arm.

He brought the food and drink over to her, laid it down on the small, round table next to where she was sitting and kissed her on the cheek.

She responded with an awkward smile.

'What's the matter?' he asked.

'Nothing,' she said, giving him another less than convincing smile. 'Thanks for getting this.'

'I can tell something's up. What is it?'

'It's nothing,' she said, more bluntly, wanting to say more, but unsure just how to open the subject up.

After that, they ate their breakfast in near silence.

'Last night was great,' Logan said, finishing the remainder of his black coffee. 'I'm not sure where you learned all that. You were like a caged tiger let loose.'

She tutted. 'Carl, I know you don't want to talk about this –'

'Then let's not,' Logan said, as though picking up on where she was going.

'Carl! Stop being so goddamn nonchalant! This matters to me, even if it doesn't matter to you!'

'I never said it didn't matter,' he said.

'Look. You can't just ignore it and hope that it'll go away. I want to know when we're going to see each other again.'

'I want to know that too. But why do we have to fight about it? Why can't we just enjoy the time we *are* spending together?'

'Well, that's just about as non-committal as you can get.'

'I didn't mean for it to be. I just want to enjoy this time together *now*. Not try to complicate things that don't need to be complicated.'

'You're right. It's not like we even really know each other that well, is it?' she said, angry as much as she was hurt. 'I mean, I don't really know who you are. And you don't really know anything about me.'

'What's that supposed to mean?'

'Well, you don't. Tell me what you know about me. I'm an FBI agent you like the look of naked and who's a good fuck. Is there anything more than that?'

He didn't say anything, just stared at her.

'There isn't, is there?' she said, angered even more by his lack of response. 'You know nothing about me. Other than my name and who I work for. Hell, you don't even know where I'm from, where I live.'

'Yes, I do,' he said. 'You live in Virginia.'

She looked at him, confusion now etched on her face. 'How do you know that?' she snapped. 'I never even told you that.'

'Yes, you did. You told me about how your dad used to take you hunting in the Appalachians. You've lived in Virginia your whole life.'

Was that true? Her thoughts immediately went back to the night before. She'd certainly talked to him about her dad. About how he'd take her hunting in the mountains. About how, on her thirteenth birthday, she'd been allowed to fire her dad's rifle for the first time. The fact that the recoil had knocked her off her feet into the wet snow. That she'd cried for days when she realised she'd killed the poor deer with that very shot.

She'd told Logan numerous intimate details about the good times she'd spent with her father.

But she'd never told him where she was from.

It shouldn't have been a big deal. But it was.

'I could have lived anywhere and gone to the Appalachians with my dad. How did you know I live in Virginia?'

Logan fidgeted in his seat, his cheeks burning red.

'I had a colleague look up your profile,' he said, unable to look her in the eye. 'Check out that you were who you said you were.'

'You what?!' Grainger said, standing up out of her seat, arms folded.

'I'm sorry. I just wanted to know who I was dealing with. Wouldn't you have done the same? But that was before any of this happened. Before me and you. It was right after you dumped me on the side of the road!'

'What else did you find out about me?' she said, a feeling of real unease creeping over her.

'It was just a simple check! It was completely innocent.'

'Well, I hope you got from it what you wanted. I'm glad it didn't put you off.'

'Jesus, Angie, you're making far more out of this than you need to.'

'I don't think I am! I think I'm kinda proving my point! We *don't* know each other. Not really. Like I didn't know that the man I'm sleeping with was going around checking up on me behind my back!'

'Look, why are we even arguing about this? We had a great time last night. We should be having a good time *now*. Can we not just enjoy this time together?'

'What, so you buy me dinner, then we go back to a hotel and fuck? Then what? *See you later?* Is that how this works?'

He had nothing to say to that. Not for the first time, his lack of response didn't calm her down at all and she moved away from the table, storming toward the bathroom door.

He jumped up after her and grabbed her arm.

'Angela. You are the most amazing person I have ever met,' he said. 'I've never felt like this before with anyone. You've made me feel alive – I mean *really* alive – for the first time in my life. And I spend every waking minute and every second I sleep thinking about you.'

The anger on her face began to ebb away, leaving a look somewhere near bewilderment. She looked deeply into his eyes and could feel tears forming in hers. She shrugged, trying to pull away from his grip. But he wouldn't let her; he held her tight.

'You've changed my life,' he said. 'For the better. I was a mess before you walked into my life, pointing that gun of yours in my face. Before you, I never had a single meaningful relationship. For the past five months I've been struggling with a condition I didn't even want to *think* about, let alone deal with. And look at me *now*. Do you know what I dreamed about last night? I dreamed about *you*. Not a nightmare. I've had nightmares nearly every time I've slept for five months. And when I don't have nightmares I don't dream at all. Last night? Last night I dreamed of me and you. *Together.*'

Her bottom lip was quivering. She tried with one last feeble attempt to free herself, but she soon gave up. Tears were now rolling down her face.

'And when I say I'm not sure how it's going to work out between us,' he said, 'it's because I'm *scared*. Scared that you might not feel the same way about me. And scared because things might not work out how I want them to. I want you, Special Agent Grainger. *Surely* you must see that by now. And I damn well know that I *need* you.'

He finally stopped his monologue.

Without saying another word, Grainger buried her head in Logan's chest. What he'd said had really touched her. It was exactly what she had hoped to hear. Because she was feeling much the same way for him, too.

Yet she knew that despite their mutual attraction, their relationship would likely never get the chance to blossom. Not now, not ever. How could it?

And as she stood with her head nestled into his chest, longing for his touch and the warmth of his body next to hers, a strange sensation crept over her: the most euphoric feeling she'd ever known, mixed in equal measure with sadness.

Chapter 57

The streets of Paris were quiet as Logan walked the short distance to the safe house – it was, after all, early morning on a weekend. The weather had returned to its seasonal self and there was a bitter wind picking up, making it feel colder than it really was. Logan hunched down into his shirt, which was the only clothing he had on his upper body.

It had been hard to leave Grainger. He wasn't even sure what he had just said to her. The words had come straight from the heart – there was no premeditation in that, no ulterior motive. It was like someone had opened him up and pulled out everything that he had been wanting to say but couldn't. Or wouldn't.

But for all of his heartfelt words, they still hadn't confirmed one way or the other whether they would ever see each other again. He couldn't understand why it was such a fraught subject. He'd tried to remain relaxed about it, although his offhand approach had only seemed to rile her. As far as he was concerned it was a no-brainer. He didn't know where and when, but what was to stop them seeing each other again?

For some reason she seemed to have got it into her head that that wasn't the case.

In a way, he could understand why the training he'd gone through all those years ago, when he'd first met Mackie, had been so concerned with trying to suppress emotions. The truth was, they were hard to deal with. He would even go so far as to say that they were a big hindrance. When you should be concentrating on catching a sadistic terrorist and all you could think about was when you might get to kiss your woman next, that could make the difference between success and failure. In a way, it already had.

And when you were kissing your woman and all you could think about was how the hell you were going to find the baddies, that was equally likely to result in failure.

Feelings got in the way. Right now, he needed to focus on the investigation. Fagan had said that Logan would be going to America. The only thing he could think was that someone had found a lead on the originator of Modena's kidnapping.

Logan reached the safe house and walked in, heading for the lounge. Mackie was there as he entered, dressed casually and standing by the desk next to Evans. Evans was on his feet too and Logan saw that he was tall and wiry; it didn't look like there was an ounce of muscle on him.

'You're looking pretty dapper there, Logan,' Mackie said, gesturing to the clothes that he had arranged for Logan at the clinic. 'Much better than that normal crap you wear.'

'You could've got me something warmer,' Logan responded, taking a seat.

Evans came around and sat next to him. Mackie stayed standing.

'You can sort yourself out at the airport,' Mackie said without sympathy. 'How's the shoulder?'

Logan still had his shoulder heavily strapped but he hadn't bothered to wear a sling; it would just get in the way.

'It hurts like hell. But the drugs are helping.'

Mackie shrugged. 'We've got a very good lead,' he said, jumping on topic. 'And with the twenty-four hours extra that we've had to dig, we think we may be getting to the bottom of this now.'

Logan's interest perked up at hearing Mackie's words, and all of a sudden his thoughts of the awkward conversation with Grainger were banished.

Mackie carried on. 'As you suggested, everything points to Selim just being a hired gun in this. But that means we're still looking for the missing link.'

'By the missing link, you mean those who put together and funded this thing in the first place,' Logan said. 'Right?'

'Exactly. Go ahead, Evans.'

'This is just preliminary,' said Evans, turning to face Logan, 'but we've identified money coming across to Blakemore. Eight million dollars was transferred into his account two days ago, right about the time you stormed his farmhouse, I'm told. A few minutes later the whole lot was wired out to another account in the Cayman Islands. From there we don't know where it went, if it went anywhere at all. We're still looking into that.'

Evans pushed some papers across the desk toward Logan. He glanced at them without picking them up, determining that they were financial records of some sort. He didn't need to inspect them any further than that. He was sure Evans and Mackie were about to tell him all he needed to know.

'But you don't think the money just went on to another one of Blakemore's accounts?' Logan asked.

'We don't know yet,' said Evans, shrugging.

'Why? What do *you* think?' Mackie asked Logan, eyeing him almost suspiciously.

'I'd bet my hat on it having gone to Selim. I think Blakemore was supposed to distribute part of the money to Selim and the others. But Selim had other ideas – he killed Reggie Graham, tortured Blakemore and transferred all the money to himself.'

'Well, that would make sense,' Evans said, picking up another piece of paper. He handed it over to Logan, who took it but didn't look at it. 'We can see a cancelled transfer for two million dollars to an account in England held by a Reginald Graham.'

'Just one cancelled transfer?' Logan queried, putting the paper on the table.

'No, there's another for the account which ended up with the whole lot. That was also for two million dollars. Straight after the cancellation, the transfer for eight million was made.'

'That account has to be Selim's then,' Logan said. 'So the eight million was transferred a couple of days ago? To Blakemore, I mean?'

'Yes,' confirmed Evans.

'So something *did* happen in the farmhouse. They weren't paid anything before that?'

'We can't identify anything unusual, no,' Evans said.

It all seemed to fit with what Selim had said.

'Well, that brings us back to the question of why they nabbed Modena,' Logan stated, looking at Evans then Mackie. 'They hadn't even been paid anything up front. A few days in and all of a sudden they're eight million dollars richer. Selim said it was for a name. But what name, and why was it worth so much money to someone?'

'Which is exactly why I've called you in,' Mackie said, finally taking a seat.

'What? You know the answer?'

'No, not yet, but we think we know where the eight million came from.'

Mackie looked over at Evans, indicating for him to continue.

'We traced the eight million back to an originator. There was quite a paper trail behind the transactions. There's money coming in and out of accounts all over the world. For many of the transactions we don't know who the bank accounts actually belong to – it's all obscured by the use of trusts, shell companies, fake names and the like. But we've found that the origin of the eight million dollars is a client account of a lawyer in New York. Alan Rosenberg.'

'A lawyer? Well, that's unexpected,' Logan said.

'Not when you find out who's on his client list, it isn't,' Evans said, pushing more paper Logan's way. 'And it wasn't eight million. It was ten. The account that paid the eight million to Blakemore is with a bank in Bermuda. We've traced ten million dollars being transferred *in*to that account. Like I said, though, it's a whole catalogue of transactions, but the ten million definitely came from Rosenberg in the first place.'

'So two million has gone to someone else?'

'It would seem so.'

'But we don't know who owns that account? The one in Bermuda?'

'No. We can see the money, but we're working on who the account actually belongs to and we need to do some more work to unwind the other transactions.'

Mackie stepped in. 'It's the link to Rosenberg that we want you to check out.'

'You said something about his client list?' Logan said.

'Yeah, this guy has a penchant for representing high-profile figures,' Mackie said, 'Usually pretty controversial figures as well. His biggest case was representing Tony Carlucci. That was also his biggest failure, as the guy is currently serving five life sentences for everything from racketeering to aggravated homicide.'

'Tony Carlucci?' Logan broke in. 'The mafia boss?'

'Yeah. Old-school Mafioso. Alleged to have headed up one of the East Coast's biggest crime families. How much of that stuff is actually real is anybody's guess, but he was certainly a pretty powerful guy.'

Logan's brain was racing. This was a lot of information to take in, but things were starting to click into place now.

'Lucky,' Logan recalled. 'That's what Modena said to me. *It was lucky.* That's the guy's nickname, isn't it? You know what these gangsters are like. Louis *Mad Dog* or whatever. Tony Carlucci is known as Lucky Tony. I remember reading about it when he went to trial. Modena was telling me who it was, giving me the answer.'

'Jesus. Modena *knew* who was behind his kidnapping?' Mackie said. 'How did he know?'

'Because Selim and Blakemore were trying to get a name out of him,' Logan said. 'They got their money when they got the information Carlucci needed.'

'So you don't just think this Tony guy's got a beef with Modena and that's why they nabbed him?' Mackie suggested. 'You know, he could hold Modena responsible for his being in jail. He wasn't the presiding judge, but who knows what kind of role Modena had to play in the investigation, the trial, even the sentencing.'

'It could be that,' Logan conceded. 'But the timing of the transfers doesn't work for me if that was the case. And wouldn't they have just killed Modena if it were? It's more than that. Modena had a name that was worth ten million dollars to Carlucci.'

'Okay. You need to go and pay Rosenberg a visit.'

'Wait a minute,' Logan said, remembering something. 'Does anyone else know about this lead? The Feds, I mean?'

'Of course not,' Mackie said, offended. 'This information is ours. No-one else will know about this until they need to.'

Logan thought back to the house in Dunkirk – holding Modena in his arms, the look on Grainger's face when he'd recounted what Modena had said. Had she known about Carlucci?

Logan got up to leave. 'Sorry, I've got to go.'

Mackie stood up. 'Logan, where the hell are you going? Your plane leaves in two hours!'

'I have to check something out. I'll be on the plane. I promise.'

When he was outside he took out his phone and called Grainger's number, but it didn't even ring out, just went straight to voicemail. He tried again twice more but the same thing happened each time. Frustrated, he stuffed the phone back in his pocket. He thought about heading back to the hotel to find her, but he wasn't sure he had time.

What did Grainger know about Carlucci?

Maybe she had been right about him not really knowing her. He didn't know what was going on, but Grainger knew something and she had kept it from him.

But there was nothing much he could do about it now. He had a flight to catch.

Chapter 58

Logan was driving the short distance from JFK airport to Manhattan in a rented Saturn, heading for Alan Rosenberg's office. He'd taken a flight from Paris just after noon, landing in New York mid-afternoon. It'd taken him longer than expected to pass through immigration and it was now early evening. He'd toyed with the idea of paying a personal visit to Rosenberg, but in the end opted for the safer course of heading to his office in the first instance. It was the weekend, and Logan was banking on the office being close to empty. He wanted to go through the man's belongings and his files, see whether there was anything in there to link Rosenberg and Carlucci to Blakemore.

Coming out of the Queens–Midtown Tunnel into Manhattan, Logan turned onto 41st Street, heading west. He called Mackie as he drove. It had been a number of hours since they'd spoken in Paris, and given how quickly the investigation seemed to be moving, Logan wanted to make sure he was fully up to date.

'Is there anything else I need to know?' Logan asked.

'Yeah, actually there is. We've got another angle to look at,' Mackie said. 'Have you come across the name Jimmy Kennedy?'

Logan racked his brain but he hadn't. 'No.'

'Well, if we're looking for a name here, that one might be it. Jimmy Kennedy used to be a henchman for Carlucci. He turned state's witness and was one of the biggest assets the prosecution had in Carlucci's conviction.'

'And he's now in witness protection,' Logan said, putting the pieces together. He had wondered what name Modena could know that would be so valuable and that of someone with a new identity was an obvious answer. 'Carlucci was paying for Jimmy Kennedy's new identity.'

'That's the conclusion we're coming to. Although it all sounds pretty elaborate that they would snatch Modena, one of the most powerful men in the country, for something like that.'

'I guess to Carlucci ten million dollars probably isn't that much to off the man who put him inside.'

'Yeah, you can pretty much believe it.'

'Something that still doesn't add up, though,' Logan said, pulling the car to a stop at a red light before turning right onto 3rd Avenue. 'What I still don't like is the missing two million dollars. If Carlucci paid ten, but only eight found its way to Blakemore, then where did the rest go? It's like there's a middleman bringing it all together, linking Carlucci to Blakemore.'

'I agree with where you're going. We're still looking into it. And hopefully the answer will become clear when you've been through Rosenberg's files.'

'And what about Kennedy? He's either already dead or he soon will be. Do you know his new identity and where he lives?'

'We're working on it,' Mackie said. 'When I get anything you can use, you'll be the first to know.'

Logan ended the call. Two minutes later he pulled up to the kerb on Park Avenue, just a few buildings down from the offices that housed Rosenberg Associates. Logan got out of the car and battled his way across the bustling pavement where throngs of tourists were travelling in force in each and every direction. On the road yellow taxis darted over lanes and pulled in and out of cross streets. Skyscrapers loomed all around, windows lit up high into the sky. Even with Logan's mind focused on the task at hand, it was hard not to feel the buzz of the city.

The busy street was a stark contrast to the building itself, which from the outside Logan could tell was relatively empty given the general lack of lit windows. Whether that was because some of the offices were untenanted or because it was quiet with it being the weekend, he didn't know. The building had eight storeys. Not a big structure, at least not by New York standards, but what it lacked in size it certainly made up for in extravagance. Logan walked in through the single set of revolving doors which opened out into an expanse of gold, marble and chandeliers.

There was a security desk at the far end of the lobby, next to two lifts. As he walked toward the desk he spotted a large notice board behind which were displayed the names of the building's occupants. Rosenberg Associates was one of two firms that took up the eighth floor.

The only problem now was how to get up there and into the office. Not only would he have to contend with the security guard sitting at the desk in the lobby but he needed a way to access the doors on the eighth floor, which he had to assume were in some way secured.

Logan reached the desk and smiled at the security guard. He was an overweight man, middle-aged, with thinning grey hair and puffy red cheeks. He had a protruding belly that hung over and completely hid the top of his trousers. Logan wasn't sure exactly what this guy would be good at keeping secure. He certainly wouldn't be a fast mover.

'I'm visiting Alan Rosenberg,' Logan said.

The man stood up, eyeballing Logan suspiciously.

'Are you? I don't remember seeing him here today. Do you have an appointment?'

'Actually I do. Henry Foster is my name. Maybe the appointment was with one of his other lawyers. It was set up by my assistant.'

'Yeah, sure,' the guard said in a manner which told Logan that he wasn't buying the story. 'Just wait there while I call up.'

The guard picked up the phone. Logan smiled at him, trying his best to appear unflustered by the situation. He really didn't want to hurt the guard, but he knew that there might not be another option. At least his calling first would tell Logan whether anyone was there or not.

The guard put the phone down without having spoken at all.

'There's no-one answering,' he said. 'I don't think I've actually seen anyone from that office today. It's probably best if you rearrange your appointment and come back during the week.'

'Look. I've travelled a really long way to get here. England, actually. I really need to get up there.'

'I'm sorry, sir. But I'm not going to let you do that.' The guard puffed out his chest as he spoke. 'Unless you want to leave a message of some sort I suggest you leave now.'

'I tell you what: you let me go up and I'll give you a hundred dollars. If you don't let me go up then I'll just go up anyway and you won't get anything.'

'Last chance, sir!' the guard hollered, voice raised. He moved around from behind the desk so that he was directly in front of Logan. His hand reached to his holstered pistol, but he didn't pick it up. It was definitely a signal of intent, though.

'Don't make this into a scene,' the guard said.

Logan really hadn't wanted to do this, but he wasn't sure he was left with much choice. He stepped toward the guard, who, on sensing that the situation was about to go awry, began to draw his weapon. Logan reached out and grabbed the guard's hand, which was wrapped around his still-holstered gun. With his other hand, Logan threw a straight forearm at the man's throat. He let go of the guard's hand and he stumbled backward, hands up to his neck, gasping for air. Losing his footing, he fell to the ground, slumping against the desk.

Logan reached down and took the man's walkie-talkie and gun.

'I ... I can't breathe!'

Logan put the walkie-talkie in his pocket, took the gun in his left hand and pointed it toward the man. He left the safety on; he had no intention of shooting him.

'You'll be fine. Unless you want any more, that is.' Logan reached out for the guard with his free hand, pulling him up to his feet. 'Come on. Let's get you over to the lift.'

The guard shuffled along, coughing and spluttering, unsteady on his feet. Logan had to take most of his considerable weight as he dragged him along. Taking the guard with him wasn't ideal, but he couldn't leave him downstairs in the lobby. Hopefully the guard wouldn't try to be a hero as Logan really didn't want to have to hurt him any further.

When they reached the lifts, Logan pressed the up button. He heard the tinkle of the left-hand lift, dragged the guard toward the opening doors and dumped him inside. He pressed the button for the eighth floor but nothing happened. He pressed it again, but still there was no movement.

'Why won't it go?' Logan said.

'You need a card.'

Logan bent down and took the man's ID card from around his neck. He inserted it into the slot in the lift wall and pressed for floor eight again. The doors closed and they were on their way.

When they reached the eighth floor, Logan lifted guard man again and began to drag him out of the lift. But the guard surprised Logan with a show of strength, flailing his arms at Logan and trying to reach for the gun that he had lost. Tired of the man's resistance, Logan took out his own gun – a Glock which had been handed to him outside the airport by a courier arranged by Mackie – and with one sweeping move he smacked the guard in the head with the metal butt. He went down in a heap. A line of red began to trickle down from the guard's thinning hair onto his face. He was going to have a pretty sore head in the morning but Logan knew it wouldn't be serious. Logan hadn't wanted to hurt him, but some people just didn't know when to give up.

He pulled the guard out of the lift and looked left and right to find the direction of Rosenberg's office. The lift bank opened up into a short corridor. There were toilet facilities in the middle, a door leading to the stairwell and a single set of double doors at each end, one for each of the floor's occupants.

A sign on the door off to his right told Logan that was where Rosenberg Associates was located. He began to pull the guard over to the door. When he reached it, he saw that there was another card slot and he used the security guard's card again to unlock the doors before dragging him inside.

The lights in the office turned on automatically to reveal a room just as spectacular as the downstairs lobby. There was marble flooring, big leather sofas, oversized paintings on the walls and bizarre coffee tables that looked more like modern art sculptures than something you would rest a hot beverage on.

Logan dragged the guard over to the reception desk and handcuffed him to the railing that ran along its top. Disarmed, restrained and out of sight, he posed no threat.

The office, which was at the front of the building, adjacent to Park Avenue, wasn't particularly big. There were just a handful of rooms off the main reception area. All but one of them were glass-fronted and contained small, open-plan spaces with modern but expensive-looking desks. The one exception was the room at the far end, which was the only room that had frosted glass. *That must be Rosenberg's*, Logan thought.

He went over to the door. It had a key card slot. He pushed in the guard's card, but nothing happened. It was definitely Rosenberg's office. He was a cautious old weasel. Not even building security had access.

But Logan didn't have time to sit around thinking about how he was going to get in. He walked back to the reception area, picked up the receptionist's chair and carried it to Rosenberg's office. He swivelled his hips sideways and flung the chair into the glass door. There was a loud bang as the chair hit and rebounded off the door. It bounced a good couple of feet away from the door, which wobbled some, but didn't smash or even crack.

Maybe all he needed was a bit more oomph.

Logan tried again, this time with a bit more venom. The door came crashing down in thousands of evenly sized pieces. He was in.

But the door had also been security-enabled. No sooner had the chair hit the ground than a deafening alarm began to wail.

Cursing under his breath, Logan hurried on into the room and began his search.

It was hard to know how much time he would have, but he had to be strict about this. The temptation would be to keep on giving himself extra seconds each time he got close to his limit. *Go on, just a few more seconds won't do any harm.* But he couldn't allow that. He would give himself three minutes only. Then he was out of there. No ifs and no buts.

The room he was now in had a large mahogany desk at its centre and a matching shelving unit that covered one entire end of the office, floor to ceiling, wall to wall, mostly filled with photo frames and fancy ornaments rather than files or books. What Logan wanted was at the opposite end of the room where there was a plain-looking gun-metal-grey filing cabinet.

He opened each of the drawers in turn, quickly filing through the contents and trying to figure what documents were in there and what kind of order they were in. There appeared to be various client files, arranged alphabetically. He went through the Cs, found one labelled *Carlucci*, a brown paper folder, and took it out. It was only about half an inch thick, so it couldn't possibly contain everything on Carlucci's relationship with Rosenberg. But Logan didn't need everything. He just needed *something*.

He checked his watch. Shit. Time was almost up. Only twenty-one seconds to go.

He opened up the file. It contained various correspondence: invoices, payment details, letters, emails. He would have to hope that this file was enough.

But as he headed back to the door, he had another thought. He looked at his watch. Three seconds to go. *Shit*, he thought – *just one last look.*

Pushing the screaming voice, the one telling him to just get the hell out of there, to the back of his head, he rushed back over to the filing cabinet. He flipped through the other drawers. No. There was nothing for Kennedy or Modena.

It had been worth a shot. Or at least he hoped it had. It had cost him an extra minute.

He glanced out of the floor-to-ceiling windows which overlooked Park Avenue and saw police cars already pulling up outside, their lights flashing.

It was time to go.

With the Carlucci file in his hand, he raced back out to the main doors. The guard was still by the desk, still out cold. Logan went right past him with barely a glance, swiped the card at the door and exited into the corridor.

He noticed that the alarm wasn't sounding out here. It must have been localised to Rosenberg's offices. Not that it helped the situation much, but at least it meant the whole building wasn't on lockdown. At least not yet. In any case, the stairs would be a better option than the lifts now. They would at least give him a chance to plan his approach once he reached the lower floors.

Logan headed to the stairwell and started his descent. He took the steps as quickly as he could, one hand holding the file, the other holding onto the handrail. His own gun was in his waistband, the other dumped back next to the security guard. There was no need to carry both.

As he approached the third floor, he heard voices and footsteps coming from down below him. Looking over the banister, he saw policemen heading up the stairs. Using the security guard's key card to unlock the door, he dived back inside on the third floor. He just had to hope that with the noise they were making, they wouldn't have heard him.

The corridor here was much the same as it had been on the eighth floor. Rosenberg Associates had occupied the front half of the top floor and he was pretty sure there hadn't been any other exits within that office area. But there was a good chance there would be one at the back end of the building.

There were no signs of people here, but he drew his gun anyway, out of instinct more than anything. He ran over to the doors to Gresham LLP, put the security guard's card into the slot and opened the door. There were already lights on in these offices.

As Logan rushed through, he nearly barged into a smartly dressed lady, probably in her forties, coming around a corner, carrying a cup of coffee. She screamed as he narrowly avoided knocking her over.

'Where's the exit?!' he shouted at her.

Her eyes focused in on his gun, which he was holding down at his side. In his adrenaline-fuelled state, face red, eyes bulging, chest heaving, gun drawn, the poor woman must have thought he was a crazed psychopath. She meekly pointed in the direction she had just come from. Without time for explanation or apology, Logan raced off in that direction, leaving the bemused woman dumbstruck.

He exited through another set of security doors and came to a service lift. Beyond that there was another stairwell. He went down the two flights of stairs to the first floor and debated for a second whether to go out there or continue. In the end he kept on going, down to the basement, which he hoped would be a car park.

His luck was in. He was right. It was only a small garage, about fifty or so spaces on a single floor. He ran over to the exit ramp, which was at the back of the building. He slowed his pace and began to walk up it, cautiously, casually, trying his hardest to temper his breathing which was racing from having run down the stairs. He couldn't see or hear any signs of the police.

When he reached the top he stooped low, underneath the barrier, out onto the busy New York street. Quickly he glanced up and down, and then smiled as he realised he was in the clear.

Chapter 59

With the file in hand, Logan walked calmly back to his rented Saturn, ignoring the police lights and sirens that were still blaring outside the office block. He got into the car and pulled out into the road, then began to push his way through the ever-busy New York traffic.

When he was a safe distance away, he pulled over to the side of the road, just shy of 110th Street, and began to sift through the file. Within minutes he had a new destination in mind.

His luck really was in. As well as containing various apparently legitimate items related to Carlucci, the file also included two pieces of paper which were of great interest to Logan. The first was a series of what looked like bank account numbers. The second was similar, but it also had a name and address on it. A name and address Logan had not come across before.

Not wanting to waste any time, he plugged the address details straight into the GPS unit which he had rented and hit the road again. He intended to call Mackie on the way to give an update, but before he got the chance to call his boss, his phone chirped.

He got a strange feeling when he saw who was calling him: Grainger.

It had been a fast and furious day – one thing to the next. Waking up this morning in a hotel room in Paris with Grainger seemed a lifetime ago. And then there was the whole question of whether she had been keeping information from him about Carlucci. But since he'd landed in New York just a few hours ago, he'd barely even had a second to think about Grainger.

Looking at his phone now, he felt pretty lousy about that. If he'd meant what he said to her this morning, about her being so important to him, about him needing her, then why had he not even been thinking about her? Missing her?

'Hi,' he answered, trying to sound more excited than he really was.

'Hi, Carl.'

'I called you this morning,' he said. 'Before I left.'

There was a moment's silence before she answered.

'Yeah, my phone was dead. Sorry about that. I'm just calling to see how you are.'

He wanted to ask about Carlucci, what she knew and how. But it wasn't something he wanted to do over the phone. He hated phone calls because there was no way to control a conversation. Not like when you were face to face with someone, looking them in the eyes.

'Yeah, sorry,' he said. 'It's just been so hectic here.'

'So you're making progress then? What have you found?'

It seemed strange having this conversation with her now. Four days ago, when they'd been the dynamic duo, it had been them against the world. But now, she was suspended and was well and truly out of this investigation. She had also been keeping something from him. So as wrong as it felt to now want to keep his cards close to his chest, he wasn't really sure what would be gained from telling her the discovery about Carlucci and Kennedy.

Perhaps there was some of the old Logan left after all.

'No, we haven't found much yet,' he said, not happy about lying to her, but knowing that it was the best option. 'We're just following up on some leads. Not much more to tell than that.'

'Oh. So the link to Rosenberg didn't help in the end then?'

Had he told her about Rosenberg? He couldn't remember.

'No,' said Logan. 'Rosenberg didn't have anything.'

'Oh.'

She sounded disappointed. Was it disappointment that he hadn't found anything, or that he wasn't telling her anything?

He was torn. On the one hand Grainger had kept information from him, so this was only quid pro quo. But then, he supposed, she had as much riding on this investigation as he did. She'd gone through a lot on this case too. In a way, with all the help she'd given him, she had a *right* to know what was going on. But it was too late to take back the lie now. One thing he'd learned a long time ago was that lies could take you forward, but they could never take you back. He'd always hated that saying. You usually only ever thought about it when you knew you were about to come unstuck.

'And what are the other leads?' she said.

'Nothing substantial. Might not be anything,' he said, cringing as he spoke. 'Where are you anyway? It must be pretty late there.'

'Oh, yeah, er, it is pretty late. I'm just in the hotel but couldn't sleep. Seems kinda funny not to have you here.'

'Yeah. It is. Look, I should go.'

'Okay.'

'It was really good to hear from you. I mean that. You just made my day a whole lot better.'

'Yeah. You too, Carl. I hope you find what you're looking for.'

So did he.

As soon as they'd hung up, Logan began to dial in to Mackie. He was greeted by the blaring horn of a large lorry in the adjacent lane as he clumsily drove one-handed, trying to start the call.

When Mackie answered, Logan began to explain what had happened at Rosenberg's office.

'I found a name and address and a whole list of what I think are bank account numbers,' he said.

'What's the name?'

'Greg Dennis. Doesn't ring any bells to me. And there was nothing else in the file I took with that name on it. But I'm heading to the address now.'

'Okay. What are the numbers? Read them out to me.'

Logan turned on the overhead light and, without stopping the car or even braking, did his best to read out the numbers to Mackie while keeping straight on the road.

'Okay. We'll check out Dennis and these numbers.'

'The address is in Binghamton town,' Logan said. 'It's in Broome County, New York.'

'Right. That'll be enough for us to narrow down our searches on him. We have something for you as well.'

'What is it?'

'We have Kennedy's new identity. He lives in some hick town in Ohio now. His name is William Button.'

'How did you find it?'

'Remote access. The same way Blakemore and Selim got it. Modena must have given them a username and password for the system, but these guys then went to town hacking through restricted databases until they found what they were looking for. So it seems Modena mustn't have known exactly where to find the answer himself. It took quite a bit of effort on the part of Selim and Blakemore to find it. They did a really good job of hiding their tracks too. Must have had some proper techno whizz kid in their ranks. The Americans had no idea the data had been hacked. I don't think they would ever have known about it if we hadn't gone looking for it.'

'They know?' Logan said, not liking where this was going.

'It was the quickest way for us to do it.' Mackie said, almost apologetically. 'We've had help from the DOJ and the US Marshals Service. It's their witness, after all.'

'So everything we know is all out in the open now?' Logan said, angered at the thought that Mackie had turned over their leads before he'd had a chance to finish things off. But also embarrassed because it meant that it would have been plain to Grainger that Logan was lying to her on the call they'd just had – assuming she was still being kept in the loop by the FBI.

'Kennedy's their problem,' Mackie said. 'This thing is almost over now. It's not really our territory anymore. This could just as well be handled by the police or Feds or whoever. I'm going to give you a few hours on Dennis, but after that we're closing it down. The Feds are already taking over on locating and protecting Kennedy, so there'll be a team arriving at his door any minute to take him somewhere safe.'

Logan felt his stomach clenching, the feeling of failure rising. Mackie never gave jobs away like this.

'So it's over?'

Mackie sighed. 'You've done your job, Logan. It's time to close it down now. But I won't tell the Feds anything on Dennis until you've checked him out.'

'Why?'

'Because I want to know if he's the right man before we hand that information over. If he's not, and this investigation takes another turn, then I want us to still be ahead of the curve. If it's Dennis that's the last missing link here, the Feds can have him.'

'But you don't think it is?'

'Well, until you told me about the guy just now, it wasn't a name on anyone's radar, as far as I know.'

'So who's on the radar then?' Logan quizzed. He had the feeling that Mackie wasn't telling him the whole story.

'There isn't anyone else yet,' Mackie responded.

Logan wasn't convinced.

'You've got four hours, Logan,' Mackie said, and then he hung up.

Logan put the phone down and sighed. It was now all or nothing. He had a hunch that Mackie wasn't being entirely straight with him. And neither was Grainger.

But he was the one who was moving the investigation forward now. And he was the one who would finish it.

Even though there was no reason to suspect there was any heat on him, Logan resisted the temptation to speed as he travelled down the freeway. There was no need to draw unwanted attention to himself. The town where he was headed, Binghamton, close to the city of the same name, was a picturesque place with less than five thousand inhabitants. Most of the townsfolk were relatively wealthy, either retirees or businessmen and women who commuted into nearby cities.

It was a long drive, and Logan was travel-weary and hungry by the time he arrived. His arm was aching more and more as the minutes went past. He'd lost his medication somewhere between landing at JFK and all the excitement in Manhattan. His head hurt and his body was weak. He knew that he should rest.

But he was so close that he wasn't going to stop. He *couldn't* stop now.

The road he'd been taken to by his GPS was near to the town's high street and consisted of a row of well-presented terraces. Many of them housed fashionable-looking art and antiques shops on the ground floors. The road seemed to lose its attractiveness, though, the further away from the high street you went. By the time Logan arrived at the address he was looking for, the well-presented terraces were in a more rustic state. Not decrepit, but certainly not as well kept.

The address he was looking for, 257b, was above a grimy-looking hardware store. From the front, it didn't appear that anybody was home. There were no lights on in the apartment.

Cautious as ever, Logan continued driving around the block, to look for a back entrance. But there wasn't one. The backyards of the buildings on this street backed directly onto the yards of the buildings on the parallel street. That provided at least some extra comfort in that there was one less escape route if the apartment's occupants tried to flee from him.

He completed his circuit of the block and parked up on the opposite side of the street to the hardware store, which had long been closed up for the night and was completely dark inside. The street was quiet, with little traffic about and few pedestrians. It wasn't late into the night, just approaching ten p.m., but what small town has a thriving nightlife? And for Logan, it was better this way – fewer potential witnesses, and less potential collateral damage.

As he opened his door to get out, Logan's phone went. Lifting it out of his pocket, he saw that it was Mackie calling.

'Logan, where are you?'

He sounded rushed, like he had something urgent that he needed to say.

'I've just arrived at Dennis's address.'

'Shit. Logan, things aren't quite how we thought.'

Logan was momentarily distracted by movement off to his right. The apartment door opened and a figure came into view. But it was too dark to make the person out.

As Mackie carried on, Logan was only half listening.

'Kennedy is gone. No-one has seen him since this morning.'

Logan's ears perked up a bit. 'He's gone? As in, snatched?'

'Well, more than likely, yeah.'

Logan was still staring over toward the apartment door. The figure began walking toward him, or toward his side of the street at least.

'Logan, are you even listening to me?'

Logan didn't respond; he was too busy focusing on the figure. Was it Dennis?

'Yeah, I'm listening. Go for it. Something about Kennedy?'

But he wasn't really listening at all. He was readying himself for action – his free hand creeping toward his Glock handgun.

This could be it.

'Logan, Dennis is –'

But Logan didn't hear the end of the sentence. He'd hung up the phone already when the figure, walking over to a car that was parked a few yards up from him, came into view, caught in the glare of a street light.

He could hardly believe his eyes.

It was Grainger.

Chapter 60

Logan stepped out of his car, almost unable to believe what he was seeing.

'Angela ...'

She hadn't spotted him and she jumped at his voice, looking as shocked as he was.

Logan's phone rang again. He took it out of his pocket and turned it off without looking at the caller display.

'What are you doing here?' Grainger asked, incredulity in her voice. He walked up to her. Neither of them was smiling.

'No, what are you doing here?' Logan said. 'You said you were in Paris still.'

'Er, actually I said I was in my hotel room.'

'You said it was late at night! Either way, you had me believe you were in Paris. Why would you do that?'

'I'm sorry, Carl. I really wanted to tell you. But you weren't exactly being straight with me, were you?'

'What the hell do you mean by that?'

'You knew far more than you let on,' she said, looking hurt. 'Otherwise why would you be here?'

'No, Angela. The question is why are you here? We both know I'm on this case still. You should be suspended.'

'Do we have to do this in the street? You're making a scene.'

'Fine, let's get into my car,' Logan said, looking around him.

He couldn't see anyone milling about, but still she had a point. He stomped back to his car and got in. Grainger followed timidly and got into the front passenger seat.

'So?' he said, not wanting to replay the same question another time.

'I'm back on the case. Given the investigation was ongoing, they fast-tracked my review. I think they realised we'd actually got much further because of how we did things. I still got a pretty severe reprimand, but the main thing is, I'm back.'

It sounded believable enough, so why did he not buy it?

'Why didn't you just tell me? Why lie?'

'Because you were the reason they reprimanded me in the first place! I've been warned about my future conduct. I can't mess up again. There really wouldn't be any way back if I did.'

Without any sympathy in his voice, Logan said, 'That still doesn't explain why you're here. How did you find this place?'

'Because this house is the registered address for some of the bank accounts to which money related to the Modena kidnapping was transferred.'

He nodded at her response. The FBI had certainly been doing their homework. Or had Mackie let on more to them than he had led Logan to believe? Mackie had already told Logan the Americans were in the loop now. But he had assured him he would give Logan four hours on Dennis. Had he lied? Or just changed his mind? Maybe that was what Mackie had just been calling about.

'You already knew about Carlucci, didn't you?' Logan said. 'I could tell Modena's words meant something to you.'

Grainger was looking down, avoiding his gaze. She didn't say anything.

'Why are you keeping things from me?' he said.

'I'm sorry, Carl,' she said. 'Don't hate me. I just ... I just didn't know what to do. I couldn't tell you.'

'You knew about Carlucci. What else do you know?'

She didn't offer up anything else. She looked up at him. He thought he could see her eyes beginning to well up. Despite his instincts screaming at him, Logan started to feel bad for her.

'We've connected this house to a Greg Dennis,' Logan said, trying to move back onto an even keel. 'Any ideas on who he is?'

'He owns the place, apparently,' Grainger said. 'I got here half an hour ago, but there was no-one home. I broke in, but the place is empty. There's nothing in there. Doesn't look like there has been for a while.'

'Perhaps there never was. It may have been a dead-end lead in the first place.'

'Possibly. So how did you wind up here?'

'I'm guessing the same way you did. The paper trail.'

'Yeah.' She turned her body to face him, a look of hurt in her eyes. 'Why did you lie to me earlier?'

'I don't know,' Logan said, looking away from her.

'It's good to see you,' she said. 'I really mean that.'

He stared back at her and she gave him a smile which sent a tingle all the way through him. But the smile was gone again in a flash. The lingering awkwardness between them was obvious. The level of trust can never be quite the same once you've been lied to. And both of them had lied. Unfortunately the two negatives didn't cancel each other out. If anything, they made the situation that little bit worse.

'So what do you know about this Greg Dennis?' asked Logan. 'Does he even exist?'

'Yeah, he does. Not much known about him, though. Pretty much a clean record.'

'A clean record?' Logan said. 'That doesn't really make sense, does it? You'd expect whoever was behind this to be someone kind of obvious. Someone with a beef against Modena or Kennedy. Or both.'

'That's what you think? It's about a beef with one of those two?'

'What else could it be?'

'No, I don't know. Nothing.'

'You do know something, don't you?'

'Yeah, what I just told you.'

'No, Angela,' he snapped, raising his voice. 'What are you not telling me?'

'There's nothing, Carl!' she protested. 'Why are you speaking to me like this? It's really not how I imagined seeing you again would be.'

Even though a large part of him didn't trust what she was saying, for the first time in the conversation Logan felt like an idiot. She was right. After all the things he'd said to her yesterday, back in Paris, he should have been delighted to see her. He should have been swinging her around in his arms.

But he knew why that wasn't the case. Her story just didn't add up. As much as he wanted it to, it just didn't.

'I'm sorry,' he said, trying hard to sound sincere, though he wasn't feeling it one hundred per cent. 'And you're right. It is good to see you. It's just unexpected. My mind is so focused on getting Dennis or whoever the hell else it might be that's still out there.'

'Mine too,' she said, still looking a little hurt. Then she smiled and said, 'But don't you at least want to say hello to me properly?' She leaned over to him and closed her eyes.

Feeling somewhat awkward with the proposition, Logan held back. Grainger put her lips onto his and despite himself Logan felt a surge of electricity. He was about to close his eyes and kiss her back, then had a sudden change of heart.

But as he went to push her away, he felt something cold touch his wrist as she tugged at his arm. When he heard the metallic clicking sound he immediately got it.

Grainger moved back as Logan looked down at his right hand. 'What the hell!'

She'd handcuffed him to the steering wheel.

Chapter 61

'I'm so sorry, Carl. I really am. I never thought you'd get here so quickly. I just hope you can forgive me.'

Grainger whipped the keys from the ignition and jumped from the car.

'Angela, don't do this!'

Logan was incensed. He shook his hand back and forth against the cuffs, getting more and more angry with each thrust.

Grainger rushed over to her car, parked further down the street in front of Logan's, not once looking back toward him. She got in and sped off into the distance.

'Fuck!' Logan bellowed.

Amidst all the thrashing, his confused mind tried to make sense of what had happened. Had Grainger found Dennis? Did she know where he was? Was all of the lying and conniving so that she could take the credit for finding the bad guys before he did? Perhaps it was him who had just been a good fuck, while she was only intent on furthering her career. Would she really do that to him?

But then, from all the turmoil in his mind, the answer came to him. Something she had said to him. Something that had meant so much to her. Something he had been able to relate to equally: 'Every day I think about what it would be like to find him, to come face to face with him.'

For Logan, it had all been about Selim. For her, it was the man who killed her father.

Kennedy. It was all about Kennedy.

He had to find her. He had to stop her.

Logan reached for his Glock with his free hand, feeling a surge of pain from his damaged shoulder as he twisted. The gun slipped from his grasp and landed in the foot well. With the wheel giving him little space and leverage, he struggled awkwardly trying to pick the gun back up again. Eventually he managed it.

He pointed the Glock's barrel to the chain that connected the two cuffs. He turned his face away as he pulled on the trigger, well aware that in the confined space he could end up with shards of metal and plastic flying into him.

The blast from the gun rang out, deafening in the confined space. His right wrist fell free. Logan's ears were ringing. The noise would surely alarm the residents of the nearby houses and apartments. He had to expect that within minutes the local police would turn up.

He immediately whipped his head down and yanked off the plastic panel beneath the steering column exposing a cascade of wires. Seconds later the car's engine rattled to life. He was ready to give chase. But Grainger would be miles away already. And he didn't even know where she was going.

No, that wasn't strictly true. He had a good idea of where she would go. He just didn't know how to get there.

He had to call Mackie. He needed his boss's help to catch up with Grainger before it was too late. Logan was still in disbelief about what had just happened, but finally everything was starting to make sense. And all of the unanswered questions in his mind were being resolved.

Every day I think about what it would be like to find him, to come face to face with him.

Then I guess we really are the same.

But he and Grainger weren't the same. Not at all. That was clear to Logan now.

Revenge had driven both of them. But to very different outcomes. Kennedy was the man that killed Grainger's father. And a whole sorry scheme had been concocted to achieve her vengeance. Carlucci, himself wanting Kennedy dead, had provided the funds to recruit the crooks – Blakemore and Graham – who would snatch Modena and obtain Kennedy's new identity. It almost sounded simple. But from there, Selim had become involved and it must have seemed to Grainger like the plan was going astray. Which would explain her desire to team up with Logan and ensure Modena was rescued from Selim. She had probably never intended for Modena to fall into the hands of a sadistic terrorist. Not that it made what she had done any more palatable.

Logan took his phone out and switched it back on. There were ten missed calls from Mackie. Logan pressed redial and Mackie picked up on the first ring.

'Logan! Where have you been?'

'It's a long story.'

'Look, we've found out about Dennis ... You're not going to like this –'

'Mackie, I already know. Greg Dennis was Angela Dennis's father. Angela Grainger.'

'Shit. How did you know?'

'Because she was just with me. At Dennis's address. She cuffed me to my car.'

'What! Where are you now?'

'That's the thing. I don't know where I'm going. Not exactly. I think Grainger's still got Kennedy. I'm pretty sure he's still alive.'

'Why would he still be alive? She probably killed him the first chance she got.'

'No, I don't think she did. This is all about her father. Getting her own back. She's taking Kennedy to somewhere that was special to her and her dad.'

'Did you actually go into Dennis's place?'

'No.'

'No?! For all we know Kennedy may still be in there! Get yourself back there and check it out!'

'I'm telling you, he's not there. I just know it.'

Mackie sighed but Logan knew he had his attention.

'Look, we need to do this urgently,' Logan said. 'Send a team or whatever you want over to that property, but I'm going after Grainger. I need you to pull up any property owned by Greg Dennis or Angela Dennis or Angela Grainger near the Appalachian mountains.'

'That's a pretty big area, Logan! It covers multiple states, for Christ's sake!'

'I know, but that's where she's going. Just trust me. Try Virginia first. She lives there. Then work out away from there.'

The short period of silence that followed told Logan that Mackie wasn't sure, but also told him that his boss was coming around to the idea. Otherwise he would have blown it away without even thinking.

'Okay. I'll get someone onto it right away. You do realise you're lucky she didn't kill you? Anyone else in that position and she would have put them down.'

Could Grainger have done that? To him? He really didn't know right now.

'I'm heading in the right direction, more or less. And I have a GPS. I just need the final address.'

Logan heard rustling on the other end. He assumed Mackie was relaying instructions to someone else. Eventually he came back on the line.

'Okay, just give us a few minutes. Land records are pretty easy to trace. Hopefully it won't take long.'

'How did you find out about Dennis?' Logan asked.

'Two different people found it at pretty much the same time. We had some people looking into Greg Dennis, like you said, and we found there was a Greg Dennis who had been an FBI agent killed by Kennedy. Or executed, I should say. Dennis was investigating the mafia at the time, but hadn't banked on meeting one of their hit-men. We also found out the same thing through looking into Kennedy's past. Dennis's murder was one of the key crimes that the Feds had on Kennedy. They had enough to put him away for life, but in the end they gave it all away for some dirt on Carlucci. It didn't take long to spot the link between Greg Dennis and Angela. Grainger is her married name.'

'I know. I figured that.'

Logan heard his phone bleeping. He looked at it. Low battery.

'Shit. I need to ring off – my battery is almost flat. Call me when you have the location. Do it soon. I don't want to go off course. It's a big place out there.'

Logan hung up. Should he turn the phone off altogether? Doing so might save a bit more battery. But then he'd have to keep powering it back on to check if Mackie had called. Better just to leave it on for now and hope Mackie got back to him soon.

If they didn't find an address for him, he really would be out of luck.

With nothing but the road ahead of him, he was unable to stop his mind going over everything he knew, or thought he knew, about Grainger. She was the first person he'd really opened up to in his life. And what was she? A murderer? Some sort of psychotic? Did she actually keep the likes of Blakemore as company? Or had the scheme just spiralled far out of her control? Even if that was the case, her actions were still beyond reckless. How many people had died? And all so she could get to Kennedy.

Logan just couldn't believe he hadn't seen it. Had never even imagined it. Not one sodding bit.

As he replayed his time with Grainger, everything started flooding back to him. All of the little hints as to what was really going on. When he thought about it, there had been plenty. Her leaving him stranded while on the way to Blakemore's. How Blakemore had been fatally shot while Logan had run after Selim. How Grainger had miraculously found the address where Selim had taken Modena. The look of recognition at Modena's words about being lucky. And how she had been so cagey and awkward about when they would see each other again. Because she knew that once her scheme was out in the open, they had no future together.

And now he was feeling like the biggest fool who'd ever walked the earth.

His attraction to her had been real. But what had she seen him as? Just another cog in her wretched plot? Or had some part of her really felt for him like he had for her?

Despite everything, he really hoped it was the latter. Because he couldn't ignore the feelings he had for her. They were still there. And he knew that the biggest concern right now was how this was going to end. If it came down to it, could he take her down?

He didn't even want to think about that.

Chapter 62

13th October

The trip was long, the roads quiet. Miles went by without his seeing any other cars. Logan was no longer keeping to the speed limit like he had earlier. He was pushing the car as hard and fast as it would go. Each time he saw the nearing taillights of a car in front, he half wondered whether it might be Grainger's. But it never was; each car that came and went only resulted in disappointment.

What would he have done if one of the cars *had* been hers? Shoot her there and then? Ram her off the road? Ask her nicely to pull over?

In the end, he hadn't needed to make that decision.

After travelling on wide freeways for the first hour or so, the roads had eventually become narrower, darker, more desolate. Even with the bright light coming down from the moon there was little to see around him. Dense forests surrounded the roads for much of the journey, and whenever he reached a clearing in the trees, the horizon stopped abruptly in the near distance with the murky silhouettes of the surrounding hills and mountains.

In the daytime, the setting would have been magnificent. Travelling alone at night, the vast, unknown blackness was much more sinister.

Despite the long, tedious and lonely trip, made worse by Logan's already weary state, he was surprisingly alert and ready – wired, heart racing, mind on overdrive. It felt like he had a steady stream of caffeine and adrenaline coursing through his blood. It should have been a good feeling. But it wasn't.

With help from Mackie and the team, he'd finally been given an address in the northern part of the Allegheny Mountains about an hour earlier. The GPS had done the rest.

Finally, over four hours after leaving the Dennis place in Binghamton, he was driving through Linville, the nearest village to his destination. His head was still in utter confusion. Over the course of the drive he'd even begun to question whether he'd somehow been wrong about coming here. Maybe Grainger was still back in Broome County. And maybe Kennedy was already dead after all, just like Mackie had said. But the reports from Mackie were that there was still no sign of Kennedy. He'd also been told that it appeared Grainger had been staying at the apartment in Binghamton.

And as he arrived at his destination, the lake house Grainger had talked about to him so fondly when they'd been together in Paris, his uncertainty was put to rest when he saw Grainger's car parked up on the gravel driveway. The house, which was an oversized log cabin, was one of five on this part of the lakefront, all in a row, separated from each other by a good few hundred yards. Space wasn't an issue out here. There was just so much of it. It was clear that each plot carried a large acreage.

Dense forest lay behind, leading into the mountains. In front was the shadowy expanse of the lake, its dark, inky water shimmering in the moonlight. Wanting to approach the property quietly, Logan parked his car out on the carriageway. He felt a chill as he stepped out of the car. Not from the weather, even though it was probably five degrees cooler here than it had been in New York, but because of the eerie setting. This really was about as remote and isolated as it got.

It took him back to a conversation he'd had with Grainger about where Selim would run to. Grainger had been surprised that Selim would take Modena to a residential area rather than the middle of nowhere. Now Logan knew why. Because to her, this was always going to be the rendezvous for this final act. Remote. Deserted.

There were lights on in the cabin. He walked up the steps which led to the raised porch that ran the entire length of the lakefront side of the property. When he reached the top, he slowly put his hand out to the door handle and turned it. It was unlocked.

Slowly he pushed the door ajar and stepped in, gun out but pointed at the floor.

As he glanced around the room, he spotted Grainger. She was standing no more than six or seven yards away from him beyond a sofa, an elaborate oak-and-red-brick fireplace behind her, and pointing a gun at his head.

'*Carl*?' she said, in an exasperated tone. 'How did you find me?'

'I'm good at this, remember?'

'Put the gun down. We don't have to do this.'

'No, *you* don't have to do this. I really do. It's my job.'

Logan took a step forward, toward the sofa that separated the two of them.

'Don't move!' Grainger screamed.

He stopped. From this angle he could see the bound and gagged figure curled up on the floor by her feet. It must have been Kennedy. The man had a bloodied face. Logan wasn't sure what other injuries he had, but he was still alive; his eyes were wide open and his nostrils were flaring widely.

Logan looked back up at Grainger.

'Don't look at me like that, Carl. I'm not a bad person. This man killed my father!'

Kennedy squirmed and moaned but both Logan and Grainger ignored him.

'How many other people have died, though, because of what you've done?'

'That wasn't my fault!' she protested. 'Blakemore wasn't supposed to do it like he did. I was never responsible for the way it panned out. When Selim became involved, it changed everything. He was the one who made it like it was. They were never supposed to kill anyone.'

'How could you even deal with those people?' Logan said, disappointment in his voice and hurt in his eyes.

'It was all Blakemore. I hired him and he brought in all the others. Somewhere along the line, the whole plan got corrupted.'

'Yeah. And look how it turned out.'

'I was trying to do the right thing,' she said.

'Somehow I'm struggling to see that.'

'How can you even *say* that? The whole time I was trying to rescue Modena because I knew what Blakemore had done, what Selim was doing, was nothing like what had been planned. And when you turned up, it seemed like a good opportunity. Work with someone else. Try to regain control.'

'You used me. I saved your life and all the time you were just using me.'

'You did save my life! And you don't know how grateful I am. Lorik had no idea who I was because he was nothing to do with me. Blakemore hired his own men, including Selim. Then when Selim took Modena, I led you straight to him. I didn't want that animal anywhere near Modena!'

'You knew where Selim had taken him all along, didn't you?'

She bowed her head, ashamed. Though he wasn't sure for which part.

'Yes. There never was any evidence at Blakemore's. I wrote the address on that piece of paper and gave it to you because I wanted you to help me get Modena back. Don't you see? I was *trying* to do the right thing.'

'And Blakemore?'

'What about him?'

'You killed him, didn't you? And you lied to me. You made me believe it was Selim's man who did it.'

'Yes. I shot him. He was a terrible person, Carl. He didn't deserve any better.'

'No, you just wanted to eliminate a potential witness.'

'Blakemore had it coming his whole life,' she spat, angered. 'His death at my hands was much more pleasant than if we'd left him to Selim.'

'What about laws? Have you completely forgotten who you are? What you do?'

'What about them?! *You* don't abide by them! Tell me, how are we different? You go around killing the bad guys too. But you feel you're justified because you do it for your goddamn country and someone's given you the order. Do you make a moral judgement before you do it? No. You go ahead and kill whoever you're told to because that's what you're paid to do. And you think *you're* justified! Ha! Well, *I'm* justified!'

'It's not up to you, though.'

'Then who is it up to? They're bad people! This man killed my dad.' She laid a kick into Kennedy's side and he let out a long groan. 'Not just my dad – he's killed dozens of people! And he gets to live his life as a free man because he did *one* good thing. That's just not good enough for me. And if you were the man I thought you were, it wouldn't be good enough for you.'

Grainger's words resonated with him. Logan didn't want to agree with her, but in many ways he did. He had never hidden who he was. Under different circumstances he would have had no qualms about putting a bullet into the likes of Kennedy.

But the way she had gone about it had seen innocent people hurt and killed. He had never expected that of her.

He looked down and saw that Kennedy was staring at him, a pleading look in his eyes. It made Logan feel uncomfortable and he shifted to the side so that Kennedy's face was hidden from him behind the sofa.

'You played me, Angela,' Logan said, unable to hide his anger. 'That's what hurts the most. My feelings for you were real. And yet all you were doing was using me to achieve your own goals.'

'That's not true. It's just not true.' Tears began to fall on her cheeks. She sniffed. 'God, why'd we have to happen, Carl? Why'd it have to happen like this?'

Despite everything, seeing Grainger so upset made Logan feel for her.

'Remember what you said to me yesterday?' Grainger asked.

Of course he did. He'd opened his heart up in a way that he'd never done before. Would he ever get the chance to do that again?

'I've never felt so confused,' she sobbed. 'I wanted to push myself away from you. I knew I couldn't get too close. But you pulled me in too deep.'

'That's why you were fighting with me?'

'Yes! Exactly. But when you said those words to me, my heart just melted. I've never felt like that before. Ever. It was the most incredible feeling. And yet it was the saddest moment of my life. Because I knew that I would never be able to feel like that again. Please, Carl. If any of what you said to me was true, you won't stop me now. You can't.'

'I meant every last word of it,' he said with bitter disappointment. 'Every last word.'

'Then please don't stop me. Just let me do this. What difference does it make now? What difference does it really make to you? Kennedy is a bad man. He deserves to die.'

Logan could hear Kennedy moaning at her words, attempting to shout out. He tried to block the murmurings from his mind.

Grainger's bottom lip began to quiver. 'He's a killer, Carl. *He killed my father.*'

Her pleading voice was getting weaker. She looked close to a full breakdown. He wanted to hate her for what she had done, for the way that she had used him. But just watching her made his heart feel like it was splitting in two.

'Wouldn't you have asked the same of me if we were in a room with Selim?' she said. 'Wouldn't you have asked me to let you do it? To let you kill him in cold blood?'

He didn't even have to think about the answer to that one.

'Of course I would,' he said.

'And yet you didn't even have to. I watched you, Carl. I was there, at the door, the whole time. I watched you with Selim. I gave you the chance to do what you had to do.'

He felt his legs go weak. He hadn't noticed her at the time, but he had seen her at the door straight after he'd shot Selim. She hadn't stopped him. She hadn't even tried.

'So how is it different?' she said.

'Because I would have stopped if *you* had asked me to,' he responded, without even thinking.

'Carl, don't you see?' she said. 'Don't you know what you mean to me? I would *never* have asked you to stop. I knew what killing Selim meant to you.'

Her words hit him like a freight train. Because he knew that she was right, and that he had no choice. What he'd told her yesterday, he'd meant every word. His entire adult life had been empty of emotions. They had only known each other for a few days but with her he'd felt so much. He'd felt truly alive for the first time. He still wanted her. He still needed her.

And he knew that he couldn't stand in her way now.

Logan slowly lowered his gun and dropped it to the floor. He turned away from her, one last stand of defiance. He heard the wails of Kennedy, who must have realised that his time was now up.

The single gunshot made Logan jump.

He turned back around, trying his best to avoid looking at the corpse on the ground. Kennedy *was* a bad man, Logan tried to convince himself. He *did* deserve to die.

Just like Selim did.

He looked into Grainger's pleading, bloodshot eyes. He loathed her for what she had done. Not just the destruction she'd caused to innocent people, but the way she'd used him. But she looked so vulnerable. Part of him just wanted to take her in his arms. Tell her that he was there for her. In spite of everything, he just couldn't ignore the attraction that was still there.

Maybe they were even more alike than he had realised.

He took a step toward her. She spoke to him, her voice nothing more than a whisper. He hadn't heard her and wasn't sure what she had said.

It was only when he saw her hand moving, rising, that his brain deciphered the words.

I love you.

He felt his heart flutter.

But before he could respond, she pointed the gun at him and fired.

Chapter 63

When Logan arrived back in England three days later, his left leg was still heavily bandaged and he was unable to move around at all without crutches. As well as muscle damage, the bullet Grainger had fired had severed some of the nerve fibres above his knee. It would be a long and slow process to get back to full strength.

It wasn't just his leg that had been damaged. A small part of him had died following the encounter with Grainger. It was a part of him that he hadn't even known existed. And he wasn't yet sure what that meant for him.

In a way, Grainger had begun his re-awakening. Before her, his entire focus had been on pain and suffering – both his and his enemy's. His need for revenge against Selim had been all-encompassing and he'd been struggling to get the remnants of his life on track. Selim was dead and buried now, thanks to Grainger's help. And it felt like he could finally start to rebuild his life again. But she'd also brought something else to the table. She'd given him hope.

It may not have been her intention – it almost certainly wasn't – but in the time they'd spent together, she'd shown him how to control his feelings, how to feel new emotions. His feelings were no longer an explosive combination of hormones and chemicals that he had no control over and that he had to keep bottled up. They were there to get him through life, to help him live. Not all of his new-found feelings were positive; he'd also had to deal with the embarrassment and disappointment of how his time with

Grainger had panned out. But his new found self did, at least, make him a real human being again.

The darkness that had once clouded him was gone for good, that was for sure, but his rehabilitation was still a long way from complete. Could he ever have feelings for another person like he'd had for Grainger? Only time would tell, but her betrayal had cut him deeply. For now, he was locked in mourning. It was as though someone close to him had died. But he still believed that, because of Grainger, the dark old days were long gone.

After two days of gruelling debriefing following the showdown with Grainger, Logan was finally back in England. He'd agreed to meet Mackie, who had also returned home having spent the previous two days in America, for a drink.

'I can see you're still hurting,' Mackie said. Logan assumed he was talking about his leg, but he couldn't quite be sure.

'How did we miss Grainger's deception?' Logan asked.

They were sitting in the corner of a coffee house near to the JIA offices. It was early morning and they were the only customers.

'We didn't miss it. We got there.'

'Is there anything on where she's gone?' Logan said.

'Nothing at all. She must have had an escape planned because she's just vanished. There's no trace of her anywhere.'

'Just one thing, though ...' Logan said, a thought that had played on his mind for the last three days coming back to him. 'Where *did* the other two million dollars go? The two million that didn't wind up with Blakemore?'

Mackie sighed. 'It certainly didn't end up with Selim. And I don't think it ended up with Grainger either.'

'So she didn't take a cut?'

'Doesn't look like it. The two million didn't end up in any one place. It was bounced around all over. But most of it was used setting up the whole scheme. There are endless transactions it went toward: setting up shell companies, trusts, bank accounts, fees, expenses. All of the stuff that was needed to try to keep the trail clean.'

For some reason, that made Logan feel better. Grainger had never gone into any of this to try to make herself a few bucks, unlike all of the other participants. It had always been about getting to the man who had destroyed her life. He really could see the parallels between her life and his. Even though what she had done had caused far more damage than she could ever have intended.

Did the end justify the means?

No, despite his feelings toward Grainger, he didn't think so. He could still sympathise with where she had started from, though. And he did believe in the ends that she had achieved – getting her revenge on a man who had destroyed her life. But he could never agree with the way that she got there.

'Poor old Modena must just have been a good fall guy,' Logan said. 'There must be numerous people who could have got the information on Kennedy. The whole scheme was designed to be more elaborate than it needed to be, just to deflect away from her.'

'It certainly was elaborate,' Mackie said. 'A lot of people lost their lives to get to just one. Most of them were bad, granted, but not all of them. Not the agents at the start who were protecting Modena. Selim must've thought he'd struck gold when he got wind of the scheme.'

'I wonder if he ever knew it was Grainger behind it?'

'I doubt it,' Mackie said. 'Sounds like she kept her head low. That was the whole point. Making it look like the plot was down to someone else, Carlucci, so that we'd never find her. But we did find her. And in the end, it's hard to see how else she could have seen this panning out.'

Logan finished the rest of his coffee and shifted in his seat to reach down to take his wallet out of his pocket. Even the slight movement sent a bolt of pain shooting through his leg, making him grimace.

'You need to take some time off,' Mackie said. 'Get that arm and leg sorted out in the meantime.'

'I don't need any time off.'

'You can't walk, man!' Mackie argued. 'I want you fresh. Even if it's just until the crutches are gone, I want you away from here.'

'This isn't over yet, Mackie,' Logan said.

'For you it is. Grainger isn't our problem. Unless we're asked to look into her disappearance, and I doubt we will be, you're not to go anywhere near it.'

Logan heard the words but he didn't have to agree to them. And he could tell that Mackie understood that.

Mackie sighed. 'Just take a few days' rest. Why don't you go on holiday? Back to Vegas or somewhere. I'll even pay for it if you promise not to contact me while you're there.'

'And do *you* promise not to contact *me*?'

'I'm not sure I'd go that far,' Mackie said smiling.

'Well, it was worth a try.'

'So you agree?'

'Yeah, fine. I'll take a few days off. But this isn't over. Not yet.'

Mackie sighed again. 'Why do I not doubt that?'

The JIA may not be looking for Grainger, but Logan didn't care. Grainger had betrayed his trust in the most grievous way and he could never forgive that. But she was out there somewhere and she was alone. His heart went out to her.

He had to find her. He knew that. And he knew that one day he would.

The only question was what he would do when he came face to face with her again.

A note from the author

Thank you for reading *Dance with the Enemy*. I do hope you enjoyed it and would be very grateful if you could write a review. It needn't be long, just a few words. Reviews make a huge difference to writers and help other readers discover new books.

Look out for the return of Carl Logan in *Rise of the Enemy* - out now!

To find out more about my other releases, just carry on reading, or head to www.robsinclairauthor.com, where you can also subscribe to my mailing list for up-to-date information on releases, promotions and competitions.

I also welcome your feedback, comments and questions. You can get in touch with me via my website or on social media:

Twitter: @rsinclairauthor
Facebook: fb.me/robsinclairauthor

Agent Carl Logan returns in

Rise of the Enemy

Read on for more details...

Prologue

Dance with the enemy and your feet will get burned. An old friend once said that to me, many years ago. The same old friend who was now sitting in front of me, across the table of the café. I think he'd misquoted the saying, but it always stuck with me nevertheless. And recently, his words had come back to bite me with a vengeance.

I'd made the mistake of getting too close to people I thought were friends. People I trusted. Angela Grainger was one of them. We'd had a connection like I'd never had with anyone before. I still thought about her every day. Mostly, despite myself, I still thought of her fondly. But she'd betrayed me. Betrayed my trust. I'd let her get too close and my feet had been burned.

The man sitting before me was another one. Grainger's betrayal was something I would never forget – it still dominated my mind. But in many ways the betrayal of this man hurt the most.

He was the person I had trusted more than anyone else in the world.

I never imagined that we would end up like this. Talking in this way. The accusations. The insinuations. Speaking to each other like we were natural enemies rather than two people who had worked so closely together for nearly twenty years.

They wanted me to kill him. Until a few days ago, the mere suggestion would have been laughable. Something had changed, though. I didn't know what and I didn't know why, but our lives would never be the same again. The fact we were sitting here like this told me that.

And if it came down to it, I would do it. I would kill Mackie. My boss. My mentor. My friend. Because it might be the only way for me to get out of this mess alive.

***

To carry on reading head to Amazon.com where a longer sample is available.

345

Money. Murder. Revenge.

How much pressure can one man take, before he breaks?

DARK FRAGMENTS is a pulsating psychological thriller from Rob Sinclair.

Read on for more details...

Book description

Outwardly, Ben Stephens appears to be a normal, hard-working family man. In reality, his life has been in turmoil since the murder of his wife, Alice, seven years ago. The killer was never caught.

Now re-married - to the woman he was having an affair with while still married to Alice - Ben's life is once again spiralling out of control, and he's become heavily indebted to an unscrupulous criminal who is baying for Ben's blood.

When Ben's estranged twin sister, a police detective, unexpectedly returns to his life, asking too many questions for comfort, it becomes clear that without action, Ben's life will soon reach a crisis point from which there will be no return.

In order to avoid falling further into the mire, Ben must examine the past if he is to survive the present - but just how much pressure can one man take before he breaks?

Dark Fragments is a fast-paced thriller with a blend of mystery, suspense and action that will appeal to readers of psychological thrillers, as well as a broad section of crime, thriller and action fans.

DARK FRAGMENTS is available in ebook and paperback now! Head to amazon.com to find out more.

Printed in Great Britain
by Amazon